ROYAL GAMBIT

Also by Daniel O'Malley

The Rook

Stiletto

Blitz

ROYAL GAMBIT

DANIEL O'MALLEY

LITTLE, BROWN AND COMPANY

New York Boston London

The characters and events in this book are fictitious. Any similarity to real persons, living or dead, is coincidental and not intended by the author.

Copyright © 2025 by Daniel O'Malley

Hachette Book Group supports the right to free expression and the value of copyright. The purpose of copyright is to encourage writers and artists to produce the creative works that enrich our culture.

The scanning, uploading, and distribution of this book without permission is a theft of the author's intellectual property. If you would like permission to use material from the book (other than for review purposes), please contact permissions@hbgusa.com. Thank you for your support of the author's rights.

Little, Brown and Company
Hachette Book Group
1290 Avenue of the Americas, New York, NY 10104
littlebrown.com

First Edition: July 2025

Little, Brown and Company is a division of Hachette Book Group, Inc. The Little, Brown name and logo are trademarks of Hachette Book Group, Inc.

The publisher is not responsible for websites (or their content) that are not owned by the publisher.

The Hachette Speakers Bureau provides a wide range of authors for speaking events. To find out more, go to hachettespeakersbureau.com or email hachettespeakers@hbgusa.com.

Little, Brown and Company books may be purchased in bulk for business, educational, or promotional use. For information, please contact your local bookseller or the Hachette Book Group Special Markets Department at special.markets@hbgusa.com.

ISBN 978-0-316-56810-4 (hc)

LCCN is available at the Library of Congress.

1 2025

MRQ-T

Printed in Canada

For Charles Reeves & Ross McAlpine

It is an old maxim of mine that when you have excluded the impossible, whatever remains, however improbable, must be the truth.

—"The Adventure of the Beryl Coronet,"
Sir Arthur Conan Doyle

That's all very well, but what do you do when nothing is impossible?

—Detective Constable Andrew Chuah, formerly of the Metropolitan Police, now attached to the Checquy Group

ROYAL GAMBIT

1

For the rest of her life, whenever Louise remembered that moment, she would feel a horrendous stab of shame through her heart. Shame because her first thought was not for the well-being of her brother Edmund lying sprawled on the floor but because, in a flash of selfish insight, she thought only of the implications for *her,* what it might mean for the rest of her life.

She was moving forward before that thought left her. For all that her horrible egocentric mind was screaming about the future, everything else was focused on her brother.

"Oh, Jesus, Ed! Please! *Please!*" She fell to her knees by him, afraid to touch him. He was on his back, an expression of pain frozen on his face. His blond hair, usually parted meticulously, was all awry. One of his eyes was slightly open, and the sight of the blank, unfocused pupil turned her stomach. She hesitantly took his arm. It was horribly heavy. She felt his hand and thought it was warm. But he was not breathing.

"Fa!" she screamed. It was instinct, not thought. Her father would know what to do. He always knew what to do. But for all the things her father was, he was not a doctor. *He must have learned some first aid, surely, during his time in the army,* she thought frantically. She tried to remember her own training from the Girl Guides. She had vague memories of a little her and Alix and Imogen giggling while they contemplated giving the kiss of life to a limbless mannequin.

I don't think any of us ever did get that badge in the end.

But now she was looking down at her brother's graying face and wondering if she should be breathing into his mouth or pounding on his chest.

"*FA!*"

And her father was there, but for the first time in her life, she saw fright on his face.

"Oh, my boy," he said weakly. "Oh, no." He knelt and took Edmund's hand, feeling at his wrist.

"Fa," she said, "should I—should I get them to call for—"

"Yes—no, wait!" he said sharply. "Where is Odette? Is she here?"

"Odette?" repeated Louise blankly. Odette Leliefeld was the girlfriend of her younger brother Nicholas. She was pleasant enough, from Belgium. "Yes, she's here, I saw her earlier. She came to watch a film with Nicky."

"Get her," Fa said in his military commanding voice. "*Now.* Not a word to anyone else."

"But why?"

"Go!"

Bewildered, Louise ran out of the room and down the hallway. She flung open the door to Nicholas's bedroom, but it was empty, and she ran on. With every step, she was aware of time wasted. Time that might make all the difference. They should be calling for a doctor. Why was she chasing about after this girl? Edmund was... was... She flinched away from the thought.

Finally, she burst into the lounge, and the girl was there, seated on a sofa and paging through a book. She looked up in surprise.

"Louise?" she said, and Louise bit back a moment of irritation.

"Where's Nicky?"

"In the garden," Odette said. Her Belgian accent was noticeable, but she spoke English fluently. "He had to take a call, so we paused the movie." Her eyes narrowed. "Something is wrong. What has happened?"

"It's Edmund, something's... I found him, and—" Louise wanted to weep. "Fa said to get *you*, but I don't understand why."

"Where is he?" said the girl. She stood, so smoothly that the motion was almost alien, and Louise took an uncertain step back. Odette's usual calm mien had been replaced by something sharper, focused.

"The library," Louise said. "He wanted to borrow a book." As if that were an important detail.

The girl was already moving swiftly. She was past Louise and running down the hallway before Louise could get to the door. By the time Louise caught up, Odette was already on her knees by Edmund's sprawled figure. She had peeled open his eyelids, and her face was close to his. Then she placed two fingers against his neck, feeling for a pulse.

"We've already *done* that," said Louise impatiently. Odette ignored her, and a faint line appeared between her brows. For a single, crazy moment, it seemed to Louise as if the veins in the girl's two fingers swelled up and then shrank. Her head was tilted, as if she was listening intently. She shook her head and took her fingers away, and Louise caught a glimpse of something glistening on her brother's throat, like a spot of liquid.

"Odette?" said Louise's father, and she held up a hand to quiet him. She leaned forward and, to Louise's shock, kissed her brother full on the lips, and then on the brow. As she drew back, she licked her lips a little, and made a sound of frustration. Then she tore open Edmund's shirt and carefully placed her hands on his chest.

All right, good, she's doing CPR. Finally, it's making a bit of sense. Except that Odette was not pushing on Edmund's chest in any sort of rhythm. Instead, she pressed down firmly and held her hands there. The muscles in her wrists jerked, there was an odd squelching sound, and Odette drew her hands back quickly, clearly braced for something to happen.

But nothing did. Edmund just lay there.

"Fuck," the Belgian girl said quietly. Louise noticed that her palms were red and swollen. Odette wiped her hands on her skirt and then slapped Edmund's face hard. "Edmund! *Edmund,* wake up!"

Odette took a deep breath and placed her hands on Edmund's chest again. Louise could see her straining, and then her shoulders slumped. She was breathing heavily, and when she looked up at

Louise and her father, she was pale, and dark patches had appeared under her eyes. There was a look of immense sadness on her face.

"Anything?" her father asked in a small voice. Odette shook her head.

"I am so sorry, sir," she said. "He's gone."

"Oh!" exclaimed her father in pain. "Oh, my boy!"

"What are you *talking* about?" demanded Louise. "We have to call a doctor! I don't understand why we even brought you." She broke off as her father closed his hand tightly on her shoulder. "Fa?"

"Nothing more could have been done," he said. There was an inexplicable air of finality in the way he said it, as if Edmund had just been worked over for hours by a team of experts, instead of getting pawed and kissed and slapped by his brother's unemployed girlfriend.

"What?" exclaimed Louise.

"Thank you for your efforts, Odette."

"Sir."

"What?" repeated Louise. "What do you mean?" It was as if they had all gone mad.

"Oh, my darling," he said to her, and pulled her close. "I'm so sorry. I am so, so sorry." The defeat in his voice was what broke Louise, and she began to weep against his chest. Only distantly did she hear him speaking.

"Odette, you'll need to call someone. We'll have to..." He broke off, and with her cheek against his chest, she felt it as he swallowed. "We'll have to tell them that the Prince of Wales has died."

2

Alexandra "Alix" Victoria Dennis-Palmer-Hudson-Gilmore-Garnsey, twelfth Lady Mondegreen, lay limply in her bedroom in the east wing of Wyndham Towers, sweating in the horrendous summer heat, and asked herself yet again why she'd come home.

And why has no one, in a dynasty that stretches back to the time of Good Queen Bess, ever bothered to have air conditioning installed here?

Her trip to the Towers really was an extremely poor idea. She had a perfectly nice, painfully expensive flat in London, one with air conditioning and her stuff and easy access to entertainment and, most importantly, a complete lack of family members. She had two weeks' leave that she'd been told it would be wise for her to take, she had a goodly amount of money in the bank that would have enabled her to stay in comfort in any part of the UK or Ireland (she was not permitted to go anywhere else without written permission from the Home Secretary), and she had no boyfriend to object to her taking off.

So why had she felt compelled to come to the most isolated part of the Scottish-English border and be awkward and uncomfortable among her family while dying of heat exhaustion in a sweltering ancestral pile?

Admittedly, Wyndham Towers *did* come furnished with a pack of absolutely lovable dogs, four of whom had realized that Alix had one of the house's few fans in her room. Accordingly, she was currently framed entirely by panting dogs.

On each side, she was boxed in by a Scottish deerhound, John on the left and Lulu on the right, while a border collie named Wompus had ensconced himself between her knees, his fur slowly welding itself to her skin. Finally, a dense little nugget of a Cairn terrier, Poppy, had inserted herself between Alix's pillow and the wall, so it looked as if she were wearing an amiable brindle fur hat.

And the house *was* lovely. All pillars, porches, and parapets, it was the brainchild of the eighth Lord Mondegreen. He had engaged some genius of an architect in the late 1820s to produce a family seat worthy of a centuries-old family who'd just made an astounding amount of money through something cunning involving copper mines in some other part of the world.

The previous version of Wyndham Towers, which had accreted over the centuries, had reflected a mishmash of period styles, with an emphasis on being able to retreat into it and hold off the most immediate threat, ranging from border reivers to salesmen. It had served its purpose, insofar as the Mondegreen line had survived, but it wasn't what you might call *gracious*.

The new house, however, was one of the nation's foremost examples of "Jacobethan" architecture. It would have received far more attention if it hadn't been so remote that even the most dedicated of architectural historians couldn't bring themselves to visit. The nearest town was an hour and a half away and always gave the impression of being in the last stages of some terminal disease.

Of course, it was entirely fitting that Alix be there. As the Right Honourable the Lady of Mondegreen, she was a *Laird o Pairlament* in the Scottish peerage. Wyndham Towers was her ancestral manse, and it was proper that she spend at least part of the year there. Especially, she reflected grimly, since the family had only been able to avoid selling the place off by selling *her* off.

"Alix!" She opened her eyes and found her mother standing in the doorway. Charlotte, the dowager Lady Mondegreen, was tall, slim, beautiful, and convinced that the world existed entirely for her convenience. "I've been calling you! Telephone!"

"Who is it?"

"It came in to the library phone."

Oh, thank God. Some sort of supernatural emergency that will take me away from here. She felt a little guilty about her relief at the prospect of escape from the bosom of her family, but not terribly so. She hauled herself off the bed, peeling her legs away from Wompus, who opened his eyes, regarded her balefully, and then rolled over onto his back, letting the breeze from the fan play across his belly. John and Lulu sighed heavily and spread out a little more so that they resembled piles of extremely regal laundry.

Because of the house's remoteness and the surrounding hills, the mobile phone reception was shit. There were two landlines: one that anyone could (and did) pick up an extension for and eavesdrop, and one in the library that the government had installed at substantial expense and from which the entire household was forbidden to make outgoing calls. Alix had a sneaking suspicion that her younger sisters, desperate for privacy, violated that prohibition fairly regularly, which meant that every personal conversation with a boyfriend or bitchy gossip-fest with a schoolmate that Cecily, Lillian, or Frances had conducted on that line had been recorded and analyzed by government agents, with transcripts that would reside in secret archives until the end of time.

Alix closed the library doors. The telephone was waiting, off the cradle.

"Hello?" she said when she picked it up.

"Identify."

"Pawn Alexandra Mondegreen. ID code 45 Fatalistic Aureate 85 Zulu." There was a pause as the listening computers analyzed her fricatives, labials, coronals, dorsals, pharyngeals, laryngeals, and accent and decided that it was indeed her.

"Hold for Lady Farrier."

Oh, hell. If it was the Lady calling, rather than the Rookery, then it was a political rather than operational matter.

"Alexandra?"

"My lady."

"You're needed in London." There was no expression of regret for disturbing her compulsory vacation leave. Any such expression would have been patently insincere anyway. Alix was there to be summoned.

"I'll leave right away," said Alix. She looked at the clock. *If I call British Rail now and ask them to stop at the halt, I'll be able to catch the train in half an hour.* The estate had its own little platform on the rail line that the trains would stop at if given sufficient notice. "I'll call once the train is approaching London, if the office could send a car to Euston."

"No, we need you immediately," the Lady said. "A helicopter will be there in...twenty minutes."

"A helicopter?" repeated Alix. "Coming here? All right, ask them to land on the south lawn. Will there be room for luggage?"

"It'll be just you, so yes, but there won't be time to change once you arrive. You'll come straight to the palace." Alix winced. It was *that* kind of emergency.

"A formal event?" Experience had taught her that trying to put on makeup and do her hair in a helicopter inevitably led to a look best described as "electrocuted clown."

"No," Lady Farrier said. "But dress...soberly."

What does that mean?

"I'll be ready, my lady." When she opened the door, her mother was standing right there, and she flinched back. "Mummy!"

"Hello, darling," her mother said brightly. "Was that the office?"

"On the official office phone?" asked Alix. "Yes, it was."

"Going back to London?"

She hesitated. "Yes. Sort of official emergency."

"Of course." Her mother smiled. "Did I hear they're sending a helicopter?"

"Mummy, you really shouldn't be listening in on these calls."

"Do you think there might be a spare seat?"

Cecily, Lillian, and Frances greeted the news of their sister and mother's departure with no expression at all. It was apparently no more than they expected. They didn't even come to the windows to watch the helicopter land or see their sister rush across the lawn in a dark gray suit while their mother teetered behind her in heels and a bright summer dress, her bag in one hand while the other held her hat on against the downwash. To Alix's mortification, the pilot did not seem surprised by the addition of her mother to the passenger manifest. Indeed, he seemed almost to have been anticipating it.

Apparently, word about the dowager Lady Mondegreen has gotten around the office. The Checquy had confronted the greatest supernatural horrors of history head-on, without giving an inch, but when it came to her mother, it was just easier to pre-capitulate.

The journey was tedious. There was no briefing packet to read, and so she had to sit and watch her mother blithely reading glossy magazines she'd brought with her and drinking her favorite melon-flavored bottled water, which, to Alix's horror, had been waiting for her in the helicopter. Alix then cringed when they arrived at the heliport at Battersea to find two cars waiting for them.

"Oh, isn't that nice," said her mother. "They could have just dropped me off at the flat on the way." The possibility that this detour might have been *out* of the way did not occur to her. "Well, bye, darling." She gave an air-kiss out of the side of her mouth without bothering to turn her gaze away from the car.

"I'm over here, Mum."

"Hmm?"

"Never mind," sighed Alix, as her mother got into the car and was whisked away without a backward glance. "I suppose we'd better go," she said to the driver of the other car.

"The Lady *is* waiting, Lady Mondegreen," he agreed.

"Lady," not "Pawn." Alix felt the familiar stab of embarrassment, anger, and sadness but didn't try to correct him. She would have just gotten the usual blank stare.

"You know I'll have to sit in the back, right?" she said.

"Of course."

"It's just for the look of the thing."

"It's fine, my lady."

There was no briefing packet in the car. Alix turned on her phone, but there were no coded texts from the Rookery masquerading as messages from friends. She resorted to checking the mainstream media, but the big news was all happening elsewhere in the world.

Not even a hint of something that might be a cover-up. So perhaps this isn't a heightened alert situation where they want subtle protection for the royal family. Is something going on at the palace?

She had the royal diary and the court circular bookmarked on her phone, and neither mentioned any specific engagements that evening. In fact, the royal diary revealed that there was nothing scheduled that day except the Princess of Wales opening a women's shelter in York.

"Do you have any idea why I've been called in?" she asked the driver. "Has there been some major manifestation?"

"No, it's been quiet all 'round the country, far as I know."

Then what the hell is going on?

Feeling increasingly uneasy, Alix decided to keep busy. She drafted a breezy social media update announcing to her civilian friends that she had returned to London and sent it off to an email address belonging to the Tactical Deception Communications section, known in-house as the Liars. Her draft would be reviewed by no fewer than five people, including at least one former journalist, one political scientist, one social media expert, the duty chief for the media watch room, and one manager. They had been known to call in additional experts as necessary.

It prevented any form of spontaneity, but since she was one of the few Checquy operatives who was permitted to use social media—in fact, was *obliged* to use social media—she had to do it. Sometimes they merely altered a word or two or added a strategic emoji. Sometimes, however, they changed large portions of her posts. On one occasion, to her irritation, the best photograph she'd ever taken— a magnificent shot of an electrical storm above the hills around Wyndham Towers—was replaced by an enthusiastic update about the pastries in a café that she'd never visited. Presumably, the change had been made for purposes of national security.

In any case, she would eventually receive the approved text and then have to post it herself, just to mesh with GPS expectations.

There were no members of the press at the gates of Buckingham Palace. The building reared above her, a cliff of windows and white stone, and despite herself, she felt a shiver of awe. She'd been there a thousand times. She'd spent hours wandering its hallways and even more studying its blueprints. She knew all 775 rooms, including the staff bedrooms, the principal bedrooms, the staterooms, the cinema, the post office, the jeweler's workshop, and the doctor's surgery. She knew the forty acres of grounds. And yet it was still impossible to take it for granted.

As the car turned in to a courtyard, a man was waiting to open her door. She recognized him as Pawn Anthony Whomsley, a fellow operative of the Checquy who was currently attached to the King's protection detail. He ushered her into the palace but stopped her when she went for the usual stairs.

"This way." He led her down corridors that became less and less grand and more and more utilitarian. She could remember running through them as a child, giggling madly with Louise. Locked doors opened at a swipe of Whomsley's pass as they moved out of the service areas, through the public and reception spaces, and up deserted staircases to a higher floor.

Just before they came to the royal family's private quarters, he opened a door that she recalled led to a conference room. Inside, seated at the table were the only two other people in the Checquy to have their own Wikipedia pages.

The first, Linda, the Right Honourable the Viscountess of Farrier, had the smallest page, and it really only existed because there were apparently people out there who felt compelled to catalog every member of the British aristocracy. It recorded her parentage (daughter of an earl), her spouse (the Right Honourable the Viscount of Farrier, obviously), and her two children. It noted that she had been a lady-in-waiting two queens ago; that her entry in *Who's Who* listed her charity work, including her position as chairwoman of the Foundation for Juhász-Koodiaroff-Grassigli Syndrome; and that her pastimes included quilting, dogs, and archery.

Unsurprisingly, it did not mention her ability to enter and manipulate other people's dreams, or that she was co-leader of the Checquy Group, a covert agency within the British government that dealt with, and was partially staffed by, the supernatural. Nor did it mention any of the accomplishments that had made her legendary within the Checquy: how she had tracked down an oneiric parasite that had been stalking through the sleeping psyches of the British populace for months. Over the course of seventeen weeks, it had driven thirty-eight people to commit suicide by self-immolation and left fifteen people in a state of permanent insanity. Then-Pawn Farrier had finally cornered the entity in the erotic dream of some fourteen-year-old boy in a suburb of Canterbury and, while dream women with improbable breasts looked on in bewilderment, she had torn the parasite apart with such force that everyone in the house developed epilepsy.

Nor did Wikipedia mention how, as Lady of the Checquy, she had accomplished the unprecedented and stupendous feat of gaining a budgetary supplement for the Checquy Group from the Exchequer in a recession year—not once, but *twice*! In consecutive years!

Alix had known Lady Farrier since she was six, and the two had been collaborating on responsibilities surrounding the royal family since Alix was ten. Yet she still regarded the older woman with a feeling of nervous reverence. Although they were both ladies, Linda Farrier was *the* Lady.

The Checquy had existed for centuries, and one of the quaint cultural elements that it had retained into the modern day was the nomenclature for its people. If you had supernatural capabilities, you received a chess-based title. The vast bulk of such operatives were pawns. A pawn could be a manager, a clerk, a soldier, a scholar, a maintenance worker.

Above them was the Court—the executives—consisting of rooks, chevaliers, and bishops. And at the very top, in charge of the entire organization, were the Lord and Lady (the chess theme having been strategically ignored at this point because referring to oneself as a "king" or a "queen" in the British Isles sent a very specific message).

It was archaic, and faintly ridiculous, but the terminology served as a reminder. You were special, yes. You were elite. But you were also a piece in a vast, important game, and you could be sacrificed at any time. People regarded the position with a grim pride. And this was the reason that Alix winced whenever one of her fellows addressed her as "Lady." It said that as far as they were concerned, she was not a real pawn and enjoyed unfair privileges.

The Wikipedia entry for the second woman, Odette Leliefeld, was much longer than Lady Farrier's because she was currently dating the dishy third in line to the throne, Prince Nicholas, and so was the subject of much public attention. The entry had some things right: it identified her as being twenty-one years old, born to parents who were academics in Belgium. There was palpable agony on the part of the page's editors over the fact that the circumstances in which Odette and Nicholas met was not publicly known.

In fact, the circumstances were highly classified. They hadn't sat next to each other at an officer's ball or some party, or been introduced by mutual friends. Instead, they had gotten to talking during a secret ceremony at Balmoral in which Odette's centuries-old ancestor had sworn his allegiance and that of his brotherhood of flesh-crafting alchemists—the Grafters—to the United Kingdom and the Republic of Ireland.

It had been an occasion of profound significance, and not just because two attractive young people had started chatting and arranged to go out on a date. The Checquy and the Grafters had loathed each other for centuries. For the two groups to bury the hatchet anywhere other than in each other's faces was momentous.

Alix had been present at the ceremony, about two horrified meters away from Nicholas and Odette's initial flirting, and she had been hard-pressed not to intervene with some extremely strong objections. She had known Nicholas pretty much his whole life and felt a sort of big sisterly protectiveness. Meanwhile, Odette was not only herself a Grafter with impossible surgical abilities, but her files indicated that she had a fair amount of biological weaponry tucked away inside her. Alix, like all members of the Checquy, had been brought up to despise the memory of the Grafters. It was bad enough knowing they'd be comrades without having one of them date her honorary little brother.

Now, in the conference room, the Grafter did not look like number four on the list of the World's Most Glamorous Women as voted by the millions of dedicated readers of www.elitegossip.goss.co.uk. Her clothes were rumpled, her eyes were bloodshot, and there were some odd blue streaks across her forehead, as if she'd wiped her brow with inky hands.

"Thank you, Whomsley," said Lady Farrier. "Resume your position outside the apartments." He bowed his head slightly and withdrew.

"My lady," Alix greeted Lady Farrier. "Pawn Leliefeld."

"Alexandra," said Farrier. "I'm afraid that there has been a great tragedy." Alix shot a look at the distraught Leliefeld.

"Has something happened to Nicky?"

"No," said the Grafter. "His brother."

"Edmund?" gasped Alix.

"Yes," said Lady Farrier. "The Prince of Wales has died."

"No!" exclaimed Alix. "Oh, God, what happened?" Her hands fluttered to her hair, and then she found that she was holding them hard to her chest, clutching at her blouse.

"We don't know, precisely," Farrier said. Her gaze was steely and her voice calm, but there was a sheen of tears across her eyes.

"Princess Louise found her brother on the floor of the library," Odette said. "I was here, visiting Nicholas, and the King summoned me to administer first aid." Alix nodded. The Grafters were the premier medical experts in the world, and the King knew that. "I did everything I could, but the prince did not respond. At all."

"So he was dead by the time you got there?" Alix said.

"Even if he was dead, the treatments I administered should have elicited some reaction. But there was nothing. It just seemed so wrong. I advised the King of the possibility that it might be Checquy-relevant, and then called Lady Farrier."

"I came immediately," Lady Farrier said. "Odette explained her concerns, and I authorized her to conduct an immediate autopsy."

"What?" said Alix. "Where?"

"In the library, where he was found," the Lady said.

"Are you *serious*?"

"We couldn't move him," said Odette. "The staff might have seen. And we couldn't bring in anyone else."

"You cut Prince Edmund up in the *library*? Aren't autopsies incredibly messy? Liquids coming out of people, and smells."

"I had a specially bred surgical sheet in my handbag. It absorbs any spilled blood and other body fluids," Odette said.

"Yes, but don't you need tools? Tell me you didn't do it with cutlery from the dining room."

"I always have tools," said Odette. "And it was just a basic examination. I didn't leave any marks for a surgeon to see."

"We needed to know if an autopsy by a normal doctor would reveal anything supernatural," Farrier said.

"So what did you find?"

"There were no obvious wounds to his body, so I began by examining his brain." Alix choked a little at this, but Odette proceeded undaunted. "I removed his skullcap and identified an immediate anomaly. There was a small gray pyramid emerging a few inches from the top of his brain. Three-sided, perfectly smooth."

"What the hell does that mean?"

"I don't know! I've never seen anything like it!" snapped Odette. She took a breath. "I decided not to proceed any further. I left the thing untouched, replaced the top of the skull, and welded it back together. I moved the face and scalp back into position and sealed everything in place."

"Bloody hell."

"A routine autopsy will not identify a trace of my examination," Odette said. "But any doctor *will* identify the anomaly that I found."

"A thorough examination will be needed," said Lady Farrier, "in a secure facility where more precautions can be taken. But the object in the prince's brain was undeniably unnatural, which places this within the jurisdiction of the Checquy."

"Who knows about this?" asked Alix.

"The only people to know about the prince's death are we three, Sir Henry, Pawn Clements, the King, Prince Nicholas, and Princess Louise." Alix nodded, dazed. Sir Henry Wattleman was the other leader of the Checquy. Who was Pawn Clements? The sorrow at Edmund's loss, her sympathy for his family, the shock that the cause was supernatural... it all combined to set her head reeling. *The poor King! And Louise! I should go to them.*

"What about the Princess of Wales?" she asked.

"She's away in York, opening a women's shelter," Odette said.

"Yes, but she doesn't know?"

"No," said the Lady. "No one will know until we have some answers."

She's his wife! thought Alix. *No matter what they find, he is still going to be dead.*

"First, we must know if this was an attack," Farrier continued. "It could have been a manifestation within the prince's own body. He might have had abilities that activated and killed him. Pawn Clements is now in the library, reading the history of the room to see if there was anyone else there at the time of his death."

Right. Felicity Clements, the psychometrist. Clements was a barghest— a soldier in the Checquy's elite tactical response team—but she also possessed the ability to read the history of objects and locations. It made sense to call her in to view the exact circumstances of Edmund's death. "How we will proceed depends on what she sees. If it was an attack, the royal family will be evacuated to a safe location, and the palace will go into lockdown."

"Where are they now?" Alix asked.

"They are together in the King's study, with Pawn Ganly," said

Lady Farrier. "Ganly does not know the situation, but he knows we are at elevated alert." Alix nodded. Solal Ganly was attached to the palace security team, and if there *was* some sort of attack, he could have the family safely transported to safety in a heartbeat.

Although I don't know how they'd explain to Louise how she'd been teleported to the upper branches of the nearest oak tree.

"Meanwhile, there are issues we need to address," Lady Farrier continued. "As you know, Prince Edmund leaves no heir." Alix nodded sadly. Earlier in the year, the prince's wife Gemma, the Princess of Wales, had been six months into her first pregnancy when she abruptly lost the baby. The entire nation—in fact, the entire world—had been shocked and dismayed.

"And because of the Succession to the Crown Act of 2013, Princess Louise, rather than Prince Nicholas, is the heir apparent," said Lady Farrier. "She is now the crown princess."

Oh, Lou, I'm so sorry. I know you never wanted this.

"Of course," Lady Farrier was saying, "because of his experience in Yorkshire, Prince Nicholas is aware of the Checquy."

That and he's been shagging a bio-sculpted super surgeon from Brussels for a few months.

"But," continued the Lady, "you are quite certain, Pawn Mondegreen, that the princess does not know about the Checquy?"

"Not so far as I'm aware." *Certainly not about me.*

The Lady leaned forward, her eyes fixed on Alix's.

"How do you think she will react if she learns?"

And suddenly Alix understood.

"Oh, my God. You're asking if she can be trusted."

"I'm asking if you think the future queen of the United Kingdom will have a psychotic break if she is confronted with the existence of the Checquy Group." Alix gaped at her. "There is precedent," the Lady said, "and we have to be practical."

"Edmund is dead down the hallway, freshly autopsied on a rug, and you want to know how this will impact future operations!"

A part of her knew that, of course, the Lady would be concerned for how this would affect the organization, but it was *Edmund,* a man they both knew and cared about deeply. And now he was gone, ripped away from them by something inexplicable, and Farrier wanted to talk about the *bureaucracy* of it.

"When confronted with the undeniable existence of the completely inexplicable, the vast majority of people do not react well," Lady Farrier said. "Even in calm, controlled circumstances with plenty of preparation, there are usually significant psychological repercussions. The crown princess will, of course, have to undergo a significant evaluation before we can decide whether she should be made conscious of the Checquy's existence. If it is not safe, we will have to explore alternative arrangements for the royal responsibilities." She noticed that Odette was looking confused.

"We're required to have two members of the royal family read in," the Lady explained. "And they have to be either on the throne or within the first ten in line. Currently, we have the King and Prince Nicholas, but ideally it will be the monarch and their direct heir because otherwise, they can be moved down and out as various royal children come on the scene. If we end up having to maneuver around Princess Louise, then it's going to make things very complicated, especially once she's queen. So, right now, I'm curious as to what you think."

"Well...if you're asking for a gut evaluation...I think she would be okay," Alix said hesitantly. "Louise is rational and, you know, sensible."

"Those are not always good things in these circumstances," said Farrier.

"Her brother seems to be fine with it."

"Nicholas is only doing...sort of all right," Odette said. "He is seeing a Checquy therapist a couple of times a week and he is on some quite serious antidepressants."

"But he's dating *you!*" exclaimed Alix. The other two women froze. "I beg your pardon."

"I think he finds it reassuring that my abilities are rooted in science," the Grafter said. "It may be science that he doesn't understand, but it's easier to contemplate than a man who shatters into hundreds of sapphires, or a woman with jasmine vines growing out of her mouth."

"Pawns Sanchez and Macnair?" asked the Lady. "When did he meet them?"

"He came to visit me at my office," Odette replied. "He introduced himself to some colleagues, and Sanchez was so excited to see him that he tripped down the stairs and had to be swept up."

"It's not the worst thing the prince has seen," Farrier said. "Now, back to the matter at hand. Until we have the results from Clements's investigation, the three of us and Pawns Ganly and Whomsley will be providing immediate security to the royal family."

"Shouldn't we call in troops?" asked Alix. "Or at least let palace security know?" *Or the Prime Minister?*

"The biggest story in the world is waiting for Clements to finish her work. Until we know what we are dealing with, however, I will not allow it to break."

At that moment, a faint noise of gongs came from Lady Farrier's handbag. She checked her phone.

"It's Clements."

3

The difference between the service area and the royal family's private quarters was so striking that it was like entering a new, much more expensive world. They moved down rich carpets, past art-covered walls that climbed up and up and up to high ornate ceilings. Alix's brow wrinkled; it was much quieter than she was used to.

"Where are the servants?" she asked. Usually, there were people bustling about cleaning or fetching things. "Oh, wait. It's an at-home day, isn't it? That's why the diary was empty." Odette nodded.

"Because all the siblings were in town," the Grafter girl said. "Louise just got home yesterday, now that she's graduated from Exeter and packed everything up, and Nicholas is on leave from the army, so the King and Edmund blocked off any appointments. The Princess of Wales had been booked months ago, and it's for one of her primary causes, so she wouldn't get out of it. The King wanted to cook for the family, so staff have been staying out, giving them privacy. A quiet day."

It's going to be a good deal less quiet now.

Lady Farrier led them to the door of the library, where Pawn Felicity Clements, an athletic blond woman, was waiting.

"Clements," asked Lady Farrier. "What did you see?"

"My lady, no one was in there with him when he died," said the pawn. "He was standing by a bookshelf, reading a book, and then he just collapsed." She sighed. "I'm very sorry. Of course, I can't guarantee anything, but I didn't see any other physical presence in the room."

"All right, thank you, Clements. Would you please join Whomsley outside the entrance."

"Yes, my lady," said the pawn. She put her hand on Odette's shoulder for a second and then hurried away.

The Lady dialed a number. "Tristan, is the line secure? Good. Patch me in." She paused. Alix assumed that she was being connected to the rest of the Court, the Checquy's executive leadership.

The phone beeped. "This is Farrier, I am in the family quarters of Buckingham Palace. It is my regretful duty to advise that the Prince of Wales was found dead here late this morning." She paused, presumably while the Court digested this bombshell. "Odette Leliefeld has conducted an examination and has confirmed that the prince died as a result of unnatural causes." She listened. "No, Prime Minister," the Lady said, and Alix twitched in surprise. "We cannot be certain as to the source. There will need to be a full investigation. Preliminary examination suggests that this is not the result of a deliberate action or attack, but I recommend heightened preparedness throughout the commonwealth. I propose that the Checquy should be stood up to alert status Heliotrope. Sir Henry, do you agree?... Good, then. Rooks, the command is given. Enact measures immediately.

"I will remind you that this means additional pawns in place at Buckingham Palace, Nonsuch Palace, Kensington Palace, Lambeth Palace, Number 10, Number 11, Bute House, Áras an Uachtaráin, the Steward's Lodge, and that fish and chip shop in Tunbridge Wells. Every member of the royal family will have at least one PPO from the

Checquy...I'm sorry? Oh, that's personal protection officers, they're bodyguards from the Metropolitan Police. We have a few agents salted in there.

"Bishops, you'll need to advise the Court of the Croatoan of our upgrade in alert status." Alix nodded. The Croatoan was the American version of the Checquy—in fact, it had been formed by Checquy operatives who remained when the colonies went independent. The two organizations remained close and shared a great deal of information.

"Forty-eight hours from now, barring manifestations, we will reconvene to review the situation and decide if extension or escalation is needed. I will speak with the King now and advise him of the situation, and then he will raise the alarm. Prime Minister, Taoiseach, First Ministers, I expect that your offices will shortly receive word that the Prince of Wales is being rushed to hospital. We leave it to you to gauge your response.

"In keeping with all applicable acts, because the prince's death represents a manifestation of inexplicable events, it will be announced as the result of natural causes. The bishops will coordinate the list of everyone who will be informed of the truth, but it will need to be kept to a small circle, given the prominence of the deceased. Any questions? No? All right, we'll talk again soon. Goodbye." She hung up and looked at the two pawns.

"Alexandra, Odette, you will remain here, outside the library. Once I've spoken to the family, I will call for you, Odette. I will then bring the King back here. He will call for help. The official story will be that he discovered the prince and raised the alarm. You will ensure that no one enters until the King has arrived."

"Louise will want to know what's going on, why I was providing medical care, and why it's taken so long to alert anyone else," Odette warned. "I expect she's been asking from the moment it happened."

"I will give an edited explanation," said the Lady. "Pawn Leliefeld, I will say that you have some medical training." She paused a moment and thought. "From your mandatory military service in Belgium."

"Belgium doesn't have a mandatory military service," objected Odette.

"I doubt the princess will know that. But fine, we'll say you served in the reserves. We need, however, to justify your having greater knowledge than a basic first-aid course." She tapped her lips thoughtfully. "I'll explain that we should alter the official story in order to protect Leliefeld, so that she does not receive public scrutiny as the woman who failed to save the life of the next King." Odette shifted a little uncomfortably at this. "No one blames you, but that's how it could be seen. And we'll also want to divert attention away from Louise and onto the King, who is better equipped to deal with it. It will also protect Louise's legacy. Otherwise, her discovering her brother's dead body could feature in every article and history written about her."

"Do you think they will go along with that?" Odette asked dubiously.

"Oh, yes. They're used to that sort of thing." The Lady wrinkled her nose. "After all, when Stephen the Third was dying, he was euthanized to ensure that the news made the morning papers, rather than the evening ones."

"What was wrong with the evening papers?" Odette asked faintly.

"They were judged less suitable," said the Lady. "Now, after I have spoken with them, Leliefeld, you will take the prince and princess to the lounge and sit with them while I take the King through the actual situation, and we get ready for the entire world to go insane." She moved off, leaving Alix and Odette standing awkwardly outside the library.

"You knew him well," Odette said finally. Alix looked at her. "The prince?"

"All my life, pretty much," Alix said. The Grafter nodded sympathetically.

"I only met him a few times, but he seemed very kind."

"He was incredibly patient," said Alix suddenly, surprising herself. "Even when he was a teenager, he never minded Louise and me being annoying little girls and running around the place. He didn't ignore us or tell us to leave him alone. He would play ponies or shops or school with us, and let us boss him around." She took a breath. "He was a good listener. He had me over for lunch after I graduated from the Estate, and I unloaded a bit, and he was so kind about it, just let me talk out all my worries and fears." *And now he's lying dead on the other side of the door.* She bit her lip so that she wouldn't start crying. Then she realized who she was talking to and collected herself. "Anyway, I always thought those were the things that would make him a good king."

"May I ask, Pawn Mondegreen, when did you enter the Checquy?"

Be polite.

"I was six when they became aware of me."

"But you remained with your family, no?" Alix stiffened. "Nicky says your parents are friends with the King, that you are all often present at occasions."

"My father passed away two years ago," said Alix. The Grafter opened her mouth, presumably to offer her condolences, but Alix plowed ahead. "But, yes, we've spent quite a bit of time with the royal family."

"Is this usual?" asked Odette. "I understood that children who develop abilities are removed entirely from their families? It is a complete severing of ties, with no contact."

"Yes," said Alix. She could feel a hot blush starting to burn her cheeks.

"But your family is of the aristocracy, yes? Is there a different rule for the nobility?"

"No," said Alix tightly. "There isn't."

"Ah, I'm still learning how the system works," said Odette. She did not seem at all uncomfortable, but as far as Alix could tell, the Grafter was genuinely curious, rather than deliberately pressing a finger on a painful nerve. "My eye is always caught by anomalies—it's my training, you see. And you seem to be something of an anomaly."

Presumably her training had also taught her to overcome any qualms about asking personal questions.

"Was it your family's relationship with the King?" the Grafter asked. "Did he intercede on your behalf?"

"My parents," said Alix tightly, "did not become acquainted with the royal family until *after* I came to the attention of the Checquy."

The Grafter finally seemed to realize that she was touching on a sore subject and fell silent.

The two of them stood quietly, pretending an interest in the furnishings and décor.

Alix's phone rang. It was Farrier.

"The King wishes to speak to you. Come to the study with Odette."

"What does he want to speak about?" asked Alix, but the line was already dead.

The door to the study opened as they approached, and Farrier escorted the prince and princess out into the hallway. Louise looked at Alix, bewildered for a moment and then startled as she recognized her.

"Alix?" she exclaimed, and broke away toward her. "Oh, God, Allie!"

"Oh, Lou, I'm so, *so* sorry," Alix said, and then they were holding each other tight. She rested her cheek on the top of Louise's head. She could feel the heat of the princess's tears soaking into her blouse.

Lady Farrier cleared her throat. "The King is waiting," she said. Nicholas stepped forward, and Alix transferred Louise into his arms.

"But why is—" Louise began, but the door to the study was already closing behind Alix, leaving everyone else outside.

It was not the formal office, in which the King met weekly with the Prime Minister. This was the King's actual study, a small, cozy room with a fireplace and landscapes on the walls. Framed photos were scattered about, and Alix knew that she featured in a couple of them. However, her eye was drawn to the man leaning over the desk.

James III (except in Scotland, where he was James VIII), by the Grace of God of the United Kingdom of Great Britain and Northern Ireland and of His Other Realms and Territories King, Head of the Commonwealth, Defender of the Faith. He looked like a king. Tall, broad-shouldered. His sandy hair was cropped close—he'd never let it grow since his time in the army. His face was on banknotes, his profile on coins all around the world, although she always thought the images never captured his reassuring air of calmness.

As a child, Alix had been dandled on his knee, and she still received Christmas and birthday presents from him. He was the closest thing to an uncle she'd known in her life, albeit a very reserved uncle whom she never addressed by name.

"Your Majesty." Automatically, she was doing the curtsy that she'd mastered when she was seven.

"My dear girl," he said. He came toward her, his hands out. She put her hands up to take his, but to her surprise he caught her up in a rough hug. "Thank you for coming."

"My cond—" She gulped. "My condolences, sir." She swallowed back a sob and could feel him shaking a little. Alix had never seen him like this, not even when his wife had passed away seven years earlier. Finally, she felt him take a breath, and then he patted her on the back and let her go.

"I still can't believe it. Seeing him on the floor..." He brushed a hand across his eyes. "Odette, she did her best, I could see that."

"If she couldn't help him, then no one could have."

"Lady Farrier and Odette believe that there was something... uncanny about his death," said the King. Alix nodded. "What can you tell me?"

"Nothing, yet, sir," she said. "They're certain that it was unnatural, but they'll need to conduct an in-depth examination."

"Do they think it was an attack of some sort?"

"It's possible," she said carefully. "But it could just as easily have been a random event. Nevertheless, we're increasing the security level around the country and around the palace."

He smiled weakly. "It's still strange for me to be talking to you as a soldier of the Checquy. I can remember when you first came here, just a tiny girl, making your little curtsy, almost falling on your bottom."

"My mother nearly had a heart attack. She'd drilled me for hours, wanting everything to be perfect."

"It was adorable, I thought everything went very well. You ended up calling me 'Kingy.'"

"You were very nice," said Alix. "Not at all grand and frightening."

"I wanted to set you at ease. And your parents."

"I'm afraid they were *immediately* at ease. They were ecstatic."

For her parents, becoming intimates of the royal family had been the pinnacle of their ambitions. They gloated over their standing invitations to Easter lunch at Nonsuch Palace and their regular attendance at palace receptions. At least once a year, they attended the theater with the King and Queen. They were seen in the royal box at Ascot. The sitting room at Wyndham Towers featured a large framed photograph of Lord Mondegreen, his wife, and part of Alix's shoulder seated prominently at Edmund's investiture as the Prince of Wales.

The fact that it had all been under a certain amount of duress had never diminished an iota of their pleasure.

Alix's father Peregrine, the eleventh Lord Mondegreen, had enjoyed spending money and living the life that he thought was owed to a lord. He'd attended and thrown extravagant parties, dressed in tailored clothes, traveled around the world, and driven expensive cars, despite the fact that all this cost more than he could possibly afford, especially given that doing a tap of work was not the life he thought was owed to a lord.

To make matters worse, the eighth lord (he who had commissioned the fancy new incarnation of Wyndham Towers) had been the last Mondegreen to show any facility with making money rather than spending it. Peregrine was the latest in a long line of Mondegreen spendthrifts, each of whom had been obliged to marry for money, resulting in the multiple hyphenations of their surname.

In his midthirties, having burned through a sizable portion of his inheritance, Peregrine was obliged to take stock of his situation. It was not good. The family coffers were nearly empty, the London flat had been foreclosed upon, the cars had been seized, and the bailiffs were looking speculatively at Wyndham Towers and the estates. Peregrine hurriedly followed in the tradition of his forebears. A society marriage to Charlotte Dennis and her family's banking money gained him a respite from the creditors, a wife just as eager as he to live the high life, and yet another hyphenation.

The two of them lived lavishly for a couple of years until Alix came on the scene. They curtailed their revels briefly, not out of any wish to spend time with their infant daughter but because Charlotte refused to allow Peregrine to go out without her, and also refused to go out until she'd lost the baby weight. Eventually she resumed the shape she wanted, and they found a nanny who would keep the child out of their sight for months at a time.

By the time Alix was six, Lord and Lady Mondegreen had managed to shift all of their combined inheritances out of the family coffers and into the coffers of tailors, designers, hoteliers, restaurateurs, jewelers, bookmakers, and croupiers. They were grimly contemplating selling off the Towers when they were saved by the inexplicable, in the form of the daughter they could not have picked out of a lineup.

Peregrine and Charlotte were not aware that their daughter had begun developing supernatural abilities. The Checquy Group, however, *had* become aware of the situation, and they approached the couple with a proposal.

Normally, the Checquy did not negotiate when it came to children with supernatural powers. It simply took them from their families, usually in such a way that the family did not know the child was still alive or that the government was involved in any way. Very occasionally, the child might be acquired for money—a process that, while much less complicated than stealing the child, was almost more distasteful. Whatever approach was taken, it was all done in complete secrecy and was perfectly legal, even if in accordance to laws that were themselves completely secret.

When it came to Alix, however, some clever soul identified a unique opportunity. The little girl was a member of the aristocracy, had no inhuman features or characteristics, appeared to be sane, had powers that could be devastating but could also function discreetly, and was the same age as the King's daughter.

The royal family and everyone around them was exposed to a level of scrutiny that bordered on the ludicrous. A new face in the royal orbit inevitably attracted outside attention and speculation. Security personnel were always obvious. With young Alix it would be possible to insert a Checquy presence into the close personal circle of the royal family with no questions asked. They could begin laying the groundwork now, establishing her as Louise's friend.

Later, once Alix was trained, she could attend occasions where the Checquy deemed that subtle security was needed. By then, she would be known as an intimate of the royal family, a socialite noblewoman whom no one would suspect had any combat abilities, let alone supernatural powers. The advantages of such an unobtrusive agent were clear.

In order to pursue this plan, however, she would need to remain a part of her family, minor nobility though they were. At this point, the financial acumen that had eluded Lord Mondegreen all his life manifested with such a vengeance that it practically constituted a supernatural power of his own. The Dennis-Palmer-Hudson-Gilmore-Garnseys sat down with representatives from the Checquy and hammered out the details. Peregrine and Charlotte argued that in order for their child to be a friend of the royal family, they themselves would need to be friends of the royal family, and in order for that to happen plausibly, they would need to be kept in the style to which friends of the King were accustomed.

The Checquy representatives rolled their eyes (and, in the case of Pawn Manguel, his face) but acceded to the couple's demands. The Mondegreens' debts would be paid off. They would receive lifetime use of a flat in London (whose furnishings the Mondegreens would select, and which the Checquy would pay for). They would receive a generous monthly index-linked allowance. All of this in exchange for the Checquy's lifelong ownership of their daughter.

I hope you know that despite the circumstances, I've always been very fond of you, Alexandra," the King said. "And your friendship with Louise has always struck me as completely genuine."

"I really wasn't aware of any ulterior motive in bringing us together at the time," she told him. "I was only, what? Seven? Of course, I knew that I couldn't tell anyone about being in the Checquy—*that* had been drilled into me for a year by that point. I just thought it was a special occasion."

"You've grown up with my daughter. You know her as well as anyone."

"Well...," began Alix awkwardly.

"I wish I could give her privacy, time to mourn, but who we are makes that impossible. Her life is going to change, radically." He paused. "My sister and brother always felt like the 'spares to the heir.' I have always tried to make it clear to Louise and Nicholas that they were not fallbacks, that we had them because we wanted to have them. But they have always known what came with being part of this family."

He swallowed, then went on. "Louise has never allowed being 'royal' to define her. She has built her own life, with her studies, with an eye toward something of her own. And now this has happened..." He sighed. "She will need support. Not just from her family, but from people she can trust."

"Of course, sir."

"And we do not know if Ed—if his death was deliberate. I need my daughter to be kept safe. I want you by her side." He looked at her intently. "You will be one of her ladies-in-waiting."

Oh.

No.

There was a knock at the door.

"Come," the King said.

It was Lady Farrier.

"Your Majesty, it's time."

Alix sat alone in the study. The door was ajar, and she could hear the scenario playing out down the hallway. People came rushing at the King's call, there were gasps, then frantic shouting. Lots of people moving about. She heard weeping, and then, later, distantly, the sound of ambulance sirens.

Alix could tell when word spread to the outside world. Her phone vibrated with a text message from a civilian friend. Then again, from another. Then all the messages she was not answering set it to clattering across the table like a lobster having a seizure.

A distant murmur rose outside. Alix looked through the curtains and saw people gathering at the palace gates. Members of the public looked forlornly through the bars. Sunlight flashed off phones held up to record or take photos, and she flinched back. Beyond the civilians, there were members of the press, their backs to the palace as they spoke to cameras.

Do they know he's dead? Or just that he's been taken to hospital?

The door opened, and Lady Farrier entered.

"It went as planned," the Lady said. "The prince and princess accepted the need for our official story. The King has gone to the hospital to be with the prince's body. Princess Louise and Prince Nicholas are still here. Odette has left—I didn't want her answering any questions from the princess."

"What about the library?" asked Alix. "Has it been secured for the Checquy investigation?" Despite her sorrow, her investigative instincts were unsheathing themselves, and she was concerned about the manifestation scene being disturbed.

"Once the prince's body was removed, the King ordered the room locked," said Farrier. "We'll work out the arrangements for the investigation."

"Has Edmund's death been announced?" Alix asked. The Lady looked at her watch.

"In seventeen minutes, he will be pronounced dead." Alix winced. The Lady regarded her thoughtfully. "This is going to change a great many things. I understand that the King spoke to you about being a lady-in-waiting."

"I don't want to."

The Lady looked at her with a withering raised eyebrow, but Alix was too appalled to be withered. On a day that had been full of nasty, world-altering surprises, this was the blow that struck at her own life most directly.

Alix was a foot soldier in the Checquy Group—a pawn. She was an investigator, called out to examine sites of supernatural manifestations and identify the causes. It meant lots of abrupt travel around the country, and then lots of time sifting through information, thinking about it, and writing it up.

She specialized in botany, but all Checquy operatives were trained to undertake combat if necessary, and so she was sometimes deployed to situations in which her particular abilities might be useful. Seven months earlier, she'd been flown to an oligarch's country estate in Hampshire to take point on the manifestation known informally as *Ossuarius Rex,* when the man's private museum of dinosaur bones had animated and threatened to run wild. Just sixteen days ago, she'd been called in to help with the operation that had resulted in her ordered-and-just-canceled vacation.

On top of all that, she was periodically dispatched to be a guest/secret bodyguard/informed pair of eyes when the Checquy felt that additional, subtle supernatural support was needed at a royal event.

She enjoyed her work and she was good at it. When so many elements of her life felt false, she consoled herself with the fact that what she did was important. And she wanted to climb in the Checquy, partly because of her own ambition, and partly because she desperately wanted to prove to her colleagues that she deserved her place and was worthy of respect, in spite of her title.

The Checquy was not a pure meritocracy. Some positions would only ever be available to those with supernatural capabilities—the pawns. But there were no sinecures, one had to earn one's promotions. Every advancement was scrutinized by higher-ups and discussed endlessly by the rank and file. The nature of the work meant that no job could be done half-assedly, and people who did not live up to their roles, if they survived, were demoted. The incremental advancements in Alix's career so far had occurred because she'd proved herself.

Becoming a lady-in-waiting would put paid to that. The role had changed a great deal over the centuries, even over the past few years. She wouldn't be expected to taste Louise's food or scrub her back in the bath, or even, probably, manage her diary. Modern princesses came with a full professional support team, including a private secretary and a personal assistant.

The role of lady-in-waiting, however, was exceptional. It meant being a confidante and companion to the princess, a close counselor at the heart of her court. For members of the royal family, it wasn't easy to make genuine friends, and even as they were meeting scores of people, their roles could be incredibly isolating. They needed individuals they could trust to be in their lives, friends who knew the rules. This was one of the reasons ladies-in-waiting traditionally came from the aristocracy.

There was no telling what Louise would require of her ladies-in-waiting. Until now, the princess hadn't had any entourage beyond the obligatory bodyguards. But because she was a working royal, that was going to change. A modern lady-in-waiting might shoulder some of the traditional responsibilities for the princess's wardrobe and jewels, and for handling correspondence, but she was also a representative, a deputy hostess, a messenger, a pair of eyes, a problem solver.

The job had its perks, and it was a tremendous honor, but for Alix it represented professional suicide. Because above all else, ladies-in-waiting were attendants, which meant they needed to *attend*. Alix knew that royal responsibilities would almost always take precedence over Checquy responsibilities. When called, she would have to come, and be in the public eye. There was a world of difference between being the friend and occasional guest of the royal family and being a lady-in-waiting to the crown princess. The fact that Lady Farrier herself had been a lady-in-waiting and had risen to head the Checquy was no comfort. She'd been in the role before her abilities had ignited and gotten her drafted into the Checquy. Things had changed in the thirty-odd years since she'd held the bouquets for Louise's grandmother.

In a life that had afforded Alix very few choices, becoming an investigator was an accomplishment she could take pride in. She had achieved it, rather than being born to it. She had needed to develop specific expertise and prove herself capable of working in the field and producing satisfactory results. She had beaten out other candidates for the role, convincing people who were inclined to doubt her. Now she faced the prospect of being shunted off into a professional cul-de-sac.

Forever. Ladies-in-waiting did not retire—you were in service to your lady for life. Alix could see all her plans crumbling in front of her. The expression on Lady Farrier's face made it clear that Alix's plans and her wishes in this matter counted for less than nothing. And this fact was so obvious that it didn't even need to be declared.

The ongoing silence was painful, and Alix flailed about for something to say, anything that might serve to derail this train. A possibility occurred to her.

"Also," she said cautiously, "I don't know that I would be Louise's first choice." She paused. "I probably wouldn't make the top five."

It was true. Although she and Louise had been friends for years, they were not really boon companions, despite the machinations of the Checquy. And there had been plenty of machinations.

Alix had been sent to the same school as Louise (with the Checquy picking up the tab), and they were always assigned to the same class, although Alix had missed quite a bit during her frequent absences. She had been a member of the 1st Buckingham Palace Company of Girl Guides, re-formed so that Louise could have the experience of being part of a club.

When they were small, they had played together frequently. The mandarins and strategists of the Checquy had probably congratulated each other as the two little girls attended each other's birthday parties, had sleepovers, and romped around on plenty of playdates. As they grew, they had snuck their first beers together, gone clubbing, and attended balls and weekend house parties, but eventually they grew apart. Though they remained fond of each other, they were not best friends. They had different interests, different likes.

When they graduated from high school, they went their separate ways. Louise went to Oxford to study PPE—philosophy, politics, and economics. Alix undertook a year's intensive study at the Estate, the Checquy's training facility (explained to the world as a gap year in New Zealand). Then she had moved into full-time work as a pawn of the Checquy (although as far as the world knew, she had gotten a job with the world's least interesting legal firm).

While Alix was being deployed on investigations and operations, Louise had kept herself firmly out of the papers by maintaining a small group of friends and not getting photographed drunk, doing drugs, or wearing even mildly interesting clubbing clothes.

The princess had then gone on to Exeter to study business,

leadership, and sustainability. They sent each other occasional emails, met for drinks when they were both in the same place, and gossiped about former classmates.

Now they were old friends who could slide into easy conversation no matter how long it had been since they'd last seen each other. The relationship had simply settled at a certain level of affection, and then stayed there. The Checquy Group could corral a wild horde of seizure-inducing pangolins in Dover, they could arrange the assassination of a wirry-cow in the back of her limousine in rush-hour traffic on the M5, and they could steal children from their families without leaving a trace of suspicion, but they could not engineer a strong devotion between two girls.

"The crown princess will not have a choice in the matter," the Lady said.

"Understood," said Alix dully.

"Good. Now, I must go to Apex House for the autopsy."

"What should I do?" asked Alix.

"You're to remain here in the family quarters for security," said the Lady. "You'll have your usual guest room. But for now, stay close to the princess. Same room if possible. If she's in her bedroom with the door shut, you're near the door."

What about clothes? Alix wanted to ask, but the Lady had already left the room. *Ugh, it'll get figured out.* She was about to leave when her eye was caught by one of the family photos on the wall. It was a picture from Edmund's wedding day, taken informally at the end of the day when the party was winding down. He and Gemma had been caught in midlaugh, their heads close together as they shared some private words.

They were so happy. There had been no posing. She knew, because she'd taken the photo. *Oh, Edmund. This shouldn't have happened to you.*

She turned at the sound of the door opening, and Louise strode in. Her face was emotionless.

The princess was shorter than Alix, but so were most women. Whereas Alix's jaw was so strongly defined that it only just stopped shy of being mannish, Louise's face was oval, with delicate pavonine features. Her chestnut hair hung straight and manageable, in contrast to Alix's russet curls, which had been known to catch on picture frames and pull them askew. Edmund had once remarked that they both looked like princesses, except that Alix looked like one who would have conquered Britain while wearing only blue paint and pig-grease dreadlocks, while Louise looked like one who would have died in Versailles while giving birth to the Dauphin.

For all her delicacy, however, Louise possessed tremendous strength of will, which had enabled her to set the course of her life, and bypass a great many expectations. It was one of Alix's favorite things about her.

"Lady Mondegreen," said the princess.

Oh, it's going to be one of those times. Sometimes, Louise decided that she was going to be "the princess," usually when she was pissed off.

"Your Royal Highness," said Alix.

"So, you're sleeping with my father?" Louise said coldly.

4

Covert battle instincts honed over a lifetime of intensive training and tested in the heat of supernatural battle utterly failed to help Alix respond to this development.

"I—you—sleeping—wha—what?"

Louise appeared to interpret Alix's bewildered fumbling as guilty admission.

"I can't believe you," said Louise. "You come here—I haven't invited you, and you haven't called me to let me know you're coming. Then, on the worst day of our lives, when everything is falling apart, Fa has you into his study for some alone time. I don't even want to know what you did to comfort him."

"Now, hold—" began Alix, but Louise cut her off.

"You disgust me," the princess said. "My father has informed me that suddenly I will have to have at least three ladies-in-waiting, that you *will* be one of them, and that I have no choice in the matter." Her mouth twisted. "I can only presume this is to facilitate his access to *you*."

"Lou—" Louise's face stopped her. "Ma'am, you've gotten entirely the wrong idea."

"Have I? This is going to be very convenient for you, isn't it? No one will question your presence, so you'll just be hanging around the palace, ready to be summoned to the royal bedchamber. It's disgusting, as if my father were Henry the Eighth." The contempt burning in Louise's eyes, the unfairness of it, at last burned any idea of deference out of Alix's mind.

"I can't believe you would accuse me of that!" spat Alix. "I don't want this either, you know! I don't want to spend my life trailing after you. This is going to totally fuck up my career!"

"Your *career*? Your job at that nothing law firm? You're not even a lawyer, and you're worried about your career! It's pathetic."

"*That's* how you think of me?"

Alix's "job at that nothing law firm" was her official cover. The law firm was housed in the Hammerstrom Building—"The Rookery" to those in the know. It was the nerve center for all the Checquy's domestic operations and housed several deliberately mundane cover businesses.

"What do you even do there?" sneered Louise. "You never talk about your work. You just say you do 'office stuff'!" She snorted. "Such a waste. You had all that excellent education."

"That's not my real job, you fuckwit!" Alix snapped back. "I can't believe you thought that's what I'm doing with my life!"

"Of course not, not when there's so plum a job as royal mistress."

"I'm not sleeping with your father!"

"Please!"

"I'm *not*!" insisted Alix.

"What then? What the *fuck* is going on?"

"He didn't tell you anything about this?"

"No!"

Thanks a lot, Kingy.

The two women stared at each other, panting after all their rage.

What do I tell her? I can't lie to her but I can't give her the whole truth, not without permission and clearances, and the assurance that she won't have a nervous breakdown.

"Well?" demanded Louise.

"What do you think Lady Farrier's job is?" Alix asked.

"Linda?" said Louise. "I don't know. She advises and briefs Fa on various government things. She's very quiet about it, so I assumed she was MI5 or MI6." Her eyebrows rose. "Is *that* what you do? You're a spy?"

"I work for her, but we're...a fully separate body." Alix flailed about for an explanation that might encompass the mission of the Checquy without sounding insane. "We deal with the occult."

"Like cults?"

"Sometimes..."

"Why have I never heard of this?"

"It's a peculiar organization," said Alix. "Not something we publicize. It wouldn't look good for the government." All of which was perfectly true but didn't really convey what the Checquy was or why it was kept secret.

"Why would we have a bureau of cults? Are there that many?"

"Not *so* many," said Alix, wary of suggesting that they dealt exclusively with weird little sects. "It's a legacy body. It's very old."

"How old?" asked Louise. "You make it sound like it goes back to the witch trials."

"You're in the right neighborhood," said Alix. In fact, the origins of the Checquy were lost in the mists of time and lack of effective recordkeeping, but it certainly stretched back centuries.

"You can't be serious!"

"Well, it's not like we're putting witches on trial *now*," said Alix. *If we found any witches, we'd probably sit them down and explain the juicy retirement plan they'd be eligible for if they signed up with us.* "The organization was set up with certain powers and authority, and it's proven useful. It's discreet and lets the government undertake certain operations without having to explain things."

"And you're part of this?"

"Yes."

"What do you *do*?"

"I'm on leave at the moment," hedged Alix.

"What's the last thing you did, then?"

Alix hesitated. The last thing she'd done had resulted in being obliged to take leave after she'd broken a total of fifty-eight bones, none of them her own, and several of them belonging to colleagues.

Alix had already been in a bad mood when she stepped into the briefing room at the Checquy's Leeds facility. She had been at her desk in the Rookery, working away on a report on a pot of malevolent nasturtiums in Cumbria that had been directing bees to swarm people and also steal their credit card details, when she'd gotten the call that she was required, immediately, in West Yorkshire. A plane ticket had been sent to her phone; there was a car waiting downstairs to take her to Heathrow, and no luggage or equipment would be needed.

To make matters worse, this was not a deployment to an investigation, or even a tedious assignment to act as a worker in some undertaking for which the Checquy could not just call a labor hire company and ask for some temps. This was a combat requisition.

Pawns' occupations within the Checquy were not determined by their supernatural abilities. Just because your teeth could be plucked out and thrown as high-explosive grenades did not mean you were going to be a soldier. A person's ability to transform concrete into a delicious and highly nutritious cakelike substance with a glance did not automatically get them assigned to catering or demolition. People were generally allowed to pursue the positions they wanted, provided they were qualified and competent, and there was an opening.

The particulars of one's power *did* mean, however, that one would periodically get requisitioned for a specific mission, if one was the exact right tool for the job. The woman in the Education and Training section of the Wolverhampton office who could breathe *in* fire might be called in to extinguish an unquenchable blaze in the sewers of Sampford Brett. Or there might be a supernaturally toxic building that could only be destroyed completely if they brought in Pawn Sammy Rabkin from Porlock to eat it.

Alix's abilities made her very good at damaging people, but it was not something she liked to do, so she was already feeling somewhat on edge. Then, just to make things quadruply bad, when she finally arrived at the Checquy offices, she was greeted with a sight that elicited a heavy sigh and a lip curl.

"Lady Mondegreen, I'm surprised you've deigned to join us," said Pawn Sweven, putting the slightest but snottiest emphasis on the "Lady."

"Oh, Mark, it's not just me. *Everyone* here is deigning to work with you," she replied.

She'd known Mark Sweven for years—they had been in the same class at the Estate. They loathed each other.

Sweven possessed the power to stretch and harden his skin into a startling array of shapes. He had been removed from his family and well settled at the Estate for a year when Alix arrived at the age of six and three-quarters, having undergone several months of training to make sure she didn't accidentally kill her new fellow students. He noticed her disjointed schedule of arriving for training and then departing for weeks at a time. It marked her as different.

Later, word had gotten around as to *why* Alix had such an unusual routine. That she retained a relationship with her family and was also attending a normal school had rankled some people, including Mark. He began putting about that Alix wasn't truly part of the Checquy, and that she thought herself superior because of her family and their royal connections.

The rumor spread. It was difficult to be an outsider in the Checquy, when its members included four siblings with one shared mind, a hyper-intelligent brown bear, and a boy made out of living mahogany, but apparently being a part-time student was enough to do it.

Every time Alix returned to the Estate, the situation was a little worse, with more students regarding her sidelong. As she grew older and was enrolled at the same boarding school as Louise, Alix's time with her peers became even more irregular. Her schedule was dizzying, shuttling back and forth between the Estate and Whyteleafe

School, especially as she was expected to stay on top of her studies for both institutions.

Of course, an alibi was needed for her time at the Estate. The Checquy, dubious about the trustworthiness of photo doctoring, had concocted a stratagem whereby her parents enjoyed exotic vacations, and Alix was flown in to be briskly photographed with them, and then briskly flown out again, having rarely spent more than half an hour in their company. Making close friends at either school was difficult.

Her class's graduation into the role of fully fledged pawns had meant their deployments all around the UK and Ireland, and to various international postings. She was sent to London while Sweven went to Edinburgh, and she hadn't seen him since.

Until now.

"Right, people!" said a woman with viridian hair. "Welcome to Leeds. I'm Pawn Metalious, I'm heading this operation. A quick recap: the stats boffins have identified an anomalous upturn in the number of assaults and brawls in the greater Leeds area over the past four months. Domestic violence is up drastically, but so are incidents of spontaneous random attacks."

"It's not because the Rhinos are having a bad year?" asked some wag. The city's rugby league club had been knocked out of the running very early in the season.

"It's possible," said Metalious, "but our people think it's more likely linked to this woman." A picture flashed up on the screen. A thin white woman in her fifties, with mouse-brown hair that had been ill-advisedly trimmed to ear length and then apparently ignored. She was dressed in drab clothing and had a sober expression.

"Grace Merritt. Fifty-four, single, lifelong resident of Leeds. No history of anything unusual. But her phone's location records show that she was in the vicinity of all the incidents, including the Small Champs football fight." There were mutterings. Footage of the fight had gone viral.

It had started out with two teams of seven-year-olds playing endearingly incompetent football. Then, for no apparent reason, all the children suddenly started fighting each other. The adults stepped in to break up the melee but then began fighting among themselves. The footage turned nauseatingly chaotic since the cameraman had been using his phone as a weapon. Still, it had produced some shocking images, and one shot of a father yelling while four children clung to his legs and bit him had become the basis for a popular series of memes.

The whole thing ended as swiftly as it started, with everyone abruptly stopping and looking around in bewilderment. There were a lot of bruises, quite a few bites, some bloodied lips and black eyes, but nothing worse. None of the participants was able to explain why they had suddenly felt such intense rage. It had been a madness.

"She caused that?" asked Sweven.

"We're not certain," said Pawn Metalious. "But she was there, and she didn't take part in the fight. She was also present at the Sheffield shopping center riot."

Everyone went silent. That had taken place only nine days ago and had been genuinely ugly. On Saturday morning, scores of shoppers had run amok for twenty minutes through the mall. They smashed shop windows and assaulted staff and each other. Hundreds of thousands of pounds of damage and significant injuries resulted. No one was killed, but the whole country had been shaken by an event that authorities could only put down, lamely, to "mass hysteria."

"If our analysts are right, then we are seeing an escalation of aggression-based events. The manifestations are getting bigger and more violent. This woman represents our best lead. Given the escalation, we don't have time for an in-depth, delicate investigation. However, since we don't know if she actually *is* the source, we need to be careful.

"Stage one of today's operation is simple. Pawns Sweven and Garstin will knock on her front door, presenting as police constables. They're both experienced investigators. They'll ask her some questions, keeping the mood very calm and easy."

"So you're just going to ask her questions?" a petite pawn with turquoise eyes and lips asked skeptically.

"There's always the potential for things to go badly very quickly," said Metalious. "And if this woman is knowingly activating her abilities around people, then that suggests some very unpleasant things going on in her psyche. That's why the rest of you will be in a truck across the road." Alix raised her hand, and Metalious nodded to her.

"If this woman *is* the cause of these outbreaks of aggression, should we be concerned about the possibility that she could affect *us*?" Alix asked. "It was dangerous enough when it was just seven-year-olds or shoppers, but if it's pawns, then it could get really bad." She trailed off, and everyone looked thoughtful, then worried.

"Obviously, we need to take some significant precautions. This is Pawn van der Kloof." Metalious gestured to a man in a white coat. "We don't want you all getting your hackles up, so he will administer protective medications. You've all indicated that you're willing to receive limited Broederschap treatment."

There was some muttering at this.

The *Wetenschappelijk Broederschap van Natuurkundigen* was the Grafters' full, official name, which no one else in the Checquy could pronounce correctly. When they'd joined the organization, the Grafters had brought a range of capabilities, all rooted in biological science, and all disquieting. These ranged from performing impossible surgeries to rewriting DNA.

As part of the merger, it was agreed that only the Grafters could decide who would be trained in their techniques, and who would receive the benefits. It didn't matter if you were the Lord of the Checquy, the Prime Minister, the King, or the richest person in the world, they wouldn't cure your cancer or give you a few extra centuries of life unless they wanted to.

The Grafters had offered *some* services to their new colleagues: Lifesaving surgeries that would leave no scars. Replacements for damaged limbs and organs. Fertility treatments. Flu and coronavirus vaccines of incredible efficacy. But there had been little take-up, because all the pawns had been brought up on horror stories of the Grafters.

Everyone had been given a form to fill out, detailing exactly what medical services they would be willing to accept. Most had refused across the board. Alix, however, hated going to the dentist and was lured in by the promise of pain-free dentistry. She had absently checked all sorts of boxes, including, apparently, a willingness to receive limited-duration inoculations for manifestation-deployment purposes.

Pawn van der Kloof moved around, injecting each of them with a bright pink liquid, then wiping down the injection site with something that smelled of fish.

"In a few moments, you will feel a rising sense of great calm," he said to Alix in a thick Dutch accent.

"All right," said Alix warily. "But what *is* this? Is it going to give me the strength of twenty big men?"

"No. It is a cocktail of tranquilizers, mood stabilizers, and antipsychotics," said the Grafter. "I formulated it myself with bespoke enzymes and an excellent strain of microbes."

"But there are commercially available tranquilizers, mood stabilizers, and antipsychotics, aren't there?" She didn't like the idea of having Grafter medicines and microbes washing about in her brain and altering her thoughts, even if they were bespoke.

"Such products are not nearly so good," sniffed the Grafter. "They can have undesirable side effects and can take hours or even weeks or months to take effect. These will activate very shortly." He noticed her nervousness. "The microbes are of a very fine pedigree," he assured her. "My grandfather laid out their line, and there have been no unfortunate mutations in over fifteen billion generations."

"Well, that is reassuring," she said. "How long does it last?"

"For about five hours, and then the effects dissipate completely."

As she sat back and let the stuff sizzle through her veins, Alix saw that Mark Sweven was in his underpants, standing in front of a full-length mirror. He put his hands several centimeters in front of his stomach, and his body swelled to meet his palms. It was only his skin stretching itself out, but it really did look like he was growing plumper. His new belly sagged over the waistband of his briefs.

Under his focus, his sharp chin became rounded, and then another chin was folded in under it. The angles of his cheekbones softened, some slight jowls emerged, and friendly-looking laughter lines crinkled at the corners of his eyes.

Alix had to admit that Sweven knew how to use his powers. He'd added a good twelve years to his appearance. He looked like the only threat he would ever pose was toward the contents of a dessert trolley.

There was a police uniform waiting for him, far too big for his normal size, but only hanging a little loose on him now. By the time he was done, he was the very image of an overly self-indulgent, cheerfully indolent community constable.

The truck from which the team would surveil Grace Merritt's street was painted with the slogan *Jocko's Removal Specialists — we'll move you in a jiff!* Eight soldiers, including Alix, were squished in back on benches facing each other. A double row of televisions angled down from the ceiling showing the team images captured by concealed cameras on the truck's roof. At the front of the compartment, two retainers sat side by side, facing their own bank of monitors. Pawn Metalious stood behind them, giving directions.

Retainers were Checquy operatives who did not possess any supernatural abilities and so did not receive a chess-based title. They were lured in by large paychecks and access to the greatest secrets of the world.

The combat team was dressed in baggy blue coveralls also marked with the Jocko's logo. Underneath, they wore stab vests. They did not have guns; Checquy soldiers were not generally issued firearms. All the pawns selected for the day's mission did, however, have abilities that could disable people without killing them, and without any flashy manifestations that might get caught on video.

"You know, I think it is her," said Alix. She was looking at the photo of Merritt that was displayed on one of the monitors.

"Why?" asked the pawn next to her.

"Her posture. She stands like a queen."

"I suppose you would know," said the pawn, and Alix fell silent. It was the sort of remark that would normally have her flushing in embarrassment.

I think I'm right, though. There was a confidence in Merritt's attitude that Alix knew well: the assurance of someone who knows they have a winning card up their sleeve. She'd spent much of her life around people with that attitude — not just the royal family, but those around them, the wealthy and the powerful who never needed to worry about the millions of little problems that bore down on normal people. They addressed themselves to the world differently, and Alix was seeing a similar demeanor on the monitor. It seemed entirely incongruous with everything else about Merritt, whose life seemed to be one of near-constant disappointment.

An infrared scan of the building confirmed that Merritt (or at least someone of her height and shape, and possessing the same gait) was at home, and the Jocko's Removal Specialists truck pulled up across the street and two houses down. The driver began playing with his phone, the retainers tapped away on their computers, and the soldiers watched the monitors carefully as the roof cameras swiveled in their concealed housing and zoomed in on the front door.

Chez Merritt was semi-detached, with a minuscule front garden consisting of gravel, a couple of bins, and some pots holding dead plants. Faded lace curtains hung yellowly in the windows.

It's hardly Castle Grayskull. It's not even Madam Mim's cottage.

"Ping the location of all active mobile phones in a five-hundred-meter radius," ordered Pawn Metalious.

"Twenty-seven," said one of the retainers. "Including one in the target residence."

"Take care of them. I want no live streaming. If things should escalate, we'll address the issue of any recorded footage later."

"Yes, sir. And let there be"—his finger pressed down on a button—"shitty phone reception."

That would be enough to piss me off. Maybe Merritt doesn't have the power to control people's emotions at all. Maybe she just disrupts their ability to make a call or check texts.

A police car containing the plumpified Pawn Sweven and Pawn Garstin pulled up in front of the house. Garstin was a short young blond woman with big eyes and a winning smile. She exuded a disarming sweetness that had nothing to do with her supernatural power, which was to inflict the sensation of drowning, even when you weren't. Between the two of them, they presented the least threatening image of law enforcement possible.

"Zoom in," ordered Metalious. The image closed in on the door as the two pawns approached, fuzzed for a moment as the door opened, then focused on the face of Grace Merritt.

The woman's eyes widened, and her face took on that instinctive fearful worry that manifests when people see the police on their doorstep, regardless of whether they've done anything wrong. Even if the police are a slim English rose and a man who looks like he would be very comfortable to lean against and take a nap. Then Alix could actually see the moment when the woman remembered something. She looked up, a drab little person in the doorway of a drab little house, and smirked in complete unconcern.

Oh, it's definitely her, Alix thought about saying as much into everyone's earpieces, but her certainty wasn't based on any actual evidence.

"Grace Merritt?" asked Pawn Garstin. She and Sweven were wearing cunningly concealed microphones.

"Yes," she said. "What can I do for you?"

"We're sorry to bother you," said Sweven. "We understand you were a witness to the fight at the children's football match a few weeks ago? We'd like to ask you a few questions about what you saw." Merritt's face tightened, and Alix could see the calculation in the little woman's eyes.

Pawn Sweven suddenly swiveled on the balls of his feet and punched Pawn Garstin in the chest, just as *she* was winding up to punch him.

"Ah," said Pawn Metalious. "That would seem to suggest that Merritt is indeed the culprit." There were murmurs of agreement.

"I'd have thought Garstin would be thrown back by that punch," mused someone in the truck. The pawn was standing still, with Sweven's fist against her.

"That's a good point, Crosby," said Metalious. As they watched, Sweven pulled his hand back, and Garstin teetered on her feet. He held up his arm, and the sleeve flapped down, shredded. Garstin's stab vest had not been able to withstand the three jutting spikes of skin that extruded from around his wrist.

"Right, I see what happened there," said Metalious.

The spikes on Sweven's arm pressed together and merged, making his arm into a single blade. He swung it and smoothly beheaded his comrade.

"Oh, dear," said Metalious.

Sweven was panting, with no sign of horror at having just struck down his colleague. He ignored the woman next to him, who was standing calmly. Merritt's eyes, bright with triumph, were fixed on him. She seemed a little startled but not afraid.

Perhaps she thinks this is a new part of her powers. She can alter people's minds, so why not their bodies? thought Alix.

Sweven's head snapped around to stare at the truck, as if he were gazing at them through the monitors. There was no calculation in that look, only rage. His lips drew back, baring his teeth. Barbs of skin curled up all over his face, and serrations erupted along his brows, cheekbones, and jawline.

Then he burst into motion toward the truck. As he ran, he went down on all fours and his skin spasmed around him in a flurry of spikes and blades. They shredded his uniform. His shirt was tatters hanging off the jags of his epidermis, his shoes burst off his feet.

Skin boiled out and down his arms and legs, spearing down so that he was coursing along on four stiltlike limbs. Tendrils flowed out of his body, creating a churn of motion.

"You should probably signal the Leeds office," Metalious said to the retainers. "Confirm that Grace Merritt is the culprit." One of them spoke calmly into his microphone. Sweven launched himself into the air. A deafening report echoed through the truck and it shook as he landed on the roof. The monitors swayed on their ceiling brackets. "This leaves us in a bit of an awkward position."

A horrendous bang shook the truck, and another. The image on the monitors rotated. Sweven was crouched, a mass of skin-prongs drawing up and then hammering down. With each impact, he yelled out something incomprehensible but extremely enraged-sounding.

"That'll draw some attention," Metalious remarked.

"Pawn Metalious?" said a retainer.

"Hmm?"

"Civilians are coming out of the houses."

"I suppose we can't blame them," said Metalious. "How many?"

"Eleven so far. A couple of children, the rest adults."

"Are they getting... rioty?"

"No, it doesn't appear—Wait. Yes." The retainer peered at the monitor. "Yes, they are. Some are now attacking each other, and the rest are running toward us. Oh, and our driver has vacated the cabin and is clawing at the side of the truck."

"All right," Metalious sighed. "We'll probably have to do something. Release smoke."

"Tear gas? Regurgitant?"

"Just smoke. At the shopping center, the mob didn't react to tear gas. Just obscure the truck. In fact, the whole street."

The scene on the monitors was lost in a dense gray smoke jetted from concealed nozzles under the truck. It wasn't actual smoke, but a harmless mist, and very effective as a concealing agent.

"Switching to thermal," said a retainer. Another series of thumps rained on the roof. There were definite dents now. The camera swiveled again, away from the many-limbed silhouette of Sweven that burned red and yellow on the roof, and panned around. "Merritt is still on her front step. The residents are increasing in temperature." Alix noted that two child-sized silhouettes were flailing at each other.

"HQ is asking if we want backup," said the other retainer.

"That's a puzzler," mused Metalious. "Judging from Sweven's actions, we've established that Merritt's power will affect us—even through the Grafters' medicine."

"Biscuit, Pawn Metalious?" offered one of the pawns.

"Yes, please." She took the chocolate bourbon and regarded it. "If we go out, we'll be affected. If the Checquy sends backup, *they'll* be affected." She chewed thoughtfully. "It's a dilemma." Thumps started on the sides of the truck, and it began to rock. Evidently, the community had found a target for their rage other than each other, and it was not Pawn Sweven on the roof.

"More people are emerging from their houses," remarked a retainer.

There was a sharp report above them, and they looked up to see that a small hole had been punched in the ceiling. A pink shape began to swell in.

"That's inconvenient," someone said. There were murmurs of placid agreement.

Alix bit her lip. Something about the situation seemed a trifle off.

"Sir, I think there may be a problem," she ventured.

"Hmm?"

"Pawn van der Kloof's medicine may have numbed us to an unhelpful extent," Alix said. "Under normal circumstances, we'd be reacting a bit more actively."

"Do you think so?"

"I haven't met you before, but I don't think you'd normally be eating biscuits if we were under siege."

"That's a good point, Mondegreen." Metalious took a contemplative bite of biscuit. "You may be on to something there." There was a tearing sound as Sweven forced back a section of roof. It wasn't big enough to allow his head through, but everyone ducked as flailing tendrils of skin scythed about, and several of the suspended monitors were sent crashing to the floor in a mass of sparks.

"That's interesting," remarked one of the retainers, still peering at their console. "The new arrivals aren't attacking each other, they're just milling about."

"Oh?" said Pawn Metalious.

"These are the ones that emerged after we released the smoke?" Alix asked. The retainer nodded. "So Merritt couldn't see them. Maybe she needs to see them to affect them. So perhaps if we emerge, concealed by the smoke, we won't come under her influence."

"Local fire department has been advised of the smoke," a retainer said. "They're en route."

"That won't do. Have them stopped," Metalious said. "We don't need more people getting all riled up." The retainer spoke into his microphone but looked up.

"Communications have been cut off. I think Pawn Sweven sliced through something important."

"Oh, dear," said Metalious vaguely. "All right, let's go out. The priority is to neutralize Merritt. Ideally, not fatally, but I shan't complain if it's unavoidable. We know the effect can end abruptly, so hopefully it shall do so once she's rendered unconscious. If not, once she's dead. Keep damage to civilians to a minimum, if possible."

The rear door was hauled up and smoke poured in. They could barely see a meter ahead of them, but dark, howling shapes were already emerging out of the darkness. Eyes gleamed with madness, and teeth caught the light.

I'd normally be quite afraid. Say what you like about van der Kloof's concoction, but it is very good for the nerves, Alix thought.

And then animal instinct, merciless training, and bred-in-the-bone duty combined with that most dreadful and irresistible of all human traits, the force of habit, to send her and the rest of the team vaulting forward, over the ravening denizens of Dalrymple Street, into the fog.

They landed, some crouching, some rolling, and one unfortunate pawn landing half off the curb and breaking his ankle instantly. The citizens moved toward them, and the team scattered.

Alix, ankles and will both unbroken, moved through the smoke, but not as swiftly as she would have liked. It was so thick that she couldn't even see her own feet. A shape loomed in the darkness and she braced herself, only to find that it was a beleaguered shrub.

There were screams and the sounds of fighting all around her. It was impossible to tell if Checquy operatives were fighting civilians, or civilians were fighting each other. Footsteps pattered by, with someone alternating between heavy wheezing gasps and desperate sobs. Then another someone rushed by in pursuit, panting and snarling. Neither of them could have been more than two meters away from her, but she saw nothing, and nothing saw her.

What was the number of Merritt's house? It was easy to get turned around in the smoke, especially when one had to keep changing direction to avoid the sounds of other people committing violent atrocities. An eddy of breeze parted the smoke before her, revealing a nightmare. Bloated, pulsating, a wedge of flesh standing on two legs. At the top of the mass, a pair of blue eyes stared at her.

"Mark," she said. Pawn Sweven was no longer a man. Splashed in blood, his hide bristled with blades and spikes and hooks that shifted about, retracting and extending and flexing. He'd lost his pants, but folds of skin draped down his lower half like layers of mismatched skirts.

He lunged at her.

She dove to the side and rolled under a flailing tentacle so studded with spikes that it looked like barbed wire made of meat. His momentum carried him forward, and before he could turn, she was scuttling in, under the protrusions of his torso, to close her hands around his ankle. She yanked and sent him momentarily off balance, but Sweven did not fall as she'd hoped. Instead, struts spooled out of his body to hold him upright and bring him to a halt.

All right, no choice.

"This gives me no pleasure," Alix said. "Although it probably *would* if I weren't hopped up on Belgian alchemy."

She activated her powers.

Energy ignited within her and rushed through her skin to pour into Sweven's body, dashing joyfully along his bones. She had an instant perfect vision of his skeleton, unchanged within the bubbling mass of skin.

Remember, you don't want to kill him, she told herself firmly. *And if we come out of this alive and sane, you don't want him utterly crippled. That'd just make you even more unpopular at work. You want to take him down, and be sure of it. Remember, some of those shoppers kept ravaging even after they'd sustained some pretty serious injuries.*

So, with a mental twist, she directed the energy to three strategic spots.

There were three loud *cracks* as, deep within his flesh, Sweven's leg broke in three places. *That should be enough to stop him,* she thought, as he howled and tore himself away.

It was not enough. He pivoted on his tendrils and his one good leg, bristling with quills ready to lash out, but she was already gone.

If we survive, that can only endear me to him further, Alix thought as she tried to hurry on through the smoke. Using her power was always draining, and she felt as if she'd just sprinted around a track. She stubbed her foot against something and crouched down to see that it was a young man lying in the street. His expression was savage, and his throat had been torn out.

There was the distant sound of fire engines approaching. The truck's communications had been disabled before the retainer could call them off. *We need to wrap this up. Otherwise, everyone who comes within sight of Merritt is just going to make the problem worse.*

A mailbox informed her that the next house was Merritt's. As she drew closer, she saw the woman, not three meters away, still standing on her doorstep. Alix crouched behind the waist-high wall that separated the two driveways and watched.

Merritt stood at ease, as if she'd stepped out for a breath of fresh air rather than unleashing a horde of berserkers in a residential neighborhood. She took in the sounds of the chaos in the smoke with the air of someone listening to a piece of pleasant music. A scream echoed down the street, and Merritt pressed her lips as if trying to hold back a laugh.

Someone came out of the smoke and ran toward the woman—a dark blue shape with one gloved fist clenched and the other hand bare, reaching out toward her. Alix recognized it as Pawn Jake Kosloski, who could temporarily overwrite his opponent's mind with a copy of his own personality. The only catch was that he needed to touch his opponent to make it happen. He was straining with all his might to reach the stoop.

Merritt made no motion, didn't clench her fist or nod her head. Her expression remained relaxed. Just as Kosloski was about to touch her, the pawn came to a dead halt, falling to his knees at her feet. Then he rose, turned, and ran off howling into the smoke.

So fast. Kosloski was only inches from her. And now he's out there, doing violence to other people, possibly using his powers to copy himself onto them, making the situation worse. I can't rush Merritt. I can't take the chance of her turning me. The prospect of unleashing her abilities on civilians and allies without any restraint was too hideous to contemplate.

She crouched down lower, nose to her knees. She needed to muster her resources. Killing at a distance with her power would leave her completely drained. *You will have one shot at this.*

Even worse, there was the very real possibility that she would kill others. Unless she was touching the subject, her power would boil out of her in all directions, unguided, random. It would hit hardest those closest to her, but there was no way to tell how far it would go or what damage it might do. It was a problem she would have agonized over if she weren't floating in the warm cotton wool of mood stabilizers. *I don't see another option.* So she twisted her mind into the necessary shape.

The power came. She felt it surging in her body, a churn that grew more and more intense. She uncurled a little to look over the wall, and then both she and Merritt flinched as a massive blue flash silently lit up the smoke. Clearly, Pawn Bethell had used her power, and was making no effort to keep it subtle.

I can't wait. But will it be enough? The energy battering inside her was not as much as she could muster, but there was no more time. She took a deep breath.

And then Merritt turned and saw her. Their eyes met and Merritt's power took her.

Red rage ignited within Alix, burning away the Grafters' chemical calm and dissolving her intentions toward Merritt. Snarling, she looked around and hated every living thing she saw. The dim figures in the fog. The dog that trotted by. The only thing she did not hate was Merritt, and that was because as far as her perception was concerned, Merritt did not exist at all.

Alix no longer cared about directing her power responsibly. She hated the hazy figures in the distance, hated them with every fiber of her being. She wanted to harm them, and the force that had built up within her was harmful, and so she released it. She fell to her knees as it erupted out of her. An invisible, untouchable cloud of energy, unmeasurable by scientific instruments, spread out from her, unguided.

It found Merritt.

The woman jerked suddenly, then again and again, as the power of Alix's unleashed will tore through her, ricocheting through her bones. She flailed as if she were being shot or struck all over her body.

The overwhelming hatred that had saturated Alix's mind was wiped away, leaving only a dazed exhaustion. She felt as if she had vomited up a thunderstorm.

There were shrieks from the smoke, as the energy found other victims, but the sound of their cries was nothing compared to the thunder cracks throughout Merritt's body of bones fracturing and snapping.

Panting, Alix watched the woman fall to her knees. Somehow, through the havoc being wreaked inside her, Merritt's eyes were able to focus and meet hers. They stared at each other through the smoke, and then Merritt's face stretched nauseatingly before tearing a little down the middle as, with a report, her skull cracked in two. She collapsed.

Silence. The smoke drifted about. And then more screams as people emerged from their madness and found themselves in the middle of a nightmare.

5

"Alix?" said Louise, and she snapped back from her memory.

"Sorry," said Alix. "I was thinking. The last thing I did was deal with a violent little group that was attacking people."

"There's a centuries-old government force that deal with cults," said Louise.

"The occult," said Alix, not wanting to get trapped in too specific a story.

"I don't believe it."

"Yes, that's a very common reaction," Alix agreed. "It makes the job much easier."

Louise's eyes narrowed.

"I need some proof. Do you have a badge or something?"

"No," Alix said. Checquy passes were all plain white except for a serial number and a phone number to call if found.

"So you take care of cults and extremists around the country," said Louise. "Secretly."

"Yes. It's classified. If word got out, it would look bad."

"Then why would they want you to be a lady-in-waiting?" asked Louise.

"I'll be your primary contact about this sort of stuff, and give you briefings on any...such events."

"So you'll be my mystical advisor," said Louise scornfully. "Like Dr. John Dee."

"Who?"

"What kind of occult specialist are you? John Dee was court astronomer to Queen Elizabeth Gloriana. He was also, like, a magician, alchemist, and astrologer."

"I deal in current events," said Alix.

"Fine."

"I'll also provide extra security," said Alix.

"*You?*"

"I'm trained to deal with threats. Look, you know how even normal people can fixate on royalty." Louise nodded reluctantly. "You're going to be a magnet for freaks, religious or otherwise." She looked at the princess sadly. "I'm sorry that you have to be queen. I don't think it will make you happy."

"Of course not," said Louise, and she sounded incredibly tired. "Nicky and I always knew how lucky we were. Edmund was the right kind of person. But how many people are like that? *I'm* not. Nick would be miserable." She grimaced. "I probably shouldn't be saying these things."

"That's the point of a lady-in-waiting, I suppose. Aside from carrying all your gifts, I'm someone you can bitch to safely."

"Yes, okay."

The two women stood in silence for a few moments. The princess looked at Alix self-consciously.

"Um, sorry about accusing you of sleeping with my dad."

"Especially when a much more reasonable explanation was already so obvious," said Alix dryly. They exchanged small nods, but to Alix's regret, there was not even an awkward smile, let alone the usual hug.

Too many things had changed in just a little bit of time.

For the rest of the day, to Louise's increasing irritation, Alix shadowed her. At first, it was Nicholas, Louise, and Alix in the lounge, the brother and sister sitting silently and trying not to cry while

Alix sat sympathetically nearby. No one knew what to do. Louise turned on the television, and then turned it off immediately when a picture of Edmund appeared on the screen. No one said anything. Their phones kept chiming with messages and calls, which no one answered.

Eventually Louise announced that she needed some air, and went out into the garden for a walk. Alix trailed her at a discreet distance. Louise looked back at her several times but said nothing.

When Louise returned and rejoined Nicholas in the lounge, so did Alix. When Louise got up to go to the bathroom, and Alix followed as far as the door, there was an irritated look from the princess, and a bland smile from the newly appointed lady-in-waiting.

When Louise emerged, she opened her mouth to say something, and then closed it again. It was clear that she wanted to tell Alix that while she appreciated the support, she didn't need an attendant in her own home, and perhaps Alix could bugger off or at least give her some space.

But she didn't.

Possibly it was because of good manners, or possibly Louise was still feeling a little on the back foot after incorrectly accusing Alix of sleeping with her father. So they stayed together, and the awkwardness and irritation grew and grew until eventually Louise took refuge in her bedroom, pointedly saying she wanted some time alone, and then shutting the door more firmly than was necessary.

Alix took up station outside the bedroom, on a chair that predated both the Napoleonic Wars and the concept of lumbar support. Her phone battery was running low, so all she could do was sit and smile faintly and nod to any staff that passed by.

The King did not return in time for dinner, and Louise did not emerge from her room, instead having a tray brought to her. When she opened the door to take the food from the footman, she saw Alix sitting there, and her face soured. The door was briskly shut again. Alix took the opportunity to ask the footman for a sandwich and a phone charger, and resisted the urge to ask for a chamber pot.

Finally, Pawn Whomsley arrived to take over the night shift, and Alix was able to go to the guest room usually assigned to her and pee before collapsing onto the bed. She turned on the television and was confronted by the barrage of coverage about Edmund's death. There was a huge amount of footage of the crown prince, and she watched as the news went through his entire life.

He was a baby in his mother's arms at the hospital.

"Prince Edmund, first in line to the British throne, has died at the age of..."

He was a little child in designer dungarees walking unsteadily across red carpeting toward the cameras.

"Doctors have identified a brain aneurysm as the cause..."

He was a teenager, walking down the high street of Harrow-on-the-Hill in his morning coat, carrying his monitor cane.

"Behind me tributes are being laid at the gates..."

He was at university, playing football and splashed with mud.

He was in a black suit at his mother's funeral, holding Louise's hand.

"...found by his father, the King..."

He was in his army uniform, riding on a tank.

Then dancing badly with the girl who would one day be his wife.

"...nation reels with the shock..."

Alix caught a glimpse of herself on the screen as they showed Edmund's investiture as Prince of Wales.

He was in his dress uniform, getting married in Westminster Abbey.

"His wife, Princess Gemma, was in York at the time, and was hurried away..."

He was solemn at the ANZAC Day commemorations at Gallipoli. He was laughing with someone in a receiving room. He was grim, holding his wife's hand shortly after the loss of their baby.

"His sister, Princess Louise, is now first in line..."

Alix sat, watching and crying, until she fell asleep.

The next morning, she woke up mired in her own hair, which, overnight, had escaped the hair tie and matted itself into a thicket around her head.

"Oh, fuck."

Then she realized that the reason she had awoken was her phone attempting to drill a hole into her left eyeball as it vibrated.

"Oh, fuck." She fumbled under her face and answered. "What?" she croaked.

"Pawn Mondegreen, I am connecting a call from Lady Farrier."

"Oh, *fuck*."

"Quite," agreed the assistant. "Connecting now."

"Pawn Mondegreen" came the Lady's voice.

"Yes, my lady. I'm here. I'm awake."

"I should hope so, it's eight in the morning." Alix opened her eyes. The Lady's claim appeared legitimate—morning light was streaming in through the windows, and birds had the bad taste to be tweeting—but it seemed impossible. "Odette and I are en route to Buckingham Palace."

"Yes, ma'am."

"We'll meet with you in the conference room."

"I'll be ready," said Alix, but she'd already been hung up on. She realized she had nothing to change into, and her outfit now looked exactly like it had been slept in.

Is it worth showering if I'm just going to be putting on the same dirty clothes? Or should I spend that time getting coffee?

Fifteen minutes later (five of which had consisted of her fighting with her own hair), she was in the conference room, facing Lady Farrier and Odette, sipping coffee, and trying not to think about how she smelled. Next to her was a suitcase—someone had gone to her London flat and packed some clothes.

"Pawn Claes carried out the autopsy," Odette was saying.

"Pawn Claes," repeated Alix. "Right." She'd never met Naomi Claes but knew the name. According to awed office chatter, she was a Grafter who had been born with a male body and had set about rectifying that error by her own hand as soon as the opportunity existed to do so to her own standards and expectations. Apparently she looked to be in her sixties but was actually in her four-hundred-and-nineties.

"They found nothing abnormal, no apparent cause of death,

except in the prince's skull. The pyramid that I saw in his brain turned out to be the corner of a perfect cube of gray granite, 7.62 centimeters on each side, right in the center of his brain."

"*How?*" asked Alix. Odette shrugged.

"No entry wounds, obviously. The surrounding brain tissue was undisturbed. The bone of his skull was completely intact with no signs of any interference."

It's like a locked room mystery. If the locked room were someone's skull.

"It's possible the brain tissue had been transmuted into stone. Or swapped places with it."

"God. Could it have been Edward unknowingly having powers and accidentally igniting them?" Alix asked.

"It doesn't seem like a very beneficial ability," said Odette.

"There are precedents for people and animals being consumed by their own abilities," said Farrier. "Although we haven't seen this particular phenomenon before. It's not listed in any of the records."

"Remember that poor boy in Wolverhampton who cut the top of his own head off with his tongue?" said Alix.

"Last month, a woman in Ennis stabbed what she thought was an intruder, but it turned out to be herself two minutes in the future," said Farrier. "Then, while she was looking down at the body in shock, she got stabbed by her own past self."

"My God!" exclaimed Odette.

"Yes, it was quite bad," agreed the Lady. "And so confusing for the investigators. When we sent in Clements to watch it in the past, she had a migraine for hours." Alix noticed Odette wince a little at that.

Glad I wasn't working on that one, she thought.

"So," continued Farrier, "we cannot be certain whether it was the result of the prince developing abilities or whether it was caused by someone or something else. The public story, however, is that the prince died of a brain aneurysm. The Prime Minister will be recommending a period of national mourning beginning today and lasting until the day of the funeral."

"How long will that be?" asked Alix.

"A week is usual," said Lady Farrier. "Meanwhile, we will

undertake a full investigation. Given the high profile of the subject, we'll need to be exceptionally discreet."

"Who will be made aware of the truth?" asked Alix.

"I will be informing the King right after this," Farrier said.

"Is the prince's wife going to be told?" asked Alix.

"Absolutely not," Farrier said. "She is unaware of our existence, and I see no reason to read her in now."

"And the crown princess?" asked Odette.

"She'll have to be told the truth eventually, right?" said Alix. "About everything."

"Not necessarily," said Lady Farrier.

"She's going to be queen!"

"Not every monarch learns of our existence," said Farrier. "The King's mother was never informed, and there's concern that knowledge of the Checquy's operations may have contributed to George the Third's instability." She sighed. "People can be even more brittle nowadays. They're often unable to cope with revelations that contradict their lived experience. I blame television and the Internet, frankly. People think they know everything. In the old days, if you told someone they had been attacked by a monster, they were more able to cope with the idea."

"Anyway, we will not inform Princess Louise for the moment. When — *if* — we do brief the crown princess, it will be in a controlled manner, with significant preparation," said Farrier. "In the meantime, Alexandra, you'll continue here in the palace, shadowing the princess and providing immediate security."

Up until she banishes me, thought Alix grimly. It was clear that Louise was beginning to look upon her as a constant reminder of how horribly things had changed, and how oppressive life was going to become.

"Odette," Lady Farrier continued, "has Prince Nicholas been in touch with you?"

"He called me last night," Odette said. "He'd like me to be here."

"I'll leave you with Pawn Mondegreen, then. There are pawns among the security teams as well. Pawn Ganly is coordinating our presence here." She looked at her watch. "We are still operating under alert status Heliotrope until at least tomorrow afternoon."

They all looked up as the distant sound of bells began tolling across the city.

"His death was announced last night," said Alix. "Why are they only ringing now?"

"They've judged there's been enough time for word to have filtered out, so there won't be any confusion as to what's happening," said Lady Farrier. "This was the hour of the prince's birth."

It was a different palace from the day before, when the family had been enjoying their at-home day. Now the presence of staff was noticeable, all of them wearing black armbands. Nicholas came down the hallway to meet Odette and Alix. His eyes were red, and when he and Odette hugged, it was an embrace of comfort rather than romance. He smiled weakly at Alix.

"It's good to see you both. It's pretty grim here." He picked up Alix's suitcase. "Gemma is staying with us—it's too empty at Kensington. Her parents and sister are coming this afternoon. They'll be staying until the funeral." He looked around.

"Fa told me that Ed—" He swallowed. "The death was something in your job's neck of the woods."

"It looks that way," said Alix. "Louise doesn't know anything about it," she warned. "Just the official story. She doesn't know about the Checquy at all."

Nicholas nodded. "What do your people know?" he asked.

"It's early days," said Alix, and she put a hand on his shoulder. "We'll be doing everything we can to get answers."

There was an air of stunned sorrow throughout the building. The staff walking the halls were all subdued, with faces drawn. People spoke in hushed tones. One or two people were weeping quietly.

She recognized several pawns dotted around the place. They were in palace uniform, but their eyes were those of soldiers on duty, always scanning. She nodded slightly to each one, and received a faint signal of acknowledgment.

When Alix arrived back at her room, she was greeted by a maid who was unpacking her clothes. Alix showered, tamed her hair, and texted Pawn Ganly for a location on Louise so she could resume her attending duties. Ganly reported that Louise was in a private meeting with her father in his study. Alix sighed, thinking of the uncomfortable antique sofa outside that door.

Having missed breakfast, she took the scenic route to the study, via a breakfast room where there were generally some pastries under a cover. She was selecting a Danish and deliberately avoiding any glimpse of the ironed newspapers laid out on a side table when a footman entered.

"Lady Mondegreen? The King would like you to join him, the crown princess, and the Princess of Wales in his private study."

Sighing, Alix realized there wouldn't be time to finish the Danish before she got to the study, and put the cover down.

Alexandra, thank you for coming." The King was welcoming, and Gemma, Edward's widow, smiled at her. Louise, however, only gave her a tight little nod. "Please take a seat with us. We are discussing how we will be proceeding," said the King.

"I don't see that she needs to be here for this," said Louise.

"Louise," said the King sharply. "Alexandra is part of this team, and decisions made here will affect her as well."

Like you wouldn't believe, thought Alix sourly, but she kept a blank look on her face as Louise flushed and nodded.

"So," said Gemma, breaking the silence diplomatically. "Another thing we'll need to start thinking about is Louise's role going forward as the Princess of Wales."

Gemma, the current Her Royal Highness the Princess of Wales, was not one's typical Disney princess. Short and muscular, she had met Edmund in the army. Of equal military rank, they had worked in the same office and discovered over the course of several arguments that they adored each other. When Captain Gemma Tidyman, the daughter of a plumber and a community nurse, was unveiled as the sweetheart of the heir to the British throne, she had drawn the startled fascination of the entire world. The couple resigned their commissions from the army, were wed in Westminster Abbey, and maintained a warm but not too available public profile. They were a team that did an unreasonable job well. Alix liked Gemma—they'd met quite a few times at various occasions—but they hardly knew each other.

"Gemma, *you're* the Princess of—" began Louise, but the other woman cut her off.

"Louise, you will be the first modern woman to be Princess of Wales in her own right, not because she's married to the Prince of Wales," said Gemma. "You are now the heir apparent; people will need to see you in that role, and this will be a meaningful part of that process. I will gladly give up the title."

"Dear, dear Gemma, this is so good of you," said the King. "I know Edmund would be bursting with pride." He leaned forward and took her hands. "You will always be a princess, and a Royal Highness. And, of course, you will always be a part of this family."

Louise reached out and put her hand lovingly on Gemma's shoulder. It was an intimate, meaningful moment, and Alix felt so tremendously uncomfortable being there that she had to look away.

Which was when her phone rang.

They all three looked at her, and burning incandescent red, she stammered out an incoherent apology and fumbled madly for her phone. When she got it free, she saw that the call was from Lady Farrier.

"I'm so sorry I have to take this please excuse me I'm dreadfully sorry." She backed out of the room, clipping a table painfully with her hip and knocking over several framed pictures of beloved royal family members.

Outside, she leaned against the wall for a moment, panting in embarrassment. Once she had control of herself, she answered.

"Hello?"

"Why on earth did you take so long to answer?" demanded Lady Farrier.

"I was with the King and the princesses."

"Are they all right?"

"They're fine. Why?"

"Eight years ago, a man was found dead with a granite cube in his head."

"*What*? Where? Who was he?"

"It happened in America, so it wasn't in our records. The team working on the prince's death put in a request to the Croatoan for any similar events — it's standard procedure — and they came back to us almost immediately."

"Jesus Christ," breathed Alix.

"We haven't received all the details yet — they'll be couriered to us from Washington, D.C. But they confirmed several key elements, including the placement and orientation of the cube. Even the measurements were the same."

"So this means..."

"It means," Lady Farrier said, "that the prince's death was not brought about by himself. Someone murdered him."

6

*B*loody hell.

For a panicked moment, Alix thought of raising her power. It wasn't an instantaneous process. It took a few seconds' concentration, and if trouble did arise, it would be good to have it immediately to hand. It was the supernatural equivalent of drawing your gun and taking off the safety catch.

On the other hand, just holding the energy ready took a toll on her, and she couldn't just release it to dissipate harmlessly. She either had to direct it out into something living, or else absorb it back into herself, which would leave her throwing up on the floor.

You've no reason to think you're at risk of immediate attack. She looked around. Suddenly, the hallways seemed incredibly threatening, for all their tall ceilings, plush carpet, and gorgeous paintings. *This means that anyone could be the murderer. It could be Elsie, who's dusting a lamp just a few feet away. It could be Greg, who's hoovering the carpet.* She turned her head in the other direction. *It could be that man walking toward you.*

Wait—who is that?

She squinted at him. She didn't recognize him. In fact, as he approached, with a strangely intent look on his face, he didn't look at *all* familiar. Tall, broad-shouldered, in his forties, the man stalked down the corridor with the bearing of a person who had been taught how to fight. His business suit was brand new, and the lights gleamed off his freshly shorn scalp.

Settle down, you don't know every member of the staff. So just calm yourself.

Even as that man comes closer and closer, and is looking at you in an odd way.

In a really odd way.

Oh, God, he's going to kill me!

She was torn between summoning her power or implementing one of the special martial arts in which she'd been instructed—the one that focused on using one's mobile phone as a weapon.

As the man with the strange gaze drew level with her, she was braced to deliver a quick, merciless strike to the throat, a blow that would crush both his windpipe and her mobile.

When did I last back up my phone?

"Lady Mondegreen," he said.

"Yuh?" She was too taut to actually speak, every muscle and instinct poised to destroy him.

"I wanted to confirm that you don't have any dietary restrictions for dinner with the family this evening?"

"Nuh." She was deflating as she realized that he actually was vaguely familiar. She rallied and collected herself. "No, thank you. I'm sorry, I know exactly who you are, but your name has flown out of my head."

"Alastair, my lady."

Alix, you're a goddamn moron.

"Of course, *Sir Alastair*, I'm sorry." She laughed weakly. "It's been such a chaotic time."

"Of course, my lady."

"Pawn Mondegreen? Hello?" said Farrier's voice faintly. Alix realized that, in her heightened state of alertness, she had completely forgotten she was still on the phone to her commanding officer.

"Yes, my lady," she said.

"Are you all right?"

"I'm fine." *I only nearly killed the King's private secretary in the hallway is all.* "Do the Americans know who committed the other murder?"

"No, they investigated but finally concluded that it was a case of someone's own powers killing them. They had no previous incidents to make them think otherwise."

"What are my orders?"

"Stand fast for the moment. You're in a secure building with fifteen pawns and retainers on the floor with you."

"I'm not sure we're as safe as you think," said Alix.

"Explain."

"Someone killed Edmund in these apartments. No one reported seeing anyone unusual, and there are quite a number of people wandering around here."

"You think perhaps a member of the staff?" asked Farrier. "A servant?"

"Or a member of security," said Alix. "I think we need to keep the family isolated from all non-Checquy staff." Even as she was proposing it, she realized the difficulty of what she was suggesting. *We can't keep them all wrapped up in cotton wool for the rest of their lives. We can't even do it for more than a day or two. Especially now, when everyone in the world is staring at them.* "The other death happened in America?"

"Yes."

"What kind of background screening do palace staff go through? Do they have to provide travel histories?" The Checquy, like many other high-security government agencies, required detailed personal histories of new entrants. They had to provide lists of every place they'd ever lived, every country they'd ever visited, every person they'd ever had sex with, and the kind of pornography they enjoyed (if any).

Alix herself had never had to undergo the process, since she'd been an asset of the Checquy since before she could do much of anything interesting. Her parents, however, with their decadent, jet-setting, massively social, not especially monogamous, and increasingly financially desperate (and therefore vulnerable to coercion) lifestyles, had probably been an absolute nightmare for the personnel department.

"Everyone in the palace has to undergo positive vetting," said Lady Farrier. "That includes information on every overseas journey they've ever taken. We'll check travel histories, see if any of the current staff was in America at the time of the other death." Alix heard papers being rustled. "Yes, if there was anyone in... Columbus, Ohio, at the correct time, we'll move on them immediately."

"Over eight hundred people work in the palace," Alix said. "They should start with those who have most recently joined the staff. Until then, I recommend that we urge another at-home day, keep everyone out except our people." She could almost hear the Lady wincing down the phone.

"It's going to be very disruptive," Farrier said, "but it makes sense. I'll contact the King and explain the situation. The order will need to come from him."

"I'm just outside his study," Alix replied. "I can take this phone in to him." She knocked gently but heard no answer. She entered only to find that she was intruding on yet another deeply personal moment.

The King, the Princess of Wales, and the crown princess were all standing together, hugging each other. The two women were crying softly, and the King looked distinctly wet about the eyes.

It took all her strength, all the resilience and courage that the Checquy had drilled into her, to respectfully clear her throat. The King looked over at her.

"I'm so sorry, Your Majesty," she said quietly. "It's Lady Farrier." His arms tightened around the two princesses, and when they looked up at him, he let them go. Louise looked around, saw Alix with the phone, and her mouth twisted in outrage. Alix made the most expressive "I'm sorry" expression she could muster up. It felt like she was going to sprain her own face.

"My dears, please give me a moment. Alexandra, please stay." The princesses exited and Louise sighed as she closed the door. The King took the phone from Alix and listened. "Yes, Lady Farrier?" He paused.

"I can do that," he said finally. "It's going to be very inconvenient for a great many people, though. Is another at-home day totally necessary?"

Alix could see the moment that the King learned his son's death had been the result of murder. The blood drained from his face, and he swayed on his feet. For a moment, she thought she might have to step in and support him. Alix's phone dropped from his suddenly limp fingers.

She went to pick it up, but he was already there, retrieving it and clenching it in his fist.

"When was this? Where?" he demanded. He turned his back to Alix as he continued to ask questions for which there were not yet any answers. His grip tightened on her phone so fiercely that she thought he might break it. "And while we're waiting for this American courier? I mean, what are you people doing *right now*? I see. Yes. Yes." He took a deep breath.

"Linda," he said. "I have always given the Checquy a great deal of latitude. I have never inquired too deeply into your operations. That is not going to happen here. As of today, I will expect a daily briefing on the progress of your investigation into my son's murder."

He paused as she said something, and then he shook his head. "No. Let me take this opportunity to remind you of the rights and privileges that my rank entitles me to with respect to your order. I will be kept apprised of *every* development of this investigation."

Alix barely dared breathe. She'd never heard the King use that tone. She'd never heard *anyone* use that tone to the Lady of the Checquy. It was like watching a policeman slap one of your parents.

"*Every* detail, Linda. I want to know what progress has been made each day. Now, where is this team based?... Excellent." He looked at his watch. "It is now eleven thirty a.m. This afternoon, I will come to the Hammerstrom offices to meet with them. At one o'clock. And I look forward to receiving the first report this evening, no later than six thirty p.m. Goodbye."

The King hung up the phone. His shoulders slumped and his head bowed, the image of a man reeling from despair. He picked up his desk phone and spoke into it. "Have Sir Alastair come to my private study immediately, please." For a moment, she thought he had forgotten about her. Then: "Alexandra?"

"Yes, my King?" She winced. It wasn't how one was supposed to address him, but it just came out.

"Please, go and stay with my daughter. Don't leave her side. Keep her safe."

"Yes, sir." She hesitated. "I just—"

"Yes?"

"I need my phone back is all."

Later that afternoon, Louise sat in the lounge, so Alix was also obliged to sit there.

"Lady Mondegreen?" Alix looked up from her computer. A plump pawn whose name she couldn't remember was at the door. "The King has returned and would like to speak with you." Louise rolled her eyes.

"Thank you," said Alix.

After his call with Lady Farrier, the King had met with his team and declared his intention to tour a government office no one had ever heard of. He also abruptly instituted another at-home day tomorrow with no staff permitted into the family's private quarters.

The announcement that the King would be slipping out for a few hours in secret, unaccompanied by his usual entourage, had nearly pushed a couple of senior functionaries into cardiac arrest. His only attendants for his secret excursion had been a close-protection officer from the Checquy—Pawn Ganly with the tree-focused transportation power—and a Checquy driver who could render a car and its occupants completely intangible for as long as he could hold his breath.

Alix remained in the family quarters to continue providing close protection to Louise. Louise had not been noticeably grateful or pleased with this, but since the princess still didn't know the truth behind her brother's death, Alix was trying mightily not to resent her attitude.

Now, as she entered the King's study, Alix dropped her habitual curtsy.

"Dear girl, when you're a guest in my home, you needn't curtsy every time you see me."

"Sheer force of habit, sir. How was your visit to the Hammerstrom Building?"

"Very interesting. Not nearly as bizarre as I expected."

"They may have gotten some of the more outlandish staff out of the way," said Alix.

"Very tactful of them. Although truthfully, I was a little disappointed. I was prepared for something out of Lewis Carroll or Robin Jarvis to come burbling down the corridor."

"It's a big deal to have the King visit," she said. "I don't think a ruling monarch has come in years."

"I met the team investigating Edmund's death," he said. "Lady Farrier explained that the circumstances of the..." He broke off for a moment and swallowed hard. "Ahem. The circumstances of *the murder* are being kept classified, even from the rest of the Checquy." He looked at her. "They gave me a report, all their findings so far. Have you seen it?"

"No, sir."

He passed over a folder.

"Have a look. It's very well put together."

It would want to be. Alix knew that the investigative staff must have been frantically pulling together materials in time for the King's visit.

"It includes a detailed autopsy report, but I didn't look at that, just at the summary."

And you think I want to look at it? But it didn't matter whether she wanted to; *he* wanted her to.

"You can read it in here," the King said. "Louise, Gemma, Nicky, and I are going to go out to greet the public, accept their condolences in person."

"Sir, I don't know that that's the best idea," Alix said. "We're still worried about your security."

"I know," he said wearily, as he stood up from his chair. "But there are some things we must do."

That's their duty. It's not enough for them to lose a son and a brother and a husband. They have to be seen to be bereaved.

Steeling herself, Alix sat down in the King's chair and opened the file.

The first page featured the coat of arms of the United Kingdom, with the lion and the unicorn supporting the quartered shield depicting various lions and a harp. Alix always had the impression that the supporting lion was staring out at her in particular and judging her, while the unicorn was looking at it skeptically. The entire page was bordered in a thick, bite-your-eyes red-and-white-checkered strip. Legal warnings declared the contents to be classified under various laws and acts. It was practically a crime to be in the same room as the file, and anyone who found it was to contact HM government via the below telephone number and to look no further. To anyone not brought up in the Checquy, it would have been terrifying, but to Alix, it was as familiar as reading Once upon a time.

The file was a jumble of detail and vagueness. The King had asked for a thorough report, and the Checquy, perhaps frightened by his newfound assertiveness, had given him far more than Alix would have anticipated.

First was a brief timeline of the known events surrounding the Prince's death. Alix's eye caught on her own name — 13:47 *Alexandra Dennis-Palmer-Hudson-Gilmore-Garnsey (P) arrives at Buckingham Palace* — but the timeline only extended back twenty minutes before Louise discovered her brother's body. Evidently, a great deal more work had to be done.

Next she scanned the list of people on the investigation team, with a bio for each one. In keeping with the uncertainty of what to provide, no biography contained any mention of supernatural abilities, although it did include the subjects' blood types, length of service, and phone numbers. She recognized several names, including the team leader, Hannah Smith, who had a very good reputation.

Then she came to the autopsy report.

It gave the facts in cold, merciless language. The lack of obvious wounds, bruising, signs of a struggle, or trace of anything under his fingernails. Blood toxicology showing no foreign substances and no unexpectedly elevated or lowered elements. The weight and condition of organs. The contents of his stomach: a breakfast of fruit salad, toast with Marmite, and a cup of coffee. The status of his lungs and heart: no flaws, condition consistent with a man who partook of regular physical exercise.

The word *unknown* featured a great deal.

Despite herself, Alix smiled at Pawn Claes's exquisitely baroque sixteenth-century signature on the confidential death certificate.

When she came to the photographs, she hesitated but then clenched her jaw and grimly turned the page.

"Oh, *God*."

It was horrible. The wonderful man she'd known since she was a girl was laid out, a pale, vulnerable corpse on a stainless steel table. He was naked, his face expressionless, with no sign of what had made him who he was—the poise, the humor, the kindness. She'd always thought of him as reserved, but now, seeing his face still, she realized how vivid he'd been. His hair was mussed as she'd only seen a few times, when he'd been playing football or had peeled off his helmet after riding.

There was a card with finger- and toe prints, then more photographs: the Y incision, his insides, close-ups of his blank, staring eyes. And then, finally, the incision across the top of the head, the flaps of scalp pulled over the face and back over the nape of the neck. The skullcap removed to reveal the red-stained beige brain, with an unnatural point of gray stone emerging from the top.

Alix gasped back a sob. *Why would they include these? Why would you put these in front of a grieving father?* But she already knew the answer. He was the King, and he had demanded to see everything.

The report described the stone: a smooth granite cube, each side 7.62 centimeters by 7.62 centimeters. The faces were perfectly smooth without any tool marks. Chemical composition and geological analysis did not identify a site of origin. No sign of crushed tissue, suggesting that brain matter had been transmuted into granite or swapped with it, presumably instantaneously.

The notes on the American cube were brief, but Alix was not surprised. Like the Checquy, the Croatoan refused to transmit any material via the Internet—the risk of interception was just too great.

Instead, a few details had been relayed over an encrypted telephone line and been kept to bare bones.

Case matching your description found. Male, 21, Columbus, Ohio, eight years ago. Particulars of anomalous object match perfectly. Full file en route via safehands courier.

After that, there was a section of operational planning material that had clearly been written frantically, with a good deal of copying and pasting and hasty updating from previous documents, albeit by someone who knew how to sound convincing. Lots of dot points that would form the structure for an effective investigation—the sort of thing Alix had read a thousand times before. She closed her eyes, then hurriedly opened them again as her mind flashed back to the autopsy photos.

I shouldn't have looked at them. She'd had nightmares after some Checquy operations, but the memories of those photos would be haunting her for a lot longer than even the manifestation with the giant white blood cells that had poured up out of the well in Plockton and absorbed twenty-seven people, six dogs, and forty-eight deer.

The King entered.

"How was it, sir?" she asked. "Outside?"

"It was very good to see the people, to see how strongly they felt about Edmund," he replied. "It wasn't easy, though." She nodded sympathetically. "Now, you've reviewed the file. What did you think?"

"It's very early, but the investigators are laying out strategies and avenues of action. They have very good people on this. They're who I would want investigating."

"I've requested that you be added to that team, Alexandra."

"What?"

"My dear girl, I know that I've already interfered unforgivably in your life, having you brought here for days at a time and appointing you a lady-in-waiting to Louise. But that's only a part-time job."

Yes, but I already had a full-time job.

And a part-time life.

"When do you think it will start?" she asked. "The waiting on the lady bit, I mean?"

"The funeral will be in six days, followed by another week of royal mourning. There will be some engagements during that time, as is judged appropriate. I want to let Louise recover, but she'll need to start assuming royal duties, get herself in the public eye. I want her attended by a lady-in-waiting for each event, get her used to being accompanied, and the public used to seeing it. Most people won't notice, but the press and royal watchers notice everything."

"That makes sense."

"In the meantime, I will feel a great deal better knowing that you are part of the team working to bring Edmund's killer to justice. I'm sure the rest of them are excellent, but we know you, and you genuinely cared about Edmund."

"You know I'm a specialist in botany?"

"Yes, but you're also trained in general investigation," said the King. "And you have experience with several major projects."

Have you been reading my file?

"Of course, sir." It was the only thing she could say. "But it will need to be approved by my superiors." *Maybe they'll find a diplomatic way to say no.*

"I spoke to Lady Farrier, and she's consulted with Sir Henry and the rooks. They've all agreed."

Of course they have.

"Alexandra, I'm accustomed to being handled," said the King. "It's one of my key responsibilities, allowing others to handle me."

"Sir," said Alix cautiously.

"I will not be handled when it comes to this investigation," he said. "I will be relying on you to make certain that does not happen."

"They wouldn't keep things from you," protested Alix, not at all certain that they wouldn't.

"There is a difference between concealing things and omitting things," said the King. "I receive my daily red boxes, and my Checquy despatch box, and I have to assume I'm getting a good overview, but I'm certain that in criminal investigations, the next of kin get handled. Elements are glossed over or played down. Details are buried. I know the tricks."

"I won't be in a position to change a report, sir," said Alix. "Everything will go through the team leader and the Court before it gets to you."

"But you will see the final version?"

"Yes," said Alix reluctantly.

"Then I want you to take note, and when you and I meet, if there have been omissions, I expect you to provide me with the details."

The King wants me to be his spy in the Checquy.

"Do you want me to continue staying here overnight?"

"You're more than welcome, of course, but with all the security the Checquy have installed, I shan't say that you must."

"In that case, it will be easier for me to be back in my flat, if only for getting to and from the office."

"That's entirely reasonable," the King agreed. "I'm very grateful for all your support, Alexandra." He clasped her hand in his for a moment, and she bowed her head a little.

"Take care of Louise and Nicky, sir," she said. "And let them take care of you as well." He smiled and nodded, and she departed.

Alix returned to her room to repack her things, which in the interim had been laundered, even though they had already been clean. As a result, everything looked better than it had when she purchased it. *Is it possible that they re-dyed this shirt?* As she was transferring her freshly ironed socks and underwear to her suitcase, her phone rang.

"Pawn Mondegreen?"

"Yes."

"This is Pawn Hannah Smith. I have just been told that you will be joining my investigation."

"I've just been told that, too," said Alix carefully. She wasn't certain how delighted Pawn Smith might be to have someone foisted onto her team.

"That's why they call us pawns, isn't it?" said Smith. "Move us about as they see fit. The whole team is meeting at the Rookery in an hour. I've brought some more people on, so it'll be the first time everyone's together."

"I'll be there," Alix said.

7

The Hammerstrom Building represented either the apex or the nadir of human decorative ingenuity. Tremendous amounts of architectural and aesthetic expertise had gone into the facade. It was just that all the talent and skill had been devoted to ensuring that the building was the blandest, least engaging structure in the area, if not the world. The eye didn't just slide over it, it *hurried* over it, desperate for something better to look at.

A passerby's attention was far more likely to be caught by the small encampment of protesters outside the front entrance who strove to convince the public that contained within this building was a secret government agency that concealed deep and significant truths. They had never enjoyed any success—practically all the followers of their social media page were identities fabricated by the Checquy to keep tabs on them.

Once she was past the protesters and through the false lobby into the actual lobby, Alix asked where Pawn Smith's team had been assigned. She was unsurprised that they had been allotted a space in the heart of the Rookery, in what was referred to as "the Box Room." It was a large, undistinguished area where temporary special task forces were housed.

Usually at least three such projects were occupying the Box Room at any given time. It was a fluid space, which meant that overnight, internal walls could be torn down, thrown up, and regurgitated by industrious Rookery facility staff to suit shifting needs and parameters.

As the layout changed and corridors and doors vanished overnight, strips of different-colored tape were constantly being laid down on the carpet, tracing new routes to offices that had once been a minute's walk from the lift but now required one to weave through a maze of new hallways.

Alix picked out the designated strip of lime-green masking tape from a rainbow of options on the carpet and followed it through the paint-smelling maze of bland corridors, and finally to a door with a barcode label stuck on it, and the traces of many previous labels that had been laboriously scraped off. Beside the door was a sensor where she had to swipe her pass to enter. There were no windows to the outside world, but the open-plan space was fairly big and furnished with battered chairs and desks set about in little clumps. Some were unoccupied, but five people were seated, intent on their work.

The first person she saw upon entering was Mark Sweven, typing briskly on a laptop computer.

Oh, there is no God.

He looked up, and a sour smile spread across his face.

"Lady Mondegreen!" he said loudly. At this, the others in the room—two men and two women—looked up. "I heard that the King had interceded on your behalf and ordered you put onto this team." Alix could feel her lip curling, but no stinging riposte occurred to her, since this was true. She settled for "Hi, Mark, how's the leg?"

"Healing away," he said. He reached down and picked up a crutch. "But still broken in three places, thanks very much."

"Any time," she said. "Do we have assigned seats?"

"We do indeed," said a voice behind her. "You'll be sitting next to Sweven, since you know each other." Alix turned, recognizing the voice and the Irish accent from the phone. Pawn Smith was a short woman in her late forties, with closely cropped dirty-blond hair and a rosy complexion.

"Splendid," said Alix. "This should be a *cracking* good time, eh, Mark?" She patted him on the shoulder, and he flinched a little. She felt his skin prickle through his suit coat, not enough to draw blood but enough to put some holes in the wool.

"Mondegreen, you're the last to arrive, so let's all go to the conference area, and everyone can introduce themselves."

Pawn Smith had her own tiny office with a door, and there were some unoccupied desks in the bigger room. The conference table was off to the side and was by far the nicest piece of furniture in the place, presumably in case the team had to brief anyone important. The team of seven fit easily around it. They were a mix of races and ages, and Sweven was the only one she knew.

"I'm Pawn Hannah Smith, team leader. I've been with the Checquy since before I was born, thanks to ultrasound technology, which proved that my mother was not crazy and there was something strange going on inside her. I started out in element and materials analysis, and for the last ten years, I've been deployed around the country managing investigations. When I'm not doing that, I'm based in the Limerick office."

Smith was known to be very good at her job. Her supernatural ability was also legendary. The previous year, on the Isle of Mull, she had been forced to take on a boobrie by herself after it had killed or crippled the rest of her team. In a fight in the hastily evacuated car park of a scenic lookout, she'd demolished three cars, a campervan, and a *Polly's Frosty Treats 'n' Hot Dogs (Tobermory style!)* ice cream truck before, with a single swipe, taking off the boobrie's head while it was manifested as a gigantic water bird.

"And I've got a husband, and two daughters in secondary school."

Smith nodded to the next person: a portly woman who was wearing a lab coat and turned out to be the Grafter, Dr. Claes. It was pronounced "Klahs" and, to Alix's disappointment, was not one of those Dutch names that required the speaker to make sounds that did not exist in English.

"Naomi Claes, I joined the Checquy with the rest of the *Wetenschappelijk Broederschap van Natuurkundigen* a few months ago. I joined the Broederschap in 1531, and my first specialty was human chromosomal redesign, although we did not call it that then. I spent a century working on interspecies surgical transplantation with a focus on mammalian-botanical fusion. My formal titles include *Meesterbeeldhouwer van vlees, botten en pezen,* and I am also a *Hormonenbrouwmeester.*"

There was a stunned silence. Alix could feel her head cocking to one side like her dog Wompus's whenever he was confused. *Did she just describe herself as a brewmaster of hormones?*

"Ah," Claes said. "We are to include a personal element. My husband and children have been dead for several centuries, of course. I have never remarried. But my direct female descendants continue to draw funds for their education from an ancestral trust." She beamed. "I have no contact with them, but I understand there are about a dozen now."

"Only the females?" asked someone cautiously.

"I ensured that my descendants would only bear daughters. And no more than two. I have always been concerned about overpopulation."

"Thank you, Claes," said Pawn Smith, who was trying to rally in the face of rather more startling revelations than one usually got in a professional introduction—even a Checquy introduction. "Next round the table is Scagell."

"Ta," said Scagell, who was a lean white man in his fifties, with a shaved head, dark-rimmed round glasses, and the most magnificent nose Alix had ever encountered. He looked like a bird of prey that had gone into academia. "Mike Scagell, I've been with the Checquy since I was three when I set off a series of small explosions in a farmers' market in Wells. No one was killed—they were more like firecrackers going off—but I lost an eye." Alix could just make out the faintest mottling of long-ago burn marks. Presumably, he'd been fitted with a false replacement eye. "I don't remember it. The Checquy investigated, found me, and took me in."

This, of course, was a polite code. The Checquy hadn't taken him in, they'd just taken him.

"After the Estate, I studied psychology and I now conduct criminal and supernatural profiling. I'm in the Norwich office, but do consultations around the country. I also have a small public practice where people who think inexplicable things are happening to them can come and talk about their concerns. It's led to identifying several manifestations and a few new entries into the Checquy ranks. My husband Leo is also in the Checquy. He's back in Norwich, looking after our dog and three horses."

Next was a man of East Asian descent, a couple of years older than Alix. He introduced himself as "Detective Constable Andrew Chuah, with the Metropolitan Police, and now of the Checquy Group." His accent was central London.

A retainer. Alix was a little surprised—he seemed a bit young to have been recruited from the Met. Law enforcement retainers were usually brought in later in their careers, once they'd built up a useful network of contacts in addition to experience in their area of expertise.

"This is actually my first case with the Checquy," he said. "I've been at the Rookery less than a week." There were some commiserating noises around the table. "Yeah, it's been educational."

You poor bastard.

To be a retainer, one needed not only to be outstanding in one's field (or, preferably, on the track to being outstanding in one's field, so that one could leave it without too many questions asked), but also to possess a very specific kind of resilience.

You could usually spot newcomers by their wide eyes and the stilted walk of someone devoting all their concentration and muscle control to not flinching. Chuah seemed to be quite relaxed for a newbie, although admittedly no one around the table was displaying any overtly unnatural qualities.

"I served in uniform for two and a half years, and then joined the Criminal Investigations Department, attached to Homicide and Serious Crime Command. After I helped track down a couple of men who'd been murdering shopkeepers, I got offered this role."

I bet he did a lot more than help in the tracking-down. Alix realized that it was her turn to introduce herself. It was always tricky, deciding how much to say, but with Sweven sitting at the end of the table, she decided it was best to put all the awkwardness out there.

"Thank you. I'm Pawn Alix Dennis-Palmer-Hudson-Gilmore-Garnsey, which is too cruel a name to make people remember, so I use my family's other name, which is Mondegreen. Technically I've been with the Checquy since I was six, but in a bit of an unorthodox situation." She explained about her parents and her connections to the royal family. "I'm an investigator out of London. My specialties are botany and horticulture, and discreet bodyguarding, but I think it's my knowledge of the palace and the royal family that is probably most relevant to this investigation."

At this, she paused and looked around to gauge reactions. They ranged from a curled lip on the part of Sweven to a placid nod from Claes. The others, however, all looked rather disapproving.

"I should probably add that I'm the one who broke Mark's leg," she said, nodding over at him. "But, in my own defense, we both got commendations for that." She smiled brightly at Sweven, who was looking daggers at her.

The next introduction was a tall Black woman in an exquisitely cut suit. She was in her thirties, and when she spoke, it was with a Jamaican accent.

"Bertina Weller. I came into the Checquy when I was five. I was in hospital having my appendix out, and one of the nurses noticed that I'd left footprints scorched into the floor between my bed and the lav. So the Checquy came and got me, and I never went home again. I specialize in forensic accounting, deep diving on personal and institutional finances." She smiled. "Don't worry, I'm here to track down our killer, not audit any of you. I've got a live-in boyfriend back in Newcastle who's learned that I work strange hours, which is all right because he's an artist, so he works strange hours himself."

Sweven's introduction was a little subdued, as he described himself as "a generalist investigator, with specialization in human-on-human supernatural violence." Apparently he had a girlfriend back in Edinburgh. She was a medical student.

"Thank you, everybody," said Pawn Smith. "This is going to be a high-pressure investigation, a lot of early mornings and late nights. The King has requested a daily progress report, and I want to make damn certain that every evening, he sees progress. On the upside, we have direct access to Lady Farrier, who will requisition whatever resources we need, including more people, if necessary."

There was a murmur of appreciation around the table at that. For all its astounding capabilities, the Checquy was still a government agency, which meant there were never enough funds or staff for a project, unless you got Pawn Beynon, whose homunculi could at least help with the filing.

"Now, to the investigation itself," said Smith, in the tones of a woman who has been here many times before. "We need to establish some assumptions, while remembering that we may have to jettison any of these if necessary. Firstly, I'm going to posit that the suspect is a human being." Everyone nodded. It didn't go without saying. Supernatural manifestations could originate from anything, including animals, inanimate objects, specific locations, and completely random circumstances.

"Second, that the suspect came in close contact with the prince."

Again, it made sense. It was suspected that some unsolved manifestations were the result of people's supernatural abilities stretching across large distances, but most people's powers required them at least to be able to aim at their target. And even if people's powers didn't work that way, their minds did. "I'm not saying there had to be physical contact, although if we can, I'd like to track that."

Alix winced. Edmund was known for making himself available to people, and he shook a lot of hands.

"If someone was in the same room as him, we must know about it," continued Smith. "If we can get footage, so much the better. Mondegreen, your first task is to obtain the prince's schedule for the week leading up to his death. That will be the initial framework for the investigation. At the moment, our only lead is the other case in America. If any of the prince's contacts were in America at the time of the previous murder, then we put them under the microscope."

Alix was busily taking notes, and added the arrow and exclamation point symbols that meant a task she'd been assigned.

"I want you all to familiarize yourselves with every element of this investigation," Pawn Smith said firmly. "That said, no case information leaves this room. Because of the high profile of the victim and the current media frenzy, I want complete discretion from you all." There were obedient noises from around the table.

"Good. The file you've put together today contains a list of avenues of investigation and who is assigned to each." She looked at her watch. "An eighth member of our team is arriving soon, from America." There were noises of interest.

"He'll be arriving at Heathrow early tomorrow morning. He's acting as courier for their file on the previous cube and our liaison to the Croatoan. Because we believe the two deaths are related, the Americans are opening a fresh investigation into the Ohio death. It's been eight years, so I'm not relying on them, but one can hope. Now, you all know your tasks. Mondegreen, come with me, please."

Alix followed her into her office.

"Will you be able to handle being part of this team?" Smith asked.

"Sir?"

"You were friends with the victim."

"I'll be fine," Alix replied. "There is something you should know, though." And she explained about the lady-in-waiting appointment. "So, it means that periodically, I'll be required to take time away to attend the crown princess."

"We'll have to make it work," said Smith. "However, we will be interviewing the family members, and I don't think you should be present for that."

"I totally agree," said Alix. The relief was like sinking into a hot bath and then peeing in it—mildly guilty, but undeniably pleasant.

"That said," continued Smith, "I expect that you will be continuing to see the royal family, especially in the course of your lady-in-waiting...ing?" Alix nodded. "I appreciate that they are close friends of yours, and you want to provide support. That is commendable, but I'm concerned about any conflicting loyalties."

"You don't need to worry on that score."

"No?"

"No," Alix said firmly. "My priority is finding who or what killed Edmund."

"Good," said Smith, "because when you are with any member of the royal family, I expect you to observe them for any insights you can provide to this team."

All the relief that Alix had just felt vanished abruptly, like sinking into a hot bath and then having someone else come in and pee in it.

"Anytime you visit the palace or meet with one of the royals, I want a report."

"Yes, sir," said Alix sadly.

"If you can do this, and do it in a professional manner, it will reflect very well on you and boost your possibility of advancement in this organization." Despite herself, Alix felt her hopes flare at the thought. Every promotion she'd ever gotten had taken longer than everyone else's, presumably to show that there was absolutely no favoritism because of her title.

But you might actually get to climb because of this! she told herself.

And all you'll have to do is take advantage of the trust of people you care about.

No, it's not a betrayal, you're investigating a murder. And these are orders.

"Now, for our interviews with the family, I'll be coordinating with Lady Farrier," said Smith. "We'll need to be delicate. What can you tell me about their awareness of the situation?"

"To start, the King knows about the existence and the nature of the Checquy. And that the prince's supernatural death was a murder."

"All right, and the princess?"

"She's now the crown princess," said Alix. "And she now knows that there is a government agency that deals with the occult, thanks to my panicking when she cornered me. But she doesn't know that the supernatural is real. She may very well soon be learning more, though." Smith looked up, questioning. "Lady Farrier is gauging how Louise will react before deciding whether to read her in."

"Right, I knew that," said Smith. "Well, this is useful. I'll be asking you for further input as we proceed."

"Of course," said Alix, although she wasn't thrilled at the prospect.

"Now," said Smith. "The timeline of the victim. Highest priority is the hour before the prince's death, and then moving backward to the previous forty-eight hours, and then the whole previous week. The first group we'll have to look into is whoever he had contact with in Buckingham and Kensington Palaces. Thoughts?"

"Hundreds of people work in the palaces, but they're very organized places," Alix said. "If we start with the heads of departments, they can provide lists of everyone who has been in the palaces during that time period and give us access to personnel records. And people can't just wander about wherever they want. You need to swipe a pass to enter different areas, and those records are retained, so we'll be able to track movements. I know who to talk to."

The team leader nodded thoughtfully. "Once we've identified people we want to interview, we'll need a cover story for why we're doing so, so that they don't know we're investigating a murder."

"That's easy. We use the unquestionable power of royal whim."

The King seemed rather pleased at having something to do.

Early the next morning, word went out from the King's study in Buckingham Palace, urgently summoning the Lord Chamberlain, the Master of the Household, the Private Secretary to the

Monarch, the Principal Private Secretary to the Prince and Princess of Wales, the Captain of the King's Guard, and, from the Metropolitan Police, the Deputy Assistant Commissioner responsible for Protection Command, the Commander of Protection Command, and the head of the Royalty and Specialist Protection branch of Protection Command.

Between them, they oversaw the management of the palace, from the "below stairs" operations and personnel, the administrative offices, and the security of the royal family to the sovereign's connection to the House of Lords. These were the people whose orders, once given, would flow down to touch every staff member in the palaces. Also summoned was Nicola Rimes, the terrifying Director General of MI5. All of the attendees were important in their own right, but not all of them were aware of the existence of the Checquy.

A freshly showered and mildly rested Alix sat in a little flunky office next door to the King's study, her eyes glued to a hidden spyhole. The connecting door was concealed by a bookcase. This gathering of people in dark suits was, she supposed, as close to a meeting of the royal court as she was ever likely to encounter: the King, surrounded by advisors and senior officials, giving his orders. Still, looking at the gathered group, she was struck by the difference between what she saw and her childhood imaginings of a royal court.

For her, the word *court* evoked a time when the monarch *was* the government, when he or she held a great deal of power and wielded it. A time when a ruler was surrounded by a multitude of specific servants—cofferers and cupbearers, dapifers and doorwards, and a Groom of the Stool—and, above all, figures of power wielding authority at the King or Queen's behest. Figures like Thomas Cromwell or Cardinal Richelieu. Elizabeth Gloriana had had her own spymaster, Sir Francis Walsingham, as well as the court astrologer Louise had mentioned: John Dee. In France, a family called the Rossignols had served as cryptographers to the court at Versailles.

Seated at the head of the long table, the King began speaking. "My son's death was found to be the result of an aneurysm. History has shown, however, that there are always parties ready to believe the worst. Accordingly, it is imperative that we be able to demonstrate that there is no suspicion of malfeasance surrounding his death. Confusion and suspicion around the succession is too dangerous to be permitted. This nation is far from being a united kingdom. Fractures and divisions abound — there are any number of movements and individuals that could seize upon this as an opportunity." He paused and looked around, but no one looked skeptical or surprised. "If ever someone seeks to question my daughter's right to the throne, I want her forearmed to quash those questions. To that end, I will now turn you over to Mrs. Rimes, of the Security Service."

"Thank you, Your Majesty," Rimes said. "The Security Service will be assembling as complete a record as possible of the days leading up to the prince's death. This record will be held in secret, to serve as a protection should ever any objection be raised. Agents will be arranging meetings with you over the coming days, and we appreciate your assistance."

"Now," said the King, "this is far more tradition than law, but it is something I want done, and I want it done with the utmost discretion. If you must delegate tasks, then I know you will do so with caution, keeping the reasons for those tasks quiet." He paused. "Any questions?"

There weren't.

The various officials moved out of the room, with the silence of people who have just been given a task and are unsure whether it is very important or completely ridiculous. Rimes stayed seated.

"Alexandra, you can come in," the King said in the direction of the spyhole. Alix opened the bookcase door. "Do you think they bought it?" asked the King.

"Yes," said Alix.

"I wouldn't have," sniffed Rimes.

"Yes, you would," the King said. "People want to believe that a king's orders are full of import — it's part of the glamour of the crown. It's bigger than any of us, and why one must be so careful when asking for things." The spymaster shrugged. "I am grateful for your help, Mrs. Rimes."

"I am committed to the security of this nation, Your Majesty, and all its citizens." She turned her attention to Alix. "Lady Mondegreen, given that I have claimed responsibility for the Checquy's actions, I trust that its agents will conduct themselves as befits employees of the Security Service. So far as the official record is concerned, if questions are ever asked, your people work for me."

"I expect this makes rather a nice change, Mrs. Rimes," said the King. "Aren't you normally claiming that people *don't* work for you?"

Rimes gave him a smile. "Indeed, sir."

The King shook hands with the Director General. He nodded to Alix and left the room.

Rimes turned to Alix. "Lady Mondegreen, tell Linda that if there's anything else I can do to help, I shall. I don't envy the Checquy this task."

You won't be doing any of the interviewing of palace staff," said Pawn Smith later that morning when Alix entered her office back at the Rookery. "I'm under strict instructions. As far as anyone is to know, you are just a lady-in-waiting."

"I understand," said Alix.

"So you'll be transcribing and filing materials brought back to this office."

That sounds like a great way to advance my career, thought Alix dispiritedly.

"Meanwhile, the representative from the Croatoan arrived at Heathrow early this morning. Pawn Ken Padilla of Columbus, Ohio. He handed over the file on the previous manifestation, and then I sent him off to his hotel—he was falling asleep from jet lag. You'll meet him tomorrow."

"What does the file say?" Alix asked.

"Take it, and see for yourself." Alix took the file, and herself, off to the kitchenette to have a read over a bedraggled takeaway Thai beef salad she'd picked up on the way in.

The file looked much like a Checquy file, with similar dire warnings emblazoned on the outside. The first page identified it as *File DBGSCB-93, covering the death of Jordan Wu, Male, 21 years old on*

November 9, *eight years earlier,* at 62 North Third Avenue, Apartment L, Columbus, Ohio 43212.

Precis

Wu, a student at Ohio State University, was discovered unconscious on the floor of his apartment's living room by his roommate Joshua D'Cruz (21) at approximately 5:30 p.m. There were no apparent wounds, but he was not breathing. D'Cruz dialed 911 and, under instruction, could not find a pulse. He provided rudimentary CPR until EMT assistance arrived.

Wu was transported to the Ohio State University Hospital Emergency Department and received immediate attention. Subject did not respond to any measures. Pronounced dead at 6:15 p.m.

Autopsy

Autopsy revealed a granite cube lodged in the center of the brain, with one of the vertices emerging from the top and grazing the inner surface of the skull. The medical examiner evacuated the examination room, the room was sealed, and the Croatoan office in Columbus was contacted.

Croatoan pathologists took over the autopsy, removing the cube and conducting a thorough examination of the body. No other anomalies were identified. Analysis of blood and stomach contents revealed no inexplicable or illicit substances.

Item: Cube

Each face of the cube measured three inches by three inches. No apparent entry wound, or any signs of surgery for implantation.

Chemical analysis of major and trace elements of the cube revealed no information about possible origin.

Research into Croatoan archives yielded no known previous manifestations or operatives with similar characteristics.

Victim Context

Interviews with Wu's family, teachers (from elementary school onward) and friends (from nursery school onward) revealed no known previous manifestations of any sort.

Interviews with D'Cruz's family, teachers (from elementary school onward) and friends (from nursery school onward) revealed no known previous manifestations.

D'Cruz and other friends advised that Wu had no known enemies.

Site Context

D'Cruz attested that the apartment door had been locked when he returned home, and no keys were missing. A review of Wu's cell phone, email, social media, and online calendar revealed no expected guests or appointments.

The subject's residence and car did not reveal any anomalous substances or conditions. Many fingerprints were present in the apartment, consistent with a party having been held there the previous night to watch the Ohio State v. Rutgers football game (Ohio State won, 56–21).

Conclusion and Cover

Given the lack of any subsequent manifestations (locally or nationally) featuring similarities over the following three months, and lack of suspects with a motive for murder, the manifestation was ruled as a likely unique occurrence, and the investigation closed.

Wu's death was announced to have been the result of natural causes: sudden cardiac death from undiagnosed Brugada syndrome.

There was a lengthy section on the cube, giving its composition and a description of its surfaces (which were just as uniform and unmarked as the cube that killed Edmund). Various tests, including a dissection that revealed it to be solid granite throughout, showed no bubbles or areas of greater density. The object emitted no radiation and tested as perfectly normal granite. After the examination, the (now bisected) cube had been placed in secure holding facility 17A, wherever the hell that was.

There were photos of the autopsy, with the now-familiar sight of a cube poking out of a human brain. There was no question in Alix's mind that the features of this death were exactly the same as Edmund's.

Right down to the lack of clues. No leads, no nothing.

"Excuse me, Lady Mondegreen?" Alix sighed and looked up to see Chuah, the retainer.

"Look, I don't know what Sweven has told you." She grimaced a little. "Although I can probably imagine. But please don't call me 'Lady.' Pawn Mondegreen. Or just Mondegreen. Or just Alix."

"Sorry," he said. "I'm new. I was told that we keep our previous titles. Should I not have introduced myself as Detective Constable?"

"No, it's fine. Retainers keep their titles, but pawns are supposed to leave everything behind us—it's about committing ourselves to the Checquy. And it's doubly appropriate for you to keep your title since, technically, you're still part of the police force."

"Are you not still part of the aristocracy?" he asked.

"I am," she conceded, "but you earned your title. I just got mine by emerging from a particular womb. Hardly a notable qualification."

"Right. I just wanted to check that I understood correctly on something. You knew the prince personally?"

"Yeah, most of my life," said Alix.

"I'm very sorry for your loss," Chuah said.

"Thank you."

"This can't be an easy assignment for you."

She shrugged and smiled, but could feel how unconvincing it was. "It's there to be done," she said. "Did you read the American file?"

"We all did."

"Nothing jumped off the page for anybody? No clues the Yanks missed?" He shook his head. "I suppose it was too much to hope for." She stood. "I'd better come help with those staff travel history files."

It took the team until late into the night, but eventually they concluded that out of all the employees in Buckingham and Kensington Palaces, there were four people whose travel histories placed them in America at the time of the Ohio murder. None of the four were of particular prominence, but the team recommended that they be interviewed and cleared before being permitted to resume regular duties.

After that, Smith sent everyone home.

8

The next morning, several text messages informed Alix that materials were waiting for her at Thames House, the headquarters of MI5. The investigation team were not the only ones who had put in a late night. She messaged Smith to let her know that she would be picking it all up on her way into the office.

When she arrived at the Rookery, with several password-protected thumb drives clipped together and strung around her neck, there were still a few minutes before the daily meeting, but it was empty. *Was I supposed to be somewhere else?* She could see that people *had* been in since last night. There were new materials stuck up on new whiteboards, and she wandered over.

It was the standard mishmash of an investigation just commencing—notes and pictures stuck up like a stalker's moodboard. The first whiteboard had a large picture of Edmund at the top. Alix recognized it as his most recent formal portrait. He was wearing a dress military uniform: scarlet coat with gold braid and medals. His face was solemn, gazing off into the distance beyond the camera. It was handsome, a portrait of a prince, but it wasn't the Edmund she'd known. Underneath the photograph was written, in marker, *HRH Prince Edmund,* the dates of his birth and death, and then bullet points about his death.

The next board that made her catch her breath. SUSPECTS was

written across the top, and it featured familiar faces: Odette. Nicholas. Louise. Gemma. The King.

Behind her, she could hear the team entering the room, and various people pausing as they saw her examining the photos. In her peripheral vision, she could see Sweven looking at her. He was practically salivating for a reaction. She refused to give him one.

"We just went out to get coffee," said Andrew Chuah. "We weren't sure when you were getting in." He looked up at the board. "These are the people we know had access to him on the day."

"Yes," Alix said. Part of her was outraged on behalf of that little mourning family she had seen holding each other. But the greater part of her recognized the logic of it all.

Remember, to these people, they're just suspects. They're not really real. And they have to be suspects to you as well.

"You can add a couple of others," she said with all the calmness she could muster. "I've got the names of the staff who brought and cleared his breakfast, the driver who took him from Kensington to Buckingham, and the security guards. Also Meredith Hamilton—she's principal private secretary to the prince and princess. They had a catch-up meeting before he left."

The next board was titled MOTIVES. Her eyes scanned the headings. *Succession. Money. Political. Personal. Insanity. Feeding on collective despair of populace. Takeover by marmot empire.*

"We're just spitballing at this stage," said Scagell, the psychologist. He was peeling a mandarin and popped a segment into his mouth. They all looked around as Smith arrived, accompanied by a short, slender twenty-something man of Latin descent.

"Good morning. This is Pawn Ken Padilla of the Croatoan." Everyone introduced themselves and received a firm, warm handshake. Alix regarded Padilla with interest. He was the first Croatoan operative she had ever met, and she understood that they did things differently over there.

"Hi," said Pawn Padilla. He introduced himself, explaining that it was his first time in England and offering his condolences and those of the entire Croatoan. His specialty, he explained, was site investigation.

Smith gestured toward the conference table, and they all moved across to it.

"Good work last night, getting through those personnel records," Smith said. "The four individuals we identified are being interviewed now, so the palace doesn't need to have another at-home day. Now, let's go around the table to report any progress or developments. Claes?"

"I have been advised that preparations need to begin for the lying in state and funeral, so they are requesting the return of the body. I would like one more detailed examination before we release it to royal undertakers. This would take the rest of the day. It will be our last opportunity to dismantle the body completely."

"I can justify that," Smith said. "You'll commence straight after this meeting?" Claes nodded.

"A thought," said Alix. "There is quite a lot of ceremony before the funeral. First, the body will be laid for private viewing, and then a public lying in state in the Palace of Westminster."

She noticed that Pawns Claes and Padilla looked a little confused.

"That's the Houses of Parliament," she explained.

They continued looking confused.

"The building with Big Ben." They nodded. "It'll be open for the public to walk by the coffin to pay their respects. They're expecting at least a couple hundred thousand people. My question is, do we think it will be safe to have the prince's body inside that coffin?"

Everyone looked thoughtful. When it came to the supernatural, you could never assume that death meant the problem was over. Sometimes it was just beginning. The Checquy used a complex, extremely thorough process for disposing of bodies, be they operatives, enemies, or victims. It generally started with reverently and respectfully putting several bullets in the head of the corpse, and culminated in incineration and scattering of the divided-up ashes from different locations.

"Are you proposing that we put an empty coffin in Westminster Hall?" asked Smith.

"If there are concerns about the body representing some sort of danger," mused Claes, "there are measures we could take."

"Oh?" said Smith.

"For instance, how *much* of the corpse would actually need to be present at the funeral?" asked Claes. They all looked at her, faces changing as they absorbed the implications of the Grafter's question. Everyone then turned to Alix, who did her best to appear unappalled.

"I don't know of a required minimum percentage, but I can ask the Lord Chamberlain."

"Claes, please take extra care to check for any potential dangers," ordered Smith. "Once we have the best understanding of the situation, we'll make recommendations." She went on. "Now, the investigation. Let's continue round the table with progress. Scagell, did you have a question?" He had raised his hand.

"Are we assuming that the prince's death was a deliberate action?" asked Pawn Scagell. The psychologist was leaned back in his seat, still eating his mandarin.

"I believe we must," said Smith. "The prince is too prominent for us to imagine that it was just a random flaring of powers. But add 'random' to the list of motives, and write me a paragraph for the daily report."

"I love making work for myself," muttered Scagell.

"Mondegreen," said Smith. "What do you have for us?"

"First and foremost is the prince's timeline for the day of his death and the previous day."

"And?"

"The day of his death is easy to scrutinize, at least from an investigative point of view," said Alix. "No appointments. He came over to Buckingham Palace right after breakfast. I've got a list of everyone known to have been in contact with him, and it's pretty short. None of them were in America at the time of the first murder, although of course we'll still need to interview them and do background checks."

"I sense that the day before is not as convenient," said Smith.

"Not nearly as convenient, no. The prince was the hardest-working member of the royal family," Alix said. "His schedule was always full. That day began with a meeting at Kensington Palace for his foundation. Just ten people, most of whom were office staff. Then he and the Princess of Wales attended a morning tea for war widows. The two of them had lunch in a private room at a restaurant in the City. After that, he gave a speech at a primary school to the year six students about having adventures and being kind, and how it was probably time for them to start wearing deodorant. That evening, he attended another reception for entrepreneurs developing small businesses outside London. That was at the Hartcher Hotel."

"Those all sound very... full of people."

"A few hundred guests at each event," said Alix. "Plus waitstaff and security. Plus bystanders. *Plus* the diners and staff at the restaurant. And God alone knows how many kids he met and high-fived or bumped fists with at the school. Every day of the previous week is like that."

"This is going to be a nightmare," said Smith.

"Count yourself lucky there was no palace garden party that week," Alix said. "Those have thousands of guests."

"The three classic elements of a murder are means, motive, and opportunity," said Smith. "At the moment, means is our weakest area. With the information we possess so far, we don't know *how* someone's power manifested to cause the prince's death."

"Hundreds of people apparently had opportunity," mused Chuah.

"Correct," said Smith. "But it's not realistic to research the travel history of every person who met him, especially since we don't know what time frame we're working within."

"But hundreds of people wouldn't have a motive," said Alix. "Surely if we can identify those with a motive, we can then eliminate them if they weren't in America for the previous murder."

"Unless it was a professional assassination," said Padilla.

It was an alarming thought. It took a very special and, thankfully, very rare kind of person who, when they discovered their supernatural powers, decided that the best way to use them was to kill people for money.

"After all, it's more likely than some random Buckeye getting a power, killing someone, waiting a few years, and then killing the Prince of Wales for no apparent reason," said Padilla.

"Sorry, what's a Buckeye?" asked Alix.

"Someone from Ohio," said Padilla.

"Is that sort of thing common in America?" asked Chuah. "Supernatural assassins, I mean?" He frowned, and then looked rather unnerved. "Wait, is it common *here*?"

"No," said Smith. "We keep a very close eye on such things. I've already consulted on the possibility with Sir Henry. He's spoken with his contacts in law enforcement, criminal enterprises, and the military and intelligence services. So far as we know, there's no one advertising the kind of skills that would have caused the prince's death. Which isn't to say that there isn't a professional assassin out there who isn't on our radar."

"So we're back to motive, then," said Weller, who, judging by the intense movement of her pen, was either taking very detailed notes or drawing hyper-accurate portraits of everyone present.

"We should start with the most likely suspects and eliminate them one at a time," said Chuah.

"Which would be?" asked Alix.

"Did he have any enemies?"

"Personally? Not that I'm aware of."

"I'm seeing a lot of vitriol online," said Sweven. "People saying how glad they are that he's dead."

"Let me see," said Alix, and Sweven passed over a tablet.

"Lots of talk about how he was the scion of a bloated legacy of racism, colonialism, genocide, and oppression," he said.

"Oh, yeah, that," said Alix. "That's not new—they get that all the time." Sweven looked a little thrown by her unconcern, but he rallied.

"They're saying that the current king should be the last king," Sweven continued, very deliberately not looking at Alix. "That it's a good opportunity to let the monarchy die off, along with the whole system of aristocracy and privilege. Could bespeak a possible motive."

"He was a public figure. Lots of people disliked him or were fixated on him because of what he was," said Alix.

"Most murder victims—even public figures—are killed by someone close to them," said Chuah.

"Most murder victims aren't the heir to the British throne," replied Alix.

"Lots of royals have been assassinated throughout history," said Sweven slyly, "many of them on the orders of their relations."

"Right, and poisoning by a rival used to count as a natural cause of death for a pope," said Alix scornfully. "Centuries ago, but not now." She didn't just say it because Sweven was a dick; people allowed the centuries-old history of an institution to impinge on the way they saw it today. Lots of people were disappointed when they saw that the King didn't wear a crown daily.

"We need to eliminate the family as suspects anyway," said Smith. "Let's start with the obvious one: Princess Louise."

"Why is she the obvious one?" objected Alix, and realized everyone was staring at her. "What?"

"She does gain rather a lot as a result of her brother's death," said Pawn Weller. "For a start, doesn't she start receiving funding?"

"From the Duchy of Cornwall, yeah," said Alix. "It's one of the two royal duchies, and it's the source of funds for the heir apparent. Millions and millions every year."

"That's quite a bit of motive to begin with."

"Louise was never short of money," said Alix. "She inherited millions from both her grandmothers, along with a country house in Devon and a townhouse here in London." To her disconcertion, Weller scribbled down some notes at this, and circled something twice.

"So, she had enough to hire an assassin, then," said Sweven.

"I suppose," conceded Alix.

"And quite aside from the money, she'll also get to be queen," he pointed out.

"Yeah, that's got to be the primary motivator, obviously," said Pawn Padilla. Alix snorted. "What?"

"Louise doesn't want to be queen," she said.

"You're kidding," said the American. "Who wouldn't want to be Queen of England?"

"Anyone who knows anything about the job," said Alix. "It's a *terrible* position, and Louise knows that better than anyone. Trust me, quite aside from losing her brother—whom she adored, by the way—

this is the worst thing that could have happened to her. She had plans."

"Plans for what?" asked Padilla.

"She was going to use her status to bring attention to a lot of major issues, and her connections to rally action and funds to address them."

"Can't she do that as Princess of Wales?" asked Padilla. "Hell, she'll have a planet-sized megaphone as queen!"

"There are a lot of constraints when you're that high up in the hierarchy. The monarch is not supposed to be political, and they have to be sensitive to national interests. You can't just denounce a company that employs hundreds of British citizens, or criticize government decisions. There can be major repercussions, and even just expressing an opinion can get you a lot of blowback about not knowing your place."

"She wasn't worried about any of that if she remained a princess?"

"Louise was going to be in the sweet spot. Not a working royal, but still prominent enough to use her position, and independent enough not to worry about people's reactions."

"Wouldn't her family object?" asked Weller, wide-eyed.

"Edmund knew what she was planning, and I think he approved—would probably have worked with her on the sly. That whole family was raised to believe utterly in the importance of service." Everyone around the table nodded, although Chuah was a little hesitant. Duty was something everyone in the Checquy, and apparently the Croatoan, could understand.

"Now she'll be gagged," said Alix. "She'll still be able to do a lot of good, but there are going to be many restrictions on her."

"It sounds like you're very convinced, Mondegreen," Smith said. "But we have to examine the princess more closely. Do we have the travel records for the royal family?"

"No," said Alix, blushing. It simply hadn't occurred to her. "I'll get them immediately."

"First priority today, please," said Smith. "We'll need those records before we interview them. Now, Weller? Thoughts?"

"I'm working on drawing together and examining the princess's finances," said the pawn. "I want to check for any unexplained expenditures or funds that are unaccounted for. And once she starts receiving funds from the Duchy of..." She looked over to Alix.

"Cornwall," said Alix miserably.

"Yes. I'll scrutinize those too. She could have borrowed against her prospects."

Smith took everyone else's progress reports and handed out follow-up assignments before turning back to Alix.

"Now, Mondegreen," said Smith. "You will need to remember that the princess is a suspect. When you see her, you must observe her carefully and discreetly, and be alert to anything that may provide insight to this investigation."

"Yes, sir," Alix said, woodenly. The rest of the team was staring at her.

Do they doubt my commitment? Do they question my loyalty? Judging by their faces, they absolutely did.

"We'll also need to examine the finances of the Princess of Wales, Prince Nicholas, and the King."

"I'll need additional staff," said Weller.

"You have people in mind?" Smith asked. Weller nodded. "Write me a list. We'll get them."

"Why would the Princess of Wales want her husband dead?" asked Alix.

"We will be looking into that," said Smith, "using our newfound authority as fictional agents of MI5 tasked with assembling information regarding the prince's death. With the royal family, there's always someone watching. We will talk to the people who serve them, the people who drive them, the people who guard them. I want a detailed portrait of the prince on every level. Did he have any known stalkers? Any infidelity? Gay lovers? Catamites? Are there any illegitimate children, ready to muck up the line of succession?"

"I—" began Alix uncertainly, before trailing off and shrugging uncertainly.

"Then we will assemble similar portraits of the princesses, Prince Nicholas, and the King."

"I don't know whether the staff will give us that level of information," said Alix weakly. Except that she did. The King had ordered them to cooperate fully.

"Will you be including all this in your report to the King?" asked Alix.

"I'll be including everything except the fact that we're investigating him," said Smith. "You don't tip off a suspect."

The next few days were a whirlwind of interviews for everyone but Alix. Each morning after the team meeting, those not busy dissecting the prince's finances would proceed to whichever palace housed staff that required questioning. Armed with the dreadful authority of the King's orders, they were ushered into rooms, given coffee, and met by team leaders and the heads of organizations. Then, selected members of domestic staff, administrative staff, and security staff were brought to them.

Introduced as agents of MI5, they gave the interviewees assurances about complete confidentiality and co-signed multiple documents affirming that all information provided would be classified at the highest level. They then interrogated their subjects about various aspects of the royal family's lives, with a particular emphasis on any vulnerabilities that might have led to the prince's death.

Of course, their lines of inquiry were never explicit. Instead, they followed a script that drew upon Scagell's psychology training, Alix's knowledge of the palaces and their dynamics, and covert interrogation techniques developed by the Checquy. It was so tactful and couched in innuendo that the interviewees often didn't realize they'd been coaxed into revealing important information.

All the recordings were brought back to the Box Room and dumped on Alix's desk to be reviewed. It fell to her to run the recordings through the transcription software, which didn't cope terrifically well with the broad range of accents across palace staff. Everything needed to be checked, and summaries written. Time was of the essence—as many interviews as possible needed to be conducted in the week before the funeral—and so Alix sat at the desk with headphones on, playing back and typing long into the nights.

Most of it was so profoundly boring that she had to elevate her desk to "stand" mode so that she wouldn't fall asleep. To her secret satisfaction, no information suggesting familial murder emerged. Edmund had left no by-blows wandering around, Gemma was not concealing any lovers, and the King did not have any substance-abuse hobbies. Louise's and Nicholas's finances were perfectly straightforward, with every penny accounted for.

But while she was pleased not to have uncovered any skeletons in their closets, Alix felt uncomfortable assembling dossiers on people she knew. Reading through transcripts of Nicky's text messages and the daily logs of Louise's protection officers felt distinctly wrong. It was mundane stuff, but some things she didn't need to know, like Gemma's visits to a therapist since the loss of her baby, the King's use of antidepressants and hemorrhoid treatments, or Nicholas's frequent typos when sexting Odette.

After a few days, just before the morning team meeting, Pawn Smith told Alix to go up to Rook Thomas's office. Alix hastily regretted her wardrobe choices and took the elevator to the top floor. She was ushered in by a retainer, only to find the rook standing over a table covered in street maps, talking to Lady Farrier.

"Mondegreen," said the Lady. "Rook Thomas and I are going over the plans for the funeral tomorrow, and your role."

It's tomorrow? Alix thought, aghast. She had been distantly aware of arrangements being made, but the pressing need for investigative progress had consumed all of her attention.

I haven't even reached out to Louise or the King, not for days, she thought guiltily.

Meanwhile, the world had continued to reel in shock and dismay. Thousands had passed through Westminster Hall to pay their respects to the coffin containing most of the prince. Claes's dismantling of the corpse had revealed no cause for concern, but the Checquy had gone a little overboard in implementing safety measures. Tradition already called for British royals to be buried in lead-lined coffins. Tradition did not call, however, for those coffins to be steel-reinforced, with additional linings of green wood, copper, silk, and slate. Nor were they usually laboriously soundproofed and then welded shut.

The body had been manacled inside the coffin and a steel sphere locked around the head, from which all the teeth had been removed—although they had been included in the coffin in a small box with an explanatory note, just in case some form of later identification proved necessary.

The cube removed from the prince's skull remained in Checquy custody and was still undergoing a battery of tests in the hope that it might yield some clue.

"We are deploying a substantial force at the funeral," said Rook Thomas. The rook was a petite woman, with unremarkable features and unremarkable brown hair, but her blue eyes were full of focused intelligence, and there was usually a wry half smile on her lips. "It's a major potential target, and much of the world's attention is going to be focused on it."

Alix nodded.

"We will have operatives within the crowds along the procession route, observing and standing ready to provide tactical support if any disruptions occur. We'd be doing this even without the supernatural element of the prince's death. But if the killer wants to target anyone else in the royal family, now would be a good time."

"Do you really think so? Why?" asked Alix.

"If the prince's murder was committed to affect the line of succession, then the princess, the King, and Prince Nicholas remain targets," said Lady Farrier. "This would be an opportunity for another target to die in plain view of millions of witnesses, with no apparent violence."

"The killer must know that the cube has been discovered," added Rook Thomas. "The fact that the prince's death was attributed to natural causes has shown to the killer that we are unwilling to publicly acknowledge its true nature. If it happens again, we have a cover story prepared: that the royal family has a previously undiagnosed vulnerability to aneurysms, not unlike the problem of hemophilia that plagued the royal houses of Europe."

But this means we're covering up the killer's crimes. We're actually helping them.

"That said," interjected the Lady, "we have no evidence that the prince's murder was committed to put a specific person on the throne. We must also acknowledge the prospect of another motive, or a random madman. In either case, it's entirely possible that they'll be present tomorrow. Murderers can be drawn to crime scenes or their victims' funerals. Which means you'll need to be on your toes for any eventuality."

"Why me?" asked Alix, with a sinking feeling.

"You will be attendant to the Crown Princess Louise," answered the rook.

My first day of professional waiting as a lady.

"This is especially important because of the scrutiny on all the attendees of the service," Lady Farrier said. "Commentators will be identifying every person who enters for television viewers. There will be some Checquy operatives seeded in with the security personnel, but not as many as we would like. You will be the person closest to the royal family, so if something *does* happen, you will be the last line of defense."

Wonderful.

"Style your hair so as to conceal an earpiece," said Rook Thomas. "You'll be kept abreast of every development throughout the funeral. Should there be an attack, your first priority is protecting the King and Princess Louise in as discreet a manner as possible."

"Of course." She hesitated. "Should I perhaps have some sort of weapon? I'm not saying a gun," she added hastily. "But maybe a little Taser, or some tranquilizer thing?"

"Absolutely not," Lady Farrier said firmly. "The sight of a lady-in-waiting pulling out a weapon would not be acceptable under any circumstances. You have a cover to maintain."

"And if something does happen?" Alix asked. She didn't have to ask, she knew the answer, she'd known it since she was nine, but she wanted someone else to have to say it, to acknowledge it.

"You put yourself between your protectees and danger," said Lady Farrier. "You shield them. You evaluate, and if you can get them to a safe place, you do so. If you need to engage the threat, then you do so. You were trained to fight, Alexandra, and to kill. And even if you weren't, you have a power inside you that should be able to break any assailant without leaving behind evidence."

Right, if they get within touching distance, Alix thought. Otherwise, using her powers was simply not an option. *I'd be at risk of crippling or killing everyone around me, including the royal family and thousands of members of the public.*

"Remember, Pawn Mondegreen, there will be snipers on buildings all around you," the rook said kindly. "And soldiers, police, and Checquy pawns everywhere."

"Yes, of course," said Alix. She would have to rely on them. *Just like everyone else does.* "It's fine."

"Good," Lady Farrier said. It was unmistakably a dismissal. Alix returned to her desk in the Box Room, where all eyes were upon her. It was clear her colleagues knew what she would be doing tomorrow. She couldn't tell whether they approved.

Over the past days, she'd noticed a distinct coolness toward her from the team, a situation she was all too familiar with. They didn't meet her eyes or call her by her first name, and she knew that she hadn't been invited to at least two group steppings-out for coffee. She grimly suspected that there had been a couple of after-work visits to the pub without her as well.

You should be used to it by now. And Sweven probably hasn't helped. He and his friends throughout the Checquy were always eager to spread some venom about her if they could. The only way to get through it was to be patient, to give them no additional reason to dislike her, and not show any sign of how much it hurt.

The most rankling irony about the situation was that as a child, Alix would have been thrilled to go to the Estate and not return home. Her parents had been completely uninterested in her or her sisters. The cooks, nannies, and maids who kept the children alive were all pleasant enough, but they came and went frequently. Her sisters had each been sent off to boarding school as soon as was legal, so the whole family only ever really gathered together during the holidays.

Alix wandered over to the kitchenette, where Chuah was making coffee while Claes leaned against the countertop.

"Can I make you anything?" Chuah asked her.

"If you're offering, I'd love a latte, thank you."

"Sure. So, Naomi, you were saying about Sweven's leg?"

"Yes, it is ridiculous that he is stumping about on crutches. I checked his records, and it is three perfectly simple breaks. Beautifully done, by the way," she said, nodding to Alix.

"Uh, thanks," said Alix.

"Right," said Chuah. "It was you who broke his leg? I wasn't sure if you were joking."

"No, it was me. It happened during a mission. He'd fallen under the influence of the target."

"Mental," he said. "The things you people accept as a matter of course."

"Mark wasn't too accepting of it," said Alix. "Not at the time, and not since."

"You know he's not your biggest fan," Chuah said, and she nodded. "Anyway, was it karate? All you pawns seem to be martial artists."

"We're all trained in unarmed combat," said Alix. "I actually do study karate, but that's not how I broke his leg." She debated what to tell him. Generally, people in the Checquy weren't shy in talking about their abilities, but the retainers could be funny about them—especially new arrivals.

Still, better he hear it from me than from someone else.

"I create an energy inside myself, and when I release it into someone else, it churns through their skeletal structure. It's painful and distracting to the target, and if I do it hard enough, it can break their bones."

"That's wild," he said. He didn't seem appalled, just interested. "Very cool."

"Thanks," she said. It had always struck her as rather a hideous power. She'd spent years refining her control of it, but it was not something she reveled in. It was also a frightening power and probably didn't encourage colleagues to regard her with any more friendliness. Even in the Checquy, some things made people uncomfortable.

"And Naomi," Chuah was saying, "your lot are the Checquy's super surgeons, right? So one of you fixed Sweven up?"

"If one of the Broederschap had fixed him up, he would not be on the crutches," sniffed Claes. "I could open his leg and fix it right here in the office—there wouldn't even be any stains on the carpet."

"So, then, why?"

"They are afraid of us," said Claes.

"We're still getting used to each other," said Alix.

"It's all magic to me." Chuah shrugged.

"I do not do magic," said Claes sharply. "I engage in scientific practices that are, as far as the mainstream community is concerned, far too advanced to be understood."

"Yeah, all right," said Chuah, who did not seem overly concerned. Alix diplomatically changed the topic of conversation.

"Chuah, are you settling in all right?" she asked.

"Three weeks ago, I thought I had an interesting life," he said. "I was a cop working on a string of murders. That's pretty interesting, right? Then I get drafted into magic MI5, and I'm assigned to *this* case. So now I know what interesting really means, don't I?"

"What do you think of the case?" asked Alix. She was curious to hear what a law enforcement officer made of the situation.

"It's a bloody hard one. I feel like we're just flailing around in the darkness. All the standard techniques—we can't rely on them, can't take anything for granted. No murder weapon. No witnesses. The only clue was inside the victim's brain, and we don't know how it got there. We've got a woman who can look back in time, and she says there was no one in the room when it happened!"

Claes nodded pensively.

"Look," Chuah went on, "most murders, you want to have a lead in the first twenty-four hours. You talk to the last person who saw the victim, get a picture of their day, get a picture of their life, and put together a theory about what happened. And almost always, it comes down to love or money. They've got a spouse or a lover who feels the victim has done them wrong, or they've stolen someone's money. Or someone wants to steal their money. Sometimes, it's the odd random attack by a crazy person. But this one? It may be political, it may be the line of succession to the throne, it may be a professional killer." He made a face. "After a week of interviews, none of these looks more plausible than any other. So, all we can do is keep following every possible lead."

"And what if it was a crazy person?" asked Alix. "Or a random uncontrolled flaring of someone's powers?"

"Then it's going to be very hard to find them."

9

Alix was de-linting her funeral hat when the intercom buzzed. To her astonishment, the monitor showed her sister standing outside the front door of the building, looking rather sullen.

"Frances?"

"Can I come up?"

"Sure." She buzzed open the street door. Her seventeen-year-old sister arrived, dragging a little suitcase on wheels. "This is unexpected. Have you run away from school?"

"We're here for the funeral, and I didn't want to share the pull-out bed with Cecily," said Frances. Alix nodded in understanding.

With the Checquy picking up the tab, the Mondegreen parents had taken up residence in a luxurious Knightsbridge flat, and then decorated in such a way as to encourage parties while discouraging houseguests, including their own children. When Peregrine had passed away, his study had been turned, not into a guest room, but into Charlotte's new dressing room. Cecily, the youngest sister and the one most jealous of her space, usually claimed the only sofa bed for her own and defended it tooth and claw. There was one non-sofa-bed sofa, and the older two usually used a coin toss to decide who got that, and who had to curl up in the gigantic bathtub with some pillows. So it was entirely reasonable for Frances to stay at Alix's, if not for the fact that they hardly ever spoke and she'd never been there before. The two sisters regarded each warily.

"I'm glad I was here," said Alix. "You didn't call ahead."

"I don't have your number," said Frances.

"Oh." Alix realized that she didn't have Frances's number either. "You're welcome to stay, of course. The guest room's through there," she said. "Would you like a drink?"

Because I abruptly really need one.

Alix's relationship with her sisters was fraught. After the Mondegreens had sold off their daughter's future for a stipend and a bunch of perks, they had gotten to thinking. One daughter had proven lucrative. Who knew what these "Sheck-eh" people might pay for the next one? The prospect of additional wealth proved to be a better aphrodisiac than a combination of oysters, Barry White, and extract of Sudanese blister beetle. Half an hour after the subject was raised, Lady Mondegreen was pregnant.

The next daughter, Frances, was the subject of much expectant observation by the Mondegreens—far more than their first daughter had ever received. Their unfamiliarity with how children developed meant that they made weekly calls to their contact in the Checquy, who dutifully trundled over to the flat and then advised them that, actually, babies were supposed to do that. And that. And that.

Frances's failure to develop unnatural skills or features immediately did not daunt her parents, especially since, with visions of private jets dancing in their heads, they had set about getting pregnant again just as soon as was practicable. In due course, Lillian became the newest member of the family and proved to be an exquisite little baby, but not to a supernatural extent.

By the time Cecily arrived on the scene, the Mondegreens' hopes were getting rather dampened, and Lady Mondegreen was extremely tired of being pregnant, giving birth, and getting nothing out of it except a child. They agreed to stop and just enjoy the profits their first child brought them. Their disappointment, however, had always colored their interactions with their three youngest daughters. The girls' impression of somehow not having lived up to their mysterious sister had made family gatherings extremely tense.

As far as Alix was aware, her sisters didn't know anything about the true, paranormal nature of the Checquy or her parents' arrangement with the government. But they would have needed to be lacking all sorts of faculties not to pick up that Alix's situation was significantly different from their own and always had been. Quite aside from the age gap, and the fact that Alix would inherit the title and the estate, there were all sorts of factors that had pushed them apart.

Firstly, there had been the issue of school. The Checquy required that Alix attend the same elite boarding school as Princess Louise and picked up the tab for her but was not willing to pay for all the daughters. The parents Mondegreen had not been willing to pay Whyteleafe School's astronomical fees, so their younger three had gone off to a different (but still expensive) school.

Once Alix graduated from secondary school, she hadn't gone to university but had segued into full-time Checquy operations. Her sisters were aware that she had some sort of hush-hush job with the government, and it was implied that she got it through family connections. They were not, however, the sort of family connections that the other three girls could rely on. As a result, Alix always felt uncomfortable around her sisters. They, meanwhile, usually regarded her with blank expressions and never asked her any personal questions.

Now Frances was in her living room, with a glass of white wine in her hand, moving around and examining the décor. Alix watched her with wary interest. They were unmistakably related. They had the same rampant ruddy hair, same Roman nose, same hazel eyes. It almost seemed impossible that Frances couldn't reach inside herself and pull out an incredible churning power to break people's bones.

She's what I might have been. If I hadn't been born the way I was. It was a new thought.

"So how's school?" Alix asked. "Final year! That's exciting!" She paused. "It is your final year, isn't it?"

"It is."

"That's exciting," Alix repeated. She wasn't sure what to say next.

"And, lady-in-waiting," said Frances. "Congratulations. Mummy is ecstatic, of course. I suppose you'll be on duty tomorrow, at the funeral?"

"Yes, it's my first day. It would be nerve-racking enough, without the whole world watching."

"I'm sorry about Prince Edmund. He always seemed very nice." The junior Mondegreen daughters hadn't spent nearly as much time with the royal family—another factor that had highlighted their differences. "How is the family?"

"They're getting through it," said Alix. "Lots to adapt to."

Frances nodded. "Right."

"Would you like anything to eat?" asked Alix.

"I'm good," said Frances. "Had a kebab on the way over."

"Oh, nice." There was no response. "Kebabs are great."

"Yeah."

They stared around silently. Alix felt a stab of guilt. There were so many colleagues in the Checquy who would have done anything for the opportunity to connect with their birth families, and here she was, wondering if feigning narcolepsy was a realistic strategy for getting away from the tension.

"I should get to bed," she said abruptly. "I have to be up early."

It was still dark and the city was silent when the palace-sent car quietly rolled up. Alix was standing ready, her funeral dress in plastic dangling on a coat hanger from one finger, her overnight bag slung over her shoulder, and, cradled in her arms, a hatbox that was unique for being used to store an actual hat rather than sewing supplies or old letters.

Frances was still asleep but had been given a key to the flat, the code to the alarm, and the number for Alix's mobile phone. Little as it was, this represented a distinct improvement in Mondegreen sororal relations.

The streets were empty, except for the occasional street-cleaning truck or cab trundling by. The closest streets had already been closed off, but Alix's driver had a pass, and at her request, the car drove by Westminster Abbey, where bleary-eyed police had already taken up position. The authorities were expecting large crowds for the funeral, and many people had already staked out their spots by the barricades that lined the route. Some had little tents, and some were nodding in camp chairs. At Buckingham Palace, moonlight glistened off the plastic of all the bouquets spreading out from the fence.

A waiting footman took Alix's accoutrements and promised to deliver them to the private apartments where she was to join the family.

"I'll be right up," Alix assured him. She needed to check in with the Checquy's palace security office. The liaison to the palace did have an update for her, and it was not good news. Rather than driving with the ladies, she was to join the royal family in marching from Westminster Hall to Westminster Abbey, and then, after the funeral service, in a procession from Westminster Abbey up Horse Guards Road, and then along the Mall toward Buckingham Palace.

Hell. Quite aside from the prospect of marching in front of thousands of people, it would mean that the entire royal family would be exposed for much, much longer than if Louise were being driven about in an armored Rolls. *And I'm the last line of defense.*

Plus, I can't do it in these shoes.

She had brought heels that were elegant and easily kicked off for combat but not at all appropriate for a long march along the Mall, let alone the cobblestones outside Westminster.

In the apartments, the butler advised her that no one else was up yet.

"I think I'll need to go home anyway," Alix told him. "I didn't know that I'd be marching today, and I don't have the appropriate shoes." She winced. "Although I don't know if I'll be able to get home and back in time, if the traffic is already picking up."

"I think we'll be able to solve this problem from within the palace, my lady," the butler assured her. "May I inquire as to your shoe size?"

Dubiously, she gave it.

Is he going to raid someone's closet? Boarding school had taught her that Louise's shoes could not be squeezed onto her own feet.

Alix decided against trying to go back to sleep and instead settled herself in the lounge, on a lounge, to read the papers.

"So, you're on the clock today," said a voice. Louise was standing in the doorway, in her pajamas and dressing gown. Alix had dropped the paper and risen in order to curtsy before Louise could wave her not to.

"Your Royal Highness, good morning," she said. "I'll be attending you throughout the day, yes."

"And is this in your guise as lady-in-waiting, or as bodyguard from the weird secretive esoteric government agency?" asked Louise.

Be nice to her. This is going to be one of the worst days of her life, and she has to endure it in front of the entire world.

"Both," Alix replied in as level a tone as she could muster. "Two for the price of one." And then, because she couldn't quite help herself: "Neither of which costs *you* anything."

Louise sniffed. "I'm up to my ears in government agents. A couple of them came from MI5 and asked a lot of questions about Ed's death." Alix nodded. "Fa said that it's important to establish all the circumstances surrounding his last days, just to pre-empt any questions that might arise. It seemed paranoid to me, but I thought I would humor him."

She sat, which meant Alix could also sit. "You should probably know, I've chosen two additional ladies-in-waiting. If I have to have them, I'm not going to have every single one chosen for me."

"Indeed," Alix said, over a little flash of hurt. "So, who are the other lucky ladies?"

"The first is Siti Amarah."

"I don't know her," said Alix.

"You don't have to," said Louise. "Anyway, she's going to be Mistress of the Robes."

"Groovy," said Alix. The Mistress of the Robes was the senior lady-in-waiting. The title came from days back when the holder was responsible for managing the princess's clothes and jewelry. Nowadays, the role mostly involved appearing at some state occasions, and scheduling the duties and appearances of the other ladies-in-waiting.

"So, who is she? Is she a duchess?" In modern times, the Mistress of the Robes had usually been a duchess.

"No," said Louise. "She doesn't have a title. She's an artist. I know her from Exeter."

The newspapers are going to love that. Any deviation from tradition meant coverage and commentary, although no one could be sure how the public would react.

"An artist, great," Alix said. "And she can afford to take on the role?" It was a tacky question, but ladies-in-waiting didn't get paid. It was one of the reasons that they were mostly aristocrats, or at least women who didn't need to hold down jobs. Most people couldn't give up hours and hours, and sometimes days and days, for no pay.

"Not particularly, no," said Louise. "Her career is just starting out, and her family can only support her so much. But I've gotten her a grace-and-favor for two years." These were apartments or houses that the monarch could provide, rent-free, to whomever they wished. Sometimes they went to relations, sometimes to employees, sometimes to people in gratitude for services rendered.

"One of the palace apartments?"

"No, it's a townhouse near here. It'll enable her to paint without having to get a part-time job. Plus, I'm paying her a small stipend out of my own money."

"Cool, like an artist's grant," said Alix.

"Sort of. She's talented, and I like her a lot." She paused. "And I can trust her."

"Are you saying you can't trust me?"

"I assume I can trust you to do your job," said Louise flatly.

"Fine," said Alix, equally flatly. "When do I meet her?"

"I'm having a lunch so you can all meet each other," said Louise.

"All?"

"There are two others," she said. "Imogen Canley-Vale and Henrietta West."

Alix had known Imogen for just about as long as she'd known Louise. She'd been one of the Buckingham Palace Girl Guides. The Canley-Vales were an old family and had been intimates of the royal family for generations. Imogen was the kind of aristocratic friend whom everyone would expect to be a lady-in-waiting. She had long straight blond hair and an upturned nose, rode horses, and had sufficient money that she could afford to donate her time to charities that didn't actually involve coming in direct contact with the disadvantaged.

The name Henrietta West sounded vaguely familiar, but at that moment, Alix really didn't feel like prying details out of a Louise who seemed to be gloating that she'd been able to select women who weren't Alix.

"I look forward to the lunch, whenever it happens," said Alix. "But in the meantime, I think breakfast is ready. If you'll excuse me. Ma'am."

Breakfast was a buffet set out for the royal family, which today included Gemma's parents, sister, and lady-in-waiting; and the King's sister, Princess Helene, who had come down from Scotland with her two sons. And Alix. Conversation was quiet. After breakfast, the King asked Alix to join him in his study. She caught a glimpse of Louise rolling her eyes.

"Louise seems a little out of sorts," the King remarked. "And not just in the way one might expect on the day of her brother's funeral."

"I think she regards the idea of a government organization that deals with the occult as somewhat absurd," Alix said, "a waste of taxpayer money. That, combined with the fact that I've been foisted on her as lady-in-waiting, makes my presence fairly irksome to her." She delivered it as calmly as she could, but it *did* hurt a bit.

"She'll get over it," said the King. "Meanwhile, I'm very glad you're joining us today. Your support means a great deal."

"It was an honor to be invited, sir." She braced herself.

"I've been receiving the daily reports from your office." He gestured toward the two despatch boxes on his desk. One was covered in red leather, marked with the royal monogram. Such a box, filled with government documents from different departments, was delivered to the King every day. It was iconic.

Next to it was a much shallower box, which was as far as it was possible to be from iconic while still actually existing. It was also covered in leather but was a rather battered and unprepossessing graybrown, fading at the corners. Alix knew that its appearance belied its composition. Whereas the red boxes were made of pine and lined with lead (so as to sink if thrown overboard in the event of capture), the Checquy despatch box was constructed of titanium. It also featured a locked inner box, emblazoned with dire threats and warnings, just in case the bland outside lid should ever be opened by an unauthorized person.

"Your team has gathered a great deal of information."

"Yes, sir." She was beginning to sweat. It was coming, she knew, the moment when the King would ask her about the investigation, sidestepping the chain of command and using her as his personal contact to get the inside track.

Just because we're pawns doesn't mean we can't see what moves will be made.

Alix understood. She could imagine the pain of having to wait and do nothing while a lengthy process clicked along, undertaken by people who had not known his son.

"There do not appear to be many leads," he said.

Alix was tempted to take the route of centuries of courtiers and bureaucrats and give a safe, soothing, but noncommittal answer.

> *Every possibility eliminated brings us closer to the truth.*
> *We still have many avenues to pursue.*
> *Our best people are working on it.*
> *We remain cautiously optimistic.*
> *This is a long process, and we will follow it to the end.*

They were all true enough, but they did not answer the unasked question. He was afraid that no one would dare tell him the truth, the real, unvarnished truth. Even though he was the King, or because he was the King, they would not give him bad news.

The Australian public service, she knew, had a phrase they invoked when describing their responsibility to report to their superiors: "Frank and fearless." For all sorts of reasons, she owed it to him to be frank and fearless.

"There are no leads," she said.

"Yet," he said, almost pleading.

"There are no leads yet," she agreed.

"No suspects."

"You know there are suspects, sir." *They're your family.* "But there is no evidence pointing to any suspects in particular," she said. He looked a little relieved.

Is Louise on his own list of suspects? He must have one. The King had been interviewed by Pawn Smith, with Bishop Attariwala—a member of the Checquy Court—attending. Information from the conversation—nothing particularly interesting—had been added to the timeline, but the actual transcript was kept locked away. *One of the benefits of being King.*

Does he look at those around him and wonder? Does he turn over the possibilities in his head? When he lies awake in the darkness of the night, is he afraid that his daughter might have plotted his son's death for the throne?

"It's not going well, though," the King said.

"No," she agreed. "I'm sorry."

"How is that *possible*?" he exclaimed, and slammed his fist down on the Checquy despatch box. "How is it possible that my son, the Prince of Wales, *my son* has been murdered, and they have found *nothing*?"

Alix shot a nervous look at the door.

"This is the way it works," she said. "You put the best people on it, and you let them work."

"They have been working for days!"

"I know."

"And they've made no progress at *all*?"

"They'll keep working," she said. He looked at her, desperate. *Frank and fearless.* "We'll keep working." She could promise this, but she could not promise him answers.

He covered his eyes with his hand. She could only sit uncomfortably while he pulled himself together. Finally, he looked up. His face was calm.

"We'd better get ready," he said. "We have twenty-five minutes before the cars take us to Westminster."

Alix curtsied and departed. For a moment, she leaned against the closed door, her eyes shut tight as she took several deep breaths.

God, that was horrible. Then she opened her eyes to find the butler waiting patiently.

"Sorry," she said. "It's just the funeral and..."

"Not at all, my lady," he assured her. "It's a difficult day for us all. Now, we've sourced a pair of shoes that I think might suit." He held up a wooden box, and Alix took it gingerly. It was highly polished and lacked any marking.

She ran a cautious finger over the wood. *Is this ebony?* Inside was nestled a delicate pair of ankle boots with a sculpted but low and broad heel—ideal for walking on cobblestones without spraining an ankle or losing a shoe.

"Perhaps you should try them on here," said the butler. "If they don't suit, we can find others." Alix sat on the uncomfortable antique sofa and put the boots on. Almost inevitably, they were a perfect fit.

"They're ideal," she said faintly. "Whom should I thank for these? I'll get them back immediately after."

"No, no," said the butler. "You're to keep them."

"Oh," said Alix. "Thank you, then." He smiled and nodded. She headed to her room to get changed. Her painfully expensive yet extremely restrained outfit had been laid out for her, and her hat was waiting in its box. She regarded it grimly.

As a pale-skinned red(ish)head, she had been indoctrinated from an early age to seek out broad-brimmed hats lest she burst into flames, or at least char, but on this occasion she needed an unimpeded field of sight, so the brim extended out only a little way. Thanks to the exuberant nature of her hair, she had to take certain precautions. She spent several muscle-straining minutes binding her curls down into a shape that allowed her hat to sit on top of her head and not look like it was being engulfed and pulled down into the mass, never to be seen again.

The whole ensemble was an armor of sorts, although only an emotional one, since it possessed no shielding capabilities whatsoever. Alix had suggested that, since the royal family was under threat, it might be wise for the King, prince, and princesses (and Alix herself) to wear some sort of discreet protective gear under their funeral clothes, but that had been vetoed on the grounds that they would be scrutinized by every journalist, fashionista, and royal-chaser on earth, and they couldn't take the chance of showing fear.

Alix stood in front of the mirror and scrutinized herself for any flaws that would be broadcast all around the world. Her reflection was acceptable, but she thought that, in her mourning clothes, with her hair pulled back and the most subtle of makeup, she looked like a black-and-white photo of herself.

She decided to take advantage of her last opportunity to visit the lavatory, and resolved not to drink any water.

It was going to be a long walk.

10

The ceiling of Westminster Hall hung high above them, an intricate sculpture of gigantic oak beams.

"Mondegreen, stop looking up at the ceiling and pay attention to your surroundings," said a voice in her ear. She twitched guiltily and resisted clapping her hand to her earpiece. Next to her, Olive Claybourne—Princess Gemma's lady-in-waiting—shot her a curious look, and she smiled weakly.

To make matters worse, every Checquy operative on the radio band would have heard her being rebuked. Fortunately, that would only have been a comparatively few people—there were so many pawns and retainers deployed that they had set up encrypted channels for different areas. A huge command trailer had been parked in a service alley filled with people listening to headsets, talking in hushed tones, coordinating movements and observations, and switching people's access to different channels.

Flushing, Alix turned her attention back to the situation at hand.

Over the last several days, hundreds of thousands of respect-payers had walked past the coffin on its high catafalque, which had been draped in purple cloth, on a red platform, with four soldiers standing guard, one at each corner of the coffin.

The coffin itself had been lavishly decorated with all sorts of symbolism. It was draped in the standard of the Prince of Wales, and placed on top was a wreath of white roses and oak leaves and then, on a cushion, the coronet of the Prince of Wales. Also on the coffin lay an unsheathed 1897 pattern infantry officer's sword and its scabbard, reflecting his military service.

The King, Nicholas, and Gemma were in military dress uniform reflecting their service. The other men wore black morning coats. Louise, like the other women, wore a black dress and a hat, since she had never served in the military, nor had she received any honorary ranks.

Then doors were opened, and soldiers entered. Eight pallbearers stepped forward to lift the coffin from its platform, shoulder the weight, and carry it through the hall. They had selected especially beefy soldiers for the task, almost glowing in their red coats, their hair cropped close. They were large men, but they still strained under the weight of the coffin, with its hidden infrastructure.

Count yourselves lucky, lads. There were some in favor of placing plastic explosives and a remote detonator in there, just in case.

The funeral party followed them outside, and Alix squinted in the sudden bright light of day. She wore no sunglasses—no one in the procession did. Their eyes, their emotions, any tears, would be on display for the world to see. Dazzled, she was blinking furiously, so that she had a momentary confused impression of a mass of color and movement, before it resolved into thousands of silent people. Before her was the gun carriage with the pallbearers carefully easing the coffin into place. Soldiers were drawn up in ranks at the front and rear of the vehicle.

The flanks of the black horses hitched to the carriage glistened in the sunshine. One of the horses stamped and snorted until its rider, a soldier gorgeous in black with cords of gold, placed a comforting hand on its neck.

On both sides of the carriage were soldiers in dark dress uniforms with sashes across their breasts, medals shining, and swords held low at their sides. Then, flanking them, were Welsh Guards in their red coats and tall bearskin caps with green and white plumes providing a slash of color on the left side. Alix's eye was caught by their guns, held in the "reverse arms" position reserved for armed guards escorting a funeral casket—the weapon held under the left arm with the barrel pointing behind.

The King, Gemma, Louise, and Nicholas were being directed to their places behind the carriage.

"Lady Mondegreen, Mrs. Claybourne," another courtier said, "will you come forward, please. You'll each be walking behind your respective princesses."

My princess. *And what does she think of that?* Alix felt a stab of guilt. Louise was probably not thinking about her at all, but rather about doing her duty at her brother's funeral.

Alix followed Olive Claybourne. Since the King and the Checquy had insisted that Alix be present, Gemma's lady-in-waiting had been included, on the grounds that two would look less peculiar than one. Next to her, Edmund's best friend, a solemn-faced soldier with eyes red from tears, would be walking behind the King. Behind Nicholas, his cousin, Prince Jerome, stood calmly.

Alix looked down. Sand had been spread thickly on the cobblestones of New Palace Yard, to ease the footing of the horses and the humans and to assist the carriage in rolling smoothly. It flared bright under the hot sun.

Behind her, dignitaries and members of the royal household were put into position in the procession. Alix was conscious that pictures were already being taken and that television cameras were recording. She needed to keep her eyes forward, but the temptation to scan the environment for any potential threats was strong.

Rely on your comrades. There were calm voices in her ear as the Checquy operatives in her area spoke to each other. If something *were* to happen, she would need to take only a couple of steps forward to be able to cover Louise.

Ahead of them, she could hear the deep-throated cry of military orders.

"FUNERAL PROCESSION!"

Oh God, let me get this right.

"SLOOOW! MARCH!"

They stepped forward as one. All Alix's drill instincts snapped into place. She may only have been a part-time student at the Estate, but she had done plenty of marching. Her instructors, many of whom had come from the military, insisted that it was a core element of training and discipline, and as a result, each Checquy student could have marched in the Royal Edinburgh Military Tattoo. She noted a brief moment of hesitation on Louise's part, but then the princess fell into step.

Ahead, the pipe band was playing. Her eyes were on the back of Louise's neck, and then she looked ahead and saw the spectacle before them. The pipers, the drummers, the officer in plumes on his horse, and then the green gun carriage that had carried two kings and three queens in its time.

They were on paved road now, and on their right, as they marched along, were drawn up more soldiers in red, their bearskins standing proud, but a massive banner lowered to drape in a display of sorrow on the ground. Beyond them, thousands of people, standing silent. *So many!* It was only three hundred meters from the Westminster Hall to Westminster Abbey, but the march seemed to be taking hours. Any one of the onlookers might be the murderer, hidden in the mass, preparing to strike out at them.

Pawn Clements's vision of Edmund's death had shown him suddenly clutching at his head, then falling down dead. What would Alix do if Louise crumpled to the ground? Or the King?

"*Funeral procession is at the Abbey,*" announced her earpiece.

They stopped. The pipe band peeled off and took up position, so that the music continued and echoed off the buildings of Westminster. The gun carriage had halted in front of Westminster Abbey. The coffin was slid off the carriage, and with small, almost mincing steps, the soldiers drew it away. As one, they hoisted it onto their shoulders and moved in step into the Abbey.

Alix had been in Westminster Abbey many times, but it had always been full of tourists. The only time she had seen it as it was now, with chairs set up, full of seated dignitaries, had been for

Edmund and Gemma's wedding. Then, a red carpet had been laid out over all the engraved memorial stones of the floor. Alix had sat with her preening parents and along with the whole world had watched the couple pledge their troth.

They had been so much in love, and she had been so glad that Edmund had found someone he could be happy with.

Now he was dead in that box.

It was that thought, and the sight of his widow taking her seat, that almost broke her.

She choked back a sob, and her eyes were hot and swimming. *Do not cry.* Television cameras were dotted around the Abbey, in hides painted to look like bricks, poised to capture images for the world to gape over. She would not be the one to give the press their juicy sorrow picture.

When Alix's father died, she'd been surprised by the level of grief she'd felt. When she'd delivered his eulogy, Alix had kept a thumbtack in her pocket and had pressed it against her fingertip to stop herself from crying. She was wearing gloves now, but she dug the nails of her thumbs into the sides of her forefingers hard enough to hurt.

Alix took in no details of the service. She stood and sat automatically when everyone else did so. During the hymns, she concentrated on the voices coming through her earpiece. A constellation of Checquy officers was spread through the crowds outside, monitoring and reporting to coordinators.

The funeral came to an end, and everyone stood as the coffin was carried out. Alix and Olive took their places and followed. The coffin was again placed on the gun carriage, but this time the horses were gone. Instead, 138 junior sailors were in their place. Tradition called for the gun carriage at state funerals to be drawn by ratings, ever since the funeral of Queen Victoria, when the horses had spooked and some obliging young men from the Royal Navy had stepped in. Although Edmund had not lived to become king, his and his wife's military service and their support for the armed forces had prompted a diffident offer, which Gemma had gratefully accepted.

"*Cortege is departing the Abbey,*" a voice noted in her ear. "*Commencing march to Hyde Park Corner.*"

It was a long march. First, up Horse Guards Road, with St. James's Park on the left. They passed the Horse Guards Parade on the right, where the King's Life Guard was turned out, mounted on gorgeous horses to give a Royal Salute. The procession turned onto the Mall, and ahead of them, the crowds were now vast. A mass of faces.

There must be hundreds of thousands.

Yet there was hardly any sound. Just the wind, and the rustling of leaves and of people's clothes, the grinding of the carriage's wheels on the road, and the measured tread of the procession as it marched. Half a mile ahead of them, at the end of the red-colored road, stood Buckingham Palace.

The sun beat down on them, and Alix's black clothes felt heavier and heavier on her. Her hat shielded her from the worst of the glare, but her hair was wet underneath.

A muttered man's voice with a strong Dutch accent came in her ear.

"All Checquy, this is Kehden. I have suspicious movement on the Mall."

Do not look around. Keep in step.

"Copy that, Kehden," said the controller. "Details?"

"White male moving through the crowd on the northern side of the road," said Kehden. "Midthirties, slim build, about five foot ten. Close-cropped brown hair, thigh-length brown coat, odd body language. He's furtive, looking around. He's about ten meters from the head of the procession, back a few rows."

"Any sign of weapons?"

"His hands are in his pockets," replied Kehden.

Alix swallowed. *Stay calm. There are a lot of people here. Inevitably some of them would look furtive. It means nothing.*

Except that even now there might be someone in that ocean of faces building up the energy and the will to reach out and kill.

Now would be an ideal time. Especially if you could do it without touching the target, without any sign that you were involved. Millions of witnesses would see the victim go down, but no one would see the cause.

"Any signs of escalation?" asked the controller.

"His body temperature is rising, his heartbeat is elevating."

Christ. Despite herself, her eyes flickered to the side, searching for a furtive-looking man with brown hair. She couldn't pick him out of the thousands of faces.

"He's moving closer to the barrier," said Kehden sharply. There was the sound of a sniff over the earpiece. "I detect hormones of excitement. He is building to some action."

"Kehden, approach," said the controller. "Quietly. We don't want to make a fuss if we can help it. Adjacent agents, move in to support. Mondegreen, be ready to protect the royal family." Alix spread her fingers out in the signal of acknowledgment.

"Proceeding," said Kehden. Over the earpiece, Alix could hear him pushing through the crowd. Distant jostling and complaints. She was poised, ready for an alert to come.

I move forward and cover Louise's body with mine. Hustle her forward, put the gun carriage between her and the attacker. Then go back for Nicky and the King. The Checquy had wanted the King to be the priority, but he'd threatened significant repercussions if his life was put ahead of his children's.

Alix's own life was not a priority, but she'd always known that.

"He's almost at the barrier," said Kehden. "He's taking his hands out of his pockets!"

Alix's heart was pounding, but she maintained her slow, dignified pace.

Be ready.

There was a sound off to their right, just a few gasps and a little movement. She was braced for the order, or a bang, or a flash of light, or the scream of a horrified crowd that would jolt her into reaching out and putting her hand on Louise's shoulder just that bit too late.

"I have him sedated," muttered Kehden.

Alix let out a deep breath. They marched on, but she caught the sound of a slight disturbance in the crowd behind them.

"It's fine," an Englishwoman was saying in her ear. "We're with St. John Ambulance. It looks as if he's just dehydrated." Presumably she was offering an explanation to the civilians.

"Support staff move in to assist with the removal of the detained," the controller said. Alix realized that her back was soaking wet with sweat, and she was grateful that her dress was black and would hopefully conceal it.

Was it him? Have they got the killer?

As they came to a new segment of the route, the operators in the trailer switched her to a new channel. They marched on, past Buckingham Palace, where the Union Jack flew at half-staff. They came to Hyde Park Corner, where a hearse and a convoy of cars was waiting. The coffin was once again transferred, and the back of the hearse dipped noticeably under the new weight.

As the rear door closed behind the coffin, a dry voice spoke in her ear.

"The procession is completed, coffin is secured."

Alix relaxed a little. The hearse would drive, with a security escort, to Nonsuch Palace. The family would join it later for a private ceremony as the coffin was interred in the vault in St. George's Chapel. Now they were getting into waiting cars to be driven to Buckingham Palace for the dignitaries' lunch. She joined Olive in the car that was waiting for them.

"Water?" offered Olive. A tall, plump woman, she always tended to tower over Gemma. As a result there were a multitude of photos of the Princess of Wales in which Olive formed the entire backdrop.

"Please," said Alix, and she took the bottle with a hand that she realized was trembling with tension.

"You okay?" asked Olive.

"I—Yes, thank you," said Alix. "Sorry, just...I was really focused."

"I don't blame you. Thank God it's over," said Olive.

"Did you hear that someone in the crowd fainted?" asked Alix.

"I'm not surprised. It's so hot, they'll probably be keeling over in waves. I was ready for something to go wrong."

At the palace, everyone repaired to their rooms for a rest. Guests would not be arriving for an hour. Alix dialed a secure number.

"Pawn Alexandra Mondegreen, ID code 45 Fatalistic Aureate 85 Zulu."

"Proceed," said a man's voice.

"Checking for updates."

"I expect you're wanting to know about the man they took into custody at the procession," said the voice. Was it her imagination, or did he sound *amused*? His informality was a breath of fresh air after such a somber and rigid morning.

"Yes, it happened right by me."

"Oh, I know. They had him out of the crowd immediately and transported to a temporary questioning facility. The Grafters revived him, dosed him with some sort of truth serum, *and* had Doc Crisp there with his fingers on the man's pulse points."

"And?"

"Nothing supernatural. Turned out he was the world's unluckiest pickpocket."

"Seriously?"

"Yep," said the man, and she could still hear the grin in his voice. "Sebastien Chuzeville, professional pickpocket. He actually came over from Paris just to work the funeral crowds."

"No!"

"Oh, yes. They found seven wallets he'd slid into the lining of his coat through a slit in his pocket, including one that belonged to a pawn who'd been in the crowds and never even realized he'd been robbed."

"So they're turning him over to the police?" asked Alix.

"I'm hearing rumors that he might be useful to have on the books. He's got nothing inexplicable about him, but he's got quick, soft hands, and we do have specialist retainers."

"I can see how that might be useful," said Alix. There was definitely precedent—the Checquy was always on the lookout for expertise, no matter how unorthodox. In the Second World War, they had brought an actual London crime lord into their ranks, and that woman had proven an absolute godsend.

"Nothing else to report," the voice went on. "No manifestations in Westminster. In fact, none around the country. It's like everything stopped to pay its respects, even the supernatural."

"That's a nice thought," said Alix.

"You did a good job, by the way," said the voice. "We were all watching on the telly. You didn't put a foot wrong."

"Thank you," she said, trying not to be surprised by the kindness.

By the time the guests began to arrive, everyone in the royal party had taken advantage of the break to have a little cry, touch up their hair or makeup (if they had either), touch base with the posted sentries, and go to the toilet. They gathered in an anteroom. On the other side of the doors, they could hear the sound of a crowd assembling.

"Here we go," Alix heard Louise mutter to herself. It was another performance, but if the funeral and the procession had been for the entire world, this was for a very select, very important audience.

The doors opened.

The reception hall was full of people, and they all turned. The great and the good were collected, with only minimal overlap between the two. Foreign royalty stood with prime ministers stood with ambassadors, aristocrats, politicians. Celebrities preened next to oligarchs and magnates whose massive contributions to strategic charities meant they really *had* to be invited.

Alix was under strict instructions by Lady Farrier to remain close to the princess, but Louise had made a rather curt remark telling her not to just hang around. Alix settled for standing behind the princess, out of her line of sight, but ready to step forward if called, or if someone needed to be discreetly subdued with an armlock or a pointedly threatening remark.

People pressed forward, eager to greet Louise, introduce themselves, express their condolences, and do their best to insinuate themselves into her long-term memory. Everyone wanted to shake her hand, to be seen shaking her hand, while laying the groundwork for a future connection. Alix began taking mental notes of those who seemed unusually pressing in their approach to Louise but gave up almost immediately.

If a desire to get close to the princess makes someone a suspect, then this entire reception needs to be listed on a whiteboard in the Box Room.

Louise was drawn forward by the tides of the crowd, which meant that Alix needed to keep moving without shoving any sheiks or stepping on the foot of a Serene Highness.

To Alix's disconcertion, people were also approaching *her*. She knew some of them vaguely and some gave the distinct impression of knowing her, even though she was quite certain they'd never met. Sometimes it was an actual dignitary, sometimes an aide or a deputy or a spouse. Their conversation was, for the most part, fairly predictable. Greetings, condolences, sympathies for the family, observations about how well it had all gone. But all of them took special care to make sure she knew their names and what organizations or businesses they represented. She was acquiring business cards at a phenomenal rate and was grateful that she'd brought her little clutch handbag to the reception, since otherwise she'd have been left holding an increasingly large stack of extremely expensive and strategically valuable cardboard.

Evidently, word has gotten out about my new position. So far as she knew, there hadn't been any formal announcement, but either the news had been passed along powerful grapevines or her position in the funeral cortege had prompted people to ask questions and get answers. She grimly suspected that if she Googled herself now, she'd find many, many more mentions. To her profound relief, no one so much as hinted any knowledge about the Checquy or her position in it. *This is all because I'm a lady-in-waiting.* To these people, she was now a direct connection to power and influence. It wasn't a very comfortable feeling.

Through it all, her eyes kept snapping back to Louise, like a mother constantly keeping tabs on a toddler who was a little too interested in an uncut wedding cake. After the Japanese ambassador bowed to her and moved away, leaving behind the most exquisite business card she'd ever seen, there was a gap in the conversation. Alix took the opportunity to snatch a glass of water off the tray of a passing waiter, and turned to find her mother standing beside her.

Lady Charlotte Mondegreen was magnificent in a funeral outfit that had cost a great deal more than her daughter's and looked it. It was not ostentatious, but it looked *good*. And so did its occupant. At forty-eight, she was slim and beautiful and possessed thick raven-black hair that showed no hint of gray, did as it was commanded, and had not been passed on to any of her daughters.

"Mummy! Hi."

"Hello, darling." Her mother swooped in to purse her lips in the vague region of her daughter's cheek. "It's so nice to see such good people here to pay their respects. I've been catching up with ever so many." She lowered her voice. "And well done you on being made lady-in-waiting. Everyone's very pleased."

"They are?" asked Alix.

"Oh, yes, your people have already contacted me, and there's going to be a nice little addition to my monthly honorarium."

There it is.

"That's good," said Alix flatly. There had been no mention of any nice little addition to *her* salary.

"I saw the King, the dear man, and he mentioned how glad he was that you'd be able to support the princess."

Tall doors were opened, and the gathering of several hundred people flowed on into the dining room and found their assigned seats at the various tables clustered around the head table. Alix had been placed with a combination of elderly aristocrats and ambitious businesspeople. She chose to see this as a sort of deputy hostess assignment—a mark of trust and responsibility rather than a punishment—and so she gamely tried to make conversation. She was starving, and when the first course was placed in front of her, she almost made a mewling sound of delight. She was about to take a bite of the excellent-looking salmon tian with fennel and apple salad when she was interrupted.

"Lady Mondegreen?" She looked up to see one of the staff standing at her shoulder. She could not remember his name, but he had been two years below her at the Estate. She also knew that, despite his slender frame and rather high voice, he was actually the strongest person in recorded history. He bent down to speak to her in a low tone. "Word has come. You're required immediately."

"But, I..." she began. It was incredibly bad form to leave a royal event before the King.

"The King has given his permission," said the pawn. "Lady Farrier has spoken with him." She looked over at the King's table and caught his eye. He nodded tightly in benediction. Alix made her quiet apologies to the rest of the table, citing some vague emergency. No one seemed particularly interested—they were all focused on their meal or their networking. Alix stood and curtsied to the King. She caught a flash of Louise's startled face as she turned.

"Do you know what it is?" she asked the pawn as they moved away.

"They said to tell you that there has been another cube."

11

Please, God, let this one give us a clue. Let us find something.

She stood in the palace courtyard and watched the car that had been sent to fetch her glide forward like a long designer shark. A footman stepped forward to open the door for her, glanced inside, and then recoiled. Alix was hard put not to follow his example.

From the outside, the stretch limousine was the personification of comfort and sophistication. The dark tinted windows concealed the fact that it was crammed full of red-faced people and luggage, like a clown car whose occupants were escaping an oppressive regime. The floor was covered in hard black equipment cases with duffels and backpacks and laptop cases stacked on them, and the people who peered out at her all had yet more bags on their laps.

"Don't hang about, get in!" barked Smith. The pawn was clutching two menacing duffel bags. "Otherwise things will start falling out."

Alix gulped. Just inside the door there was a space amid the massed materiel and personnel that was about her-sized, and so she crammed herself into it. She braced her foot against the floor and pressed herself up hard against Pawn Smith. The footman pushed the door gingerly, and she could feel it pressing against her.

"I'm very sorry, ma'am," he said.

"It's fine, just push," said Alix tightly.

"Everyone hold your breath," ordered Smith. The footman looked around, planted his shoulder against the door, and shoved. Alix could feel her bones folding, until the door finally, unwillingly clicked shut. The limousine moved off, and everyone relaxed as much as they could, considering the car was holding the massed bulk of Alix, Smith, Sweven, Sweven's crutches, Chuah, Scagell, Claes, Padilla, and, seemingly, all their worldly possessions.

How am I going to get my seat belt on? she thought, and then decided that in the event of an accident, she'd either be shielded completely by the mass or crushed by it into a fine paste.

"Here, take this," said Smith, and she tilted slightly in her seat, so that one of the duffels toppled over onto Alix's lap. It clanked as it fell onto her, and judging from the way it dug into Alix's legs, it contained a selection of appliances, shackles, and hardcover books.

"Hi, everyone," said Alix. There was a chorus of slightly compressed greetings. "This is a very nice, if slightly unorthodox transport."

"I thought it might be appropriate for picking you up from the palace," said Smith. "We needed something that could carry us all, and all three of the Rookery's mini-buses were checked out."

"So, there's been another death?" asked Alix.

"Yes," said Smith. "Here." With some difficulty, she fished a folder out of one of her duffels and strained to pass it over to Alix, who rested her elbows on the duffel in her lap and began reviewing the material, which was pretty scanty.

It had happened late that morning. The victim was Ian Blanch, a civilian, fifty-seven years old. A prominent businessman, he had died in his home in Winchester. His wife, the only other person in the house, had found him collapsed in the kitchen with no apparent sign of injury.

After the paramedics and the A&E doctors failed to revive the victim, someone entered the details into the NHS database, and various highly specific medical minutiae of his death triggered all sorts of administrative trip wires and alerts that had been laid down throughout the British medical system (and the veterinary industry, just to be sure) after Edmund's death.

Frantic orders were sent to the Royal Hampshire County Hospital, and Blanch's body was retrieved from the morgue, where it had been waiting patiently for an autopsy. A quick MRI by a Checquy-cleared technician revealed a cube of granite in the center of the man's skull, and all hell promptly broke loose. The Winchester Checquy field office received a terrifying telephone call from Rook Thomas. Pawns descended upon the deceased man's house and removed the mourning and bewildered family. A perimeter was established, and no one would be allowed in until Smith's team arrived.

"We don't consider this good news, do we?" said Alix carefully.

"Absolutely not," Smith replied firmly. The other occupants of the car exchanged guilty glances.

The occurrence of another death by brain cube was, of course, cause for significant concern. It was a dreadful tragedy, a failure of the Checquy's mission to protect civilians from the supernatural, and it represented a chilling escalation of events.

And yet, for all that, it did open up a bit of hope for the team's stalled investigation. No one wanted to say it, but another death might mean more clues. The victim's timeline had to be less challenging than Prince Edmund's. At the very least, it might reveal some sort of pattern or connection: a shared enemy, a common acquaintance.

"That's all we know at this point," Smith said. "Pawn Weller is back at the Rookery with her squad of financial researchers, pulling together a dossier on the victim."

"Do we think it's coincidence that this death happened on the same day as the funeral of the first victim?" asked Alix. "Sorry, Padilla, the first *British* victim." The American pawn waved a forgiving hand.

"No," said Smith. "We don't think that."

"How *was* the funeral?" asked Padilla. "You looked good."

"Thanks," said Alix. "It went smoothly. Ish."

"I always end up critiquing funerals," said Padilla. "I'm always thinking '*That's* the music you picked? *Those* are the photos you showed?'" The American pawn shook his head. "I've got my funeral playlist all chosen, and I've picked out pictures that I look good in." He turned his attention back to the tablet that perched on top of the luggage that covered him. "This was amazing, though. I've never seen anything like it. I don't think my funeral is going to match up."

"So, no notes for improvement, then?" Alix asked, and he smiled.

"No notes." He paused. He looked over at Alix. "*You* got a bit of coverage, you know." From further down the limo, Sweven snorted.

"Ugh, really?" sighed Alix.

"Yeah," said the American. "You're not the main story, don't worry, but people wanted to know who you were. Quite a few of them. All around the world."

I suppose it was inevitable. I was standing right behind Louise.

"An international profile!" exclaimed Sweven false-brightly. "Gosh, isn't *that* exciting! Although..." He trailed off, sounding thoughtful. "I hope that's not going to be a problem. I mean, for deployments and so on. Will there be a danger of people recognizing you?"

Alix shot him a look, and he gazed back at her, wide-eyed and innocent, before a smirk ran across his face.

"I'm sure people aren't going to be focusing on me," she said. "This is just a brief flash of interest." To her horror, Smith was looking thoughtful.

"Also," said Padilla, "quite a few people are talking about your boots."

"Oh, fuck them!" exclaimed Alix. Everyone in the limo stared at her, but she didn't care. "What is *wrong* with people? It was a funeral! For the Prince of Wales! That's what's important. And people are talking about my *boots*?"

"Don't worry, they like 'em," said Padilla. "Some of the fashion blogs are trying to identify who made them." He scrolled down further. "There's already some rigorous debate on social media going on around... '#mysteryboots' Who *is* the designer?"

"I have no earthly idea," said Alix. "Someone at the palace brought them for me." She tried to look down at them, but the strata of luggage prevented her.

"They are cute," said Padilla. "Although I thought your hat was the best part." He looked over and winced. "It's getting a bit crushed, by the way."

"Crap." Alix fumbled it off her head and onto the lap-duffel. She'd been told that her go bag from the office would be transported for her—it was probably buried in the luggage of the floor. "Is there anything to eat? I got pulled out of lunch before I could start."

"I have some mandarins," said Scagell from the other end of the limo. "Would you like one?"

"Bless you," said Alix. The fruit was passed with difficulty down the length of the car, and she peeled it gratefully.

When they arrived at the heliport, the driver came around to open the doors, because none of the occupants could reach the handles. Cases and operatives spilled out of the car onto the pavement.

The pilot fussed for quite a while getting everything and everyone onto the large helicopter in such a way that it wouldn't be unbalanced and spiral down into the Thames, killing them all. Alix thought she could hear the blades straining to get them airborne. Soon they were roaring over a green patchwork of fields and irregular blobs of woodland.

Mercifully, several large SUVs were waiting in the paddock where they landed to transport them and their stuff. Once settled in an SUV, Alix took a moment to check her phone. She'd had a grim presentiment in the helicopter, and it was turning out to be accurate. Her social media following on various platforms had tripled in the hours since the funeral. Most of them were people she had never heard of, but a few were fairly prominent.

"Pawn Mondegreen," said Claes. She was leaning in through the car door but did not get in. Alix looked up guiltily from taking in the many queries from complete strangers about her boots. "May I ask a favor?"

"Sure."

"There is a piece of equipment that must be set up at the scene, but I have been detailed to conduct the postmortem of the victim." She pointed to a case by her feet. Black, ridged, it was about the size of Alix's torso. "Would you deploy it? It is simple. It just goes into the room where the body was found, and the doors must be shut so it can gather trace evidence in the air. You can be in there while it does its work."

"I'd be happy to," lied Alix.

"Thank you. The instructions are inside. It is very easy."

Chuah and Scagell were driven off to interview the widow Blanch, while Claes was ferried away with her multitude of luggage to conduct the postmortem. The rest of the team was driven to the Blanch residence by Pawn Gary Roscoe, the head of the local Checquy office.

"What have you told the family?" asked Smith in the front passenger seat. In the back seat, Padilla, Sweven, and Alix were crammed together, and Alix was wondering how she'd come to be sitting in the middle with the tops of Sweven's crutches in her face.

"Only that there have been irregularities about the death," said Roscoe. "We weren't certain whether you wanted to imply murder or accident."

"It'll have to be murder," decided Smith. "If we want a thorough investigation, and to ask the right questions."

"So, it actually *is* murder, then?" asked Roscoe.

"Yes," said Smith. "I'll need to speak with the local police chief, tell him it's all hush-hush."

"The house is being guarded by our people," said Roscoe. "We'll provide any support you need. Also, Pawn Felicity Clements is being brought in. She should be arriving in a couple of hours."

The Blanch house proved to be large: seven bedrooms, a study, a library, seven and a half bathrooms, a pool, a pool house, a sauna, a home cinema (in addition to the vast televisions in the lounge and family rooms), a beautiful kitchen, a dining room, a second, less beautiful kitchen where cooking actually got done, and extensive gardens. Two pawns in police uniforms were stationed at the front gate, and another in a police dog uniform was patrolling the back garden.

"Nice," said Padilla. "What did this gentleman do for a living?"

"Executive in a tool manufacturing corporation," said Roscoe.

"Longtime resident of Winchester, though I think he spent a lot of time up in London."

They went around to the back garden, where a white tent had been set up to act as a staging area. Everyone delved into their go bags and kits and began donning Tyvek overalls and masks. Even Sweven's crutches were swathed in plastic bags so as not to track any contaminants into the house. Alix nipped behind the locked pool house to change out of her funeral dress and the infamous boots and into the rumpled, slightly musty clothes that she kept in her go bag.

It was eerie walking in through the Blanches' back door. Crime scenes always had that feel of a place holding its breath, but private houses even more so. The team moved quietly, respectfully, and the rustling of their coveralls was the only noise.

They first moved into the fancy kitchen, where Mr. Blanch had died. The notes from the paramedics did not say where in the room he had collapsed, and the whole place was in a state of significant disarray, as the paramedics had shoved things about. Unsurprisingly, no one had taken any photos at the time.

"When Pawn Clements arrives," said Smith, "we'll get her to mark out where the body was."

"Do we know what he was doing at the time?" asked Sweven.

"Making tea," said Smith. "Mondegreen, you're good to set up Claes's...item?" Alix nodded unenthusiastically. "We'll give you the kitchen, then. When you're done with whatever it is, do a survey-scan of the room, and then start gathering samples of all the food." Alix brought in Claes's mysterious case, her own equipment bag, and the large cases containing the survey-scan equipment. She closed all the doors.

Cautiously, she unlatched the plastic case. There was a box on top, flush to the surface, and when she lifted it, mist coiled out of the interior. She flinched back. Nestled amid bags of dry ice was a curving lump about the size of a cat covered in limp, light brown-gray fur dotted with droplets of ice. A furry tail at one end curled away under the thing.

"Oh, God!" She'd been hoping that it might just be some sort of cunning alchemical appliance, but there was definitely a creature in there. "I'll address you in a moment," she said to the thing, which lay still and, thankfully, did not reply.

The box that she had lifted out contained a few objects in foam recesses—a metal thermos-like cylinder, a folded plastic sheet, a neatly wrapped towel, and a small plastic box that rattled when she picked it up. There was also a laminated piece of paper with the instructions, which she read through carefully.

Steeling herself, she lifted the thing gingerly out of the ice. "This is so *gross*." Weighing about four kilos, it was rigid, and the cold of it bled through the latex of her gloves. The long furry tail hung down, and she wanted to gag. It took all her strength not to drop it but to place it gently on the kitchen counter. It lay there, facedown, like a lump of frozen bath mat.

The next step was to dry the thing with the microfiber towel. Biting the inside of her mouth so that she didn't throw up (a measure that was not in the instructions), Alix draped the towel over the stiff little body. She was the veteran of a thousand dog-bathings and dryings, but it felt very different when the object of the exercise was rigidly frozen.

Join the Checquy! You too can confront supernatural evil, fight for the safety of society, and briskly towel-dry an oversized dead rat.

When the thing felt dry, she sat down on a chair and grimly laid the towel out on her lap. She turned the cold, hard thing over and saw that it was not just a ball of cold fur, like a dead tribble. This was an animal that had furry limbs, a head, and a face. It was somewhat pear-shaped and had a short, broad head with a snubbish muzzle and plump cheeks. Rounded ears sat on top of its head, and its eyes were, thankfully, closed. Its black lips were drawn back, revealing flat teeth and gums so pale they were almost white.

Alix laid it on her lap, on its back, supporting its head like a baby. She took a deep breath and pinched the ends of its ears firmly between her thumb and forefinger. Almost immediately, she felt a wash of heat blossom.

Warmth was spreading through the creature. She could feel it becoming less a frozen thing and more like an actual animal. Its limbs lost their rigidity and twitched a little. With a sigh, it drew in breath, and its lips relaxed down over its teeth. Its eyelids fluttered, then opened to reveal black beady eyes. It focused on her, and then its lips drew back again, this time in what looked like a smile.

It's a quokka! Alix realized. She'd seen pictures of the little Australian creatures. It was adorable.

"Hullo," she said to it delightedly. It continued to smile up at her, and its little ears twitched. "Do you talk?" It didn't reply. "Do you understand me?" It cocked its head at her. "Well, that is okay, because you are great anyway. You are just great! You are!"

Still supporting it with one hand, she reached out with the other for the thermos and flipped the lid off to reveal a thankfully normal-looking rubber nipple (it *was* Grafter equipment, after all). She presented it to the quokka, which reached out and held the bottle in its little paws. A contented look settled across its little face as it began to suck. "This is the best thing I've ever done for the Checquy," she told it.

When it had finished its wake-up beverage, the quokka waited while Alix reviewed the instructions. The next part required her to speak some Dutch phrases, which were written out phonetically.

"*Bereid?*" she asked. It nodded a little nod. Clearly, it knew what to do better than she did. "Okay, *staart*." Its tail, longer than she suspected was normal, curled up. She held the creature under the kitchen's hanging light fixture until the quokka's tail coiled around the cord and it lifted itself up. Carefully, half-afraid that the weight of the little beast might pull the fixture down, she moved her hands away, ready to catch it, but everything remained intact.

"*Initiëren.*"

The creature's eyes closed and it began to pant rapidly. It spun slowly on its tail. Her only moment of fear was when it paused and coughed a little *chuff!* before resuming its hyperventilating. After several minutes, it stopped panting, opened its eyes to look at her, and chirped.

"You're done?" Alix asked. It chirped again, so she took it in her hands, and it released itself from the lamp. "Good job." The instructions told her to give it a treat from the little plastic box, which it chewed while she scratched its head between its ears. "It doesn't say what I'm supposed to do now, so I'm going to hope that you're happy just sitting on the counter while I do my work."

She put it on its towel and stroked it again. It sat and watched her as she set up a tripod and a horrendously expensive camera-like piece of equipment with multiple lenses and lots of gears visible through its transparent plastic carapace.

Once she set it going, the thing would turn about on top of its perch, panning its lenses up and down, taking photos and shooting out low-powered lasers. It would capture a detailed scan of the entire room, and the final result would be a three-dimensional record of the crime scene that could be moved about and scrutinized from the comfort of one's own ergonomic chair. The pictures it recorded were of such high resolution that the title of every book on a shelf would be readable.

"You and I need to step out for a moment," she told the quokka, which consented to be picked up and taken out the back door of the house. After they heard the scanner's distant little beeps indicating it was finished, she had to return and repeat the process a couple of times, setting up the device in different parts of the kitchen to ensure that there were no gaps in the recorded imagery.

After that, the quokka supervised while Alix took testable portions of every product in the Blanches' cupboards, fridge, and bar trolley.

"Now I have to find Smith, but I don't like the idea of leaving you alone," she told the quokka, "so you'd probably better come with me." She scooped it up, taking care to support its hindquarters. She passed Sweven, who was processing the living room. The two of them ignored each other.

As she moved from room to room, Alix took in impressions of the house and of the Blanches. Everything she saw spoke of a moneyed family. The rooms were large, clean, comfortable. Family photos from vacations showed two cheerfully rotund parents with two slim teenage boys and a slim younger girl, all with brown hair, and all looking genuinely well-adjusted, healthy, and pleased to be in each other's company.

This is what a normal happy family looks like, she thought. *Try not to compare and contrast with your own.*

Ian Blanch and his wife each had their own study-sitting room. In Mr. Blanch's, a vanity wall exhibited his framed diplomas and certificates for contributing to this or that cause. Alix scanned the photos of Mr. Blanch at various events, mostly charity functions, as he smiled and shook a dignitary's hand. Sometimes his wife was present in the pictures, sometimes not. None of the photos showed any member of the royal family.

"I'm not seeing any sign of a connection between this guy and Edmund," Alix remarked to the quokka. She passed back through the kitchen, where Pawn Clements was sprawled on the floor laboriously drawing an outline around herself with marker.

"Wotcher," the barghest said from floor level. "That's a cute little beast you've got there."

"A quokka," said Alix. "Grafter tech."

"Nice to see they don't just make sea monsters," said Clements.

"Did they drag you out of some covert strike to do this?"

"Training in the Brecon Beacons. They sent a helicopter."

"Us too," said Alix. "You've already watched the victim's death?"

"Yeah."

"Anything helpful?"

Clements shook her head. "Same as the first one. Poor man's just standing at the counter, making tea, and then suddenly falls down dead. No one else was in the room. Only other person in the house was the wife."

"Did you see her reaction when it happened?"

"Genuine shock and horror," said Clements. "I mean, maybe she faked it, but why would she? There was no one else in the house to see her."

They shrugged, and Alix went out the back door to the garden.

"What the hell is *that*?" asked Smith when she saw the quokka. "Is that Claes's equipment?"

"It is!" said Alix.

"Is it one of those smiley little animals from the Internet?"

"It is!"

"Can I...pat him?"

"I think he would love that!" said Alix. The quokka preened

under Pawn Smith's caress. Padilla came forward and tentatively patted it.

Alix handed the chest of her samples over to a representative from the local office, to be couriered back to the Rookery for analysis. She did not hold much hope, though—Checquy examination of Edmund's food and possessions had revealed no unusual substances.

"We'll be heading off to the Winchester office soon," Smith said. "We can leave our equipment. There will be guards around the clock, and we're going to be here a few days." Alix was relieved. The prospect of repacking and hauling it back and forth was tiresome, especially after the day she'd had.

The team arrived at the local office, an unassuming warehouse on the outskirts of town. Alix knew that beyond the shabby windowless cladding and the incredibly bland lobby, it was actually one of the most heavily fortified facilities in the country—a bunker of corridors, barracks, arsenals, and investigation facilities. It was designated as a "fallback fortress" if ever major disaster struck or social order broke down.

Claes was waiting for them in the garage and took the quokka from Alix.

"Was he good?" she asked.

"He was very good," said Alix. She paused. "Is he going to be all right?"

"What do you mean?"

"Well, he's been inhaling evidence."

"He is designed very carefully. The gathered substances are filtered away into special pouches. He was very difficult to produce, and very expensive, so I've put in multiple redundancies to keep him safe."

"How do you get the samples out?" asked Alix.

"He will pass a series of plastic pellets later this evening," said Claes. "I'll set up a litter tray wherever we're staying."

"Gotcha," said Alix. She'd had a secret concern that the quokka would have to be opened up somehow, or that he might even be disposable. That was one of the things about the Grafters—they were so matter-of-fact about cutting into flesh and twisting life.

"The difficult part was engineering a bowel that would produce an unscrewable capsule," said Claes, stroking the quokka. "Of course, that's not all he does. He has also registered and recorded all the scent-signatures in the house."

"He's super useful," said Alix, leaning forward to bump noses with the quokka. "How did the postmortem go?"

"Not unexpectedly, unfortunately," said the Grafter. "Blanch's death matched that of the Prince of Wales in every way. A cube of stone in the center of his skull, with no clue as to how it had come to be there. As inexplicable as the first, with no leads beyond the fact of its existence." She looked over to the conference room. "Do you think they would mind if I brought this little fellow into the meeting?"

"I think we're all going to need to have him there," said Alix. "I have a bad feeling this will not be very encouraging."

It was not.

Preliminary investigation had not identified anything that pointed immediately to a suspect, a motive, or a means. The most promising avenue had been Chuah and Scagell's interview with Mrs. Blanch, and that was not fruitful except in comparison to everyone else.

"Mr. Blanch and the Prince of Wales had never met," said Chuah. "At least so far as Mrs. Blanch knows."

"You didn't just ask if he knew the Prince of Wales?" asked Smith.

"No, we thought that might give the game away, somewhat," said Scagell. "Especially given the funeral was today. We were establishing Blanch's contacts—business, social, charitable. He's quite a high flier in corporate circles, and we threw the royal family in as a possibility, along with some prominent industrialists, politicians, scientists, academics. When we mentioned the royal family, she opened up because they'd just been watching the funeral procession on television. If they'd known the prince, if they'd ever met him, she'd have mentioned it."

"How did she strike you?" asked Smith.

"Shocked, distraught, bewildered by the news that it might be foul play," said Scagell. "So far as she could see, there was no reason to think that her husband had been murdered."

"And had she noticed anything unusual at the scene?"

"No, and we took her through a thorough checklist. No odd sensations, nothing remarkable about the way he was lying when she found him. Not even any strange smells or sounds."

"What about before? The hours and the days leading up to it?"

"Nothing," said Chuah. "Her husband hadn't mentioned any new acquaintances, hadn't taken any unusual trips or talked about any out-of-the-ordinary business dealings."

"No enemies?" asked Smith.

"Maybe business adversaries," said the retainer dubiously. "He's CEO of Kabriolet, a corporation that manufactures various industrial tools. We're talking millions of pounds in holdings. Not in the top ten of the country, but significant."

"And no money problems?" asked Padilla.

"Not that she knew of," said Scagell.

"Did Edmund perhaps have any investments with this Kabriolet?" suggested Alix.

"I'll get Pawn Weller to check through the prince's holdings for any financial connections," said Smith. "Also the King's and the princess's. Anything else?" Everyone shook their heads. "All right," sighed the team leader, "it all needs to be written up for the King's daily report. You've got forty-five minutes to get down everything you've accomplished today, and note all analysis and test results that are still pending."

After the team had frantically written up and sent off the report, they were ferried to a hotel. In the lobby, Smith surveyed her group. Everyone was visibly exhausted. Even the quokka, nestled unobtrusively in Claes's coat, was lacking some of its customary *joie de vivre*. Alix thought she heard a small marsupial snore.

"Normally I'd suggest we all go to dinner," Smith said, "but you look knackered, so get room service, and get some sleep. We'll meet here after breakfast." Everyone made limp sounds of agreement and shambled to the lifts.

After a long shower and a bowl of Bolognese that in no way made up for missing a Buckingham Palace lunch, Alix found that she was not sleepy. Tired, yes, down to her marrow. Sleepy, no. She puttered around the room, unpacking her clothes and putting them in drawers. She examined the #mysteryboots and found the tiny letters VRI embossed under a flap, but the Internet knew of no such shoe brand. She turned on the television and flinched away from footage of the funeral — especially when she caught a glimpse of herself looking blank-faced. She decided to go down to the hotel bar.

She found that Pawns Scagell and Padilla had had the same idea and were seated on a couch, the former with a whisky, and the latter with something clear and oily in a martini glass. They nodded in greeting, and once Alix had been furnished with a brandy, she joined them.

"What are we talking about?" she asked.

"Guess," said Scagell. "We were just saying how nothing promising came out of today." He grimaced and took a drink.

"Nothing *obvious*, certainly, but we've just started looking," objected Alix. "We've only spent part of an afternoon on this man."

"I suppose," said Scagell. "Chuah said that with most murder investigations, there's usually something that stands out about the victim — a cause for the killing. But just like the prince, there's nothing here."

"But this is a manifestation murder," said Padilla. "It doesn't have to make sense. After all, none of *us* make sense."

"The means of killing these men may not be explicable," said Scagell, "but it's not random enough to be just a phenomenon. It's an entity that's doing it, and it's targeting people. Individuals."

"All males, all adult," said Alix. "And that's about the only common feature, so far as I can see. Taking into account the American killing, we can't even say that they were all the same race or age or marital status."

"I sent a message to the embassy," said Padilla. "Washington will investigate whether Blanch had any connections to the victim in Ohio."

"I don't think we should focus too much on the American death," mused Scagell. "The time gap between him and the two here — it's too much. I think that the first victim was the initial manifestation. Whoever was responsible, they learned they could do it from that experience."

"And then they didn't do it again for eight years?" asked Alix.

"I don't know." Scagell shrugged. "Maybe it festered away inside them, and now they've come to terms with it. Or it's broken them, and now they're doing it again as acts of madness."

"Is that the official terminology?" Alix asked.

"I suppose correctly it would be 'acts committed in a state of diminished responsibility,' but it's been a long day, and this is my second whisky." Scagell sighed. "I can come up with any number of plausible profiles, but without more information, there's no way to be sure."

Alix and Padilla both nodded knowledgeably at this. They were well-acquainted with situations that precluded certainty.

"The timing of this murder is troubling, though," Scagell mused. "The death during the prince's funeral is suggestive of some ritual or pattern, and that leads us to some very alarming possibilities. If we're talking about a serial killer..." He took a drink. "Well, we could be working on this for a very long time."

"This one will be easier," said Alix. "We've declared that it's a murder, so we can conduct an actual murder investigation without having to conceal our actions. Already we've been able to do things like take fingerprints and unleash a quokka without having to sneak past guards to do it."

"You know," said Padilla, "there is something I could try."

"Yeah?" said Alix.

"It's a thing I can do with my powers," said the American. "I've never tried it for an investigation, but it might yield something."

"That sounds...not incredibly promising," said Alix, "but anything's worth a try at this point." She had no actual idea what the American's abilities were.

"Exactly," said Padilla. "I'm going to ask Pawn Smith if we can go over to the house."

"What, *now*?" asked Alix. It was past midnight.

"I'd need to do it at night anyway," said Padilla. He called Smith and explained the situation. "Yes, ma'am, I will. Thank you." He hung up, and looked over at the two British pawns. "Want to come?"

12

A warning was sent ahead of them, and a Checquy guard in a police uniform was standing by the front gate when they arrived.

"Anything doing?" asked Alix.

"Nothing," sighed the pawn. "I'm keeping a watch out here, and Kalu's prowling around the back, but there's been no activity." He rolled his eyes. "That hasn't kept the neighbors from walking by and asking. I've seen a lot of curtains and blinds twitching. All of them probably watch *Midsomer Murders* and *NCIS* and are ready to solve it themselves."

"Have they said anything useful?" asked Scagell.

"Nope. No useful gossip on affairs, signs of money trouble, or domestic violence. Not even any tales of late-night shouting or quarrels."

"Well, we're not going to be too interesting ourselves," said Alix. "We'll be around back. Please see that we're not disturbed."

The Blanches' back garden, which had seemed pleasant in the afternoon, was now a mass of menacing shadows. The moon glimmered off the swimming pool, but with all the lights off in the house and no outside lights turned on, they all had to step carefully. No one wanted to turn on their phones' flashlights in case the neighbors saw and called the police.

"Evening," said a voice, and they all jumped as a short Black man appeared from the impenetrable darkness by the potting shed. "I'm Kalu. We're supposed to give your investigation all the privacy you require, but what do I need to know?" Alix looked to Padilla, who had been reticent on what he was actually proposing.

"I'll be turning into a tree," the American said. His companions, completely taken aback by this revelation, did their best to appear nonchalant.

"Indeed," said Kalu after a pause. "Will I need to worry about any glowing or sounds that might attract attention?"

"Nope, it's pretty quiet," said Padilla.

"Ah, good." He paused. "Can I watch?"

"Sure," said Padilla. "I don't even need to get naked." The guard nodded and stepped back into the shadows.

"I didn't know you turned into a tree," said Alix. "Do you turn into anything else?"

"Just this one kind of tree," said Padilla. *Fagus grandifolia.*

"American beech," said Alix. "Cool. Do we need to dig a hole?"

"I just need a bit of open space. That lawn beyond the pool looks fine."

"What will being a tree do?" asked Scagell. "It's impressive, but how is it going to help our investigation?"

"I'll experience the world differently," said Padilla. "I have different sensory apparatus. I might be able to pick up traces or signs that people can't detect. Also, I can communicate with other trees."

"You're going to ask them if they've seen anything strange?"

"Trees don't see," said Padilla. "But they may have observed something."

"How long will this take?"

"It depends," said Padilla. "Time feels different. I don't notice the hours as much, let alone minutes. If I haven't gotten what I want by dawn, I'll turn back." He walked to the proposed spot, and the other two held back cautiously.

Padilla stretched his back up straight. He rolled his head, cracking his neck loudly.

He hasn't even taken off his shoes. I would have thought that would be the minimum requirement for turning into a tree.

Padilla smiled at them, and the tree began to take his place, shading into the world around him like a pencil sketch taking on more and more form and detail. The American's skin did not become bark, his arms did not rise up into branches, his hair did not become a cascade of leaves down his back. Instead, he was simply less there, less in focus, and a young sapling, barely taller than him, was more and more solid in his place, becoming the reality.

Then, once there was no sign of the pawn, the sapling began to grow, so that what must have been years and years of growth occurred before them in just a few seconds. The trunk grew thicker and stretched up. New branches emerged, divided, and divided again, as the tree grew taller and taller. Leaves opened up with a soft pattering sound like rain as the branches spread out. They rustled gently in the breeze, so that the bare, moonlit lawn was now dappled in a thousand shadows.

And then, as if it had always been there, the beech was still, unchanging. Taller than the house, its roots spread out across the lawn.

"*God*," breathed Alix. "That was pretty amazing."

"Yes, indeed," agreed Scagell.

"I can see why he needed to do it at night," said Alix. "This would definitely have gotten some attention." The other trees in the garden were dwarfed by the towering beech. "What do we do now?"

"I suppose we wait," said Scagell. They carried some sun lounges over from the pool area and set them up facing what was once Padilla. It was a warm summer night, and the stars were bright overhead. They sat for several minutes, staring expectantly and reverently at the beech, but after a while, their attention began to wander. After all, for all its miraculousness and majesty, it was, when you got right down to it, a tree.

Scagell delved into his satchel and offered her one of his ever-present mandarins.

"Thank you."

They sat quietly for a while longer, eating their fruit and taking care to spit the pips into a little bag so that they didn't leave anything for their teammates to excitedly find the next day and mistake for crucial evidence.

They sat in a silence that felt somewhat companionable, and Alix fought to stay awake. A couple of times, she stood up and swung her arms, but she could feel the day and the night catching up with her.

Then, a new problem made itself known.

"I really need to go to the toilet," she said.

"Solids or liquids?" yawned Scagell.

"Gross."

"Are we talking a fine slurry?"

"Really gross! And liquid."

"There's a whole garden."

"I am not pissing on a crime scene," Alix said haughtily. "Besides, there's the question of Padilla." She nodded at the tree.

"What about him?"

"I don't like the idea of him, maybe, absorbing it up from the soil."

"Go to the end of the garden, then. The far end."

"No! Who knows how far those roots reach? Plus, he said he was going to be talking to the other trees. What if one of *them* sucks it up, and then tells him?" She looked at her watch; it was now almost four in the morning. She called out quietly. "Pawn Kalu?" He unfolded himself out of the darkness, giving the Padilla tree a wide berth. "Hi. Do we have keys to the house?"

"It's a crime scene," objected Scagell.

"We've processed all the toilets," said Alix, "so it should be fine. I won't be flushing away evidence." She sighed. "And I'll write up a statutory declaration for the file, asserting that I have used the downstairs guest toilet."

Alix did not turn on the lights—her eyes had adapted to the dimness of the garden. She moved through the kitchen into the darkened hallway. She made her way carefully along, managing to slam her knee agonizingly against only one table. Finally, she came to a lavatory.

Rather than shutting herself into a small room with no windows, fumbling for the light and losing her night vision in the process, she identified the toilet's location with a gently questing foot and decided not to close the door.

I am so tired. After finishing, she sat there for several minutes, elbows on knees, chin on hands, eyes half-closed, too exhausted in her bones and her brain to stand, pull up her pants, and flush.

A shape moved silently past the open door.

Alix's sleepiness burned away instantly.

What the fuck was that?

Had a person-shaped shape really just walked past the toilet in which Alix sat, pants down in the darkness, as vulnerable as she had ever felt? She strained her ears, but heard no sound.

Calm down. You were three-quarters asleep — you can't be sure.

And if it was someone, it was probably the pawn who had been standing guard out the front. Or maybe his relief has come, and they're just doing the rounds.

Except that no pawn doing the rounds would walk past an open door and not check the room. Only someone fully confident of an empty house would walk like that. And besides, the thing, if it was real, had not been wearing a police uniform. She'd had a fleeting impression of dull black, except for a smear where its hands would have been — something a little shiny, catching a glint of light from the front of the house.

She listened, holding her breath, afraid to close her eyes. The silence of four in the morning in an empty house. Silent except for the beating of her heart in her chest and in her throat.

She heard the faintest sound, as something moved from carpet to the kitchen tiles.

It's real.

Maybe it's the murderer.

Alix let out her breath, slowly, quietly. She rose and pulled up her jeans, conscious of every whisper of sound.

Sheer force of habit led her to turn and lower the toilet lid, but her tension ensured she did it silently. She was on the verge of pushing the flush when she came to her senses.

Could you please try not to be a complete moron?

Alix moved as she'd been trained, placing each foot softly. She peered around the door. The hallway was empty.

She debated calling for help — her phone was in her pocket, and at that thought, she hastily drew it out and muted it. The odds of it chiming at this hour with a text were minimal, but she wanted to take no chances.

What is wrong with me? I have backup! And a phone! She hastily texted Scagell.

IN THNK THERES B AN INTRUDER IN N THE HOUSE.

Damn typos.

Come on. How long does it take a text message to travel twenty meters? She stared at her phone and checked her watch. Thirty seconds went by.

A minute.

SCAGRLL ARE V YOU THERE?

Another thirty seconds went by. No reply.

Jesus, what if something has happened to him? If there was an intruder, they had gotten past the Checquy guard at the front. How? Was that poor kid, whose name she couldn't even remember, lying sprawled on the lawn with a block of stone in his brain?

Could it also have killed Scagell and Kalu? She couldn't take the risk of calling Scagell, but she could easily imagine him, still on that lounge chair, his dead eyes staring up at the stars while Padilla-as-a-tree unwittingly stood over him. She looked up at a noise from the kitchen.

I'll have to go by myself. Do I go in primed?

If ever a situation called for her to have a weapon ready, it was now. She opened herself, and felt the energy rise in her skin. She allowed only a little, nowhere near what she could summon, but enough to severely inconvenience a person. And if she had to swallow it back herself, then she could cope with the repercussions. She moved down the hall and paused at the doorway.

It was dark, but the all-white kitchen was much brighter than the shadows of the hallway. A person stood in the center of the room clad all in black, seemingly wearing a balaclava. She couldn't tell if it was woman or man. Slim and short, it stood with its back to her and one hand held up to its face. The figure leaned forward over the kitchen island, as if peering at something.

"If you move," said Alix in a clear voice, "I will cripple you." The figure froze and brought its hand down, placing something on the counter with a quiet *tink*. It put its shiny hands up. "Hands on your head. Don't turn around."

She squinted in preparation and turned on the light.

Alix was braced for the flare, but there was an unexpected pause as the filaments in the bulb realized they were supposed to do something and then, as the light flickered, the figure spun and brought its hands down to splay its fingers at Alix. She had a brief impression of fawn-colored skin.

I warned you.

She was unclenching her powers when *something* spun out at her from those shiny hands—an expanding blurry cloud of yellow-white lines like webbing. It closed around her head, a torrent of soft, yielding fibers hitting her full in the face, and she fell back, choking and bewildered as it layered itself over her eyes and mouth.

Alix clawed at her head. It felt like fishing line, but softer, and it was tangled all over her head and shoulders. She could see snatches of the room through the snarl, and a dark silhouette bearing down on her. She opened her mouth, and the tickly feel of the threads against her lips and in her mouth made her want to vomit.

She coughed and retched. Her power was raging wildly inside her. It hammered at her insides and grated on her bones. She knew distantly that she needed to push it out of her body, but she was gasping and gagging and that stuff was in her mouth and the energy was rushing back and forth in her body and she couldn't concentrate.

"Help!" she choked through the mass on her face. "Help!" Panicked, she was wrenching at the mass, desperate to get it off.

"Mondegreen, I'm here," said a voice.

Scagell.

"What is this?" he was asking. "What happened?"

"Someone was here," she exclaimed. "Go after them!"

"Kalu, go." She heard the guard's boots pounding away. "Mondegreen, be still, I'll get this off you."

"What *is* it?"

"It looks like hair," he said, and Alix retched again. "Don't throw up if you can possibly help it." Horrified by the thought of puke getting caught in the tangle, Alix bit down on her lip, hard. "It's coming off." The horrible tangle came away, and she gasped in air.

"Oh, God, thank you!" There were still blond fibers wound in her hair and around her neck.

"You all right?"

"Yeah." The raging energy inside her had settled, soaked into her. Soon enough it would bring its own problems. *So I need to move quickly.* "We should get after them. Kalu may need help."

"You're certain you're good?"

"Absolutely," she said. He helped her to her feet. They hustled down the hallway. The front door was open. Kalu was on the lawn, kneeling next to the still body of his fellow guard. "Is he dead?"

"Irregular pulse, ragged breathing," said Kalu. "I'm calling for help."

"Where did they go?"

"That way," said Kalu, pointing down the street. "But I've got to help my lad here."

"Let's go," said Alix. She and Scagell took off in the direction Kalu had indicated. The road rose in a slope to crest a couple of dozen meters away. Their feet slapped on the pavement, and Scagell's satchel bounced crazily on its strap.

"I texted you. Where were you?" asked Alix as they ran.

"I fell asleep," replied Scagell.

"Padilla?"

"Still a tree."

"Right."

They came to the crest and looked down on the street stretching ahead of them. Streetlamps cast narrow pools of light, and the houses and their gardens were dark. Here and there, cars were parked on the side of the road.

"There!" exclaimed Alix. Ahead of them, almost at the bottom of the slope, a black-clad figure was moving away.

Gotcha!

"Freeze!" she shouted. The figure increased its speed. It was moving off to the side of the road. "They're going for that car!" A black sedan was parked between two streetlamps.

I can't just use my power. It'll hit Scagell, and maybe even civilians in the houses around. She pushed herself into a harder sprint.

Scagell, although a good twenty years older than her, kept pace. Without pausing in his run, he dipped into his satchel and produced one of his ever-present mandarins. Suddenly, the fruit flared with blue light through his fingers. Scagell bounded into the air, and as he landed, his off hand swung up, whipping down and back, followed by a windmilling motion of the stiff arm holding the mandarin. It was a motion familiar from a hundred summer days on the playing fields of the Estate, and a thousand afternoons with the television on in the background: the classic action of a cricket bowler.

The glowing fruit flew from his fingers, blurred through the air, and struck the front of the car. The mandarin exploded in a cloud of vivid blue fire that engulfed the vehicle. The blast of it roared out into the night.

*Oh my G—*Alix began the thought but was cut off when a shock wave of heat struck her. The intruder was blown backward off their feet by the force of it, but what brought Alix to her knees was a sudden, overwhelming feeling of shame. Not shame about any specific thing, just a sudden, stomach-turning sensation that wiped away thought and sent her cringing and holding her head. It faded almost as soon as it had occurred.

"Was that you?" she asked Scagell breathlessly.

"Blue fire and guilt," he said, grinning. He had drawn another mandarin from his bag and tossed it in the air to catch one-handed.

"Very cool," she said, standing up. She looked around. The blast had blown out several windows of houses. Burglar alarms were screaming, babies were screaming, lights were coming on in bedrooms, and the black car was on fire, now burning orange-red, the blue flames having given way to regular old car fire. "Not very subtle, but very cool." Then she gasped, and put a hand to her stomach.

Oh, no. Her reabsorbed power was churning through her muscles and her organs. It was going to take its toll shortly.

"Are you all right?" he asked.

"Fine. But let's get this wanker quickly, before civilians appear on the scene." *And before I'm completely laid out by my own bloody powers.*

Seven meters away, the intruder was getting to their feet. From the light of the car fire, she now could see their silhouette clearly enough to tell that it was a woman.

"I'd be very grateful if you didn't come easily," Alix called out. "I'm really eager for an excuse to fuck you up."

"Alternatively, you can come with us peacefully, and not get fucked up," said Scagell.

The figure stared at them, silhouetted by the burning car behind her. She brought her hands up, holding them out to her sides, at chest height.

"Good," said Scagell.

"Wait," said Alix. The intruder was holding something in one of her hands, and as they watched, she slowly used the other hand to point at the something. From what Alix could tell, the something was a clear glass globe, about the size of one of Scagell's mandarins. She peered at it and could see nothing inside. "I don't understand what you're saying here." The intruder now held her arm out to the side, her fingers curling down around the globe-thing. "Are you saying that you'll drop it?" The figure nodded. "And this is some sort of threat?" She nodded again. "That empty glass ball is a threat?" Another nod.

"What do you think?" Scagell muttered out of the side of his mouth.

"I think we've got a few seconds before the locals appear on the scene," said Alix.

"I think it's a bluff. We've already seen this person's ability, the thing with the hair," said Scagell. "Go on two. One..."

"But..." began Alix. *Why would someone have an empty glass ball on them for no reason?*

"TWO!" Scagell moved forward, the mandarin in his hands already starting to glow with blue light. Alix was two steps behind him when the figure dropped the glass ball.

It shattered.

And then Alix wasn't there anymore.

13

*T*he room was dim, lit only by flickering candles that Alix could not see. She lay on a hard surface. Her wrists and elbows were bound down. Metal bands across her forehead, throat, and chest prevented her from sitting up. She could feel a similar pressure across her waist and knees. Her bare feet dangled off the edge.

There was a foul taste in her mouth, and her throat burned. She panted and stared up at the ceiling. Plaster, with ornate eyes painted on it that stared down at her. There were footsteps in the room. She heard the clink of glass on glass, and someone muttering to themself.

"And how does it taste?" the someone called out. It was a man, English.

"Bitter," she said. "The foulest thing I ever tasted."

"I'm not surprised," said the man. "There are many foreign herbs and rare minerals in it. But each one's properties are well established. It is in combination that I believe we shall see something new. An alloy of qualities. How do you feel?"

"I'm a little afraid."

"So must every explorer feel, traveling into a new land." He came into view. He was thin, in his fifties, with a graying mustache and a pointed beard that reached down his chest. His brow was high, and he wore a black skullcap. "Simply because this undiscovered world is not across the sea, but inside our own bodies and souls, does not make it any less an adventure." He patted Alix's forehead. "And how is your body?"

"There is a shuddering in my belly, and my bowels."

"I shall make a note of it." He turned away. "Do not worry if something should happen. This table will scrub clean."

"That is a great comfort," said Alix, and the man laughed. "I can feel my eyes watering," she said. "But I do not feel that I am weeping."

"Excellent!" said the man. "This is what I had hoped for. As we take so much of the world in through our eyes, through our mouths, and through our ears, it is logical that some of what is inside us will issue forth from our head." He came over, and Alix felt cold metal on her cheek as he gathered up her tears.

"And will you take aught else that issues from me?" she asked. "Is that why the trembling of my guts troubles you so little? You think they will yield something new and remarkable?"

"I will take a little of everything you can give."

"Will you cut me for my humors?"

"I will take some blood, but not too much. I am doubtful about the theory of the four humors. I elect to make my own discoveries. Hence our work this evening."

"What do you think will come of this?"

"We shall see," he said, as the cold metal of his little spoon gently touched her eye.

Alix opened her eyes with a gasp. She was not in some room, bound to a table, with an old man collecting her tears. She was lying in the street, with the dancing orange light of a car on fire just on the edge of her vision.

Her body hurt, but it was not the twisting of her stomach that she'd felt only a few moments ago on that table. It was the familiar pain that came of letting her powers run rampant through her body, plus a few new aches that she assumed came from falling down on the road.

What was that? Was it some illusion? A dream? It had been vivid, undeniable, far sharper and more realistic than any dream she'd ever had. When she'd spoken to the old man, it had not been with her own voice. It had been a man's voice. *What did that woman and her glass ball do to me?*

At the thought of the intruder, she jerked up and looked around. There was no sign of the black-clad figure.

She turned her head painfully and looked to Scagell. The other pawn was laid out on the road, facedown. His arm was flung out before him, and she remembered that he had already been transforming another piece of fruit when that woman dropped the glass ball. The mandarin must have fallen out of his limp fingers when he had gone down, and rolled away to explode a few meters from them.

That must be why my ears are ringing and I feel like I've been gone over with a riding crop. Fragments of what she presumed were pulp were scattered all about a smoking patch on the road, and they were still burning blue with a festive Christmassy smell.

With a groan, she pushed herself onto her knees and crawled over to Scagell. She hastily rolled him onto his back and winced at the bleeding graze along the length of his nose.

"Scagell," she said. "*Scagell,* you need to wake up!" *What was his first name again?* She slapped him lightly on the cheeks and shook him. He opened his eyes.

"He'll check my humors," he muttered, and she froze.

So it wasn't just me who saw that strange man.

"Scagell, look at me," she said. He blinked, and then his eyes focused on her.

"Mondegreen." She smiled weakly. "What happened?"

"Well..." Alix looked around. Between the burning car, the flickers of blue fire on the road and lawns, and the shattered windows in the houses, the place looked like an extremely unorthodox war zone. God knew what the inhabitants thought was going on. "Things got a little bit buggered."

Pawn Hannah Smith was renowned for her expertise and experience, but she did not arrive at the scene exuding an air of professional insouciance and unflappability. Rather, it was one of barely contained rage. Those who knew about her supernatural ability eyed her warily, just in case things were about to get a great deal more surreal.

Pawn Claes was with her, looking unfairly bright-eyed, probably thanks to some gland that manufactured espresso and expressed it right into her brain. She was *sans* quokka, but she did have a large satchel, presumably carrying several billion dollars' worth of potentially world-altering intellectual property, and possibly some more marsupials.

The scene they discovered offended every instinct of a Checquy operative to keep a low profile. Three ambulances, two fire engines, and four police cars were parked in the middle of the street, lights flashing. Once the authorities had arrived and the burning car and the scattered fires had been extinguished, people had come warily out of their houses in their pajamas and dressing gowns. Some were now receiving medical attention for shock and cuts from flying window glass. Some were weeping. Others were giving excited statements to the police. Smoke still hung black and heavy over the street, and there was a strong smell of cooked citrus. Apparently just one supernaturally charged mandarin was enough to make a whole street smell like it had been doused in mulled wine.

Scattered throughout the morass were local Checquy operatives who were doing their best to secure the scene without attracting attention or getting photographed. The bravest pawn presented himself to Smith and Claes and guided them to the gutter, where Scagell and Alix were seated near the ambulances. Scagell's scraped nose had been treated with iodine, but there was no dressing, so it stood out orange-brown and horrible.

Alix's head was tilted over a basin as she retched, despite having already lavishly emptied her stomach into the gutter. The energy of her power, which she had reabsorbed, had taken effect, and now she was trembling like someone who has eaten a plate of bad oysters. Padilla, who had arrived several minutes after the pawns resumed consciousness, was holding her hair back.

"Sir!" exclaimed Alix. "I think it was the murd—Oh, God! *Hurghk!*" She bent her head back over the basin.

It fell to Scagell to give the report.

"I want all three of you transported to the local hospital immediately," said Smith when he was finished. "You need MRIs to check for any foreign materials in your brains."

"I don't feel anything wrong," protested Alix from the depths of her basin. Her head felt fine, apart from all the liquids that were coursing through its lower stories. All she wanted was to pursue her usual reaction routine, which was to take a long, shaky shower, gargle with ice-cold water, and then curl up naked in a nest of towels next to the toilet and pass out.

"Yes, you look like nothing's wrong," said Smith.

"This is *meant* to happen," said Alix. "It's what happens when I—I—*hcurck!*"

"And I didn't even *see* this person," said Padilla. "Plus, I was a tree at the time, I didn't have a brain."

"I don't know why—" began Smith.

"*Hccurrrrck!*"

"I don't know why you would think this wasn't an order," said Smith. "But to be clear, I am ordering all three of you, as well as the guards posted at the house last night, to have MRIs, unless you want Claes to crack open your heads right here and now. Or I could do it myself, albeit with a great deal less finesse." Alix, Scagell, and Padilla made obedient noises. "Claes, go with them, and review the results."

* * *

A few hours later, scrubbed, brains-declared-cube-free, but not rested, Alix, Padilla, and Scagell arrived back at the Blanch house. Smith assembled a team meeting in the dining room.

"I'm glad that you three are all right," began Smith. "No one will be facing disciplinary review over what happened. A situation emerged, and you responded to it. The Liars are spinning their stories, trying to keep the events of this morning separate in the public consciousness from the story of Mr. Blanch's murder.

"The current story is that the car belonged to a drug dealer who was driving by in the wee hours, and that some of the"—she waved her hand vaguely—"drug materials being transported ignited and caused an explosion. The drug dealer fled the scene."

"Why a drug dealer?" Padilla asked.

"The idea is that we will blame any civilians' unusual experiences on the vaporized dispersal of said drugs," Smith said. She shot a pointed look at Scagell. "This includes reports we've received of people being overcome by a brief but intense feeling of guilt." Scagell shrugged, unconcerned. "Some residents recall seeing strangely colored lights about the place. There are also accounts of people passing out for several minutes and hallucinating that they were someone else."

"So civilians had the same vision as Scagell and I?" asked Alix. Scagell had told Smith about their shared vision while Alix had been attempting to vomit up her ankle bones.

"Apparently, whatever it was, the effect stretched several dozen meters," said Smith. "Fortunately, many people's recollections are so muddled that they're not sure whether they were dreams, a vision, or a hallucination. We are encouraging them not to speak about the details of their, ahem, 'drug-induced' experiences, in case it prompts flashbacks and trauma in others."

"Nice," said Padilla.

"Meanwhile, this intruder raises all sorts of questions. Who is she? She successfully subdued Checquy officers, evaded the local authorities, and deployed supernatural capabilities. These factors in themselves would require an investigation. Mondegreen, you got the best look at her, I understand?"

"Yes. Regarding supernatural capabilities," said Alix, "the thing that gets me is that there were two distinct attacks. The hair coming out of the hands, and then the, um hallucination... bomb?" She bit her lip. "The hair looked like an innate capability, but the other thing was the result of an external device."

"It gave the *appearance* of an external device," said Scagell. "We can't be certain that it wasn't a bit of theater, and also part of her power."

"I suppose that's possible," said Alix dubiously. "But they are still two radically different abilities."

It wasn't unheard of for supernatural entities (Checquy-affiliated or otherwise) to have more than one power, or to find multiple, sometimes completely disparate applications for their power. A man in the Checquy's Porlock office could breathe out a mist that could be used to extinguish fires, suffocate people, and dry-clean clothes.

"If it was a *device*," said Smith, "then it would have been fantastically valuable. We'll come back to that. Now, the intruder?"

Alix quickly described the person.

"Could you see their skin color or hair color?" asked Chuah. He was taking notes in his little police notebook.

"Her face was completely concealed, and it was dark, and then everything happened very fast. But her hands were uncovered." Alix closed her eyes to remember. "Sort of a yellow-brown color? It didn't automatically make me think of a specific race. The hands had an unusual texture, weirdly shiny."

"That could be a symptom of her supernatural ability," said Claes. "Especially since the hair she produced came from her hands."

"But since she wasn't wearing gloves, there may be fingerprints!" Alix realized. "She put something down on the counter when I confronted her."

"We haven't found any items," said Sweven. "She must have taken whatever it was with her. But we're dusting for fresh prints."

"Can we talk about the likelihood that she was the murderer?" ventured Alix. It felt as if they'd been dancing around the most important element of the whole encounter.

"We can't take anything for granted," said Smith. Alix gaped at her, but the team leader remained calm. "Take me through your reasoning."

"Okay," Alix said, deliberately calming herself. "So, with the first murder, with Edmund, we put it out that it was from natural causes."

"Technically, the first murder was *our* murder," said Padilla. "The one in Columbus."

"And *your* lot, the Croatoan, put it out that it was natural causes," remarked Scagell.

"Exactly!" said Alix.

"Exactly what?" said Scagell.

"Up until now, it's always been reported as natural causes. For all we know, this murderer doesn't know anything about her powers, except that they kill people. I mean, when I use my power, I'm definitely aware of it happening. Is it that way for everyone here?"

Everyone nodded. There was precedent, though, for people deploying their supernatural power without realizing its effect. She knew of a girl at the Estate who'd unwittingly infected people with an increased likelihood of dying in an automobile accident.

"But maybe this person doesn't know what she's doing," Alix went on. "Not exactly. Think about it: the first person dies, back in Columbus, the student. Maybe our target knows she's done something and it's caused that death. Maybe she doesn't, and it takes another death to figure it out, or confirm it."

"What other death?" said Sweven.

"A death we don't know about. Maybe it didn't take place in America, so the Croatoan never learned of it." She looked to Padilla, who gave her a wry little smile acknowledging her diplomacy. "Maybe no one but the killer knows about it," Alix continued. "The point is, between the student's death and Edmund's death, the killer learns that she can kill people with her powers. But she might not know exactly *how* it works." Everyone was staring at her.

"Picture it: someone falls down dead, and you know you caused it. Maybe you felt a frisson in your brain, or you wet your pants, or you had your hands on them and there was a blinding flash of indigo light or whatever, and they're dead. You run away. Or you only learn later that they died.

"Regardless, you're not in a position to know exactly what mechanism caused them to die. Either way, you wait, petrified, to hear what the news will say. You wait for the cops to come banging on your door. And then the authorities declare that the death was due to natural causes. So, now, as far as you know, you can kill someone in such a way that it looks natural, maybe from that disease the Americans blamed it on."

"Brugada syndrome," said Claes.

"Right. In fact, maybe you think you have the power to inflict Brugada syndrome on people."

"Except that we said the prince's death was caused by a brain aneurysm," said Sweven.

"Okay," allowed Alix. "Another natural cause, then. But nothing that looks like murder. Why would you assume you could put cubes of stone in someone's brain?

"I don't know what the killer did in the eight years between the Ohio death and Edmund's. After all, maybe she didn't intend for the kid in Columbus to die. She'd have had to spend some time coming to terms with her power. Maybe she spent some time going nuts." She looked to Scagell, who shrugged and nodded a little. "Who knows how any of us would have reacted to our abilities without the Checquy to guide us? Or the Croatoan?" she added.

"Thanks," said Padilla.

"So maybe her power manifested, and then she went insane. Like that chef in St. Ives who could suddenly hear the thoughts of plants and so started serving vegan steaks," said Scagell.

"That doesn't sound *that* insane," said Chuah. "Wait, if he could hear plants thinking, why was he serving *vegan* steaks? Did he not like what the plants were thinking?"

"He was serving steaks made of vegans," said Smith heavily.

"Jesus," said Padilla.

"Regardless," said Alix. "This person has discovered she can kill people. Maybe she denies it for a while, or develops psychological problems. But eventually she emerges with the idea that she's the perfect killer. Put yourself in her shoes. You're a ghost, you leave no trace. After all, you've killed the heir to the throne of the United

Kingdom, and there's been no hint, *anywhere,* that they're looking for you. But then with Mr. Blanch, word goes out that it *is* murder. Suddenly, you're doubting yourself, your mystic immunity. What if you're no longer untraceable? What do you do?"

"You panic," said Chuah. "And you start to wonder what clues you may have left behind."

"Exactly!" said Alix triumphantly. "So you come back to the scene of the crime, checking for evidence of your involvement, and unexpectedly there's a massive scuffle with some unexpectedly supernaturally powered people. You get your stolen car blown up by a citrus fruit and, and..." She trailed off.

"And now you know you're being hunted," said Sweven. "And that the hunters have their own unnatural powers."

"Right!" said Alix, eyeing Sweven warily, ready for his dickitude to manifest itself in some dicky follow-up. "So the woman Scagell and I fought last night was the murderer."

"Ahem," said Padilla. "I was also there."

"Mate, you were a tree," Scagell said. There were some smiles around the room. Padilla had clearly reached the point of acceptance by the group where he could be good-naturedly teased. A point at which Alix only sort of found herself. Maybe.

"Or perhaps the killer doesn't know they're the killer," suggested Sweven silkily. Everyone looked at him.

"What?" said Alix, her train of thought completely derailed.

"Well, think about it," said Sweven, his eyes wide. "The killer wasn't in the room with the prince, or with Mr. Blanch. We don't even know if they were in the room with the American student. Perhaps they know they've experienced something, but if they're not at the scene, then how do they know that their experience caused that death? Perhaps they have no idea."

"And one of those deaths just happened to be the Prince of Wales?" objected Alix. "What are the odds of that?"

"Perhaps his death was just as likely as that of anyone else this person encountered." Sweven shrugged, seemingly detached, but he didn't take his eyes off Alix's. "As random as any of the others."

Alix struggled with the idea. She couldn't help but feel that *of course* Edmund's death was significant. For it to be some random tragedy made no sense. He was the Prince of Wales! First in line to the throne! Was Sweven doing this just to needle her?

Don't get emotional, she told herself. *If you show you're taking it personally, the rest of the team will doubt your professionalism. They won't respect you. Which might be just what Sweven wants.*

"And you think a supernatural burglar happened to break into the house of a supernaturally murdered victim, the night after a public announcement that he was murdered?" she asked coolly. "And she happened to head right to the room where the murder happened?" Sweven shrugged again. "She *has* to be the killer," Alix said, trying not to grit her teeth. "And she has to know it."

"We can't be sure," said Smith. "But this person is a lead we need to follow. And she has left all sorts of evidence around the place."

She looked over to Sweven, who held up a large clear plastic bag full of a tangled mass of hair. It looked like he'd shaved an Afghan hound.

"Several meters of blond hair from the kitchen," he said. "I didn't see any follicles, and it's probably contaminated with Lady Mondegreen's DNA, but..."

"Claes will look at it," said Smith. "By the way, the MRIs confirmed that the guards from last night are also free of brain cubes."

"Do we know how the guard at the front was immobilized?" asked Scagell.

"Preliminary bloodwork revealed no toxins or anesthetics," Claes said. "I looked him over and found no signs of blows to the head or deprivation of oxygen. He resumed consciousness about twenty minutes after your nighttime street duel. He doesn't remember anything—just standing on the lawn, and then waking up to find me looking at him." She shrugged. "I've arranged for him to be sent to the Comb for an in-depth examination. We'll see if anything comes of that."

The Comb—the Checquy's primary research and analysis facility—was notorious for providing observations, descriptions, and extrapolations but no actual explanations. The supernatural tended to resist the scientific method.

"If the intruder *is* the murderer, what clues was she worried about?" wondered Chuah.

"A piece of equipment?" suggested Claes. "Like this glass sphere Mondegreen described. Perhaps a booby trap in the kitchen that could have put the cube in his brain when he touched it. Something not obvious."

"Are there such things?" asked Chuah. "Magic objects?"

"There are items that can have supernatural effects," said Smith. "They're rare, but they do exist." She paused. "We'll have to examine the scene of the prince's death again, see if there might be such a booby trap there."

"Maybe the prince wasn't even the target, then," said Sweven slowly. "He was only in the library by chance, after all."

"None of this meshes with the details I picked up last night," said Padilla.

"From when you were 'questioning the locals'?" asked Smith.

"It's information I got from the trees in the backyard, yeah," said Padilla. "Now, keep in mind that trees don't think or communicate like us," he cautioned. "It's not like taking a witness statement. I can't ask if they saw anyone weird hanging around the neighborhood."

"So, why bother?" asked Chuah. "No offense, I'm sure they're lovely...individuals, but...?"

"They have radically different sensory apparatus from us," said Padilla. "They can detect things we can't."

"So, how do they sense things?" asked Scagell.

"A few different ways," said the American. "First, when the roots spread out through the soil, they touch and wind around the roots of other trees, and we make a connection that way."

Does that sound kind of weirdly erotic? Or am I just really in need of a boyfriend?

"There are also pheromones," Padilla continued. "Trees release them into the air—these mists of information—and they transfer data and commentary by absorbing the mist from others."

Okay, that's definitely kinky. Then Alix realized that the previous night's tree pheromones had probably been misting onto *her* as well, and she choked a little.

"So, trees trade concepts and impressions," said Padilla, "along with complex chemical analysis of soil, astronomical and climate observations, mathematical equations, and some juicy gossip about the cherry trees four miles to the southwest."

"And what did you learn?" asked Smith.

"Well, to begin with, those cherry trees are *biiiiitches*! Oh, my God. The shit they've been up to, you would not believe." Everyone stared at him. "Sorry, it's like *The Real Housetrees of Winchester* out there."

"Pawn Padilla," prompted Smith flatly.

"Right. Okay, the trees said, and I'm paraphrasing, that they sensed a significant flare of unorthodox radiant energy from the house in the daylight phase of the preceding global rotation, just prior to the apex of the sun's transit."

"Is that yesterday morning?" asked Smith, frowning.

"Yes."

"So..."

"So, I think the radiant energy burst they experienced was when Mr. Blanch died."

"So, they were witnesses," said Smith. "Sort of. Good. Did they sense anything else? A presence that might have been the murderer, say?"

"No. Trees don't really notice people very much, unless the humans are doing some significant pollarding. But they *did* say that they've been sensing that specific energy sporadically for quite a while, on a much smaller scale. And then on the day of Mr. Blanch's death, it abruptly flared.

"I can't be certain, but I think that since Mr. Blanch was visiting the house on an irregular basis, the energy had been present on him for some time beforehand—as if he'd been infected earlier."

"How much earlier?" asked Smith.

"At least one complete lunar cycle," said Padilla.

"That's like a month!" exclaimed Chuah. A grim silence fell over the room.

A month! They were aghast at this revelation. All their meticulous work tracking down Edmund's every move—the long lists they'd assembled of people who'd possibly met him—now seemed pointless.

Then, nauseated, Alix thought about the other implications. A seed in your brain, radiating out an energy that only trees noticed. You'd be walking around for weeks, unaware, and then suddenly this thing flared and you were dead from a cube in the brain.

Is that what's going to happen to me? I would know if I had something wrong with my brain, right? I mean, I do feel a little fuzzy, but that's only to be expected. I've been up for how many hours? Was there a headache starting in the center of her head? *You are panicking. They checked your brain.*

Except they checked for cubes. Not weird energy.

With an effort, she dragged herself back to the conversation.

"...and we'll need to review Blanch's diary for at least the past three months," Smith was saying, "to see if he and the prince attended any of the same events. It's possible that this wasn't a deliberate act but just a manifestation that infected both of them."

Oh, good, more looking through people's social diaries.

"Which could mean that other people out there have this energy in their brains," mused Claes. "Chuah, Scagell, when you spoke to the widow, did she mention whether he'd been experiencing any headaches or behaving oddly?"

"Not that she knew of," said Chuah.

"The prince hadn't complained of any symptoms either," said Smith. "And Princess Gemma hadn't noticed anything. All right, we'll have to give this some thought. Also, it means that our best witnesses in this investigation are a pair of elm trees. We'll need to make protection arrangements for them."

"Tree bodyguards?" asked Chuah.

"Or is it something like the witness protection program?" asked Padilla.

"Yeah, we could move them and set them up with a different identity," said Alix wryly. "Dig them up, trim them strategically, and give them a new life as some larches in a park in Monmouthshire."

"Obviously, we're not going to move the trees," said Smith. "We need to ensure that there's to be no landscaping that might hurt them, and that they can't be cut down or"—she waved vaguely, obviously having no idea about what one did with trees—"pruned."

"How are you going to explain that to Mrs. Blanch?" asked Alix.

"Someone will think of something," said Smith, in the tone of a person who was inclined to delegate the problem to the next team member who annoyed her. Everyone strategically shut their mouths. "Now, what else?"

"Did the glass ball give us any useful information?" asked Alix. "Or at least its fragments?"

"Preliminary lab work has revealed no residue in it," said Smith. "Analysis of the glass hasn't identified any specific source, and it's not antique. It's just unremarkable glass, so far as we can tell."

"What about the intruder's car?" asked Scagell.

"Ah, yes. Despite your best efforts at demolition, Pawn Scagell, we were able to lift quite a bit of identifying information from its charred carcass," said Smith. "Chuah?"

"License plate matched a vehicle reported stolen yesterday lunchtime from the city of Swindon, fifty miles away," said the retainer. "It's possible that the report of the theft was a lie to act as cover, but the owner is an emergency room doctor who was on shift last night, with multiple witnesses. Still, we'll be checking for any connections between this car owner and the victims."

"Scagell, Mondegreen, Padilla, you all look exhausted," the team leader said. "Write up your preliminary reports and then get some rest back at the hotel."

"Before we go, could we perhaps ask the trees to check Scagell's and my brains for this energy?" asked Alix.

Otherwise, I don't think I'll be able to fall asleep ever again.

14

"Hello?" Alix said, not recognizing the number. She was in the kitchen of the Blanch house, getting all the surfaces clean of the luminol, fingerprint powder, various other forensic substances, and quokka footprints that two and a half days of intense forensic investigation had left.

"Lady Mondegreen, this is Miss Franklin from the office of the crown princess. You're invited to a lunch at the palace today, if you're available. All of the ladies-in-waiting will be coming to meet each other. I know it's a bit late notice, but it's just been decided." Alix looked at her watch.

"What time?" she asked, and bit her lip at the answer. "I'm sorry, could you please hold?"

"Of course."

She trotted out to the back garden and explained the situation to Smith.

"It's fine. We should be done today, so we'll be heading back to London anyway. You can go." Behind Smith, Sweven's lip curled, and Alix shot him a look as she thanked the team leader. She had no sooner accepted Miss Franklin's invitation and summoned a ride than the phone rang again.

"Hello?"

"Lady Mondegreen, this is Sir Alastair, calling from the King's office."

"Good morning, Sir Alastair. How can I help you?"

"I understand that you'll be having lunch with Princess Louise this afternoon?"

"Yes."

"Excellent. The King would like you to stop by his offices beforehand for a quick chat."

There was only one answer, naturally, but it would mean cutting things very fine. "Certainly. For how long would the King like to meet?"

"Half an hour, I believe, would be enough."

"I shall be there, Sir Alastair."

Alix was delivered to the train station just in time to run down the platform to catch the last possible train that could get her back to London with sufficient time to appear at the palace, showered and dressed appropriately, and having broken only a few speed limits and run a light that was on the pinkish side of orange.

She was panting slightly when she entered the palace. As she moved through the corridors, Alix noticed a change in the staff's reactions since the last time she had been there. Not quite a curtsy or a bow of the head, such as the King or Louise would have elicited, but a definite pause, a downward flicker of eyes, a slight nod. A deferent acknowledgment of her presence.

Word has gotten around. To be a friend of the royal family was one thing. But it was clearly something else entirely to be a lady-in-waiting to the heir apparent. She had been imbued with a new status.

This time, she was brought not to the family quarters and the personal study but to the official office — the one where the King met weekly with the Prime Minister. A double-story ceiling, white walls with gold trimmings, and deep red curtains at the windows. Portraits on the walls looked down at antiques on plinths, and on her. It was a stately, *grand* room, designed to intimidate. And it would have worked, probably, if Alix hadn't as a child played marbles on the carpet, and once spilled orange juice on one of the sofas.

Alix curtsied as the King rose from his desk, a priceless antique made from the timbers of the eighteenth-century naval vessel HMS *Incorrigible*. "Your Majesty."

"Dear Alexandra, thank you for coming."

"Of course, sir. How are you?"

"Oh, we're battling on. Things have gotten a little quieter, as they often do after these big events. The world gives us a bit of time to recover. Still, some things don't stop." He gestured toward the desk where the red and gray despatch boxes squatted. "Of course, I've been scrutinizing the daily investigation reports. My eye was caught by this person who broke into the Winchester house. You were the one who clashed with them?"

"Pawn Scagell and I both confronted her, sir," said Alix.

"It sounds remarkable," said the King. "And you fought with this person! Of course, one has always been aware of your abilities, but it's still difficult to reconcile the idea of a warrior with the young lady I see before me." He smiled. "Now, the report has been a bit coy on the matter of this intruder. Not many facts, and no analysis. What are your thoughts?"

"You know, sir, Pawn Smith would come in immediately to answer questions if you wanted," said Alix. "Even Lady Farrier and Sir Henry..."

"I feel better talking to *you* about this," said the King.

Would you feel better if you knew I was going to be writing up this conversation for Pawn Smith?

"You're a part of the firm, Alexandra. I can trust you not to shilly-shally about or tell me what you think I want to hear. Our last meeting showed me that." Alix thought of their last meeting, when he'd been so full of rage and sorrow over the team's failure to find anything.

"All right, sir," she said. "But the truth is that we don't know a lot."

"They had... abilities, though? Like your people?"

"Yes."

"And no clues toward this person's identity? I saw that fresh fingerprints had been found in the kitchen?"

"Yes," said Alix. Sweven had redusted and lifted fresh fingerprints and a palm print from the kitchen counter. "We've run the prints, and they match no record in any government database. The Americans ran them as well and came up with nothing."

"And the hair?"

"It's being examined," said Alix.

"Anything else? Any clues that could help to identify this person?"

"We have her scent profile recorded." She did not explain that it was recorded in the memory of a small, extremely personable marsupial. "We tracked her a short distance from the place where we confronted her." Alix, Claes, and Smith had gone out with the quokka late at night so that the already-bewildered community wouldn't be exposed to any more weirdness. The quokka, zipped into an adorable furry costume that made it look like an extremely shaggy terrier, had led them down several streets, until the trail went cold by the side of a road.

"She got in a car here," Claes had said.

"An ally, or just some random?" Smith mused.

"It was well past midnight," said Alix. "Not a lot of randoms driving by."

"We'll check with ride-hailing services. But we may be looking at a team of at least two," said Smith.

"So, no leads, then?" asked the King now. Alix shook her head. "I see. Thank you for telling me." He looked at a gold clock on the mantel. "I should let you go, you've got your lunch with Louise. Thank you. I'm grateful for your honesty."

"Sir," said Alix. After she left the room, she took a breath and leaned for a moment against the door behind her. *I can't do much more of this.*

"Lady Mondegreen, lunch is in the yellow breakfast room," said the waiting footman. "May I escort you?"

"That's not necessary—I know the way. Thank you, though."

Of course, Alix knew multiple ways, including the fastest route, which would have taken her down the hallway, around a corner, through a green baize door next to a bust of a bilious-looking Wellington, down two flights of stairs, and along various service corridors until she emerged from another green door, this one next to a bust of a smug-looking Pallas Athena, and situated almost exactly opposite the door to the yellow breakfast room.

Instead of that path, however, she elected to take a meandering but infinitely more scenic route, which took her down a sweeping marble staircase, through an exquisite courtyard in which Lord Palmerston had once gotten into a fistfight with the Bishop of the Checquy, along some soaring hallways, past a multitude of paintings— including two magnificent Turners, a very important Stubbs, and an often-overlooked Monet painting of ponies that a young Alix had always coveted.

"Hello, you're the first to arrive," said Louise, as Alix was ushered into the room and did her little curtsy. The two of them regarded each other warily. It was not clear how things stood between them.

"Traffic was good, ma'am," said Alix. "How are you?"

"I'm doing well, thank you," said Louise.

"Yeah, but are you actually?" asked Alix, and she caught a flash of surprise in Louise's eyes.

I can't just handle her with the same kid gloves and reverence everyone else uses. I'm supposed to be her friend, and if I can't be that, then I have to be her support. And I can't do either if we just have polite little scripted conversations where nothing actually gets said. She could see the princess debating. Then her eyes softened a little.

"It's been hard," Louise confessed. "I thought the funeral would help me move on—that's one of the points of a funeral, surely."

"Normal funerals, yes," said Alix. "Funerals where millions of people are watching you, probably a bit less."

"Millions of people were watching *you* as well," Louise said, a little archly. "You got a bit of press."

"Yeah," said Alix. "I didn't like it very much."

"Better get used to it. Fa wants you and the rest of the ladies present for all public appearances. Especially in the beginning, so that people can get used to seeing you."

Marvelous, more exposure. She must not have concealed her feelings very well, because Louise smiled a little bitterly.

"That's the machinery closing around you," she said. "I can feel it too. It's always been there, the process and procedures, the firm suggestions that aren't really suggestions. But now it's really beginning to gear up in preparation for when it all starts." Her mouth twisted. "I actually am sorry."

"Oh, I'm used to process and procedures," said Alix.

Sure you are, Louise's eyes said patronizingly.

Babe, if you only knew, said Alix's eyes back, and there was a flicker of sudden uncertainty in the princess's gaze.

"How are *you*?" Louise asked tentatively. "You bolted out of the lunch so suddenly, and you look like you've had a rough few days."

"Yeah, I'm sorry about leaving. I got an urgent call from work. Had to go out of town."

"Of course, your work." The princess frowned. "You know, my security clearance came through very, very quickly. For briefings from the police, and the MIs, and all the government departments. I got my very own red box this morning. The vetting process was much faster than I thought it would be."

"Even though you're the crown princess, so of course they're going to fast-track it?" asked Alix. "And your life has been documented and observed by officials ever since you were born, so you wouldn't be at all difficult to evaluate?"

It was probably a bit more tart than the crown princess was accustomed to, especially recently, but Alix had decided that too much deference was unhealthy.

"That's a reasonable point," said Louise. "Anyway, I *haven't* gotten clearance for briefings from your organization."

"It's a complicated process," said Alix. "Not just a case of being judged trustworthy."

"Apparently not, since I've already had two interviews with a psychiatrist, with several more scheduled."

We have to know how much we can tell you without breaking you. Plus, they're evaluating you for any sign that you already knew about the supernatural, and so might have commissioned an assassin to murder your brother.

"It seems a little ridiculous, but because we deal with some rather upsetting things, it can get a lot of people very excited, so we're very, very careful."

"Are you allowed to tell me what you're working on?" Louise asked. Alix paused and weighed how much to say.

"A murder."

"Oh. Gosh. A murder that falls under your people's responsibilities?"

"Yeah," said Alix. "I can't say more until you've got your clearance."

"I understand," said Louise. She seemed to be regarding Alix with a bit less suspicion and a bit more awe. "Is being my lady-in-waiting going to make it more difficult to do your job? I mean, aside from leaving your crime scenes to show up to various things. You've already gotten a good dose of media attention. You're a known somebody now."

"I've always been a bit of a known somebody," objected Alix. To give her credit, Louise almost completely held back her snort at this.

"Sure. But now if you're out on one of your investigations, there's a reasonable chance they'll recognize you as that lady from the television with the fabulous boots."

"Those were not my boots, by the way," said Alix. "Someone here gave them to me."

"Yeah, Muir sourced them," said Louise. Muir was a butler. "Mine wouldn't have fit, so I think he dug them up from somewhere here." Alix was about to ask for more detail when the three other ladies-in-waiting were ushered into the room.

"Hi, everyone!" exclaimed the one Alix already knew, the Honourable Imogen Canley-Vale, the cute blond ideal of a lady-in-waiting. Old family, old money.

"Good afternoon, ma'am," said a woman Alix had never met but about whom she already knew a great deal. *This is the artist friend who will be Mistress of the Robes.* Alix had received dossiers on the new ladies-in-waiting and had spent some time going over them. The trick now was not to give away how much of these women's histories she was familiar with.

Siti Amarah. Born in the city of Padang. Eldest of four children (one girl, three boys). Moved with parents to the UK at the age of twelve so that her father could take up a professorship at King's College London. Renounced Indonesian citizenship at the age of eighteen and received English citizenship. Studied painting at the Cascade School of the Arts in Edinburgh. Awarded a two-year Emerging Artist residency by the city of Exeter, during which she met the princess at an exhibition opening.

No known current romantic partners.

Social media accounts reviewed and found acceptable.

Amarah is not a practicing Muslim, although her parents and two of her brothers are.

Background check of her and her family members has yielded no concerns from MI5, MI6, or the Checquy Group.

The photo in the dossier had not shown that the woman was petite, even shorter than Louise. The cream A-line dress and the small necklace of moonstones that she was wearing contrasted beautifully with her skin and the wealth of gorgeous black hair that hung down her back.

"When it's just us, I think we should go with 'Louise,'" the princess said. "Otherwise I will go insane with power."

"Then this is lovely, Louise." She turned to Alix with a smile. "Lady Mondegreen, I saw you marching at the funeral, and Louise has spoken of you." She had a slight accent. "I'm Siti Amarah."

"It's very nice to meet you, Miss Amarah." Alix hesitated. Normally, she wouldn't use first names so soon, but after Louise's remark... "Please, just call me Alix."

"And I'm Siti," said the woman. They shook hands.

"Alix, so good to see you!" exclaimed Imogen, bouncing over to kiss her on the cheek. "This should be a good time."

"Hi, Immo," said Alix. She hugged the other woman, immediately warming to her as she always had. The little blonde looked lovely, in a beautifully cut minidress the color of a bright morning sky. With shoes the same color, she looked like a splash of very expensive summer.

Oh, the press are going to love her if she dresses like this all the time, Alix thought. *I mean, I would dress like that if I had legs that good.*

"And everyone, this is Mrs. Henrietta West," said Louise. She took the hand of the third woman, who had been hanging back, and drew her forward. Henrietta West (or "Hen" as she quietly introduced herself) was at least five years older than the rest of them, and had an air of calm about her. Short, with straight dark brown hair, pleasant features. She wore a sleeveless black dress that fell below the knee and was covered in a pattern of different-colored roses. "Hen's father was with mine in the army. That's how I know her."

"Hen, you look awfully familiar. Have we met before?" asked Alix.

"We have, but only very briefly, and I'm afraid that it wasn't under the happiest of circumstances," said Mrs. West. "My father knew your father. Lord Dolchford?" Alix nodded. Lord Dolchford and her father had both liked horse-racing, she recalled. "We attended your father's funeral."

"Oh, of course." Alix slotted Hen into her mental directory. It was a small community, really, the aristocracy. Names and faces swam past at parties and dinners and weddings and funerals, and even if you were separated by geography, word got around. You might not actually know someone personally, but gossip meant that you'd know about their divorce or triumph or scandal. In that way, it was a great deal like the Checquy.

"Thank you, everyone, for coming," Louise said. "It's good to see friends after such a grim time. And thank you for agreeing to take on this rather odd job. It means the world to me that you've agreed to do it."

Alix looked around the table at the other ladies. They all gave every impression of being delighted at being asked to take on the role—and why wouldn't they be?

They weren't ordered into this gig. For them, it will be a fun adventure. So, maybe try to see it that way as well.

Calligraphied name cards sat in little holders above the settings. Louise took her place at the head, flanked by Siti and Imogen. The table was beautifully set, with gleaming china and a small arrangement of yellow flowers that didn't obscure anyone's sight lines. Once everyone was settled and beverages had been quietly poured, the food was brought out. The main course was a pastry parcel of chicken so exquisitely folded that it felt like she'd been served some carb- and protein-based origami. Alix turned to the woman next to her.

"Siti, Louise told me that you're an artist," she said politely. The newly minted Mistress of the Robes smiled.

"Just getting started. I do landscapes in oils, which are not very fashionable, but people seem to like them. Louise hasn't told me much about you, though, Alix. Are you working?" Alix shot a look at Louise, who shrugged a little. Alix gave her cover story.

"How are your sisters, Alix?" asked Imogen.

"They're doing fine," said Alix a little guiltily. *I assume.* "How is your family?" She knew Imogen's younger sister a bit, and recalled that there was a younger brother she'd never met. Alix's mother had once said something about the youngest Canley-Vale child being quite severely disabled.

"They're all well," Imogen assured her. "Please give my best to your mother."

"I absolutely shall." The lunch proceeded nicely, and as they all got to know each other, Alix built up little mental dossiers on each of them.

Siti Amarah had a poise about her, and the air of someone who was always holding back a little. A woman of subtle but genuinely warm smiles and quiet humor.

Imogen was the one she knew best. Alix hadn't seen her much since they'd graduated (apart from exchanged nods and sad smiles at Edmund's funeral), but she was the same cheerful person with whom Alix had played tennis and gone to gymkhanas and gotten drunk in a summer house of Buckingham Palace.

Henrietta West was the most reserved of them. Very calm, with a considering gaze. She struck Alix as being the most uneventful human being she had ever encountered—an ideal candidate for a lady-in-waiting. Which was why it was a surprise when, late in the afternoon, as the remains of the dessert (a sumptuous chocolate orange cake) was being cleared away, West asked if anyone had plans for that evening.

"I don't," said Louise. The other women indicated that no one had anything that couldn't be canceled.

"Clearly, we need to bond," said West. She turned to the attendant standing nearby. "Could you fetch us some tequila, please? And some lemons and limes."

"Yes, ma'am," said the attendant. Alix detected the faintest hint of uncertain hesitation before he left the room.

"It's entirely possible that no one has ever asked for tequila in this place," said Louise.

"Will they even *have* tequila?" asked Imogen.

"Surely there's a bottle somewhere," said Hen.

"At some point, some visiting official from Mexico must have given a bottle of really good tequila as a state gift," suggested Siti.

"Can you drink state gifts?" wondered Imogen.

They all looked to Louise, who shrugged. "I know there used to be a staff bar here in the palace," she said. "But they had to close it after too many staff were getting absolutely ratted."

"At this very moment, some poor footman may well be frantically hauling his arse out to the nearest off-license," mused Alix.

"I heard there's an underground passage from St. James's Palace to a cocktail bar," remarked Louise. "But I've never seen it." St. James's Palace was the most senior of the royal palaces—it was from there that the royal court took its name: The Court of St. James's. It was still a working palace, holding some offices, and was also the London residence of several royal relations.

It was not clear how far the staff had needed to go in order to procure the requested bottle, but it *was* clear that they hadn't had one waiting nearby. Eventually, it was brought in, gleaming on a silver tray, accompanied by a plate of lemon and lime wedges.

The china teacups and coffee cups were whisked away and replaced with the most expensive-looking shot glasses that Alix had ever seen. Heavy in the hand, they had an intricate snowflake pattern along the bottom. They looked like the sort of thing a Russian duke would take his last shot of vodka in just before his dacha was overrun by angry serfs.

"Are these the state shot glasses?" she asked curiously.

"I've never seen them before in my life," said Louise.

"They'll hold tequila," said Henrietta, undaunted. She poured out the shots and handed them around. Salt was judiciously applied to licked hands, and lemons and limes were placed in easy grabbing range.

"I'm not sure this is the most sophisticated way to drink tequila," said Imogen.

"Possibly not, but it's by far the most fun," said Henrietta. "Ready? Lick! Sip! Suck!"

Alix's tongue felt like it was going to fold up on itself.

"And another!" declared Henrietta.

Several hours, and an unspecified number of shots and cocktails later, the five of them had decamped from the breakfast room to a lounge where they had sung together—or at least made noises to pop songs together—and then decamped slightly more unsteadily to Louise's suite, where they were now at that level of intoxication in which they were not at all certain whether they were still having a good time or were about to be ill.

After Siti had asked what the Mistress of the Robes actually *did*, Louise had called for some trappings to be brought out from the bit of the Royal Collection that was kept in the palace, and now all of them were wearing tiaras.

Siti was teetering about in a pair of Louise's high heels, which seemed to increase her height by a good ten percent. She wobblingly wandered through the princess's walk-in wardrobe, and occasionally had to reach out and clutch at a gown in order to keep her balance.

"I cannot believe this is all you have," she said.

"It's more than I have," said Alix from the bed that she was oozing off of, headfirst.

"Me too," said Henrietta, who was seated on the floor next to her, a bottle of tequila in one hand and a jury-rigged margarita analogue in the other.

"Are these all your shoes?" asked Siti.

"I think so," said Louise. She was lying on the floor, with Imogen's head pillowed on her stomach. "I haven't been going to enough things to justify having a lot of them."

"If these are the robes that I am to be mistress of, then...then..." Siti teetered and put a hand against the wall. "Then that is really depressing."

"I can get more, obviously," said Louise.

"We're going to need to work out your whole look," said Siti. "Probably get a stylist or something. And I'm sure there are lots of designers who—" She was cut off as she stepped forward out of one of the shoes, like a toddler in her mum's heels, and fell flailing to disappear behind the hanging gowns.

"Are you okay?" asked Louise.

"I've found some more shoes," said Siti's voice from behind the gowns.

"What are *you* doing?" Henrietta asked, as Alix pawed upside-downly at her hand for the bottle.

"I'm looking for dust on the bottle," said Alix. "I want to know if this had been laid down in the palace's tequila vaults."

"I don't think we have any tequila vaults," said Louise.

"You could have some installed," said Imogen, who was festooned in enough jewels to buy a house.

"Marvelous. That'll be my legacy," said Louise. "The spinster queen who left behind an excellent tequila cellar."

"Maybe it'll be an empty tequila cellar," suggested Imogen. "Because I feel like we're already making a bit of a dent in the national tequila reserves."

"Why aren't you going to be married?" asked Siti from the depths of the wardrobe.

"Do you not want to be?" asked Imogen.

"I like the idea of being with someone," said Louise. "*And* there's the question of succession." She winced. "But I'm not already married, and with all that has happened, how am I going to find someone I can have a real relationship with? I mean what reasonable person would sign on to this? And how can I know if they'd want to marry me for *me*?"

"You're going to be meeting a huge number of people in the course of your job," said Henrietta. "The odds of meeting someone you like have actually gone up a great deal."

"But how do I move from them bowing to me to going to dinner with me?"

"You've got a whole apparatus," said Henrietta dismissively. "Including us. We'll figure it out." She waved her hand vaguely, slopping margarita substitute across the carpet. "Remember, you're *allowed* to date." She took a contemplative sip of her drink, made a face, and then took another. "Meanwhile, what about the rest of you? Do you have menfolk?"

"Got a boyfriend," said Imogen. "He skis." The rest of them looked expectantly at her, but that appeared to be all the information that was forthcoming. It might have been all the information there was.

"No one, and not really looking," said Siti from behind the gowns. "Had enough to do finishing my residency, packing up the show, moving, and then getting this gig. For which I'm very grateful, by the way." Louise lifted a glass in acknowledgment, though Siti might not have been able to see it. "And Alix?" asked the Mistress of the Robes, poking her head at shin level out from between dresses.

"No boyfriend at the moment," said Alix. *And not particularly concerned about that fact.* She'd had two serious relationships in her life, and both had been exhausting. One had been with a pawn who had managed to disregard all the rumors about her. It had been nice for a few months, and then less nice. After an ugly breakup, she'd had to see him around the hallways of the Rookery, since he'd never had the good manners to be killed in a supernatural catastrophe. It had been a matter of singular relief when he was transferred to Bognor Regis.

The second had been a civilian whom she had met online, since she was determined to avoid any more entanglements with the Checquy or the aristocracy. He was a librarian, and the Checquy had cleared him. He'd been nice, and extremely clever — clever enough eventually to see that the story of her life had quite a few gaps in it. He'd become interested in her work, asking too many questions, and she'd had to break it off.

"I'm sure we can find you someone nice," said Imogen.

"Sure, if the opportunity arises," said Alix.

"*I* think...," began Louise. They all paused expectantly. "I think... I'm going to be sick." She scrambled to her feet, leaving Imogen's head to bounce painfully on the floor. She vanished into the bathroom, and they could hear the sound of royal retching.

"We should go help her," said Alix. "It's the sort of thing we're here for." There was a general murmur of agreement, but no one actually tried to get up. Alix couldn't speak for the others, but she felt that if she were to disrupt the delicate equilibrium of her stomach and her inner ear, she might be joining Louise in the festivities, and there was only one toilet.

Finally, there was silence.

"Lou? You okay?" Alix called.

"I think my tiara has fallen into the toilet."

Alix had been given one day off for the ladies-in-waiting lunch, but no mention had been made about the possibility of needing to sleep off a gigantic hangover courageously incurred in the service of her nation. The staff had been judicious enough not to wake the five women asleep in Louise's bedroom, but a lifetime of ingrained discipline had roused Alix.

She had just enough time to get home, desultorily shower, and get herself to the office for the morning meeting, *if* she ignored the headache and the nausea and the disinclination that all weighed her down like an anvil made of blue cheese lodged just behind her eyes and got up right that very second.

Checquy operatives could take sick days, but the culture was such that if you wanted to stay at home in bed with a mug of tea and a hot water bottle, you practically needed to be bleeding from the pores. Unless you were Pawn Orczy in the statistics section, in which case you needed to be *not* bleeding from the pores. Still, the possibility of going back to sleep was tempting, until she pictured Sweven's sneer at the news that she wasn't coming in.

Fine, I'll get up. But I should get a medal for this. She stepped over the scattered ladies, found her shoes and her purse, and put on her sunglasses before flinching her way through the corridors of the palace.

I have gotten some insights from the hair that was collected at the Blanch house," said Pawn Claes. She was scratching the ears of the quokka seated on the conference table. The cheerful little marsupial had not been put back into stasis, partly because it might be called upon at any time to help track down the intruder, and partly because everyone in the team had become extremely fond of it. It did not, however, appear to have a name, which offended some small part of Alix's sensibilities.

"There were no follicles attached to any of the hairs—it is as though they were sheared off cleanly. But there was some genetic information scattered throughout. To begin with, the hair comes from a male."

"But it was a female!" exclaimed Alix.

"Are you certain?" asked Smith. "They were wearing a mask."

"I'm fairly certain," said Alix. "Scagell, you thought they were female, right?"

"I did."

"Maybe it's a woman with the ability to produce copious amounts of hair belonging to the opposite sex," suggested Claes brightly.

"It's not the weirdest thing I've ever heard of," mused Smith. Given what she must have witnessed in her distinguished career, that was hardly a barometer.

"I lifted some genetic biography from the hair," said Claes. "Anglo-Saxon, as undiluted as I've seen in the last couple of centuries. Pure Cornwall."

"That's strange," said Alix. "I saw her—*their* hands. They were the only part that weren't covered up, I assume so they could excrete the hair without filling up any gloves. And the skin was yellowy-brown."

"Suntan, perhaps?" wondered Smith.

"Not like any tan I've ever seen. Maybe staining of some sort."

"Mondegreen, are you wearing a crown?" asked Weller suddenly. The financial expert was peering at Alix's head.

"What? No."

Except that Alix had a sinking feeling in her stomach. She hadn't washed her hair that morning—she'd been in too much of a hurry for more than a perfunctory shower to scrape off the sweat and alcohol residue, and she didn't actually remember taking off the tiara the night before. She put a hesitant hand to her hair and felt something hard lodged deep within her curls.

Oh, hell.

The group silently watched as Alix laboriously untangled her hair from around the prongs of the jewelry and produced a broad, Art Deco–style band of white gold that featured more emeralds and diamonds than one normally encountered in a government meeting. She put it awkwardly down on the conference table.

Under the lights of the meeting room, the large stones glittered like a collection of intricately cut precious stones of unspecified but obviously exorbitant value, surmounted by an insanely valuable trapiche cabochon emerald.

The table regarded the newly emergent decoration with slightly dazed wonder. Even the quokka was staring at it in awe.

"Yeah, see?" said Alix, deciding to brazen it out. "It's not a crown, it's a tiara." This did not appear to settle anyone's nerves. "And it's not mine—I borrowed it from a friend." She did not feel the need to say which friend. "You can all calm down, it's not like it's the Crown Jewels." *I don't think.* No one said anything. "Pawn Smith, would you excuse me for a moment? I need to make a quick call. I think I've just inadvertently committed a major theft. Possibly of a national treasure."

Sir Alastair received the news of the accidental jewel heist with the kind of unflappable aplomb that had probably gotten him the job. He dispatched a car to the Rookery, and the tiara was retrieved and ferried back to the palace in a locked briefcase.

"Right," said Smith, half an hour later. "Where were we?"

Where they were was not very promising. The team's examination of the life, death, and house of Mr. Blanch had not yielded an obvious enemy or guilty secret, or indeed, anything that made him a viable candidate for brain-cubing, as they had taken to referring to the process. They'd found not a single element linking him with the prince.

"Maybe it's a serial killer who's targeting rich white men," suggested Padilla.

"That should certainly settle the nerves of the Establishment," remarked Weller.

"How rich *was* Blanch?" asked Smith.

"Very, very comfortable, I'd say. Not Duchy of Cornwall comfortable," she said, looking sideways at Alix, "but he was worth quite a few million. It all goes to his wife."

"What happens to the company now that he's dead?" asked Smith.

"The Kabriolet board of directors will select someone else," said Weller.

"Who? Do they have an automatic line of succession?"

"I expect they'll have several possibilities," said Weller. "Or they might look at bringing someone in from outside. They're probably meeting fairly frantically."

"Weller, you and I will need to meet with this board of directors as soon as can be arranged. The only notable thing I can see about Mr. Blanch, apart from the manner of his death, is his business significance. Let's look more closely at who gains from his removal." Pawn Weller nodded in an unconcerned way that suggested that someone would soon be doing a lot more research and it would not be her, but rather her cohort of finance flunkies (none of whom had been invited to the team meeting). "The rest of you have work to hop to. Mondegreen, I'd like the write-up of yesterday's time with the princess while it's still fresh, please."

Alix nodded. Then she thought about the previous evening's activities.

Shit.

"Pawn Smith?" asked Alix.

"Hmm?" The team leader was reading a report.

"I've finished my report, the details of yesterday's lunch and dinner with the princess."

"You've left it a bit late," said Smith. "I'll need to review it for anything to include in the report to the King. Anyway, message me the link on the shared drive."

"It's, um, it's not on our server. It's here." She stepped into the tiny office and laid a folder on the desk. She flushed. "May I shut the door?" The team leader gestured her permission.

"Sir, yesterday's gathering was a bonding moment. It was five women getting to know each other before they start having to spend a lot of time together, them against the world. We drank, we told some stories, we drank some more, we told some very embarrassing stories, we talked about our love lives and our fears. It got very personal."

Smith raised an eyebrow but continued listening.

"For people like Louise, there isn't much opportunity to be that open, especially with people who aren't family. She put a lot of trust in all four of us. I appreciate that my position in the Checquy and in this investigation mean that I have to attend these things with a professional eye. And, of course, if I had heard or observed anything that implicated Louise—the princess—in the murder, then I wouldn't hesitate to bring it to you.

"But there are things you'd say to your drunken friends that you would never confess to your parents. Louise let her guard down among friends. And I am her friend. If I put this sort of personal, intimate material where other people—including her father—can see it, then I've betrayed her." Her cheeks were burning.

"I can see your concerns," said Smith. "You're in a difficult position, Mondegreen. Sit down." She took out a red pen and began to review the material while Alix waited.

"You've been very candid about your consumption of alcohol," said Smith. "You put down the number of drinks you consumed as 'uncertain but possibly at least sixteen'?"

"Yeah," said Alix. "I kind of... lost track over the course of the night. Although to be fair, they were none of them standard drinks." Henrietta had poured with a heavy hand, and to make matters worse, they'd gotten to that dangerous stage where they decided to create new cocktails by combining whatever alcohol was readily available.

"I appreciate your candor, but should you have been drinking at all?"

"It was a bonding experience," said Alix. "Close quarters. No way to really fake it." She hadn't drunk as much as the other women, but she had drunk a lot.

"Perhaps. Although it does rather cast your recollections of the evening into some doubt."

"My wristwatch has a recording function," Alix replied, "and I transcribed everything that was said. It's at the end of the report."

"And the recordings?" asked Smith.

"Downloaded onto a thumb drive," said Alix. "I thought we could put it in the safe, and maybe destroy it at the end of the investigation."

"If there *is* an end to the investigation," Smith muttered. She turned her attention back to the report. "There are a lot of points in the transcript at which you've just written 'incomprehensible slurring.'"

"Yes."

"Including points in the transcript when it's you talking."

"Yes."

"You have no idea what you were saying?"

"No."

Smith nodded. There was no concern that Alix might have said anything incriminating about the Checquy or the investigation—the lessons of discretion and secrecy from the Estate were so well ingrained that operatives could consume massive amounts of alcohol, throw up everything they'd ever eaten, confess to their crush that they wanted to shag them in the emergency fire stairs, and *still* be trusted not to speak about the Checquy.

"Okay," the team leader finally said. "I'll agree that the princess's concerns about marriage and her stated fears about the throne imply that she was not seeking out the role." She handed the report back. "We'll still need an official account. I've highlighted some points— nothing super personal—and your findings. Write them up into an executive summary and put it on the team drive. I'll put these pages and your recording into the safe. We'll have them if we need them, but I'm happy for the rest of the team not to read the other details."

"Do you think this is enough to dismiss Louise as a suspect?" asked Alix tentatively. She thought of the way Louise's reserve and poise— her final layers of defense—had slowly come down the night before, until she'd seen the girl she knew from school and childhood. She thought of the jokes Louise had told, things she'd never dare say lest word get out about vulgarity and black humor. She thought of the sadness and fear she'd seen in her friend and been utterly convinced that Louise was innocent.

But when put down on paper, the conversation was shorn of all that genuine emotion.

"Do you?"

"No," said Alix sadly.

15

"Alix, this is Siti Amarah calling."

"Hello! It's lovely to hear from you." It had been a week since the luncheon, boozing, and passing-out of Louise's ladies.

"I was sorry that you'd gone when the rest of us woke up."

"Day job," said Alix. "It's got some flexibility, but they still expect me to show up."

"Of course. I'm calling now because the palace is arranging some lessons for us on how to be ladies-in-waiting," Siti said.

Oh, great, Alix thought sourly.

"Oh, great!" she said, much less sourly. *I can only imagine the investigation team's reaction to this.*

"I was wondering if you could maybe arrange a day off this coming week?" said Siti. She named a date, and while she kept talking, Alix listened with half her brain while the other half immediately fired off an email to Smith asking permission. "It should be nice, we'll start with breakfast with Louise at Buckingham Palace."

When the appointed day dawned, Alix walked through Green Park to a small gate to the palace grounds, where she signed in with the guards in their little booth. She made her way unerringly and unquestioned through to the apartments, doors opening to her security pass and staff stepping aside (unless they were carrying something heavy, in which case she stepped aside before they had the chance).

"Good morning, Lady Mondegreen," a butler greeted her. "The King and the crown princess are on a call at the moment, but if you'd like to head to the breakfast room, they're just setting out the food."

"Thank you, Muir," said Alix. She'd always rather liked the man. Inevitably a little more cheerful than one expected in a butler, he was the same age as the King, and his red hair was always beautifully styled and held in a vise of pomade. "Have the others arrived?"

"Miss Canley-Vale arrived about half an hour ago."

"Lovely." *It'll be good to catch up with her.* "Oh, Muir, the boots that you'd arranged, that I wore for the funeral?"

"Yes, my lady. Were they all right? It was rather a last-minute arrangement."

"They were fine, thank you. But where are they from? Should I return them?"

The butler shrugged. "I shouldn't bother. In truth, I grabbed them from an old cupboard in a storage room and had them cleaned very quickly. They hadn't been worn in decades."

Huh. Fascinating. They're vintage! So vintage that no one's heard of them. She nodded and smiled.

As she walked down the hallway, she passed the door to the library. She turned as she heard it open behind her, and Imogen emerged. "Morning, Immo. Borrowing a book?"

"Alix, hi," said the petite lady-in-waiting. She smiled but was far from her usual sunny self.

"Are you okay?" asked Alix.

"Hmm? Yes, just, I was sitting and thinking about Edmund." She looked down. "That's where it happened, right? The library?"

"It was," said Alix. She eyed the door. She hadn't gone into the room since the day of Edmund's death.

"He was such a good man," said Imogen. "It's so sad."

"Yeah," agreed Alix. She caught her friend in an awkward hug, and after a moment of hesitation, Imogen hugged her back. "How's your family?" she asked, eager to change the subject.

"Mummy and Daddy are doing fine," said Imogen. "And Lily is at Whyteleafe, so I get emails from her asking for me to send her sweets. But you know how it's not allowed, right?" Alix nodded, remembering. "So, I have to smuggle them in to her. I've razored out the insides of every cheap thriller in the house so that I can hide chocolate bars in them and send them to her."

"That's so good of you," Alix said. She was stabbed with envy at the thought of a sibling relationship like that. *I should reach out to my sisters. After all, Frances did come stay the night of the funeral, even if it was just to avoid the sofa bed of doom.* "You have a little brother as well, right? I don't think I've ever met him."

"Jimmy, yes." Imogen hesitated. "You know that he needs special care?" Alix nodded again, although she didn't know the details. "Right, so he's nineteen and lives at home. We're lucky because we can afford the teachers and speech therapists and carers he needs." She bit her lip. "It's not easy, though. It's hard to see what he has to endure."

"Yes," said Alix sympathetically. It seemed like the only thing to say.

"And your family?" asked Imogen.

"Unchanged, probably," said Alix. "I haven't seen much of them, but you know my mother—she's resistant to developments. And development." Imogen laughed. "The sisters are fine, I think."

"And how's your job?" asked Imogen.

"Chugging along," Alix said. "There's a big project that eats up a lot of my life."

"Lucky you can get away to things like this," remarked Imogen.

"It is a nice break," said Alix, and she meant it. *Especially when there's a palace-style buffet,* she thought as they walked through the door. The breakfast room was full of morning light, with the table set exquisitely with white linen and shining china. But even more exquisite, at least so far as Alix's mouth and stomach were concerned, it was full of morning foods.

At one side of the room, a battalion of covered silver dishes stood on a long table, with delicious smells coiling up out of them. Alix could already identify the presence of sausages, baked beans, tomatoes, and potatoes, and experience had taught her that there would be eggs available in a variety of formats.

A little farther down, a large basket held a bouquet of golden croissants, with little plates of jam gathered around it adoringly, and then an arrangement of fruit so luscious that Van Gogh would have given his other ear for the opportunity to paint it. A pot of congee stood in majestic steaming splendor, with an array of vividly colored toppings laid out around it.

Beyond that, jugs of different juices, each a different color, stood on plates, condensation beading on them. Coffee, tea, and miso beckoned alluringly from polished silver pots.

"This is the most beautiful thing I've ever seen," breathed Alix. A sudden unpleasant thought occurred to her. "This isn't the sort of spread you guys enjoyed after our night of drinking, is it?"

Because that would represent the greatest injustice in the history of the world, when all I had was a muesli bar.

"No," Imogen assured her. "We had toast with Marmite, and someone vomited into the bidet."

"Oh, who?" asked Alix, intrigued.

Imogen was about to respond when... "I beg your pardon, ladies," said a servant as she maneuvered between the two transfixed women and placed yet another covered dish on the table. The two friends exchanged guilty looks.

The walls have ears, Alix reminded herself. *They may be discreet ears, but still.* She lifted the lid and almost moaned in pleasure at the sight of a mountain of kedgeree.

"Should we start now?" she wondered.

"We should wait for the others," said Imogen in an uncertain, highly tempted voice.

"But the kedgeree will be less... fresh," said Alix, hearing a slight unexpected whine in her own voice. They looked at each other conspiratorially.

At that moment, Henrietta and Siti arrived. The four of them immediately flowed into the comfortable repartee of people who have seen each other get massively intoxicated. But while there was much enthusiastic greeting and cooing over the buffet, no mention was made of digging into it while it was hot.

Siti's phone chimed. "Text from Louise. She says we should just start. She's on a call that's going to be a while." Alix felt a little sting of envy that it was Siti who had been given the heads-up.

Of course she gets the text messages. She's the Mistress of the Robes, and that's a gig you didn't even think about wanting, and wouldn't have time for. Try to enjoy what you do have—especially this breakfast.

"You know what makes this meal so much better?" remarked Henrietta, as she served herself some congee and scattered some shards of chicken into it. "The knowledge that my husband is currently eating a bowl of cold cereal."

"What does your husband do?" asked Imogen.

"He's in the army," Henrietta said. "The Blues and Royals." The Blues and Royals were a cavalry regiment, the second most senior in the British Army. They were part of the Household Cavalry, which were among other things, the King's official bodyguard. A memory stirred in the back of Alix's brain.

"Isn't your brother with them as well?" she asked.

"Yes, that's how we met," said Henrietta. "I was studying folklore at Hertfordshire, and Robert—that's my brother—introduced us."

"What were you going to do with a degree in folklore?" Siti asked.

"Oh, probably die in the streets of exposure and malnutrition," said Henrietta. Alix smiled a little. She'd read up on the ladies-in-waiting and knew that Henrietta's family were very, very comfortable.

Although I hadn't realized how closely integrated she is into the royal network. She looked up as Louise entered the room, and everyone greeted her.

After breakfast, Louise had some appointments to attend, so, full of food, the four ladies-in-waiting moved ponderously through the corridors to a meeting room where Olive Claybourne, Mistress of the Robes to Princess Gemma, would present to them Waiting 101. Olive was cheerful and practical, explaining their roles' responsibilities as companions and assistant hostesses.

"People can get very nervous when they meet a princess," Olive explained. "Your closeness to her means that you'll be in a position to help things go more smoothly. You must make all your decisions with an eye toward how it will reflect on your princess. You're a semi-public figure. If you're in a car accident, or get in an argument with someone in public, it can end up in a gossip column. You are a celebrity without any of the perks."

She paused. Her four students were sitting, semi-stunned, and only partly because of all the food they'd eaten. Olive reassured them that there would be lots of people helping to support them, and gave them her private number, telling them to call her anytime.

After she left, Siti said, "Next, we have a briefing on court etiquette from Lady Lindley, Louise's great-aunt, and then a briefing on security procedures from a representative from the Royal Protection Squad. And then lunch."

There was a weak mooing of protest from everyone.

"Or we can just sit with a glass of tepid water each."

There was a weak mooing of approval from everyone.

"Tepid water it is, then. And then to Kensington Palace to meet the administrative staff."

The other lectures went smoothly-ish. Lady Lindley was very patient and had lots of good stories about being polite to controversial leaders. The Royal Protection Squad guy explained that they would not only be in increased danger because of their close proximity to a prominent public figure, but that they could easily attract stalkers and obsessives of their own. He helped them to download an app that would enable the ladies-in-waiting to alert the Royal Protection Squad to any problems, or for them to be tracked down if they were abducted by anti-monarchists, or if they lost each other at a reception.

Afterward was the field trip to Kensington Palace. They were taken around and shown parts of the buildings and the grounds, all of which Alix already knew well. They were introduced to the office staff of the Prince and Princess of Wales, all of whose names and faces were familiar to Alix. All of them had been suspects in the murder of Edmund.

Then they were driven back to Buckingham Palace for coffee and, for those who felt they might have room, a biscuit.

"And here is your homework," said Siti, handing around some bulky folders.

"What are these?" asked Henrietta dubiously.

"Letters to Louise," said the Mistress of the Robes, "from schoolchildren, well-wishers, and so on. We're going to be responsible for answering some of them."

"Didn't we just see that she has a secretarial staff?" asked Alix.

"She does. Equerries and secretaries do the bulk of her correspondence, but we'll handle a portion of these. Louise is going to answer a few personally, so if you find one that's especially cute or meaningful, put it aside for her."

"Do we have any example replies to draw on?" Alix asked. She might be a supernatural investigator/warrior/bodyguard, but she was still a public servant and was going to spend as little time as possible coming up with new language. She'd seen an entire Checquy report repurposed simply by doing a find-and-replace to change every instance of *kobold* to *onion*, and then updating the dates, locations, and fatality figures.

"Here's one that I've written and gotten approved," said Siti. "But we don't want just form letters. So, draft up responses—reserved, but kind. When you're done, I'll check them, get them written up on letterhead, and you can sign them." Alix regarded the large bundle of letters in her folder. There were at least fifty.

This is not work I need. Not on top of my other work. She had a suspicion that Smith would not approve her writing nice little notes to members of the public during Checquy office time. *Suddenly, I'm once again the kind of person who gets homework.*

As they all left, Siti gestured for Alix to stay behind.

"Alix, Louise will be starting her appearances soon, and I have to coordinate the roster of ladies to accompany her. At first it's going to be all of us together, but eventually it will be just one or two of us at a time, especially for things that call for travel. I want to make sure that everyone gets an equal go, but the security team said there will be some events where it has to be you, although they wouldn't explain why."

"How silly of them. I have no idea why they would be so coy," said Alix.

Do I sound as fake as I feel?

"See, I have some training in martial arts, and a security clearance from work my firm did for the government, which means that I can receive briefings on current events. The King wants someone who can blend in and stand right next to Louise without attracting attention but can provide a bit of extra muscle and an informed eye if they think there's any need for heightened security."

"Oh!" said Siti. "You're like a fallback bodyguard."

"Exactly," said Alix.

"Cool. Well, our first event is next week. It's a reception for a group of ladies in Kent who do a lot of volunteer work, so you probably won't need to do any unexpected bodyguarding. The office has described it as a very easy, quiet event with no press—a way to ease Louise into her new role."

Oh, fucking hell," said Louise as she stared out the car window.

"It looks like there are some people who are very, very interested in the importance of exposing city children to the delights of the countryside," said Alix.

The event had been meant as a gentle entrée into Louise's new public role. It had not been announced ahead of time and was to be conducted without the usual fanfare and hurly-burly of a royal visit. Word, however, had gotten out. Somehow, the press had learned of the princess's inaugural nonfuneral public appearance as the first in line to the throne, and decided that it was an Opportunity. A horde of photographers and journalists had descended upon the village of Little Woldweir, eager to capture the historic event. Little Woldweir had obliged by putting on a glorious summer day, and by being extremely picturesque, with wildflowers, butterflies, and freshly painted cottages adding splashes of color.

The ladies who were being honored were not society wives doing good with copious amounts of free time and money, but farmers and farmers' wives who had brought disadvantaged children out to the countryside and into their homes for a few days, to show them a completely different way of life.

As the car pulled up to the village hall, the flock of journalists surged forward. Even through the radiant summer sunlight and the heavy tinting of the car's windows, the strobing of camera flashes was enough to make even the slightest of epileptic tendencies a genuine risk.

"Ready to go?" asked Siti.

"Yeah," said Louise. "God help me." The other ladies-in-waiting made noises of comforting reassurance.

"Don't bite your lip, you'll fuck up your lipstick. You'll be fine," said Alix. "You've got your speech, you've got your smile, and everyone involved in this event is on your side."

"What about *them*?" Louise asked, gesturing at the media clotting around the car.

"Yeah, *they'd* be thrilled if you fell on your arse in a mud puddle," admitted Alix. There was an audible gasp from the other three ladies-in-waiting that she would even dare *think* of such a thing, lest the universe hear and decide to make it happen. "So, if something *does* happen," Alix went on, "just make sure you smile and act amused. Everyone likes a good sport. Let me see your teeth."

"What?"

"Fab. And up the nose?"

"But—"

"All clean. Let's *go*." Alix opened the door. Sunlight flooded in, and Louise had no choice but to emerge to a blissful greeting from a phalanx of village ladies who had been holding back, ready to curtsy and introduce themselves respectfully, but, upon seeing the besieged car, had gamely elbowed their way through the press. The other ladies-in-waiting froze, until Alix used her elbow to lever Siti out of her seat. The others followed instinctively, and Alix brought up the rear.

Alix was torn between being utterly delighted by the hospitality and completely stressed by the fact that she was not in a position to identify any potential threats, supernatural or otherwise. On the other hand, a manifestation would have to be pretty damn persistent to get through the likes of Morag, Lucy, Shirl, Dot, Jenny, Lavender, and the rest of the Little Woldweir Farming Community Ladies, who had taken the delicate princess and her entourage completely under their wings and into their hearts. Louise's close-protection officers were expending all their might just staying near her.

"You're not wearing the boots," said the rotund lady who had companionably slipped her arm through Alix's. "Such a pity, I loved them. I thought they were really nice for that march, very sensible but so smart."

"Thank you," said Alix.

The world's interest in the boots had not died away as Alix had hoped. Instead, it seemed to ebb and flow, with #mysteryboots trending periodically on social media, when nothing significant was happening in the fashion world. No one had yet managed to identify their creator, and no one had dared take credit. Alix had tentatively asked the Liars how to respond to the barrage of queries from various columnists, editors, and designers. Mindful of Alix's relationship with the crown princess, the Liars were wary of encouraging any press attention and couldn't decide if things would be made better or worse by answering.

Louise and her team were bustled into the hall and settled comfortably on the little stage. Louise stood at the lectern with perfect aplomb.

She had her speech memorized and looked around the room as she spoke. Under her gaze, the audience nodded and leaned forward.

"The work you are doing may seem simple to you," Louise said. "But the experience you give to the children who visit Little Woldweir— the opportunity to see a different part of the world—is important. You are touching their lives and broadening their horizons."

She's good. Alix noticed the smiles and shining eyes of the ladies of Little Woldweir. Everyone was listening intently, even the photographers, once they'd gotten their shots.

"As you all know," Louise finished, "this is my first appearance in a formal capacity, and I'll confess, I was a little nervous, but I couldn't have hoped for a better experience. People talk a great deal about the privilege of this position, but your hospitality has shown me that the greatest privilege will be the opportunity to meet inspiring people like yourselves.

"Now, I understand that an outstanding morning tea has been laid on, and Mrs. Wynne has assured me that there is more than enough for all of us. So, let's enjoy!" The applause filled the hall and threatened to push out the windows. Smiling prettily, Louise shook hands again with the now-jubilant head lady, and the whole group moved over to the tables, which were straining to hold all the food.

Louise was shielded by the rule that the press did not take photographs of the royals while they were eating or drinking, but there was some uncertainty about whether that courtesy would extend to her entourage. As a result, her ladies were all careful to eat delicately, lest some journalist capture a shot of one cramming an entire scone into her mouth, or give the appearance of fellating a sausage roll.

Later, in the car, there was an air of satisfied relief.

"I think that went all right," said Louise hesitantly. They all assured her that it had gone very well, and settled back to gloat over all the jars of jams, pickles, relishes, and chutneys that had been pressed upon them as gifts.

The next morning, Alix emerged from the front door of her building and was checking messages on her phone when she heard her name called.

"Alexandra!"

And then from a different voice: "Alix!"

Then: "Lady Mondegreen!"

"Ally!"

"Oi!"

"LADY! LADY!"

"HEYALIXAlexandra*LadyMondegreen*ALEXANDR*AheyaMondegreenAlixLadyALIXwheredidyougettheboots*Alix*! Alix!*"

She looked up to find a cluster of photographers across the street. For a moment, she was frozen—a maneuver that would have had her combat instructors slapping her—and then, as she was hammered by a barrage of camera flashes, she turned around smartly, walked back into the lobby, and ducked behind a column, as if taking cover from bullets. Her heart ricocheted inside her torso, and the bone-breaking energy of her power was alert and poised, like a Doberman ready to sic 'em.

What in the hell are they doing here? Did I do something inadvertently horrible yesterday? She hurriedly rang Siti.

"Alix? Hi," said the sleepy voice of the Mistress of the Robes, who had clearly been awakened by the phone call.

"Siti, there is a horde of journalists outside my building! Tell me that there is a bunch of them at your place, too."

"Oh, God, let me check. I'm just going to peek out the window... No. There is no horde, no journalists at all. Unless they are hiding behind the bus shelter."

"But why are they here, then?" Alix asked. "Oh, God, did I flash a nipple or something?" It didn't seem likely—the dress had been entirely respectable *and* she'd been wearing a bra—but the roar of the photographers outside suggested that something interesting had happened. "You have to tell me, did I do something wrong yesterday?"

"No, I didn't think so," said Siti. "We were all fine. I didn't see any nipples. I'll check the papers."

"Okay. I'll conference in the others." Alix hurriedly called Imogen, who also hadn't been awake yet, and directed her to check out the window.

"So, are you saying that—oh my *God*!" exclaimed Imogen. "There's a swarm of them out there. Right across the street!"

Thank God it's not just me. Alix leaned back against the column, weak with relief. She stood up straight as a distressed squeak came over the phone, followed by a clatter.

"Immo! Are you okay?" She could hear a distant *"Fuckfuckfuck!"* coming over the phone. "Immo!"

"Sorry, I think they saw my curtains twitching, and I'm just wearing a T-shirt, so I panicked and stepped backward and fell over the cat."

"Are you okay?" asked Siti.

"How's the cat?" asked Alix.

"Fine," said Imogen grumpily.

Henrietta proved not to have been aware of anything unusual, having gotten up early and taken the dogs out the back gate for a walk on Hampstead Heath. She agreed to return cautiously and check the situation from down the street. If she saw press waiting, she would turn around and take the dogs for a coffee and a croissant.

"Meanwhile," said Siti, "yeah... we've gotten a bit of coverage in the press this morning."

"Good? Bad?" asked Henrietta.

"Ugly pictures?" asked Imogen.

"Nipples?" asked Alix.

"*What?*" asked Henrietta and Imogen.

"No nipples. I think it's good." Siti paused. "I think they like us. I'll send links."

"Why aren't they camped out at your place, though?" asked Alix.

"Probably because I've been moved into this flat by Louise," said Siti, "so no one knows where I am."

The grace-and-favor apartment, right.

"Once they figure it out, maybe they'll besiege this place too," mused Siti. "I'd better get in contact with Louise and the palace. I think it's obviously best not to talk to the press until we get instructions."

"I have to go to work, though!" said Alix.

And what if they follow me? She could all too easily picture the press pursuing her down the street and into the Tube, photographing her while she stood in a carriage looking pained, then following her through the City to the Hammerstrom Building, with its colony of protesters camped on the street.

There could very well be journalists camped outside the Rookery at that very moment. Her cover job with the law firm of Smith, Patel & Smith was not well publicized—not mentioned on her social media or her Wikipedia page. Her name wasn't on the firm's extremely shabby website, partly to keep her off Google, and partly because, as protective camouflage, the thing hadn't been updated since 1999. Still, the fact that she had a job there was a matter of public record—that was the *point* of a cover—although not a very interesting one.

She blanched at the idea of paparazzi hanging around, eyeing Pawns as they went in and out of the building. Eventually, those ridiculous, delusional (admittedly completely correct) protesters of *Occupy Rupert Faunce Lane* would catch their eye, and some journo would saunter over and pick up their literature, just for laughs. They would hand it to a superior at the office, just for laughs. The groups' claims were so preposterous that some editor might think of it as an entertaining human interest story, just for laughs. And then they might print it, just for laughs.

But I don't think anyone would be laughing afterward. Certainly not me.
Alix felt weak.

"No one can expect you not to go outside," Siti was saying reasonably.

Want to bet?

"Just accept that you're going to have your photo taken," said the Mistress of the Robes.

"How do you look?" asked Imogen.

"I—All right, I suppose," said Alix uncertainly. She was wearing a work suit. Her hair was behaving itself. She made a decision. "I have to go. Call me if instructions come through." Then she dialed a number that every member of the Checquy memorized before they memorized their own.

"Office of Qualifications and Examinations Regulation, notifications line."

"This is Pawn Alexandra Mondegreen." She gave her authentication code. "Can you please put me through to the Liars?"

"Transferring you to the Tactical Deception Communications section." There was a momentary pause, then:

"This is Geri Westfahl."

"This is Pawn Alexandra Mondegreen." There was a noise of recognition. "So, it seems that the press have abruptly become interested in me."

"No kidding. Have you not seen the papers?"

"Not yet," said Alix.

"Well, they're very interested in you. And your friends."

"I only just met most of them," said Alix. *Why am I setting the record straight with this person I don't even know?* "Anyway, I just got ambushed by a bunch of paps outside my flat. I'm hiding in my lobby. I need to know if they've camped out at the Rookery."

"No."

"Are you sure?" asked Alix.

"I'm looking at the cameras right now. Besides, if there were journalists out there, all the lights inside the building would have turned red, and we'd be on high alert, probably be venting that feces-based aerosol out on them and putting it about that there's been a sewage leak."

"And if that doesn't work?"

"Then we'd start pumping actual sewage onto the footpath. But at the moment, that's not necessary. So, let's see, how best to address this situation?" The Liar's tone suggested that she was viewing the whole thing as a marvelous intellectual training exercise. "Hold on...hold on...Okay, so I've dispatched a Checquy-operated taxicab that'll pick you up in about ten minutes."

"And until then?" Alix asked. "Do I just stay in here?"

"Actually, I think it would be a good idea if you give them a chance to get a few pictures and are nice to them rather than just jumping into the cab once it screeches up to the doors. After all, it's not like they're trying to snap incriminating photos of you coming out of a brothel, or drunk and disheveled. They just want pics of you existing. At least for now."

"All right," said Alix. "But what about my cover job? I'm worried this might lead them to the Rookery."

"We'll take care of that," said Geri. "We'll have a solution by the time you get to the office."

"Thanks," said Alix. "I'm so grateful."

"Not to fret," said the Liar. "We've managed that Grafter dating the prince, so this should be fine."

Alix hung up and her phone immediately pinged with a series of links that Siti had sent. Hesitantly she tapped on them. Headlines jumped out at her.

> PRINCESS CHARMING AND HER MERRY MAIDS
> WONDER WOMEN!
> NEW JEWELS IN THE CROWN
> PRINCESS STEPS OUT INTO THE LIGHT!
> ROYAL GAL PALS
> THE PRINCESS POSSE
> LOU AND HER LADIES
> CORONETS IN THE COUNTRYSIDE

They don't like us, she thought weakly. *They LOVE us. Is that actually worse?*

Each headline was accompanied by large photos of their expedition, in colors so bright they bit the eye. It was quite the prettiest group of tabloid covers that Alix could recall seeing, a selection of countryside scenes: green grass, cottages, sunshine, pretty clothes, and smiling faces. There was not an unflattering shot or a nipple among them.

As she skimmed the articles, select words and phrases caught her eye: Brave. A role she never sought. Enthusiasm mixed with dignity. Clearly, the press had decided it was going to hitch its collective wagon to Louise and her ladies.

At least for now.

Each lady had received a short profile piece, although some were scantier than others. The press had been obliged to cannibalize Siti's bio from her graduation art show. For the others, they'd turned to *Burke's Peerage, Baronetage, and Knightage,* and the *Almanach de Gotha,* or whatever meager coverage Imogen, Henrietta, and Alix had picked up in the course of their lives. Clearly, some photo editors had put the word out that they wanted fresh pictures.

Alix's own profile advised that she was employed in a small City law firm, but thankfully, it was not named. Far more attention was paid to her childhood friendship with Louise (with a stock photo of the two of them as little girls in party dresses), her parents' "long-standing closeness to the King" (with a photo of Lord and Lady Mondegreen with the King and the Queen at some event that had called for her mother to be wearing an impressive hat), and her presence in the funeral march. A picture from the previous day showed Alix chatting with the woman who'd liked her boots. Another showed her smiling and holding a cup of tea. Then there was a photo of her in the funeral procession, and a little sidebar all about the mystery boots.

She winced at one headline: MOURNING HAS BROKEN. No one was going to be happy about that. *Still, as long as it's not "Tiaras and Tequila."*

Nervously, she called Smith and explained the situation. The pawn, who had already seen some of the newspapers, did not sound impressed but acknowledged that Alix would have to be late to the office. In the pit of her stomach, Alix could sense the inevitable effect all this was going to have on her career.

Alix took a deep breath, smoothed her clothes, and went outside. She waved to the photographers, who were snapping away, and walked across the road. They kept clicking, ready to capture some good shots of her being angry and shouting.

"Good morning," she said. There was a chorus of cautious "Morning"s. "I'm sorry about ducking away before—you just surprised me. This is my first time meeting the press like this, and I hadn't even had a coffee yet." There were a couple of chuckles. "I've got to head off to work, but I understand this is your job, and you've got to get some pictures, so I'm happy to stand over by the gardens there for you until my car comes."

Much to her surprised relief, this suggestion was greeted with approval, and they moved *en masse* across the street. Alix was determined not to pose like she was on the red carpet, but she found that each photographer wanted a shot of her looking at their camera. Accordingly, she looked straight at each of them in turn and smiled, but not too broadly. When they thanked her, she asked for each of their names and filed them away in her Checquy-drilled memory.

When the cab pulled up, the driver was clearly braced for a mob scene, and seemed disappointed that none of her urban evasion techniques were going to be needed. Instead, the photographers were hurrying off to their next assignment.

"You don't think they'll trail us, then?" asked the driver.

"Always best to be certain," said Alix diplomatically. The driver brightened up and spent the rest of the deliberately convoluted journey to the Rookery checking the mirror every few moments and muttering into the microphone taped to her throat. There were at least three Checquy cars nearby, ready to roll in and use some sort of offensive automotive choreography to stymie any attempts at tailing them.

By the time Alix arrived at her desk, the morning meeting had been held, and everyone else was busy at their tasks. She was about to knock on Smith's door when her phone chimed with a fresh message from the Liars.

POST THIS ON SOCIAL MEDIA ONCE YOU ARRIVE AT THE OFFICE.

It was a picture of a mouthwatering Black Forest cake emblazoned with *Good Luck, Alix!* in icing.

The accompanying text that had been drafted for her was Last day at work! So much love and thanks to my wonderful team for all the great times! Looking forward to new adventures.

So, according to the official record, I am now unemployed.

Sighing, Alix set about posting on all her accounts. She noted that her follower count had gone up by many thousands more since she'd last checked. After she'd finished, a thought occurred to her, and she dialed Geri.

"Am I going to get any of that farewell cake?" she asked. "The one with my name on it?"

"Uh... no, it's already been eaten. It became the office's morning tea."

"Of course it did," said Alix. "Just out of interest, how many of your cover-up strategies involve cake?"

"That's classified, I'm afraid," said the Liar, who swiftly hung up.

16

Nine days after the ambush on Alix's doorstep, things had settled down with the press. The novelty of Louise and her ladies-in-waiting had faded a bit, and photographers were no longer waiting outside her flat. She'd still had to be ferried to the office in a Checquy vehicle for a few days, just to ensure that no one was following her, but the Liars were now satisfied that she could resume the use of public transport.

On this particular morning, Alix had come in to work quite a bit earlier than usual. There was a palace event that evening, which meant leaving early, which meant she needed to preempt any sniffy remarks about skiving. She found, however, that she was not the first in the team to arrive.

"Morning, Weller. You look like you've found something entertaining." The finance expert was in the kitchenette, chortling at something in the newspaper spread out on the counter.

"Saucy financial gossip," said Weller.

"Oh?"

"Yes, there's been another massive leak of information on people's offshore accounts and company ownerships. Thousands of them in European microstates." She shook her head happily. "Some of these belong to very prominent public figures. Very tasty. They're calling the whole thing 'The Principality Papers.'"

"No one we know, I hope?" said Alix.

"Worried that you'll show up?" asked Weller, looking at her archly.

"Chance would be a fine thing," snorted Alix. Every year, inevitably, she was one of the people "randomly" selected for an in-depth audit by the Checquy's dreaded accountant-inquisitors. She was certain that it was the doing of some pawn who disliked the very idea of her and was eager to find any humiliating flaws in her personal finances. To prevent the possibility of such an event, Alix was meticulous in her bookkeeping.

"You don't need to worry, Mondegreen. You're not in it, nor is your mum," said Weller. Alix, who knew exactly how much money her mother didn't have, smiled. Then a thought occurred to her.

"Any royal personages named?"

"Not the King or either of his kids. But there *is* a prince of the blood on the list. One of your protectee's cousins."

"Christ, which one?" Wordlessly, Weller pointed at the name. "Of *course* it's Jerome. There are going to be some pointed conversations in the near future."

"What's in the case?" asked Weller. Alix looked down at the green leather case that she had been trying to conceal behind her leg.

"Nothing."

"Oh, come on. Is this because I pointed out you were wearing a tiara that one time?" Alix hunched her shoulders a little. "What, is it another tiara?" Weller laughed, but then stopped as Alix looked away. "What is it?"

"... It's another tiara."

"Seriously? What is it with you and tiaras?"

"The first time was an accident, and tonight I am going to a thing, and we've been asked to wear tiaras. So I had to go plead with my mother to lend me the family tiara."

"Right. Well, you have to let me see it," said Weller. Sighing, Alix opened the case to reveal, nestled on a sculpted bed of black velvet, a platinum circlet shining with rubies and large half pearls. "*Damn.* How long has it been in your family? Like, centuries?"

"Since I was seven," said Alix. "My mum extorted it out of the Checquy. She said she needed one for royal events, and then there was specific mention of it in *Tatler* when she wore it to a ball. She said that since it had been mentioned in the press and was part of the historical record, the family had to keep it, and I think the comptroller just broke and agreed."

Prying the tiara out of her mother's clutches had not been easy, but since it technically belonged to the House of Mondegreen and Alix had promised to return it the very next morning, it had eventually been handed over with a maximum of reluctance. The family had actually picked up a few tiaras over the centuries, but they had been quietly sold off as circumstances and finances dictated.

"Credit to your mum, she knows how to work the system," said Weller.

"You want to try it on?" asked Alix. "I'll take your photo."

"You won't get in trouble?"

"Just don't put it on social media. Also, there's a matching necklace." She lifted out the tray to reveal more rubies and pearls waiting. She helped Weller put on the jewelry and adjusted it. "It looks really good on you." It did. Amid the pawn's tight braids, the jewels glistened like stars and nebulae in the cosmos. Alix had a suspicion it would not be nearly as impressive in her own ruddy locks. Her mother (who had glorious raven hair) had undoubtedly picked it solely with an eye toward how she herself would look in it.

"I'll need to borrow this for a meeting sometime," said Weller. "Just to put extra fear in my underlings. And what is this event?"

"It's a reception celebrating British women actors," said Alix. "Stage and screen and monitor. Lots of famous names and faces, including Caroline Delahunty!"

"No!"

"Yes!"

"Now I'm jealous. And you're wearing a tiara? It must be pretty grand."

"The princess said we should all wear them." In truth, Louise had said that she very definitely wanted the ladies-in-waiting to wear them, but hadn't said why. Alix suspected that, faced with the combined glamour of the British stage, the film industry, and those British actors who had made it big in Hollywood, Louise wanted to host an event that was appropriately glittering.

After all, this was going to be her first major social event. As hostess (a position as patron of the Thespienne Society having been flung at her as early as was considered appropriate), she knew it would set the tone for Louise as a princess, as well as for the future monarchy. Alix also suspected that Louise was still a little insecure in her new role and wanted to establish firmly just who was crown princess. Quite aside from the celebrated Caroline Delahunty, several of the actresses were extremely imposing figures, but there was nothing like a royal tiara of massive historical significance and a bevy of ladies-in-waiting, each wearing her own tiara, to firmly establish one's precedence.

"I thought tiaras were for married women only," said Weller, taking the jewels off and handing them back to Alix.

"Yeah, for them and the pope," said Alix. "He gets one as well."

"Typical," sniffed Weller. "There's always a man who's got to horn in on the action."

"Well, it's not actually written down as a firm rule." Alix shrugged. *And even if it were, who's going to argue with the crown princess?* "So word went out to all the guests that tiaras would be most welcome on any and all heads that choose to wear them, and everyone has completely flipped out."

The announcement had created something of a panic in certain quarters of society. The lateness of the decree that tiaras would be encouraged had meant that fashion choices made months ago needed to be adapted—in some cases radically. All the major jewelers had been caught off guard and had sold more tiaras in a fortnight than they were accustomed to selling in a year.

Late in the afternoon, after accomplishing a full day's work, Alix left the office, to only a minimal sniff from Sweven, who was grudgingly aware of how early she'd come in, since Weller had mentioned it in his hearing. A car delivered Alix to Buckingham Palace. The princess and her ladies (and her gown) were waiting in a large room where they (the ladies, not the gown) were being made up, coiffed, dressed, and shod by professionals. Alix greeted them. Louise was curtsied to (because staff were present), and cheeks were kissed, or, for those who had already been meticulously made up, hovered in the close vicinity of.

Alix was briskly settled in a chair in front of a mirror, with a makeup artist and a hair artist looking speculatively at her and talking to each other. The makeup process was paused twice as her cream-and-silver gown was fetched and held up alongside her face, and the necklace and tiara were also held up for color-complementing purposes.

"The dress is well-chosen," said the makeup artist. "Beautifully cut. Reddish hair and pale material can be unflattering, but this tone is not the same as the skin. In fact, it will bring out some color."

"And it will highlight the pearls in the tiara," the hairdresser said. It was not at all clear whether they were including Alix in the conversation, but she felt a wash of relief at their words. The gown was new and had been the subject of much agonized consideration, since Alix had had to pick it out and pay for it herself. The shop assistants had gotten very involved and spent quite a bit of time assuring her that it did not in any way look like a wedding dress.

The hair process was intricate. First, the hairdresser ran her fingers contemplatively through Alix's locks, then expertly created a thin braid across her head, before styling the rest of her hair into its chosen party format.

"You don't put the tiara on and then style around it?" asked Alix.

"We don't want to get hair spray on the jewels," said the hairdresser. "It would diminish the luster." She positioned the tiara on Alix's head, its wire base nestled strategically into her hair, and then sewed it into the braid, so that it wouldn't slip around or fall off.

Eventually, all five women were ready, and they looked—frankly—magnificent. Henrietta and Imogen were wearing family tiaras. Louise had lent something to Siti that glittered with dark purple sapphires of some historical significance. The princess herself was wearing a tiara of diamonds and shimmering royal blue Belle Époque enamel that glowed like a stained glass window, and that Alix happened to know had been smuggled out of revolutionary Russia in the underskirts of a fleeing grand duchess. The bodice of Louise's deep blue gown was perfectly fitted, leaving her shoulders bare, and then cascaded down into ornate skirts.

There had been a fair amount of discussion about the gowns beforehand. It was understood that the ladies-in-waiting should absolutely not outshine the princess, but Louise had insisted that everyone should look good on her own merits, and not be coordinated like bridesmaids. Accordingly, each had picked a color and style that flattered her, but a little private discussion without Louise present had ensured that none of them was wearing blue.

Siti wore a fascinating gown of deep magenta, with shimmering golden threads woven through in an intricate pattern. Imogen's soft pink dress made her look like a delicate porcelain sculpture crowned with diamonds. Henrietta glided smoothly in a gown of emerald green, with a gold necklace and matching tiara that, unless Alix was very much mistaken, dated back to the Victorian period.

They made their way to an antechamber. Beyond the high double doors, they could hear the sound of 165 people—actresses and plus-ones—who had arrived punctually and not had to deal with the usual obstacles of traversing a red carpet or suffering feverish inquiries from the press as to whom they were wearing.

"Ready?" asked Louise. Her ladies murmured assent. "Then let's get this party started."

And the doors opened.

There was no great fanfare, no announcements. Still, silence spread through the Blue Drawing Room, and everyone turned. Alix's stomach flipped over as she looked out on a room full of faces familiar from newspapers and television shows, magazines and movie screens. Many were surmounted by a shining ornament that sparkled in the light of the room's many chandeliers, so that a galaxy of eyes and jewels was arrayed before her.

Louise smiled, then moved to greet some hapless actress who had unwittingly been standing by the doors and was completely unprepared to be engaged in conversation by the princess. Siti and Alix remained flanking her, but the other ladies-in-waiting peeled off to circulate. Nerves were eased by waiters stepping forward to offer beverages, and after a moment, the throng relaxed into a cocktail party hubbub.

There were far too many people attending for Louise to meet every single one, but those who were to be presented to the crown princess were quietly being marshaled into position. There would be no formal receiving line, but rather several semicircles.

As Louise made her way along, the female guests knew to curtsy, and almost all of them did so with the smoothness of someone who'd done at least some practicing in the hours beforehand and was resisting all her professional urges to theatrical it up a bit. There were only a few men presented, this being an occasion to honor women specifically, and their bows from the neck were perfectly acceptable.

To each one, Louise offered her hand, and it was shaken with a light touch. Every person in the semicircle was famous. There were at least three dames who had been hailed as national icons, as well as a beloved longtime main actress from a beloved longtime soap opera, a film star who was midway through a critically acclaimed run of *Hedda Gabler* in the West End, and *the* Caroline Delahunty.

For someone trying to keep her bodyguarding instincts on alert, the presence of Ms. Delahunty was a problem. The BAFTA- and Laurence Olivier Award–winning actress was last in the queue, but her beauty and charisma and the sheer fact of her actual presence were such that Alix's eyes kept rotating away from the people Louise was shaking hands with and flickering across the gap to catch a delighted, incredulous glimpse of her.

When they made their way to Caroline Delahunty, Alix was able to stare without being too obvious about it. In her midforties but looking like early thirties, with delicate features that nonetheless exuded a strong, warm character, the actress was just as magnetic as Alix remembered from the theater. That charm always seemed to get lost somewhat in the transition to the silver screen, but in person, feeling her eyes meet yours, it was like getting French-kissed right in the brain. The actress seemed just that little bit more in focus than everyone else, especially given that she was wearing a tiara of diamonds and fire opals so large that it had to have been lent to her by some oligarch's daughter—it was simply not the kind of thing people bought unless they already possessed a sizable portion of some country's natural resources.

Alix listened to Louise make polite conversation about Delahunty's next project, and then there was a brief pause as members of the royal household finished corralling the next group to be met. Louise took the opportunity to drink some water, while Henrietta relieved Siti and Alix. A waiter approached, and Alix accepted a glass of champagne that she had no intention of drinking but which gave her something to do with her non-shaking hand.

As it turned out, in terms of breaking the ice with perfect strangers, the decision about tiaras could not have been more genius. The phrase "I absolutely love your tiara. Could you tell me about it?" had essentially replaced "Hello, isn't all this lovely?" as a standard greeting.

Alix was introduced to the minutiae and provenance of a selection of tiaras, circlets, bandeaux, kokoshniks, and a single aigrette that was supporting a small but bright plume of feathers over the forehead of a rising British Indian actress. The collected monetary value of the room's head adornments was dizzying, although she had to give major respect to the independent film actress who'd worn a pink plastic child's tiara from a corner shop.

For many of the guests, perhaps for all of them, this evening was going to be one of the greatest highlights of their life. It was splendid for Alix too; she knew she would remember it forever. But she also knew that this sort of thing would eventually stop feeling unusual or remarkable to her. Always lovely occasions, she was sure, but not quite as magical as they became more routine.

So enjoy it. And make sure that others are enjoying it.

For most royal events, there was an official photographer from whom photographs could be ordered afterward. But because this evening represented a unique merging of fashion, celebrity, and royalty, there were several photographers cruising through the crowd like dinner-jacket-wearing stealth eels. The images would show the world a princess who could not only be charming at a small village gathering but could wield glamour like an expert. Alix turned and came face-to-face with Lady Linda Farrier.

"My lady!" she gasped.

"Lady Mondegreen. Good evening." Alix's commanding officer was wearing a splendid black-and-silver-striped gown. Resting regally in her blond hair was a black tiara that had no jewels on it but shone with a fascinating luster.

"Good evening," said Alix. She looked around. "Is there a threat I need to be aware of?"

"No," said Lady Farrier. "I'm on the board of the Thespienne Society."

"Oh," said Alix. *That's not mentioned on your Wikipedia page.* "Good." She flailed around for something appropriate to say. "I absolutely love your tiara. Could you tell me about it?" It just slipped out, but it appeared that even Lady Farrier was susceptible to the charms of talking about a tiara, because she put her hand up to it and looked pleased.

"Thank you! It's been in the family for years. It's Whitby jet."

"It's exquisite," said Alix. Lady Farrier was like an Art Deco raven in a flock of theatrical birds of paradise.

"I think the evening is going very well." Farrier looked around. "I was dubious when word went out about the tiaras, but it's made for something of a triumph. The crown princess is certainly rising to her new role." She regarded Louise across the room. "Yes, she seems quite happy. Unlike her father."

"Why? Has something happened to the King?"

"No, it's not that." Farrier's lips twisted. "It's the lack of progress in the investigation."

"Is he going to replace us?"

"No, not that." Farrier sighed. "It is, inevitably, complicated. The sovereign of this country reigns but does not rule. Still, he has certain powers."

"Like curing scrofula with a touch?" asked Alix wryly.

"The Checquy have checked every monarch since Henry VII and

found that story to be untrue," said Farrier. "No, I'm talking about legal authority and control. Over the centuries, even as this country moved from absolute monarchy to constitutional monarchy, the sovereign retained some powers. Some are simply not talked about, such as vetoing laws, or pardoning people for crimes, or crown immunity." Alix frowned in confusion.

"Theoretically, the King is personally immune from all criminal and civil actions," the Lady explained. "He also can't be arrested." Alix raised her eyebrows. She'd never realized that to be the case.

"Oh, you can read all about it on Wikipedia," said Farrier. "It's just not publicized. But some of their powers remain secret, including, obviously, those related to the Checquy. We're no longer as dependent on them for funding, but the sovereign and the first in line each have a vote in the selection of the Checquy Court."

"Yes, I knew about that."

"The fact that we are still in the process of selecting a chevalier currently leaves us vulnerable. The balance of power in the Court could be shifted."

This is political, Alix realized. She had never thought of the Checquy as having those sorts of struggles. Divorced as it was from public scrutiny, from electoral upheaval, and from the rest of the civil service, she always thought of the organization as being devoted to its mission without time for political squabbles.

Farrier shrugged. "Maybe I'm overstating the situation. But the investigation is not making progress, and the King is not happy." She tilted her head suddenly, looking away in vexation, as if she had heard an abrupt sour note in the music.

"Are you all right?" asked Alix.

"Hm? I'm fine." She shook her head as though to clear it. "Now, you have responsibilities." They nodded to each other and parted.

Alix drifted, her eyes continuously catching on faces that struck a chord of recognition, before she realized that she'd seen them but never met them before.

"Excuse me," said a man behind her. He spoke with a European accent that she couldn't immediately place. "I absolutely love your tiara. Could you tell me about it?"

You have got to be kidding me. Still, she was a deputy hostess, so she put on a smile.

"Thank you, it's my mother's," she said, turning to behold a man wearing an extraordinary outfit. The first thing she noticed, because it was directly at eye level, was a black cravat with, seemingly, a small supernova nestled in it. Once she could drag her gaze away from the multitude of facets, she took in the white shirt and the black Edwardian-style frock coat fitted closely at his chest and hips, buttoned tightly, but then draping down, and down farther, out and down and down and back, to trail along the floor behind him like a river of ink. He was *not* wearing a tiara, but the diamond pin that nestled in his cravat burned with an unholy number of carats.

"Is that a train?" she asked weakly.

"It better be. I got married in it," he said. He was slim, but with broad shoulders. His vivid blue eyes were like chips of summer sky in his long, well-tanned face, and his blond hair was meticulously arranged.

"How long is it?"

"It's a little over two meters. I'd have gone longer, but it's unbelievably heavy as it is. Fourteen kilograms." He twitched his train, and she saw that it was lined with iridescent black-and-gold-checked cloth. "Still, I get so few occasions to wear it, and when my friend Harriet invited me to be her plus-one, this was the opportunity to dust it off. Especially when word came down about the tiaras. So, I've left the husband at home, and am judging everybody's choices."

"And are you in the arts?" She didn't recognize his face, although the ensemble was so eye-catching that she probably wouldn't have recognized herself in it.

"I'm a producer," he said.

And a very successful one, Alix thought. *Judging by that diamond.* He put out his hand, and with a start she saw that it came equipped with manicured nails half an inch long that looked like glass with glittering flakes of actual gold embedded in them.

Not supernatural, she decided. *Just utterly fabulous.*

"Caspian Vanacore."

A Dutch name, Alix thought. *And a Dutch accent.*

"And you're Lady Alexandra Mondegreen," he continued. "She of the famous boots."

"That's going to go on my tombstone, isn't it?"

"More likely than that tiara, I'm sorry to say," Vanacore said. "It's gorgeous, but not at all the stones I would have picked for you. Or the metal. Or the shape."

"It's my mother's," said Alix.

"I'm sure it looks marvelous on her, but when it comes time for you to pick your own, give me a call," said Vanacore. "I have strong, extremely well-informed opinions on this sort of thing."

"I can tell," she said. "Are you enjoying the evening?"

"It is inspired," he said. "A gorgeous party."

I will have to tell Louise. There could be no better endorsement than this stylish gentleman's approval.

They chatted a bit more, and then Alix realized that Siti was signaling her. She excused herself and moved over to where Louise was being shielded by her ladies-in-waiting while she took a drink of water.

"How's the reaction? Do you think it's going all right?" asked Louise.

"*He* thinks it's marvelous," said Alix, nodding over at Caspian Vanacore, looking like the couture combination of a Catholic priest and an imperial Chinese aristocrat.

"Bloody hell," said the princess. "Whoever he is, he's got taste. We couldn't do better, could we?"

"I think it's a success," said Henrietta.

"Was I all right with Caroline thingy?" asked Louise.

"Yeah, you were great," said Alix.

"My knees were knocking a little."

"No one could tell, thanks to your dress."

"That's probably why we wear them. She's amazing. When I met her, I had to remind myself how to let go of a hand when I'm finished shaking it."

"That's why she's a beloved actress."

"Yeah. Okay, last semicircle, then Fa will stop in, and then dinner. Do I look all right?"

"Show me your teeth," said Alix. "And up the nose... Yep, you're fine."

"Okay, good." Louise took a breath and became the princess again.

When the King arrived, the room paused. He moved through the crowd, accepting curtsies and bows.

And then Caroline Delahunty's orbit intercepted that of the King, the one a flowing watercolor of jewels and rose silk, the other a dinner-jacketed ink drawing by Rembrandt. When the two of them met, it was as though the rest of the world went into a soft blur. The King's calm reserve cracked, and his jaw dropped a little as he took in the beauty before him. Alix couldn't blame him. Delahunty dipped in an elegant curtsy, looking up at him through her lashes. The stunning woman in her tiara, in the palace, with the colors of the crowd washed behind her—it was a fairy-tale moment.

Oh, my, thought Alix, a little breathless. She couldn't hear their conversation, but the delight on the King's face and the demure satisfaction on Delahunty's lips suggested that both of them were enjoying themselves immensely. The King looked more animated than she had seen him since Edmund's death, and, against all his training and experience, he was ignoring everyone else around him.

With an effort, Alix looked away to check on the progress of the evening. Louise was just at the end of her final semicircle. Siti, who was attending the princess, caught Alix's eye and raised three fingers.

Three minutes. Alix nodded and moved toward the attendant who had come in with the King. She realized that it was Sir Alastair.

"Sir Alastair, we'll be proceeding in three minutes," she said. The King would not be attending the dinner, so it was time for him to make his gracious exit. Judging by the intensity between him and Caroline Delahunty, however, withdrawing was the last thing on his mind.

"Yes...," said Sir Alastair uncertainly. Alix could not blame him for hesitating to push himself into the intense little world that consisted entirely of the King and the actress. Still, the power of the schedule was inexorable, especially to a member of the royal household. So he moved forward, cleared his throat, and muttered something to the King.

There was a flash of irritation on the King's face, and she could see the effort it took him to drag his gaze away from Delahunty. His lips tightened at Sir Alastair's whisper, but he nodded and said something to the actress. She smiled graciously and the King shook her hand. He murmured something to his secretary, and then he was departing, nodding and smiling as the other guests curtsied or bowed. He looked back, and Delahunty was still watching him, even as Sir Alastair spoke to her. She nodded and accepted a card that he discreetly passed to her.

I wonder what's going on? Alix cast an eye over the crowd to see if they had noticed the passing of the card, but they were mostly watching the King depart, or had turned back to their own conversations. Still, it would have been difficult not to detect the spark that had just passed between the actress and the monarch.

Spark! More like a lightning bolt.

Since the Queen's death, the King had been alone. Alix had never seen him light up for anyone as he had that evening. Admittedly, Delahunty was quite a few years younger than he, but still...

An official was calling the gathering to dinner, and Alix slipped back into lady-in-waiting mode, helping to usher the guests through a few very grand connecting rooms to the insanely grand ballroom. The biggest of the state rooms, it was now mainly used for state banquets and investitures, and it *was* majestic—a vision of vivid red carpet and soaring white walls chased in gold, with gigantic pictures in gilt frames. Huge chandeliers hung from the distant ceiling, and enormous arrangements of flowers stood about like floral sentinels. At the end of the room, under a crimson canopy, two thrones stood on a dais.

It was dazzling—guests kept freezing upon entering, overwhelmed by the spectacle, at which point one of the ladies-in-waiting would step in, breaking them out of their daze, and guide them to their assigned seats at the single enormous horseshoe-shaped table.

As hostess, Louise was, of course, at the center of the base of the U, where everyone could see her. She was flanked by various important people from the Thespienne Society. Lady Farrier was a few seats away and had a distant look in her eyes as the doyenne of the society said something to her. Caroline Delahunty had been placed close to the princess, but not so close as to eclipse her.

Before dinner was served, Louise stood to give her speech about the astounding work of women in the British performing arts, hailing their talent, skill, and contributions to the culture. She then proposed a toast to the head of the Thespienne Society, to which everyone happily raised their glasses and sipped their extremely good beverages.

The head of the Thespienne Society, one of the renowned dames, then rose to thank the princess and to propose a toast back. Alix, who had been too busy to eat anything since lunch, was striving to figure out which muscles she had to clench to stop her stomach from growling.

Finally, *finally,* the speeches ended, and it was time for the fish course.

Alix was about to start her fillet of West Coast turbot with lobster mousse when a hesitant clearing of a throat came from over her shoulder.

"Lady Mondegreen?" She looked up to see the strongest person in recorded history looking apologetic. She couldn't even muster the outrage to reply, just looked at him with tired expectation. "Lady Farrier needs to speak with you."

Seriously? Will I never get to eat a meal in this place unless it's breakfast?

"The crown princess has already given her approval for you to step away," said the server. In fact, Louise was shooting her an incredulous look of disapproval. Alix shrugged wearily and followed the pawn.

Lady Farrier was waiting in an empty reception room.

"Thank you, Pawn Larcher," said Farrier. "Now, please fetch her." The pawn nodded and stepped away.

"Fetch who?" asked Alix.

"Did you see the King meeting Caroline Delahunty?"

"I did," said Alix. "He seemed very taken with her."

"Yes," said the Lady. "I am concerned. I have a suspicion..." She frowned. "I think that it was not natural."

"Are—Are you certain?" asked Alix. Delahunty *was* glamorous, but she was an adored figure of British stage and screen. Being glamorous was what those people did. It didn't necessarily mean that she was a malevolent entity of occult origins.

"I'm not certain, no," said the Lady. "But all this evening, I have sensed a faint"—she paused, searching for the right word—"a *pressure* in the air. Like a tone that you can only just hear. Then, when those two met, I thought perhaps it changed pitch."

It didn't sound like the most convincing testimony to Alix, but Farrier was her commanding officer. Alix was obliged to conceal her own skepticism.

"Okay. What are we going to do?"

"Meet with her," said Farrier. "Assess the situation, act as necessary."

"But right now?" asked Alix. "This very moment?" *Before I get to have supper?* "You don't want to lay any groundwork, perhaps do some reconnaissance? Have our people conduct some background research?"

"You saw the King's reaction to her."

"I did." *It wasn't that far off from my reaction to her, except that she didn't acknowledge my existence, and I'm not sexually attracted to women.*

"I asked Sir Alastair what the King said to him. He's to arrange a future meeting with her, just as soon as she would like. What if it's tonight? What if she doesn't leave the palace after the reception, but is instead quietly guided up to the residence for a drink and a conversation, et cetera?"

"It could just be the mutual attraction between two famous and attractive people," objected Alix.

"I know," said Farrier. "That's why we have to be careful. If it's nothing supernatural, then we can't afford to alienate her. But if it's something, then we need to investigate now and, if necessary, nip it in the bud."

"So, it'll just be you, me, and Larcher?" asked Alix. The Checquy presence in the palace had been lessened significantly in the weeks since Edmund's death, as new supernatural threats failed to materialize.

"Larcher should remain outside as possible backup," said Farrier. "The nature of his abilities means that if he's called in, things inevitably get broken. Or demolished." She surveyed the room, with its objets d'art roosting about on plinths. "Yes, we want to avoid that if possible."

"So, what do you think she does?" asked Alix. "Just bends people to her will through charm and charisma?" It sounded equally plausible and implausible. Famous and attractive people did this all the time. "And if it *is* a manifestation, then what if she enchants *us*?"

"I've already left a voice memo for Rook Thomas, advising of the situation and my suspicions," said Farrier. "If we show up to work tomorrow, awed and denying that there are any concerns about Delahunty, then Thomas will know we've been rolled, as it were."

"But what if Delahunty is innocent, and we're genuinely awed and deny any concerns about her because there *aren't* any concerns about her?" asked Alix.

"What? Well, in that case, we'll just need to ensure that we're properly subdued in our effusiveness."

The door opened.

17

Caroline Delahunty swept in, cheeks adorably flushed, the very picture of a fairy-tale sweet thing about to meet a handsome king. Alix half expected there to be a heart-stirring swell of orchestral music coming from somewhere.

When Delahunty saw that rather than the expected Handsome King standing by the window ready to turn and greet her, there were instead two unfamiliar women regarding her fixedly, she paused. Then she looked behind her as the door was shut.

Alix, meanwhile, was examining all her feelings to see if the slight thrill she'd felt upon seeing Delahunty was supernaturally induced or had come just because it was actually *the* Caroline Delahunty, and there was still the possibility of getting a selfie, if not tickets to something.

"Good evening, Miss Delahunty," said Lady Farrier.

"Hello," said the actress. She'd recovered from her surprise and was now standing as if she owned the place. "I had been told that the King..."

"Yes, of course," said Farrier. "However, this is a sensitive situation, and so preparations are necessary. I'm sure you understand?"

"I think so," said Delahunty, her eyes narrowed.

"It is important that you appreciate how things happen when it comes to the royal family," said Farrier. "We wish to protect everyone concerned. Let us sit, and we can explain it to you before we proceed."

"All right," said Delahunty. She allowed herself to be led to a group of chairs clustered by one of the windows.

"First, introductions. I am Lady Linda Farrier, an advisor to the King, and this is Lady Alexandra Mondegreen, lady-in-waiting to the crown princess." Delahunty nodded, crushingly giving no impression that she had any recollection of meeting Alix less than an hour earlier.

"I understand your conversation with the King was..." Lady Farrier broke off, her eyes distant. Delahunty looked at her uncertainly, and then looked questioningly to Alix, who had no idea what was happening.

Suddenly the Lady of the Checquy reached out toward the actress's face. Before Delahunty could jerk back, Farrier's finger curled in the air in front of her nose, and then, with a sudden hooking motion, swept down.

There was a noise like paper tearing, and Alix could actually see the air around Delahunty wrinkle, as though Farrier was pulling away fabric.

The lights seemed to have dimmed, and Alix felt a palpable lowering of her spirits, like the unpleasant realization that there was work she had forgotten to start and which was now due. She blinked and tried to understand what was happening.

Farrier held her hand up in a fist. Clenched in her fingers was a transparent film that hung and glistened like a sheet of slimy silk.

Staring at it in shock, Alix had the impression of cheeks and brows, and of lips moving emptily.

Did Farrier just pull her goddamn face off? The visage sagged, stretching from the Lady's hand down onto the floor, and the light oozed off it.

Delahunty slumped back in her chair, wheezing, her hands half held up to her head. Then she looked up at them, and she was no longer who she had been.

She was still a human woman, wearing that startling tiara and glorious dress, her hair still done up beautifully, but the face was no longer the same. Traces of the famous Delahunty visage remained in the brow and the shape of the chin, but the flesh was drawn painfully taut. Yellowed eyes stared, large and startled, as if the sockets had shrunk and were forcing them out of her skull. Scars and scabs dappled her brow and cheeks.

Though she was still human, this human was not well. She showed the kind of premature aging that comes from drugs or illness. Pinpricks of blood dotted her face, even her lips. Were they the result of Farrier's unexpected maneuver? Had she torn that shiny film out of Delahunty's pores?

Most shocking was the lack of charisma. The allure that had drawn the eye and the mind and fascinated them both had been stripped away.

"What *is* that?" asked Alix. Farrier sat calm and composed, her back ramrod straight, seemingly unconcerned by the sheet of... *something*... that trailed from her upheld hand. The outlines of the famous Delahunty face were still there, but the material itself confused the eyes, indistinguishable as liquid or fiber — one moment almost resembling cobwebs, the next mucus.

"Glamour, you could call it," said Farrier. "In the old sense of the word. Supernatural power to charm and enchant." She regarded it with cool interest. "Malleable, palpable illusion, but it does more than just change what we see. It changes what we *feel*. It manipulates emotion. Such stuff as dreams are made of." She smiled wryly. "Literally. Which is why I could pull it away." She regarded the shocked Delahunty.

"You used this to build your career," said Farrier. "No wonder everyone loved you on the stage. But less so on the screen, because the camera would just capture the appearance, not the"—she waved her hand vaguely—"razzle-dazzle. So you left Hollywood and returned to the West End, where you were worshipped. But the opportunity of this evening arose, and you thought it was time to focus on something else. Some*one* else. And who is more eligible than the King? Did you think you'd be the new Grace Kelly? Or just a Lillie Langtry or Nellie Clifden?"

Delahunty regarded her with hate-filled eyes.

"We wouldn't have found you if you had simply carried on acting," said Farrier. "There's been no inkling that you've caused actual harm, at least not to others. And it's clearly taking its toll on you." Alix took in the actress's face—the drawn flesh, the wounds, and that empty hunger that roiled in her expression. A thin film of sweat glistened stickily on her face, and her breath was rasping. "Are your powers doing that to you? Or have they afforded you a lifestyle that you can't sustain? Drugs? Alcohol, perhaps?"

Delahunty said nothing.

"I can see why you wanted a change. But we can't allow you to use your powers on the King. You've twisted his will, and for more than just an initial meeting and some fawning."

"Men fall for beauty all the time," said Delahunty. Her voice was no longer smooth caramel. She now spoke as though she had a mouthful of phlegm. "They don't care about the actual person underneath."

"But no one could resist what you did to him," objected Alix. "No one. I felt just the faintest hint of it, and I was reeling. I know the King. He's not the kind to be lured in by a face, no matter how beautiful. But he could barely turn away from you. Your power isn't just beauty. You smothered his will, making him adore you."

Delahunty regarded her with bright eyes, the sheen of sweat on her face, and Alix fell silent. Then:

That's not sweat! Alix tensed to leap forward out of her chair.

But here was *the* Caroline Delahunty again, standing beautiful, regal—more: *imperial*. The figure poised above them was unassailable, like a thunderstorm. Despite herself, Alix cringed back.

It's not real. You don't really feel this way! But her mind did not care, nor did her body. Her heart thundered inside her.

"No one takes from me," spat Delahunty, and Alix quailed. Whereas before she'd felt adoration, now it was a torrent of reverence. She gave out a strangled moan, and it was all she could do not to fall forward and grovel on the floor.

"Oh, no," said Farrier. She stood swiftly, her hand snatched out, there was another ripping sound, and more dream-stuff puddled to the floor. Alix felt a whiplash in her mind as her wonder was torn out of her.

The Lady of the Checquy, however, did not pause. She stepped forward, elegant in her gown and tiara of Whitby jet. Her hands still glistening with trailing strands of that stuff, she used rigid fingers to stab mercilessly at Delahunty's throat.

It was intended as a killing blow, or at least a seriously discommoding blow, and it would have been effective if not for the fact that Delahunty had been clutching her hands to her restripped face and took the brunt on her wrists.

Oh, my bloody hell! thought Alix weakly and a little incoherently. Delahunty looked at Farrier with disbelief. Alix herself felt some disbelief.

"You can't snare me in your tedious little delusions," said Farrier contemptuously, and she punched the actress in the stomach. Delahunty stumbled back, doubled over, and for a moment, it was the foul Caroline looking up at Farrier, furious. But whatever pain and shock she'd experienced, the actress shook it off, because she was already stepping back, straightening up, her beauty again unmarred. And now the entire room was unfocusing behind her, as rivulets of the substance rippled through the air and spread out around her.

The room was getting fuzzier, the walls fading away, and Delahunty drew back further, vanishing in the sudden greasy miasma that hung in the air. The room was darker, *much* darker. Waves of black mist washed around them. The walls had vanished, and Alix realized that she could no longer see Farrier standing near her.

"Lady Farrier?" she called out. She strained to hear an answer, but none came. *Where has she gone? Is she stalking Delahunty through this? What should I do?*

Alix was abruptly aware of a spreading wet coldness under her, and realized that, during the horrible overwhelming moment of awe, she'd wet herself. The chair was designed to be elegant, but also to effortlessly weather the passing of many thousands of distinguished bottoms. Accordingly, its cushion was impermeable and stain-resistant. The urine had puddled beneath her, and completely and visibly soaked the rear end of her cream-colored gown.

I am going to fucking smash her. She stood, stepping out of her heels, her gown pooling around her feet. She thought about summoning up her ability but dismissed it. She couldn't risk releasing it into the air— the cloud of her power would spread out without discrimination, just as likely to strike Farrier as Delahunty. Hell, it could pass easily through walls and smash into Pawn Larcher, any passing staff member, or the cream of British theater.

She moved forward, horribly aware of the rustling of her gown.

And then an eddy in the dark fog opened in front of her, and she could see Delahunty. The actress's back was to her, her hands clenched in fists, and she was looking about cautiously.

Gotcha. Alix lunged toward her enemy, just as the actress started to turn toward her. She tackled the older woman, and they crashed onto the floor.

Don't give her a chance to react! She'll boggle your emotions! Delahunty was struggling in her arms and was surprisingly strong, given her true, wasted form. Alix punched her awkwardly in the ribs, and as the actress wheezed, Alix moved into a new grip, placing her forearm on the blond woman's throat and pressing down.

I'm just subduing you. Putting you under. I won't kill you unless you give me a really good reason to.

Like resisting in any way.

The actress's face was wavering, and Alix felt a stab of satisfaction. *Losing control, are you?* The gorgeous features were liquid, bits spattering off as she writhed under Alix. Those magnificent eyes were unfocusing.

Almost there...

The features melted entirely, collapsing and pouring down like yogurt to reveal the face of Lady Farrier.

Alix snapped back in horror.

Is it her? Is this real? She was frozen, uncertain of what to think or do.

Alexandra.

A whisper in her mind, a thought so faint she wasn't certain it had happened at all. Except that it was not a thought in her own voice. She looked down at Farrier and her heart skipped a beat. The Lady was lying still, her eyes shut. Then she heard Farrier's voice again.

Alexandra, it said. *She is saturating the room with this stuff. It's letting her change the appearance of the place, but it also means that I can use my ability to talk to you through it, even with both of us awake. I don't think she can hear us.*

Her power produces both illusion and emotion. I can either dispel the illusion for you, or I can dispel the emotion. I can't do both, and it has to be the emotion, or you won't be able to act. You'll just be hers, and she could very well order you to kill me.

"Larcher?" Alix whispered, her lips barely moving.

I can only just block her effect on you. It's taking all my strength and focus. If Larcher comes in, she'll entrance him, and we absolutely can't have that. It has to be you.

So, you need to release me, and get her.

"Is she dead, then?" asked a voice from behind her. Alix turned her head and saw the regal figure of the actress. A blanket of reverence washed over Alix and then immediately ebbed away.

Farrier's intervention. Delahunty must think I'm on her side. So play the thrall until you can get your hands on her.

"Yes, ma'am," she said.

"Well done," said Delahunty. Despite herself, Alix felt a moment of pride thrill through her at the praise.

Alix stood up and took a step toward the still-beautiful but no longer divine Delahunty. Alix's dress was horribly soggy, and clamminess had seeped down the backs of her thighs.

"You know this place. Do you have any suggestions for how I can escape?" asked Delahunty.

"Well, ma'am...," she began, taking another step toward the actress. Delahunty regarded her, and her eyes landed on Alix's clenched fists.

Uh-oh.

Delahunty's brow furrowed, and the darkness closed in. Suddenly, red cords, like ropes or tentacles, lashed out at Alix from the ceiling and walls.

She flinched and flung her arms up to shield her face. There was no impact, of course. But it didn't matter that they weren't real. Her eyes and nervous system and millennia of evolution and years of training had insisted she defend herself. She took a step back, her body tensed for blows that never came. Then, as she looked up, Delahunty was there, right in front of her. Alix punched out and was sent stumbling as her fist passed through thin air.

Where is she? She looked about wildly, but there was no sign of Delahunty, just Farrier lying on the floor. *Did she escape? Is she invisible?*

There was a rustling to her side, the sound of expensive silk that hadn't been pissed on, and she tried to kick out at it, but her dress caught at her leg. *Dammit!* She was stumbling, trying to listen for sounds and keep her balance at the same time.

The shadows shifted dizzyingly, and for a moment, the floor pulsed and swelled like the belly of a beast breathing shallowly. Then it glistened as if covered in slime. She paused, hesitant to take a step.

She closed her eyes, straining to hear the clack of Delahunty's heels. The rustle of her dress. Her breath.

The faintest sound, away to her left, but then it was lost in the distant sound of applause as, down the hall, the dinner continued.

Then a hard pair of hands shoved her, *really* shoved her, from behind. She flailed forward, and her foot caught in her gown and sent her sprawling on the floor.

She twisted onto her back, and there was Delahunty coming down on her, her hands outstretched in the classic "I'm going to strangle you, preferably to death" posture.

But is she even really there?

Hard hands closed around her throat, surprisingly strong.

She's really there.

She could feel something on her face, warm and smooth for a moment, and then it slid greasily on her skin, stomach-turning as it smeared on her lips and cheeks. *She's pouring that stuff onto me! Into me!* The liquid was thick and slimy on her lips and she clamped her mouth shut. Then she choked and gagged as it welled up her nose.

The warm wetness in her nostrils brought a new, intense fear. *Is it seeping into my brain? Can Farrier block her power if it's inside me?* She strained to claw at the arms, to pull Delahunty off, but a rigid strength was holding her down.

Alix felt her thoughts growing fuzzy. There was a rushing in her ears. Her hands were heavy, and she felt them fall back to the ground.

Despite herself, her eyes fluttered open. The room seemed dimmer, smeared, so that all she could see in focus was the perfect face of Caroline Delahunty above her, her glorious eyes intent. She was a goddess, and to die at the hands of such majestic loveliness would be an honor...

Strike.

STRIKE!

Or you will be lost.

She summoned the dreadful energy from inside her. It boiled up into her throat and erupted out, through Delahunty's palms and fingers and into the foundations of her hands.

Alix felt the actress's phalanges, her finger bones, crack. She didn't feel it through her power, but as little reports against her neck.

Pop go the distals!

Pop go the middles!

POP go the proximals!

Delahunty screamed and went to pull away, but Alix's hands snapped up to grip her wrists.

Delahunty stared down at her. The beautiful mask wavered and oozed down.

I see you. The actress's eyes darted back and forth in panic. *And then we continue on down. From phalanges to metacarpals—the hand bones.* She could hear the bones snapping, even with Delahunty screaming and writhing in her grip. *And next the carpals.* The eight small bones of each wrist fractured beneath the gleeful chaos of Alix's power.

Delahunty wrenched herself away and sprawled on the floor in a puddle of silk. Alix was up on her knees, her right hand clenched into a fist. She was braced for another attack, but Delahunty could only curl up and cradle her shattered hands protectively.

The actress's real face was showing now, and whereas before she had looked dismal, she now looked dismal and exhausted. Whatever effort was needed to create the illusions saturating the room, it had taken a toll on her.

The beauty was already coming back, though. As Alix watched, the sheen layered itself onto the actress's face so that even through the pain and the wheezing for air, she was again becoming *the* Caroline Delahunty.

She restored her beauty first. Before she even thought of affecting me. It must be instinct. Or is it just the most important thing to her?

"Mondegreen, we can't take the chance of her entrapping anyone else who comes in," said Farrier behind her. The Lady was standing, and in her gown and black tiara she really was a figure out of dreams.

"Right," said Alix. "One move, one weird vision, and I'll snap your neck," she warned the whimpering actress. She put her arm around her opponent's neck and braced against the back of her head with her other arm. Delahunty writhed for a moment in panic as her carotid arteries were compressed, the flow of blood to her brain pincered, but she soon grew still. Farrier was standing over them, and she placed her fingers lightly on Delahunty's brow.

"Good," said the Lady. "She's truly unconscious." Alix released her grip. "I shall keep her under until someone can drug her appropriately. What *are* you doing?"

Alix was retching and scrubbing at her face. The sensation of that dream-stuff was fainter, but it was still stomach-turning. It was on her skin, clogging her throat and nostrils, but her hands were coming away clean.

"I can feel it on me!" She gagged and spat, but it was just clear spit on the floor. She snorted, and wiped her nose on the shoulder of her gown.

"Here," said Farrier. She reached out and drew a skein away from Alix's head. Alix could feel the stuff peeling off her and out of her nose and throat. "It's dissipating anyway, but hopefully this will make you feel better." She flicked her wrist and sent the material flying to land with a *splatch* on the floor. She regarded the unconscious Delahunty. "Fascinating, a power almost... adjacent to my own."

Alix took a deep, cleansing breath, resisted the urge to throw up, and got up off the floor. The two of them looked at the woman sprawled on the floor.

"That was very nicely done, Lady Mondegreen," said Farrier. "You've got real promise." Alix felt a flush of delight on her cheeks at the praise. Could this actually mean the possibility of eventual advancement, despite the lady-in-waiting thing?

After all, Lady Farrier had done it.

Then, a knock came on the door. They looked over.

"I told Larcher not to come in until we came out," said Farrier. "And to kill anyone if they came out without us." She raised her voice. "Who is it?"

"My lady," came Larcher's voice. "There is—"

He was broken off by the door flying open and a very firm-looking Louise marching in, trailed by a guilty-looking Larcher. Even if you were the strongest person in recorded history, you couldn't manhandle the crown princess. The princess took in the situation.

It was not a flattering tableau.

Illusions still hung about the room, so that the walls could not be seen for rippling darkness. The floor was mottled, as if it had been stained with slimy black mud.

Delahunty lay splayed and unconscious on the floor, with thrust-out hands that had obviously been vigorously mangled. Her aura of glamour had been shorn away, but her beautiful false visage was still intact.

Alix stood, slumped, with snot glistening brilliantly across her shoulder, bruising that she could feel rising on her face, and a massive wet patch across her rear.

Lady Farrier looked completely unmussed.

"What the *fuck*?"

Larcher shuffled in behind the princess and shut the door before any more outraged squawks summoned additional witnesses.

"Your Royal Highness," said Farrier, sounding as startled as Alix had ever heard her. "Hi!" Alix looked at her in astonishment. She had never in her life heard Farrier use that word. "We did not expect that you would be joining us." She paused. "How is the gala going?" she asked brightly.

At which point, with a sound like a gigantic sodden towel being flung on a bathroom floor, the illusions that coated the room all collapsed. Everyone jumped as the room brightened markedly. The walls were unmarred, but greasy dream-stuff lay mounded about in crumpled incriminating piles.

To her credit, Louise did not scream in terror. Her incredulous outrage seemed to counteract any fear.

"What in the hell is going on?" the princess demanded. "What is all this shit on the floors? Jesus *Christ*, is that Caroline Delahunty?"

"We felt it necessary to question Miss Delahunty here on suspicion of some ill intent." Farrier shrugged. She seemed to have regained her composure. "Matters escalated, and we were obliged to subdue her." She made it sound completely reasonable, despite the insane tableau around her.

"What did you *do* to her? Is she all right?"

"Yeah, she's fine," said Alix, with no certainty at all that she was, and no actual concern about the matter.

"Wait, what's happening to her?" Louise was peering at the unconscious woman.

Alix looked down to see that the actress's facade was sliding down off her head, like wet clay washing off a wall. As they watched, the veneer of beauty oozed down her cheek and slid onto the floor.

"That's not Delahunty," said Louise weakly.

"It really is," said Farrier.

"But her face... I mean, it just... It can't be her!" The princess peered a little more closely at the sprawled body, taking in the unmistakable dress and the even more unmistakable tiara. "What did you do to her?"

"That's what she really looks like," said Farrier.

The princess gaped at her. "It was a mask?"

"She was altering her appearance through occult means."

"Occult— You mean, like your little agency?" The princess looked at them in horror. "That's *real*?"

"Of course it's real," said Alix.

"I knew your ridiculous agency was real, but this is—this is— I mean *look at her*! And you said you investigated cults!"

"I said we dealt with the occult," said Alix.

"You said cults!" insisted Louise. "Like, I don't know, people with lots of children who only ever wear nightgowns."

"I said both. The occult *and* cults."

"No, you..." Louise seemed at a loss for words. She gestured at Delahunty. "What the *fuck*?"

"I'm sorry," said Alix. "I just—Okay. There are some things that don't make sense, and we deal with those things."

She looked over to Farrier, hoping that the head of the government's supernatural agency would step in and provide some sort of helpful, official, presumably long-established explanation, but the Lady just gave a small nod for Alix to continue. She seemed perfectly happy with this being the pawn's problem.

"Things that don't make sense?" repeated Louise incredulously. "What are you *talking* about?" It was clear that Louise was reeling from what she'd just seen. Alix felt a hint of pity for her and remembered that some care should probably be taken when stripping away someone's understanding of the universe.

"There isn't always a scientific explanation for everything," Alix said. "And that goes for people as well. Like her." She nodded at the unconscious Delahunty, who chose that moment to give a faint moan and roll over onto her side to vomit on the floor. Louise's eyes almost bugged out of her face.

"Speaking of *her*," said Farrier, and she knelt down to rest a finger momentarily on the actress's cheek. Delahunty subsided back to sleep, and the Lady wiped her hand on the prone woman's dress. "Before we have this conversation, we really ought to make arrangements about getting her out of here." She looked at her watch. "And also, Your Royal Highness, you have a reception to host."

"You want me to go back? After seeing all this?"

"Questions will be asked. Your absence will be noted."

"I'm allowed to go to the toilet," said Louise testily. "That's where I told them I was going."

"If you take too long, even more unpleasant questions will be asked."

"But what are you going to do with her?"

"We'll take care of her," said Farrier calmly. "You can put the word about that she had to leave, that she wasn't feeling well. Your Highness, you must go back, finish dinner, and then go into the state room for coffee and handmade petits fours." At the mention of petits fours, Alix's stomach, which hadn't even had the opportunity to try the fish course, growled loudly. "When everyone's left, we'll explain everything."

"Fine," said Louise uncertainly. She took a final look at Delahunty. "That's what she really looks like?"

"Yes," said Farrier.

"Blimey." She bit her lip. "Fa's not going to be best pleased."

Fa was *not* best pleased.

The King had been sitting in the residence, expecting a visit from an entrancing actress for a drink and then to see where the evening took them. Alix didn't want to make any assumptions, but the King was not wearing a necktie.

Their arrival alone would have been enough to whiplash the King's mood, but their appearance did nothing to ameliorate the situation. Farrier, of course, looked fine. Alix, however, had been obliged to shower hurriedly in the security section's locker room, and emerged to find that all there was to wear was a wadded-up track suit scrounged from someone's locker—the work clothes she had arrived in had already been couriered home. Her horrendously expensive damp gown was scrunched up in a garbage bag and had been handed off to an incredulous pawn.

Her appearance was made even more demented by the fact that she was still wearing her high heels and the somewhat askew tiara, since there hadn't been time for a hairdresser to unravel it from her hair.

At first, the King had stood, worried that they had come to advise him of some national emergency, or that something had happened to Louise. Then, when Farrier explained, "No, it was nothing like that. But I'm afraid, sir, that there has been a problem with Miss Caroline Delahunty. She was acting in a way likely to cause problems for you, and we've had to remove her from the palace," his expression changed. His cheeks flushed. He was discomfited and embarrassed, then angry.

Despite herself, Alix took a couple of steps backward as the King's voice grew louder.

"I must say, Linda, that this is absolutely no business of yours! I appreciate that you have a continued security role, but when it comes to whom I choose to meet in a personal situation, lines need to be drawn!"

"I quite agree, sir," said Farrier. "However, we uncovered certain facts that place Miss Delahunty's actions firmly within our bailiwick."

"That's preposterous!" snorted the King. "The lady is a renowned, world-famous artist, not some sort of gorgon. What on earth could she have to do with the Checquy? And what do you mean she's been removed? Did you at least call her a car?"

"Not precisely," said the Lady. "We've drugged her into a coma with a cocktail of barbiturates, and she's currently in a straitjacket, shackles, and muzzle, packed in a vinyl duffel bag in the back of a truck, and being transported to a fortified facility in Shoreditch for examination."

"My God!" The King actually staggered back a little as the parameters of the disaster shifted abruptly.

Thank God she didn't mention that I broke Delahunty's hands and choked her into unconsciousness. The shock might kill him.

"Your Majesty, I apologize—I should have been clearer. Caroline Delahunty was using supernatural abilities to manipulate people's perception of her. We suspect she has been doing this for the entirety of her acting career, and possibly before." The Lady laid out photographs of the unconscious and unglamoured version of Delahunty. They'd been hurriedly printed out in the Checquy's little palace office. "This is what she really looks like."

The King's hands shook a little as he lifted up one photo.

"So you're saying she is some sort of shapeshifter?"

"The mechanics are uncertain, sir," said Farrier. "But certainly, the face you saw, the face everyone has seen, was not her real face."

"But she was magnificent! Not just to look at, but to talk with. Charming and fascinating..." He trailed off.

"The emotions you experienced were also not genuine," said Farrier gently. "She impelled you to feel them."

"How can it not be real?" His face was red again, but now he was vulnerable, bewildered, and ashamed.

"I understand how you feel, your Majesty," said Alix. "When we confronted her, she overwhelmed me completely with adoration. I was ready to be her slave. If she'd told me to kill Lady Farrier or myself, I think I would have. But it wasn't real. It was all her power."

"I can't believe this," said the King. "I've read about this sort of thing in your reports, but I never expected to be confronted with it in my own home." He rubbed his brow. "And what would she have done, if we—if she had come up here?"

"I think we can all guess what her intentions were," said Lady Farrier.

You'd probably have a meaningless conversation which you'd have found enthralling, and then you'd have had the best sex anyone's ever had. Or at least you'd think you did, which is almost as good.

"Do you think this might be related to what happened to Edmund?" the King asked weakly. Alix felt a shock. It hadn't even occurred to her.

"We've seen no evidence of any connection, sir," said Farrier. "We'll be questioning her, however, once she's in our secure holding facility. A thorough interrogation should get us the full story."

"And then what will happen to her? Will you execute her?" asked the King. Alix and Lady Farrier exchanged glances. Killing an opponent in battle was one thing, but the Checquy was not in favor of cold-blooded executions of people with supernatural capabilities.

After all, there but for the grace of God and the Checquy goes any one of us. Some entities and people were, of course, too dangerous to be kept alive, and some especially heinous crimes brought the Checquy's death penalty. But a complicated trial system was in place to protect the accused, and judges tended toward the merciful side of the scales.

Ironically, operatives of the Checquy were far more likely to suffer the death penalty than those they confronted. Treason or abuse of power (supernatural *or* bureaucratic) brought as brisk an execution as could be arranged, the general sentiment being that if you were in the Checquy, you ought to know better.

"It's clear that she cannot continue to move about in society," said Farrier. "That could very well mean that we'll need to implement a fake death."

"But not an actual death," said the King.

"We'll let circumstances guide us," said Farrier.

"There is no question that what she has done is illegal. Even if she proves not to have murdered my son, this—this *person* used supernatural abilities to subvert my will," said the King tightly. "It's like she drugged me!"

"Your Majesty, I understand your outrage," said Lady Farrier.

"This occurred in my home! In the presence of my family! It was an attack, not just against me as a person but against my position as sovereign." His fists clenched. "I know what effect she had. I can still feel it."

"You feel the memory of it," said Farrier. "The intensity will fade. I detect no trace of her power left in you."

"And if it had continued?" demanded the King. "If she had continued to lay down those false emotions, layer over layer?"

The answer was obvious. The King would have come to adore her with a mindless devotion. He would have been her slave. At the very least, she would have lived a life of guaranteed luxury and ease. But she would also have gained unfettered access to the most powerful people in the land. She could even have become queen.

"That's why you have us," said Farrier.

"Oh? To protect me? And my family?" The two women were silent.

"You'll be kept abreast of all developments," Farrier said finally. "Your Majesty."

"You may leave."

Outside, the two women stood for a moment.

"That was *horrible*," Alix said weakly.

"It was not good," agreed Farrier. She dabbed at her forehead with a handkerchief.

"I want to go home, shower, have a stiff drink, and go to bed," Alix said.

"You can't," said Farrier. "We need to go talk to the princess."

"Oh, God. Right. Well, I really need to get something to eat first."

18

The gala had wound down by that point, with Louise and her remaining ladies having quietly made their exit and the guests departing. Alix had expected that she and the others would sit with Louise, drink cocktails (although not as many as the last time), and discuss how the night had gone. But instead, she received a text message from Siti telling her that Louise was in one of the palace's innumerable staterooms, the Little Eastern Sky-Blue Room, waiting for her and Lady Farrier.

Alix, of course, knew exactly where it was. An exquisite jewel box of a space, it was ideal for a delicious afternoon tea between world leaders and their spouses, or for two women to explain to a third that her understanding of the world was a lie, and that all around her were horrendous forces that defied rational thought and logic.

"How are we going to do this?" asked Alix. "What do we say?"

"We tell her the truth," said Farrier. "Carefully."

Louise sat alone in the darkness. She turned to look at the two of them as they curtsied.

"You can turn the lights up, if you like," she said.

"Maybe just a little," said Alix. Her head hurt, and she could feel the ache from using her powers. A dimly lit room was just what she needed.

"Did you speak to my father?"

"Yes, Your Royal Highness," said Farrier. "He is aware of everything."

"How did he take it?"

"It was difficult for him," said the Lady. "I would recommend that you not bring it up with him."

"I wouldn't know what to say! I would need to know what happened, but we can get to that later. First, obviously, I need to know about you people. What you really are."

"Entirely reasonable," said Farrier, settling herself down in a chair and arranging her skirts around her. For a moment, Alix wondered if *she* should sit without permission, and then, thankfully, the princess gestured toward a chair.

"Alix," said Louise. "*You* tell me."

Alix looked to her commander, who nodded.

"Okay," said Alix. She regarded Louise, her friend, for all the distance that had grown between them. Farrier probably had a prepared speech, one carefully calculated both to intimidate and to create loyalty to the idea of the Checquy. It would invoke all the hidden magic of the British Isles, the centuries of service, the continued dangers that brave people fought secretly every day.

Fuck it. She stretched out and kicked off her heels.

"There are people," Alix began, "who can do things we can't explain. We don't know why it happens, or how. It defies all scientific explanation, so it might as well be called magic."

"All right," said Louise dubiously.

"Now, even if you're a relatively pleasant person, well, that kind of power might be intoxicating. Maybe you don't question it, but maybe you start thinking about the implications. It wouldn't actually be unreasonable to think that you're something of a god. And if you're something of a god, then the rules of mortals don't apply to you." Louise was staring at her with wide eyes. "You can hurt normal people—steal from them, dominate them—and they cannot stop you. They're not even going to believe what's being done to them. Which is why people like us are needed, who will believe the impossible and be able to do something about it. It's maybe the highest secret in the land."

"So you and Linda and this Checquy Group fight these people, like this 'hypothetical' person you just described, or Caroline Delahunty tonight?"

"Yes," said Alix.

"What kinds of abilities do people have?" asked the princess. "Give me an example." Alix flailed about for a moment, suddenly unable to think of anything, despite the fact that the vast majority of her acquaintances fit the bill. Then:

"Like, a child who finds that, with a touch, she can break people's bones."

"So, she's strong?" asked Louise.

"No, not with her muscles. She can release a force that will travel into a person's body. She's like a battery for an electricity that can cause fractures, or snap bones like twigs." Alix took a breath. "Or even worse."

"And what do you do with someone like that?" asked Louise warily. "A little girl?"

"Six years old," said Alix. "A sweet little thing in pigtails, and a danger to everyone around her."

"Yes, but, you can't hold a six-year-old responsible for her actions. You can't just..." She trailed off. "What *did* you do with Caroline Delahunty?"

"She has been taken into custody," said Farrier. "We will evaluate her and decide what is to be done."

"I can't believe it about her. She was so amazing, just breathtaking, and then what I saw on the floor..." Louise looked at Farrier. "It wasn't just her looks, was it?"

"No, she manipulated people's minds," said the Lady. "Can you see why we could not permit her to continue to use her abilities on people?"

"Yes...," said Louise. "But what about this six-year-old girl? What would you do with her?"

"You can't expect normal parents to know how to bring up such a child," said Alix. *You certainly can't expect massively self-centered parents to do it.* "She might, at any time, without meaning to, harm or even kill another person. School is out of the question. She can't even walk down the street without being a risk to everyone around her." Louise nodded.

"But that's not the only problem," continued Alix relentlessly. "This little girl reveals a flaw in everyone's understanding of the world. Humans can't do that sort of thing, everyone knows that. But *she* can. She's a question with no answer," said Alix. "And the public doesn't do well with that. They never have. Just think about what they used to do to people they thought were witches."

"Yeah, but the world is more tolerant now," objected Louise.

"Maybe," said Alix. "Maybe they won't burn her at the stake, or hang her, like they did in the old days, but the news will travel like a plague. The Internet will catch fire from its undeniable insanity and its undeniable truth.

"If society learns about this inexplicable little girl, people will come up with their own theories — anything for their world to make sense again. They'll blame the government, or other countries, or an ethnicity or religion. They'll call her a gift from God or sent by the devil. They'll say it's the result of corporate vaccines, or polluted water. They'll fight with each other. They'll come for the girl, either to destroy her or to use her. Everything will be destabilized by one little girl. And then... can you imagine if it was revealed that there are more like her? Many more? Each one unique and inexplicable?"

"So you keep her, and people like her, a secret," Louise said.

Alix looked back at her seriously. "Maybe the highest secret in the land."

"My God. The people in your Checquy are also these... inexplicables," said Louise.

"Some, yes," said Alix. "They're found, kept safe, and taught to control themselves and protect others."

"There's an organization of supernatural operatives working in the civil service," said Louise. "That's insane."

"It absolutely is," agreed Alix.

"How long have *you* been with the Checquy, then?"

"Since I was six years old." Louise was looking at her with horror as the penny dropped. "Just a sweet little thing in pigtails."

The room was silent for a moment.

"Lady Farrier, please leave us," said Louise tightly.

"Your Royal Highness...," began Farrier.

"Leave us." Louise's eyes never moved from Alix, as the Lady stood, curtsied, and left. "Six years old," the princess said. It was impossible to read her expression, but she was speaking through clenched teeth, which did not bode well. "You're her."

"Yes."

"Had we even *met* then?" Alix shook her head. "So you've been keeping this insane secret from me all my life!" Louise was suddenly shouting. "Did my parents know?"

"Yes," said Alix. "They knew. Well, your father did. My abilities and my position in the Checquy were why our families were brought together. The powers that be wanted us to know each other."

"Why?"

"For *this*!" Alix exclaimed, waving at the room. "For tonight! So there could be a Checquy presence to protect you and your family. You weren't the only one who was groomed all her life for a job that she maybe didn't really want, you know."

"Were you ever really my friend?" asked Louise bitterly. "Or were you just assigned to me right from the beginning? Just another piece of the machine!"

"You think I've had an agenda since I was seven?" demanded Alix. She was yelling too. "You think I played with you, and told you about my secret crushes on celebrities—and that one footman—just so you'd trust me? I was a little kid, like you! I had a secret to keep, yes, but it wasn't just from you! It was from everyone!"

The princess had paused, startled by the vehemence of Alix's outrage. Alix was a little startled herself, but it was a wave she didn't feel like stopping.

"I realize this may be a difficult concept for you, but you aren't the center of my life, Louise!" She realized that she was standing over the princess. She took a deep breath.

"But you *are* my friend," she said. "Or you *were,* until you started acting like everything that's happened these past weeks was my choice, and I was doing it to use you. Instead of seeing that I had even less choice in it than you did!" She shook her head. "It's not your fault, but when you took Edmund's place, it meant that I had to do this. But I care about you. I worry about your happiness. I always have. So, of course I'm your friend." She took a few steps back and sat heavily in her chair.

"Oh," said Louise in a small voice.

"Look, we might never have met if you weren't a princess. But we also wouldn't have met if I weren't the way I am. And I wasn't under instructions to try to be your friend. They had enough sense not to do that, at least. I had to be nice, and polite, and not mention the Checquy, and not use my powers. But I happened to like you that first day." She smiled ruefully. "And almost every other day since."

"And the fact that I was a princess?" asked Louise, almost desperate.

"I was a little disappointed that you weren't wearing a big pink dress and a crown." Alix shrugged. "But after that, it didn't matter. You didn't even have especially good toys." The two of them smiled cautiously at each other.

"So you can break people's skeletons?" asked Louise. To Alix's immense relief, the princess was not regarding her with fear or loathing.

"Yeah," said Alix. "But I'm not going to demonstrate it."

"Do you have any other secrets?"

"I have a metric fuck-ton of secrets," said Alix. "And I can't tell you all of them."

"I won't hold that against you."

You say that now.

Coiled in the back of her mind was the knowledge that Louise was still a suspect in her brother's murder. But despite herself, Alix smiled. Tonight had been worth the danger and pain if her friend could now look at her, know the truth about her and the Checquy, and still smile back.

Alix and Louise talked for hours, although she had to be cautiously selective. She didn't mention Odette's true nature, and of course, there was absolutely no talk of Edmund's murder. But she explained about her own life and told quite a few war stories. It wasn't always amusing; a few tears were shed by both of them.

Throughout, she was watching Louise carefully, partly to evaluate how the information was hitting her — if it was breaking her mind — and partly to catch any indication that the princess knew about the supernatural and could have used it to bring about her brother's death. It was a hideous tightrope walk that left her exhausted, but she saw nothing but a friend who was learning that the world was ten thousand times stranger than she had ever imagined.

Still, it felt like a tremendous weight had been lifted off Alix's shoulders, and it wasn't from revealing the truth about herself and the Checquy. It was from having Louise thaw, and no longer look at her with resentment, suspicion, and contempt.

When they emerged, it was the wee hours of the morning, and Lady Farrier was seated in a chair in the hallway. The Lady appeared to be drowsing, but a moment after the door opened, she opened her eyes and stood.

"All right?" she asked.

"I think we're fine," said Louise. "Although I have some questions... But not now. When we're all better rested."

"Of course," said Farrier.

Louise and Alix sat quietly while the bleary-eyed hairdresser (who had to be earning quadruple overtime) unraveled the tiaras from their hair, and a waiting maid placed them in velvet cases to be locked away. Louise said good night, hugged Alix tightly, and withdrew.

"She seems fine," said Farrier, who was still wearing her tiara and probably had some hapless maid waiting up at home to remove it. "Not distraught. I'm sure you did a fine, tactful job. Still, I'll monitor her dreams for the next few nights. First thing in the morning, write up the details of your briefing to the princess and send the report to my office."

"Right," said Alix wearily. It wouldn't be too difficult—she'd had her smartwatch recording the entire conversation to her phone.

"After that, I'll need your write-up on Caroline Delahunty, to fold into my report."

They walked to the courtyard, where their cars were waiting to take them home. Alix crumpled down into the back seat and raised the privacy screen. She was so tired that it took her trembling hand two tries to dial the number she needed.

"Nicky? Your sister knows about the Checquy. Yeah, I told her. She may need someone to talk to tomorrow."

Just a few hours later, Alix was roused from sleep by her alarm, which had apparently been screaming bloody murder for some time. She was still in her scrounged track suit, having collapsed facedown onto the bed as soon as she got home. One high heel dangled from a foot.

Even though she was running late, still completely exhausted, with a face that throbbed abominably, and a body and mind that felt like they'd been run over a few times by a station wagon, she felt a hundred times better about everything. The relief of remembering that her friend was no longer mad at her was like a mouthful of caramel.

It was replaced with a panic that hit her like an unexpected mouthful of anchovy paste as she realized exactly how late she was. There was enough time to get to the investigation's morning meeting, *just*, if she flung herself into the shower right that very moment for a lick and a promise, skipped brushing her teeth, skipped coffee, and was willing to spend the money on a taxi. The prospect of Smith's disapproval was enough to justify all those tactics, and seven minutes later, she was in the street, hair wet, still buttoning her shirt as she waved down a cab.

The cabby didn't remark on her mildly bedraggled appearance, although he did give her a couple of wary looks in the mirror.

When she hustled into the investigation office, panting, hair pulled back in a Croydon facelift, there were actually two minutes before the meeting started, and everyone was either getting their notes together or checking their emails.

At the meeting, Alix recounted the details of the previous evening. There were shocked gasps when she revealed the beloved identity of the manifestation, and even more shocked gasps when she showed them photos of the actress *sans* glamour.

"Do you think it may be related to the prince's death?" asked Smith.

"Nothing she said indicated that," admitted Alix, "but her abilities and her focus on the King mean that it's got to be a possibility."

"According to the overnight briefing, Delahunty will be undergoing interrogation later today," said Smith.

I wonder how the Liars will manage her vanishing, Alix thought. In her memory, the Liars had successfully covered up all manner of manifestations, including the abrupt disappearance of a small military installation in Powys. But then again, Davis Barracks hadn't had a social media following of several million waiting eagerly for an update and an artfully posed casual shot of a humble but beautiful breakfast.

"Hopefully, she'll provide some useful answers," said Smith. "Still, the way this investigation's been going, I'm not going to rely on it. Mondegreen, throw Delahunty's name up on the board and check through her history for any potential connection to Ian Blanch."

Alix added this to her mental to-do list. She'd have to write her reports for Lady Farrier first.

When Alix advised that Louise was now aware of the Checquy's nature, there were some sucked-in breaths around the table. Sweven, of course, had his lips pursed like a cat's ass, but the older pawns seemed unimpressed.

"What was her reaction?" asked Scagell. "How easily did she accept it?"

"She was presented with quite compelling evidence. But she was definitely shaken."

"That's good to know," said Scagell. "It makes the possibility of her having hired a supernatural assassin seem less likely."

"I thought you said it was probably a crazy person with a pattern," said Alix.

"Yeah, well, we can't throw out any theories."

At this, Smith slammed her hand down loudly on the conference table, and everyone jumped.

"I don't think any of you appreciate just how badly this investigation is going," she said tightly. Six pairs of eyes widened. "So, I will take this opportunity to tell you. It is a matter of significant concern that we are not making any progress." There were noises of protest around the table. "You're working hard, I appreciate that. And we are gathering information, yes. Weller and her team have produced reams of financial data. We have traced the prince's every movement in the weeks leading up to his death. We've delved into the complete and, I'm sorry to say, extremely boring life story of Ian Blanch. We've scrutinized every email and text message that each of the victims sent in the past two years. We've interviewed their immediate family, friends, and the people they worked with. And we have nothing! No clues, no leads."

She cleared her throat. "All of this nothing has been noted. You know the forces at play here, and they are not happy." Alix thought of the King's rage on the day of Edmund's funeral, the way he'd shouted. She'd never seen him that way. "We need results. So, if it seems like I'm clutching at straws, it's because I am. Because if it turns out that a world-famous actress *isn't* responsible for the murder of the Prince of Wales, and we don't come up with something soon, then life is going to become very uncomfortable for us." She looked around at the team. "All right? Then move."

They moved.

The morning sun was dappling in through the leaves of the tree outside her bedroom window, and Alix floated sleepily in the happy knowledge that it was Sunday morning, which meant that she could nestle back down into her bed and sleep in before eventually migrating to the couch with a coffee, idly reading the papers, showering, meeting up with friends who were neither Checquy nor aristocrats for brunch, maybe taking in a new exhibit at an art gallery, and *then* going into the office to do work.

The phone rang. It was her sister calling, which had never happened before.

"Frances? What's wrong?"

"Nothing's wrong," said Frances. "I'm in town for the day—a few of us took the train—and I thought you and I could catch up."

"Oh." *That would be a pleasant, normal thing to do.* "Yes, that sounds pleasant and normal."

"What?"

"Sounds lovely," said Alix hastily. "Where are you?"

"In the café across the street from your flat."

That sounds less normal. When she arrived there twenty minutes later, mildly wary, she found that Frances looked equally wary. *But maybe this is a reasonable way to feel. We're both figuring out how this works. And it's nice that she wanted to see me.*

"This is a nice surprise," said Alix. "The school just lets you come to London?" She was fairly certain Frances was eighteen, but this seemed like more freedom than Alix could recall from her own school days.

"We signed out for the day, and sneakily caught the train."

"Very cunning."

"Yeah, the other girls are shopping, but I thought I'd come see you."

"I'm glad," said Alix, and meant it, although she could sense that there was something else coming. "So school is going well?" Frances nodded. "Good."

They sat silently for what felt like a few decades.

"And this is your final year?" Frances nodded. "And then off to... university?" Frances nodded. "Do you know what you want to study?"

"That was something I wanted to talk to you about, actually," said Frances. Alix could feel her eyebrows rising and, with an effort, lowered them. This had a "big sister talk" vibe, something in which she had no experience.

"Okay," she said. "I didn't go to university, you know."

"Yes, but I thought you might be able to give me some advice about money." Frances flushed. "I was talking to Mummy the other day, and I mentioned my plans for next year—and how I was thinking about going to study in America—and she just sort of remarked, almost in passing, that she wouldn't be paying for university for any of us, that there wouldn't be any money beyond secondary school."

Alix winced. The Checquy had paid the younger girls' school fees as part of their effort to legitimize the Mondegreens' connection to the royal family. They were not, however, prepared to fund them forever. If Alix had ever given it any thought, she'd have presumed that her mother, who was well aware of the situation, would have made preparations.

But of course she hasn't, Alix thought. She could picture her mother blithely dropping this bombshell on her second-oldest daughter and utterly failing to see why it might be a problem.

"Do Cecily and Lillian know about this?"

"I don't think so," said Frances. "I haven't told them. I don't know how to. And you know Mummy—she doesn't talk about money. But it's not like she, or Daddy when he was alive, were about *saving*. Money was always just sort of there, but I suppose it isn't, really. But *you've* got a job. It must be a good one, if they're sending you helicopters, and you've bought your place."

"Oh, it's not my place," lied Alix hurriedly. "Work provides it." Which wasn't true, but the implications of having spent a vast amount of money on a flat had suddenly hit her.

It was no surprise that her parents hadn't taken any steps toward helping their daughters. But Alix had never given it a moment's thought. She'd had her own problems, and a life that consumed everything.

"Okay, but you must know *something*," Frances was saying. "How one goes about getting loans. Like, can you introduce me to your bank manager?" She spread her hands helplessly, and Alix was stuck with an immense sense of pity and guilt. She'd always envied her sisters their freedom. They could be anything, they didn't have their futures foretold for them. But they also hadn't had the support and guidance of the Checquy.

"Well," said Alix, "to qualify for loans I think you need collateral.

Our family has the Towers, and some of the surrounding lands, but there's a sizable debt on the estate." She paused. "Daddy took out some loans." Frances winced. "The money coming in just about services that debt, and it will probably be paid off in about fifteen years, but if we sold now, we'd maybe have enough money for you to go to university, *maybe*. But not Cecily and Lillian." There was a silence as they both considered this grim reality.

"Of course. I'm sorry," said Frances to the table. "I shouldn't have bothered you." She flushed. "I feel stupid and useless."

"You're obviously not stupid or useless," said Alix quickly. "I'm not quite sure how it works either. But I will investigate." Frances looked up. "I'll talk to a financial advisor. We'll discuss where you want to go and find out how much it costs," Alix said. "We'll see what we can't figure out."

"If you're sure," said Frances, brightening slightly.

"Absolutely, I'm sure," Alix said. She smiled a shy little smile at her sister, who smiled a shy little smile back. She raised her cup of tea. "To your future."

After breakfast, they actually hugged goodbye, and then Frances, looking a little less worried, went off to meet her friends.

When Alix arrived at the office, she found Chuah, Padilla, and Smith already there.

"Are Claes and Scagell in yet?" Alix asked. Weller and Sweven had taken the weekend to go home. Pawn Smith had instituted a rota of weekends off, partly to blow the cobwebs out and partly so that people could see their families.

"Scagell is at lunch with a couple of civilian forensic psychologist friends," Padilla said. "He's going to very casually run some ideas about the killer's M.O. by them, and see what they suggest."

"Claes is still at church," said Chuah. "She goes to some insanely old Flemish institution tucked away in Bethnal Green. Apparently it's the closest she's been able to find to the church she grew up in."

"Nice," said Alix. She nodded to Smith as the team leader emerged from her office. "Any news?"

"The results from Delahunty's interrogation," Smith said. "She wasn't involved in the prince's death. Or Blanch's. In fact, she nearly had a nervous breakdown when we opened the subject."

"And we believe her?" asked Alix.

"Doc Crisp had his fingers on her pulse the whole time," Smith said with a shrug. "We also had a conventional lie detector hooked up to her, and Marcel Leliefeld put some sort of eel around her neck to monitor her."

"So, what was her deal, then?"

"No outside power involved, no foreign government or shadow organization trying to gain a foothold in Buckingham Palace. Just an individual who has used her supernatural abilities to get ahead and saw an opportunity to upgrade her lifestyle."

"What will be done with her now?" Chuah asked.

"She can't be released," said Smith. "She knows too much, and she's guilty of a serious crime. So, imprisonment, at least for the immediate future. They've removed her to Gallows Keep." This was the prison the Checquy maintained in Scotland. Almost as remote as Wyndham Towers, it was probably the most mercilessly secure place in the British Isles.

"And in the long run?" Alix asked. Smith shrugged.

"That's not for you and me to decide."

"But not execution," said Alix.

"I doubt it." There were centuries-old laws that allowed for the execution of captured manifestations, but nowadays, unless they represented a clear and present threat, the Checquy tended not to kill human detainees. "Perhaps there's room for rehabilitation. She's not well, not at all. But if she lives long enough, who knows? She could end up working for us."

"The King won't be happy with that," Alix said.

Smith was about to reply when they heard her office phone ring. She went inside, they heard some hushed talk, and then the team leader emerged, looking shocked.

"We have a third victim."

★ ★ ★

The third victim, Alfred "Alfie" Rohmer, was twenty-seven years old, of African-Caribbean descent, a resident of London, and already known to Alix. This did not represent a startling connection that might unravel the whole damn mystery, since he was also known to the vast majority of the United Kingdom, and to a sizable segment of the rest of the world.

Alfie Rohmer was a professional footballer, striker for the Premier League club Oakmead Maulstick. Born to a working-class family, Rohmer had accumulated wins and glories for his team and himself. He had brought the Maulers the Cup, and he had won both the Premier League and FIFA's Golden Boot. Even if you didn't particularly care about football (and Alix was more of a show jumping and ice hockey girl herself), it was generally agreed that to watch him play was to witness a thing of beauty.

In addition to his phenomenal skills, Rohmer gave every impression of being a lovely chap who always played a good, clean (if somewhat intense) game, having never received a yellow or red card. For two years, he'd been dating a music teacher who was a friend of his sister's, and there had been no hint of trouble in his personal life, not even when he was out drinking with his teammates. He spoke to the nation about the importance of keep-fit and staying in school.

He was, quite simply, beloved. A national icon.

And now he was lying dead on a table in the morgue of the Rookery, his body covered with a sheet up to his shoulders, his eyes closed, the top of his head removed, and the incriminating little stone spike of a cube's corner poking out from the top of his glistening brain.

"I really can't believe this," said Chuah.

"Did you think the murders were going to stop?" asked Alix.

"No, but this is different. This is *Alfie Rohmer!*" He shook his head. "I never thought I'd be in the same room as him. And now I'm looking at him and he's a victim! A *Checquy* victim!"

"Where did he die?" asked Alix.

"At his flat," said Smith. "Enjoying a quiet morning at home with the girlfriend, and just suddenly dead in bed."

"Did he have a connection to the prince?" Padilla asked Alix.

"I don't believe so. They might have met. I mean, Edmund attended every football cup final and England match. And Rohmer's team won the Cup, so maybe they met afterward and he congratulated them. But I don't think they were closely involved in any charities or anything. I'll check."

"Will they announce that it was a murder?" asked Padilla. "Like they did for Mr. Blanch?"

"It would spark a national seizure," said Smith. A horrible part of Alix's mind wondered if the murder of a football star would cause a bigger fuss than the murder of the Prince of Wales. "A public investigation would draw too much attention," Smith continued, "so we'll have to announce it as an accident or natural causes again. Which is going to make the investigation a good deal more difficult."

Claes entered the room. A car had fetched her from church, and she was dressed in stern but excellent black clothes, with a hat, an air of irritation, and extremely good perfume.

"How was church?" asked Chuah.

"We were only two hours into the homily," she said sourly. "And then some pawn was tapping me on the shoulder. Everyone looked very disapproving as I left."

"I'm sorry," said Smith. "Duty calls."

"It wasn't a terribly good sermon anyway," said Claes. "Standards have slipped over the centuries." She shook her head. Then she regarded the body of Alfie Rohmer and sighed. "So, another. I shall commence the examination."

"Meanwhile," said Smith, "I've paged Scagell and dispatched him to go to Crampton Hospital and interview Rohmer's girlfriend. She's still there, laboring under the misapprehension that skilled surgeons are doing their utter best to save his life."

The group stared at the corpse, which was as dead as it was possible to be without being a paste.

"The rest of you, get the equipment ready to go to Rohmer's home to begin the site investigation. Once we've gotten everything together and I've called the King to let him know about this, we'll depart."

"You're calling the King?" asked Alix.

"Mondegreen, it was made very clear to me—*very* clear—that the King wants to be apprised of developments as they happen," said Smith tiredly. "Another murder definitely qualifies."

"Alexandra, will you take the quokka, please?" asked Claes. "He's in his bed under my desk, and he is most comfortable with you."

"Certainly," said Alix, rather pleased at being *someone's* favorite.

Right, everyone ready?" asked Smith from the door of the Box Room. Everyone was. Bags were packed and the quokka was in its crate. "Good. A courier will meet us there with the keys and the alarm code."

"Were there any problems at the hospital?" asked Alix.

"Just emotional ones," said Smith.

At the hospital, Scagell had gently explained to the bereaved music teacher girlfriend that her boyfriend had died and that the cause of death was not yet ascertained. There *was* a possibility that he had encountered some sort of toxic substance, and so the residence had to be investigated as soon as possible. The girlfriend shakily handed over her keys and the alarm code, and one Checquy car and driver was ferrying them to the flat, while another was standing by to take the girlfriend to her parents' house.

Scagell had prevailed on both the girlfriend and the authorities not to announce Rohmer's death immediately, to avoid giving rise to rumors that might harm the man's legacy. When the public heard about a young footballer dying, they automatically assumed violence, drink, or drugs. This gag order meant that not even the man's family would be informed of his death. It was a cruel strategy, but it bought the team time to conduct their investigation of the premises.

Miraculously, no word of the footballer's hospitalization had trickled out, despite the fact that he had been seen by paramedics, emergency room doctors, and presumably his building security guard. It was the sort of thing that gave Alix a little bit of faith in humanity. It also gave the Liars some time to concoct a cause of death that would not raise any specter of murder, let alone a connection to the other victims.

"We'll need to work smartly," Smith said now. "When word gets out, there will be hordes of press around the place, to say nothing of bereaved fans." The team hustled down the hallway, but then Smith's phone rang. "Wait," she said. "Hello?" She sounded puzzled. "I'm sorry, could you repeat tha—" and then she dropped the phone.

"Oh!" exclaimed Alix, Chuah, and Padilla as the phone hit the floor. But Smith did not reach down, just stood there.

"Pawn Smith?" asked Alix uncertainly. "Are you all right?" The duffel bags slid off the team leader's shoulders, and she turned to them unsteadily. "What's happened?" She saw that the pawn's eyes had rolled back in her head and her eyelids were fluttering.

"Is she having a seizure?" whispered Padilla.

Smith's body jerked once, twice.

Then, with a sound like several hundred sides of beef being simultaneously ripped in half, the team leader transformed into a stegosaurus.

19

Holy... bloody... fucking..., thought Alix dazedly, her stunned brain apparently incapable of recalling any nouns with which to complete her thought.

The transformation itself had been practically instantaneous. There was a moment's blurred glimpse of expanding mass. Alix had a fleeting impression of clothes being shredded and flung away.

And then there was the undeniable and bewildering bulk of a stegosaurus in front of them. They had little mental bandwidth to take in the spectacle, however, because the abrupt existence of a stegosaurus brought with it various implications beyond the philosophical.

For one thing, the walls burst away instantly in a flying mass of dust and rubble.

Meanwhile, the creature's double row of back plates had scythed into existence and sliced up through the hanging tiles of the ceiling. Tube lights were shredded in a spattering of sparks and falling glass. It was as though a bomb had gone off, except that instead of an explosion, there was a dinosaur.

Okay. You need to respond. Okay. Alix tried to gather her thoughts. *Stegosaurus.*

Right.

She was staring into its nostrils and, with an effort, moved her gaze up to meet its eyes. Its eyelids were still fluttering, just as Smith's had been, and the eyes were rolled back, mottled green instead of white. As she watched, the fluttering ceased and the eyes snapped back down, a slash of black pupil.

There was no trace of the levelheaded, somewhat cynical team leader in that reptilian gaze. There was no hint of recognition, no humanity with which to connect. This was the mind of a creature that had roamed the world more than a hundred million years ago, and that was not very happy at this moment. *Stegosaurus stenops* took a step toward them, and the floor trembled.

How much does it weigh? Tons. Tons and tons. Can the floor support it? It appeared to be adequate, because the creature took another step toward them, then opened its mouth to blast out a growling bellow.

In its carrier, the quokka bared its teeth and made a screeching sound.

You've got the right idea, mon petit frère.

"Fucking *run!*" yelled Alix. She dropped the equipment duffel but kept hold of the quokka crate. She spun and saw that Chuah and Padilla had dropped *their* duffels and were legging it back down the hallway. Alix vaulted over the discarded luggage, while behind her, there was a crashing sound as the dinosaur began to follow them, forcing its way easily through the walls and ceiling.

A siren had begun to scream distantly. Evidently, the building's emergency system had realized that something disastrous was happening.

So, help has to be coming.

She risked a look behind her and saw that the stegosaurus had gotten up some good speed and was lumbering after her. In its carrier, the quokka was making high-pitched unhappy sounds as it jounced around.

"I know!" she snapped. Ahead was a corner, and she took it smartly.

The dinosaur did not take the corner as smartly as she had. Instead it bashed through, demolishing several walls in the process. As it turned she caught a fleeting glimpse of its massive scything tail sweeping through the revealed offices. The four spikes on the end abruptly rearranged tables into clouds of splinters, and a metal filing cabinet was rent open to send papers flying about.

Alix rounded the final corner and saw that Chuah and Padilla had the door to the office open. They gestured urgently to her, she rushed through it, and they slammed it shut behind her. Then they dashed off to the side, vaulting as one (plus quokka carrier) over Claes's desk to crouch quietly on the other side.

We need to stay quiet. Still and quiet. It was a ridiculous thought. The sirens were screaming so loudly that she could have started playing the accordion without being heard. Still, they all held their breath, even the extremely jostled quokka.

Nothing yet.

Time seemed to slow.

The sound of stegosaurine havoc on the floor, while ongoing, also sounded hearteningly distant.

"I don't think it's coming here," whispered Alix. "Yet." She winced at the unmistakable sound of a human scream abruptly cut off. Clearly someone else had been in to do work on the weekend.

They'd have even less idea about what's happening than we do.

"How did this happen?" asked Chuah. His voice was shrill and he looked decidedly wild-eyed, for which Alix could hardly blame him. It was all very well for a new recruit to come to terms with the idea that people had impossible abilities, but an actual gigantic monster suddenly exploding into existence was a bit much in his first few months as part of the Checquy.

"It's Smith's ability," she explained.

"What? To change into a dinosaur and go nuts?"

"Normally she doesn't go nuts—you get a dinosaur with a human mind. Lack of control has never been a problem. Something has gone wrong." They heard a crash from the other side of the wall. The quokka moaned in distress. Alix gave a moment's thought to taking the little marsupial out and comforting it, but she couldn't predict how it might react. She settled for making a little crooning noise to it.

Besides, if we have to run again, better to have it in something portable.

"We have to let someone know the situation," she said. She reached up for the desk phone.

"Security," said a fraught-sounding male voice. "Is this about the dinosaur in the Box Room?"

"No, there's a blocked toilet in the library," said Alix, rolling her eyes.

"What?"

"Of *course* it's about the dinosaur!"

"We already know about it!"

"Did you know that it's Pawn Hannah Smith?"

"What? No. Hell, it's one of ours?"

"Yeah, we don't know what's happened to her," said Alix, "but tell the response team to subdue, not terminate, if at all possible."

"Right, yeah," said the voice. "Hold." Then: "Are you still in the Box Room?"

"Yes."

"Can you get out?"

"Maybe...," said Alix. There were no other doors out of the section, but if the past few minutes had demonstrated anything (other than the astounding weight-bearing capabilities of the Rookery's infrastructure), it was that the walls of the Box Room were by no means an impenetrable obstacle.

"If you see a chance, get out. Otherwise, stay low, because the response isn't going to be gentle, even if she *is* one of ours."

"Understood," said Alix. The Rookery, for all its security, fortification, and discretion, was a London office building surrounded by other buildings, civilian buildings. The noise from Smith's rampage would be problem enough, but she absolutely could not be allowed to emerge into the city. "How long do we have?"

"Can't say. But it'll be soon."

"All right. Thanks." She hung up.

"What did they say?" asked Padilla.

"Help is coming, but not the kind of help that's healthy for us," said Alix. "And maybe not soon enough. So, do we stay, or do we move?"

"Go out *there*?" asked Chuah, horrified. "Can't either of you do anything?"

"I need to be touching soil," said Padilla. "And I'm not sure the presence of tree-me would improve things. Plus, I'm not sure I could stand up to Smith in her current form. She definitely looked capable of bringing down a tree."

"And they were herbivores," Alix pointed out.

The American pawn looked even more unnerved.

"My power's somewhat problematic," explained Alix. "I'd need to be touching her, or else my powers might hit *you*. If it's not touch-based, then I don't control the energy—it's just gonna run wild through walls and floors and ceilings."

"We need to get out," said Padilla. They all looked up at another crash—presumably a wall coming down—and the roar of the beast. This time, the sound was not as distant as they would have liked.

"Agreed," said Alix.

"Oh, hell," said Chuah. "Yeah, all right." They stood, and Alix hefted the quokka's carrier. They moved quietly past their desks, through the kitchenette, to the office where Weller's finance-serfs labored during the week. It had its own exit. "There are no weapons about, right? No guns or, I don't know, magic wands?"

"We don't have magic wands!" snapped Alix. Admittedly, there *were* supernatural items in the building, but it was not like Checquy soldiers each got issued a standard Rod of Invisible Lightning. "But security will be sending powerful forces, and there could be collateral damage. Everyone ready?"

"I'll go first," said Chuah.

"Good," said Alix. "Then Padilla, then me."

"But stay close," said Chuah. He opened the door a crack and peered through. He nodded, and they followed him.

The corridor ahead of them looked pristine. It was clear that Smith-as-stegosaurus had not rampaged down here.

"*Go!*" whispered Alix. They set off as quietly as they could, but when they rounded the corner, they pulled up short as they saw the destruction that had been wrought.

It was not a case of stegosaurus-shaped holes punched in walls, or even the occasional damage wrought by a trailing thagomizer. This was demolition. Walls had been pulverized, and what had been offices and soulless little corridors was now a wasteland. The floor was covered in shattered plasterboard and the remains of furniture. Classified papers were strewn everywhere, a thousand secrets scattered like leaves.

It was a patchwork of light and darkness. In some spots, Smith's back plates had carved furrows through the suspended ceiling and brought the frame and the lights down to lie tangled and smashed on the floor. In other places, fluorescent tubes dangled and twisted, some still illuminated.

Over it all, the alarm screamed.

Crikey.

There was no sign of the stegosaurus.

"Where is it?" said Alix.

"Over there?" suggested Chuah, pointing to a portion of the floor with intact walls. Presumably Smith was behind there somewhere, but they heard no rampaging over the sound of the alarm.

Maybe she's changed back into herself and is lying unconscious somewhere. Turning into a dinosaur and then charging through an office had to be tiring, surely.

"We heard people," said Padilla. "Where are they?"

"Maybe they got out."

No one wanted to say that perhaps they were smeared under the papers and the remnants of wall, or on the underside of Smith's gigantic feet.

"There," said Alix, and she pointed to the far side of the floor where an exit sign was still illuminated.

The sirens cut out. The silence throbbed in their ears.

"Do you think that's a good thing?" asked Chuah in a whisper.

"I think it means we should move *now*, and quietly," Alix whispered back. They picked their way across the debris field. There was hardly a patch of clear, level floor, and it was impossible to move silently. Debris shifted under their feet—papers, file folders, desk phones, or the shattered remains of desks and chairs.

And then the quokka snarled, a sound of macropodial fear, and Alix looked around to see a triangular reptilian head coming slowly around a corner.

Millions of years separated dinosaurs and humans, and yet some instinct coiled deep within Alix's DNA woke up in her head and screamed.

"Go!" said Alix. Chuah and Padilla looked back, then froze when they saw the dinosaur. "Take him," she said, and handed the quokka's carrier to Padilla. "Get yourselves as far away as possible." Already, the energy was building up inside her.

"What? But you've got to—"

"It's too far." She knew she was right. They couldn't outrun Smith, especially over the mangled terrain. *"Go!"* She turned and began to move toward the massive creature. The stegosaurus lurched into action, bringing down another wall as it approached. Dust rose, but Alix marched on, her advance broken only when she put her foot through a digital scanner and it skidded under her. She got to her feet and saw that the dinosaur was still plowing forward.

It came closer and closer, but now she was still. This was as good a place as any. There was a little spot of clear floor to give her a good footing. She assumed a ready stance.

I really didn't think this was how I was going to die. She clenched her fist, and her power flared inside her. *Let's see if this works.*

Now the beast was so close that she could smell it, a musty reptilian odor.

Don't get distracted. Focus. Here it comes...

It lowered its head to barrel over her, to trample her.

NOW!

She took a few steps, then leapt up and forward.

She had envisioned a maneuver like the bull-leaping fresco of Knossos. She'd flip up, using the thing as a vaulting horse. It would buy her a moment to release her power into the creature—if her power would even go into it. What came after that, she hadn't planned. All she knew was that she absolutely could not stay at ground level.

But there was nothing to grab onto, so when she launched herself up, she had to scrabble madly. She caught at the first of its back plates. The energy was boiling inside her, so she pushed it out, hoping it would find purchase in Smith. If it didn't, then it would smash back into her.

But there *was* a connection. The energy coursed out from her hand, through the creature's skin, and she could feel the map of its massive bones. The dinosaur was shaking its head back and forth violently, trying to throw her off. Every instinct screamed to just dump the energy, roll off, and run away.

Instead, aware that at any moment she might be sent flying to shatter her spine against a disemboweled filing cabinet, she directed the power, ordered it down and forward. Obedient to her will, it divided and gathered—two whirling pools like malignant chakras—in the ulna and radius of Smith's left foreleg.

The sound, when it came, even through the layers of muscle and skin, was a stomach-turning crack.

The stegosaurus bellowed. Its leg buckled and it collapsed. Alix was flung off. She tumbled through the air and smacked into the floor. She screamed as there was an unmistakable snap. Even through the pain, she was able to appreciate the irony of her own left leg getting broken.

She half slid, half rolled through debris, her leg flashing with a red-hot agony with every impact, until she slammed into detritus that used to be a whiteboard. The creature was thrashing about. It roared, and she felt a stab of pity. Pawn Smith might be somewhere in there, buried in the dinosaur, but at the moment its bewilderment was that of an animal.

Then the stegosaurus rose up. It was awkward, ponderous, taking as little weight as possible on its forelimb, but it stood. She could see the telltale twitches and jerks as remnants of her power coursed through its frame—not enough to break more bones, but certainly enough to be felt. It looked at her, and she thought she could see rage in its eyes.

For the first time, Alix thought to look for her colleagues. Through the flickering lights, she saw that they had reached the fire door and were still crouched there.

"Alix, get up!" Padilla shouted.

"Run!" yelled Chuah.

Not going to happen, kids. Her shin had snapped, and the slightest movement set the ends grating against each other. The shouting had drawn the stegosaurus's attention, and it began to turn away from her, toward the fire door. Which meant that she and its tail were shortly going to be occupying the same space.

I'm going to get thagomized.

The fire door burst open, hitting Padilla and sending him stumbling back. Soldiers poured in, all black armor and visored helmets, with green lenses glowing ominously. Some of them had guns, others did not.

They did not pause to gape at the chaos. One of them stepped forward, empty hands thrust out. Silver filaments burst out of their fingers and spiraled out through the air toward Alix and the stegosaurus. Light from the remaining fixtures glistened on them. The dinosaur snapped at one that came too close to its head, but the wirelike thread swooped around and coiled itself around the creature's neck. The other lines snapped into place all over its body, tightening around its legs and tail, then stretched back to the hands of the pawn.

"Got it!" she exclaimed triumphantly.

The stegosaurus did not give the impression of liking this new arrangement. It pulled forcefully against its bonds and yanked the pawn off her feet and into a large potted plant that, miraculously, had been unharmed up until that point. The cords evaporated out of existence.

"Peacham!" exclaimed one of the other soldiers. "You all right?" Peacham was dragging herself out of the plant and gave a thumbs-up.

"Right, that's how it wants to play?" the soldier said. He snapped the visor of his helmet up.

"No, Tindall, wait!" snapped another soldier, but a blast of crackling sky-blue fire erupted out of Tindall's face to boil across the room.

I'm not going to get thagomized, Alix thought. *I'm going to get incinerated.*

She closed her eyes.

★ ★ ★

And then opened them again when agonizing death failed to envelop her.

As the admittedly gorgeous blue fire erupted across the room, a torrent of gray clouds burst out of vents in the ceiling, filling the place almost instantly. Alix had time to close her eyes again, but she could hear the hiss as the fire was unzipped at a chemical level by the halon fire suppression system. A bellow came from the stegosaurus and was cut off abruptly.

Alix felt the cold buffeting of the halon as it roared all around her. There were distant cries of bewilderment that turned into distant coughs of bewilderment.

When tail-spikey oblivion also failed to crunch into her body, Alix opened a wary eye. Halon filled the place like fog. She opened the other eye and squinted. There was no shadowy sign of a stegosaurus, which, even in the haze, would have been difficult to miss.

Then, out of the clouds emerged a silhouette that resolved itself into the naked, human, and distinctly unimpressed shape of Pawn Hannah Smith. She was cradling a broken arm and exhibited no trace of mindless rage. She did, however, exhibit some quite mindful rage.

"What the *fuck* happened here?" the team leader asked.

Alix was rescued from the impossible task of explaining the situation by the sudden *zing*ing arrival of a dart cutting through the fog and burying itself in Smith's biceps. Smith looked down at it, and then collapsed.

Masked soldiers materialized out of the haze. One of them applied something resembling an oily black leech to the neck of the unconscious Smith, presumably in an effort to preempt any re-stegosaurization. They did not cover her nakedness, but they did lock some incredibly thick shackles around her wrists, knees, and elbows before hauling her away.

A medic appeared to take Alix's pulse and check her for wounds. She wheezingly explained about her broken leg, which she hadn't precisely forgotten about in all the chaos, but which had slid down the list of things to worry about until that moment, when the pain shouldered its way back to center stage. A soldier lifted her gently, but every movement sent a burning slice of pain through her leg and a little shriek from her lips.

"Any remaining threats that you're aware of?" someone barked.

"It was just the dinosaur," said Alix.

"We've gotten your team secured. Was there anyone else on the floor?"

"I don't know. We heard a scream, but they might have gotten out."

"We'll do a sweep. Alethia, get her out of here." The soldier carried her carefully, but the unevenness of the floor meant more agonizing jouncing. As they approached the stairwell, one of the soldiers was admonishing another, who still had smoke coming up out of his face.

"You're a bloody idiot, Tindall!" the admonisher, who sounded Australian, barked. "You know there's that halon system, we *told* you lot, and it costs the bloody earth to get it recharged."

"Well, it worked, didn't it?" the unhappy Tindall muttered.

"Are you trying to tell me that was on *purpose*?" The door to the stairs shut behind Alix and her bearer, cutting off Tindall's answer. They descended to the response center that had been set up in the office space one floor down. Chuah, Padilla, and the quokka were there, all three with oxygen masks over their noses and mouths. The humans nodded, and the marsupial gave a little smothered chirp. A sofa was cleared and Alix placed on it.

"What has happened here?" asked a petite doctor with a high chartreuse ponytail. "Halon inhalation?"

"Yeah," wheezed Alix. She was immediately provided with an oxygen mask.

"And your leg looks very interesting."

"Compound tibia fracture," said Alix through gritted teeth.

"Ah, Lady Mondegreen," said the doctor. "I shall bow to your expertise. Are you comfortable receiving Broederschap treatments?"

"Fine."

"*Jasper!*" shouted the doctor. A middle-aged white man with chestnut hair and a handlebar mustache came over, accompanied by a young Black girl who looked no older than eleven. "Broken shin bone, you good for this?"

"Yes, Dr. Basney. Now, Pawn," said Jasper, "are you ready?"

"Ready for—*HWWWWOAARGH!*" He'd jammed a syringe of vivid neon-blue liquid into her thigh, and the sensation as the liquid was forced into her leg made her want to slap herself in the face. It faded instantly, however, taking all the pain with it in a single, strength-draining surge that left her feeling like she'd just had an extremely successful bathroom visit.

Wow. That's great. I can face the trip to the operating theater with this floating in me. She opened her mouth to say as much, and then gagged as he proceeded to slit open her trouser leg from ankle to midthigh with a single easy scalpel swipe.

Before Alix could object, her attention was caught and held by the sight of one of her shin bones jutting out through the skin. The end was jagged, and there was a thought-provoking amount of blood coming out of the wound.

She then made a strangled gasp as the Grafter slit open her actual leg from ankle to knee with another single easy scalpel swipe. The skin and muscle were pulled briskly back to reveal her shin bone glistening white. The breaks in the bones were obvious and ugly, and even though Alix couldn't feel anything, her stomach was doing barrel rolls.

The hulking soldier who had carried her vomited inside her menacing black helmet-mask and had to stagger away.

The Grafter said something in Dutch to the little girl.

"*Ja, mijn Heer,*" she replied, and reached down to place her fingers—ungloved, Alix queasily noted—into the open incision and close firmly around one of the breaks. The older Grafter leaned forward and reached down.

"Now, wait a minute," said Alix nervously.

"*Nu!*" barked the Grafter.

"Sorry, what?"

As one, the master and the pupil tensed and pushed. Every instinct in Alix's body screamed at her to run away from her own leg. With a nauseating scrunching sound, the ends of the bones were forcibly realigned. There was no pain, admittedly, but there was a distinct...sensation, and

Alix had to cram her hand into her mouth to prevent herself from screaming in shock. Quite a few of the onlookers had crammed *their* hands into their mouths as well. One soldier keeled over backward.

"Very good," said the Grafter. He patted his student on the shoulder, leaving a handprint of blood and leg-fluid. *"En nu het glazuur."* The girl produced a paintbrush, along with a stoppered jar that looked like it had been living under someone's sink for a few decades. It was sealed with an actual cork, and there was a label on it with spidery writing in faded ink.

Alix forced herself to watch as the little girl carefully dipped the brush into the syrupy yellow liquid and applied a thin layer over the bone. Several squirts from a mister ensued, soaking the meat along the incision with something that looked like swamp water.

"Done," said Jasper. "I will close it up, and you will have no scars." Alix gave herself permission not to watch as he sewed up her skin. "Sensation will return shortly. You should feel no pain, and you will be up and walking in a few minutes."

"Thank you," said Alix.

"Of course. Quirine, thank the pawn for allowing you to practice on her body."

Alix smiled at the serious girl, who thanked her in heavily accented English. "Not at all. Thank *you*," Alix said, which earned her a shy smile. Then Alix closed her eyes and took a few breaths of oxygen.

"Lady Mondegreen." It was one of the soldiers.

"Hmm?"

"Just doing a quick follow-up," he said. "We've spoken with the retainer and the Yank. Can't get a word out of the other one. He's pretty shaken up — won't turn back from a dog."

"Not a dog. A quokka. And he doesn't change. He's full-time."

"I need to know if there were any other people on the floor."

"I heard some screams at the beginning, when it — when *she* smashed through the first walls."

"Do you know which office?"

"It was coming from the direction of the one with the yellow tape," she said.

"Yep, good, there were two people in there. They're both alive and accounted for."

"Any injuries?"

"One chap's got a broken arm, collarbone, and shoulder," said the soldier. "The creature caught him pretty hard, but he's declining Grafter attention. The other one got him out and is uninjured. It was just those two and your lot. We're lucky—it would have been a lot worse if it happened on a weekday."

"It's already disastrous."

"Yeah, there are going to be a lot of questions about this manifestation," said the soldier.

Oh, God, poor Smith. No pawn wanted ever to become a manifestation.

"How is Pawn Smith?" she asked.

"Heavily sedated and restrained, and en route to the Comb. The boffins will want a detailed account of everything that happened."

They'll want to interview us while it's still fresh in our minds. Everything we saw, heard, smelled. There were so many things to remember, jostling each other in her brain. Then:

"Hell! The investigation!"

"Don't worry, it'll be fine," said the soldier.

"Not yours! Ours!" She jumped to her feet, then remembered she'd just undergone radical surgery. She paused, ready for her leg to shatter under her, but it bore up with no pain or sign that anything catastrophic had happened.

Alix was obliged to assume leadership. Padilla was a visitor, Chuah was a newly minted retainer, and the quokka, for all its charm and expertise in its field, was a quokka. All three had looked startled when Alix pointed out that they still had work to do and no time to be traumatized. When it came to processing a crime scene, every moment counted, and there was no one onto whom they could foist the responsibility.

Their equipment had been the first casualty of the Jurassic office rampage, but replacements were sourced easily. When they arrived at Rohmer's building, the Checquy courier was impatiently waiting in the lobby with the keys to the flat and the alarm code, having no idea what had happened at the Rookery. The team did not feel the need to fill him in as they signed for the keys and the piece of paper with the code, and took the elevator to the penthouse apartment.

Alix had to keep reminding herself that there was no need to limp as she hauled the duffels into the living room of the tragically departed football star. She looked around the modern, well-appointed room and saw very little crossover between this place and where the other two men had died.

Though Alfie Rohmer's home was a flat, it was as luxurious as you would expect for a man who was paid a large sum every week to kick a ball into a desired location, and who had several lucrative endorsement deals—including ones for football boots, a whisky, and a fragrance—and whose (obviously ghostwritten) autobiography had been a national bestseller the previous Christmas.

The floors were marble, and the ceiling arched overhead like a miniature Art Deco cathedral. Through the massive windows, an envy-inducing view of London spread out to the horizon. In one corner was the largest television Alix had ever seen, in the center of the room was a pool table, and dotted all around was massive baggy leather furniture that looked like the shorn scrotum of some extremely fit deity. Trophies and awards lined the shelves, along with photos of his family and of him playing football. On one wall was a massive black-and-white portrait of a shirtless Rohmer, looking like a deity himself. A framed newspaper clipping featured the triumphant headline ROHMER MAULS ARSENAL FOR THE CUP!

The football player had died in bed, while enjoying a Sunday lie-in. Snuggled comfortably with his girlfriend, according to her, he had suddenly gone rigid and silent. Through the door, Alix could see Chuah grimly stripping the sheets and pillowcases and putting them into evidence bags. The quokka had already hoovered up whatever particulates had been hanging about in the air and was now sitting on a towel, cleaning its ears.

All three of the British victims died in the first half of the day, Alix mused as she set about photographing the room. *Could that be significant? What else did they have in common?*

They were male.

They had money.

They were all in relationships with women.

They were all prominent in their respective fields.

All three of them had homes in London.

But then there are the differences: Two of them white, one Black. Two of them public figures, one a private citizen. Two of them in their twenties, one in his fifties.

Two of them not the Prince of Wales.

Well, the world knows," said Chuah. He held up his phone to show a headline announcing the death of Alfie Rohmer.

The three of them (et quokka) had finished their examination of the apartment and returned to the Rookery, stopping only to pick up Turkish food on the way. Out of habit, Alix pressed the lift button for the Box Room, and when they alighted at the appropriate floor, they were greeted with devastation.

Cables snaked across the debris from wall outlets and generators to tripods supporting large field lanterns. Slump-shouldered figures in coveralls were shambling about, engaged in the hard toil of trying to clean the place up.

A woman was standing by the lift, grimly reviewing information on a tablet. She told them that since their portion of the Box Room had not been damaged by the dinosaur, there was no reason to move them. A path had been cleared to the few intact office spaces. The team shuffled sheepishly along the path, their dinner's smell of warm cheese and spicy Turkish smoked salami prompting heads to look up hopefully from their tasks, and then to lower again with disappointment.

Alix recognized some of the workers as denizens of the other Box Room offices, and nodded in passing. They were the ones who seemed focused on gathering up the thousands of papers and trying to put them back into some usable order. Other workers, however, had the grim mien of persons abruptly drafted on a Sunday afternoon for an emergency manual labor secondment. They were the ones shifting actual wreckage and debris.

Finally having arrived at their miraculously intact office space, the investigative team was now sprawled about, most of them too tired and hungry to do anything but eat pides. Scagell and Claes had joined them. The psych-pawn was drinking a glass of wine, while the Grafter was eating a garlic prawn, mushroom, tomato, and cheese pide with one hand and feeding the quokka some shrubbery cuttings with the other.

"The Liars said they were going to say Mr. Rohmer's death was due to natural causes," said Claes. "I suggested they go with sudden cardiac death as the cause."

Alix grabbed her tablet and scrolled through the coverage. It included the predictable amount of shock and distress but nothing suggesting any form of foul play.

The investigation of the flat had proved predictably dispiriting. No obvious clues had emerged—certainly nothing that linked the footballer to the other two victims. There weren't even any trees near the building that Padilla could question. They would run the fingerprints they had gathered, but Alix grimly anticipated that the death of Alfie Rohmer would prove as bewildering as the others.

Meanwhile, the question of what they would do without Smith hovered grimly in the air.

20

It was the day after Rohmer's death and Smith's manifestation. Sweven and Weller, the team members who had not been back to the Box Room yet, expressed shock at the state of it. They were wondering how to proceed without a team leader, and Alix was poised to smack down any move by Sweven to declare himself in charge, when they were summoned to the top floor. Rook Thomas and Lady Farrier were waiting for them.

"Has there been word on Pawn Smith?" asked Claes.

"Yes," said Rook Thomas. "Once secured at the Comb, she was chemically roused from her sedation, although she remained restrained and one of your colleagues temporarily disconnected her spine. The staff spent the last twelve hours questioning and examining her. Her body is unharmed—the broken arm was repaired by one of the Broederschap—and shows no sign of anything that might have prompted her actions.

"I visited her unconscious mind before they woke her," put in Lady Farrier, "and found everything to be perfectly normal."

"Since she's been awake, she seems completely rational," said the rook. "She's been cooperative but has no memory of running amok."

"So she's saying she doesn't know what caused it?" asked Alix. A memory was clearing its throat in the back of her head as she recalled the manifestation.

"No. Why, do you?" asked Rook Thomas.

"I don't know, but right before she changed, she received a telephone call," said Alix. "And I mean it was a direct segue. She reacted to whatever was said, dropped the phone, then turned and... stegged up. At the time, for a moment, I thought it must be bad news—something catastrophic that pushed her into a mental breakdown."

"Do you know who the call was from?"

"No. I thought a family member, if the news was that bad." She looked around at Padilla and Chuah, who nodded.

"I contacted Pawn Smith's family last night," said Rook Thomas. "I let them know that she'd been deployed to an emergent operation and would not be in immediate contact."

"Did Smith mention the phone call to the people at the Comb?" asked Chuah.

"I'm not seeing any record of it in the transcripts," replied the rook, scanning through her papers.

"We need to chase this up immediately," said Lady Farrier. "Rook Thomas?" The rook nodded and touched a tablet, and a voice came over hidden speakers.

"Yes, Rook Thomas?"

"Ingrid, can you please arrange a teleconference with Pawn Smith at the Comb?"

"Right away, ma'am."

"Thank you. Now, while we're waiting, you are without a team leader. We will be reviewing the situation and identifying an appropriate stand-in." The tablet chimed. "Yes?"

"Rook Thomas, I have Pawn Smith."

"Please connect us."

There was a pause, then: "Smith here."

"Pawn Smith, this is Rook Thomas, Lady Farrier, and your team," said the rook. "I'm sorry to disturb you."

"Not at all," said the pawn's voice, sounding completely unconcerned. In the background, there was a continuous beeping.

"I understand that you are a trifle discommoded at the moment, so we needn't use videoconferencing."

"The staff have very considerately brushed my hair," Smith assured them. "So, videoconference is fine."

The rook tapped her tablet and a screen descended from a slot in the ceiling. It clicked into life, displaying the image of Pawn Smith.

For a moment, it looked to Alix as though the team leader were standing at attention against a white curtain, before the other details of the image registered and she realized that they were being presented with a ceiling's-eye view. Dressed in blue pajamas, the team leader was lying on a bed, with straps pinning her down at the ankles, wrists, elbows, knees, stomach, and forehead. There was no cast on her arm.

At least three lines were dripping virulently colored liquids into Smith's arms and legs. Sensors were attached to her temples and cheeks, and a few white cables snaked down into the collar of her pajamas. Despite all the restraints, she did not seem at all troubled by the situation.

"Good morning, Lady Farrier, Rook Thomas, everyone," said Smith. "Apparently, I caused a bit of trouble. I do apologize."

Everyone made reassuring noises about how little trouble it had been, that it was nothing to worry about, except for Padilla, who looked around in astonishment at how English they were all being.

"How are you doing?" asked Claes.

"The staff here are very nice. We're trying to figure out what may have prompted my tantrum. Lots of tests."

"Pawn Smith, your team says that right before your episode, you received a telephone call," said Lady Farrier. "They feel it may have caused the, um, transformation. Do you have any recollection of that?" Smith's brow wrinkled as much as the sensor discs on her face would allow.

"I... Wait, yes. Yes! I remember! It's the last thing I recall before the room was suddenly trashed. There *was* a call."

"Who was it from?" asked Alix. "Was it personal?"

"It wasn't a number I recognized," Smith said.

"You answered a call from a strange number?" asked Padilla. "What about telemarketers?" Clearly, to the American, the threat of being hassled by scammers or someone trying to sell him solar panels was at least as severe as the threat of supernatural attack.

"I have kids," said Smith. "I'm always going to take the call."

"And who was it?" asked the rook. "What did they want?"

"It was difficult to understand them," said Smith, thinking back. "The connection was clear, but the words were strange. They were sounds I could almost understand, but not quite. They seemed to reverberate in my skull." She sounded uncertain. "It got louder, incredibly loud, as if it were filling my head up, so that it drowned out all my thoughts..."

"But it was a human voice?" asked Alix.

"Well, it was a voice." Everyone but Chuah nodded knowledgeably—you couldn't go around making assumptions about the humanity of things.

"Male or female?" asked Alix.

"Male, I think," said Smith. "Yeah. He said something, or made sounds, and then the next thing I knew, I was naked, my arm was broken, and the office was a shambles. And the next thing I knew after *that*, I was strapped to a slab, being asked questions with lots of guns pointed at me."

"This is all extremely worrisome," said Lady Farrier.

"There's definitely precedent," said Alix. All eyes turned to look at her. "Recent precedent. Isn't there, Mark?"

Sweven's eyes widened in realization. "Lady Mondegreen and I were subjected to something similar just before we were assigned to this project. We were driven into a state of uncontrollable rage, such that we attacked civilians and our colleagues."

"Oh, my God, of course!" exclaimed Rook Thomas. "The manifestation in Leeds. That woman, what was her name?"

"Grace Merritt," said Alix and Sweven simultaneously.

"What's her current status?" asked Lady Farrier.

"Dead," said Alix.

"Lady Mondegreen killed her," put in Sweven helpfully.

"Is this a common ability, then?" asked Claes.

"It's very rare for people to have exactly the same ability, but even if the mechanics are different, the effect can be very similar," said Lady Farrier. "Forcing people to turn on each other is possible by any number of means. Why, Rook Thomas here could do it to any one of us right at this moment." Everyone around the table nodded sagely, except Chuah, who looked distinctly ill at ease, and, to Alix's surprise, the rook herself, who shifted uncomfortably. "And Lady Mondegreen had her hands around my throat just a few nights ago," the Lady added easily.

Everyone's eyes turned toward Alix, who shrugged as casually as she could.

"The phone call doesn't fit. Merritt didn't have to speak to us to make us crazy," said Sweven. "It was just her presence."

"And I remember every part of being under her influence," said Alix. "What I did and how it felt. That overwhelming hate." Despite himself, Sweven nodded in agreement.

"That's not at all what I experienced," confirmed Smith. "It's all a blank to me."

"This is apparently someone whose voice can send you into this mindless rampage, then," said Scagell. "Even over the telephone."

"Then that call is the key," said the rook. "Where is the phone?"

"It's currently a silicone and plastic pancake in the middle of a stegosaurus footprint," said Alix.

"Okay, so we will need to pull the records. In the meantime, no one answer their phones."

"What? None of us?" asked Weller.

"We can't take the risk of anyone else being affected that way." Everyone looked at each other nervously.

"Do we think this is an attack directed specifically at Pawn Smith, or at the Checquy as a whole?" asked Lady Farrier.

"I don't want to order an organization-wide moratorium on using the telephone unless it's absolutely necessary," said the rook. "We'll have to reevaluate if anyone outside this room gets a provoking call. But given that Pawn Smith is attached to this investigation, I want to start by assuming that the attack—if it *was* an attack—is linked to the series of crimes you're investigating."

"Evidently, the call affected Pawn Smith's mind," said Claes. "Therefore, it affected her brain—which is the modus operandi we have seen with the three murder victims." Alix looked uncomfortably to Pawn Smith on the monitor, to see how the discussion of her brain was affecting her. The team leader looked a little uncomfortable as well.

"Do we think they might have been killed via a phone call?" asked Rook Thomas. "That might explain how the killer dealt with the difficulty of accessing the prince."

"Pawn Clements looked back in time and witnessed the collapse of the prince and of Mr. Blanch," said Alix. "Neither of them was using the phone at the time. She's at Rohmer's flat today, but..." She shrugged.

"Did the prince have a phone?" asked Padilla.

"Yes," said Alix. "It wasn't registered to his name, though. It was a business phone. Only a few people had the number, and he didn't take any calls to it on the day of his death."

"We seem to be cataloging a goodly number of abilities for this individual," remarked Lady Farrier. "Brain cubes, growing copious amounts of hair from one's hands..." Alix gagged a little at the memory. "Inducing highly specific hallucinations, and now triggering *berserkergang* via the telephone."

"But we think there may be at least two people involved, don't we?" asked Alix. "The person Pawn Scagell and I fought at the Blanch residence, and whoever picked them up after Scagell blew up their car."

"Good times," nodded Scagell.

"If the caller was the murderer," began Weller, "or one of their confederates, how did they get Pawn Smith's number?"

"How would they even know who I am?" asked Smith. "That I exist?"

Easy, thought Alix. The murderer, having barely escaped an encounter with the explosive citrus ministrations of Scagell, would have been all too aware that the murder investigation of Mr. Blanch featured supernatural elements. They could have returned to the area and joined the crowd of interested neighbors observing the Blanch house from across the crime scene tape.

Apparently, Chuah agreed. "Keep in mind, we remained onsite for two days after Scagell and Mondegreen's nighttime encounter," the retainer said. "That's plenty of time to stalk members of the team, to follow them to the hotel or to coffee shops, and to put cash in some hands for a name from the hotel register or a credit card receipt."

"But still, how could they have gotten Smith's mobile number?" Scagell asked.

Chuah shrugged. "Information is always available if you have wiles and money. All sorts of places would have the number recorded. Pawn Smith, I expect your doctor has your number? Your children's school, your mechanic, your friends."

On the screen, the pawn nodded as much as her restraints would allow. "Of course," she said, looking unhappy.

Glancing around the table, Alix saw that she was not the only one who was uneasy. For all the Checquy operatives, who were accustomed to gliding unnoticed through the world, it was a disquieting thought.

Even more disquieting was the realization that all this applied to Alix herself. Not only had she confronted the intruder face to masked face, but she had been at the Blanch residence the following day. And she was infinitely more recognizable than her colleagues, as demonstrated in the weeks since the funeral by several awkward encounters with excited members of the public in various pubs, Prets a Manger, and her local Indian restaurant.

Come to think of it, didn't I put down a contact number when I checked in at the hotel in Winchester?

"But why would they do this to her?" wondered Alix.

"Uhh... to cause harm to the Checquy?" said Sweven. "To cause damage to our facilities, possibly even bring about the death of our people. After all, they targeted someone who can turn into a dinosaur." He said it in a tone that suggested that Alix was a moron.

"But they couldn't know about the specific nature of her ability, presuming they even knew she had one," objected Alix. It might have been relatively easy to get someone's personal mobile phone number, but the details of a pawn's powers were so highly classified that they were never committed to any computer that could conceivably be hacked.

"Maybe it was just a random lucky fluke on their part," suggested Chuah. "If they knew they could make her go berserk, maybe they thought she'd just pick up a pen and run around stabbing people."

They all considered this point, and then Rook Thomas turned back to the screen. "Pawn Smith, once the doctors at the Comb have reviewed your situation to make certain there's no residual effect, we'll have you transported over to Winchester for the trees to examine you for any unusual energy traces," said Rook Thomas. "Pawn Padilla, you're happy to translate?"

"Yes, ma'am."

"Good, thank you. Pawn Smith, if the doctors and trees are satisfied, and if you're feeling up to it, we'll get you back into action. But if you need time to recover, we can certainly make that happen."

"I want to get back to work as soon as possible," said Smith.

"It shouldn't be too long, then," said Lady Farrier. "The Comb will make accurately clearing you a priority. In the interim, Pawn Scagell, as senior operative, are you comfortable acting as team leader?" Presumably, Alix mused, the term *senior operative* referred to years served rather than age. Otherwise, the centuries-old Claes would have been leading.

Right, I have a list from Rook Thomas," said Scagell when they were all back in the Box Room. "To begin with, everyone, put these on your phones." He handed out bulky nylon cases with Velcro fastenings. "These will remind you only to answer calls from numbers you know."

"Do they do anything else?" asked Padilla.

"No."

"Not true," said Sweven. "They also make the phone too big to put in a pocket."

"That is an inconvenience we must endure," said the man who carried his phone in a satchel filled with mandarins. "Now, a few other things. The Telecommunication Privacy Intrusion section in the Rookery is accessing Smith's phone records to trace the source of the call."

"Do you realize this could crack the case?" said Padilla. "A phone call from the murderer! Or at least the murderer's accomplice. If we can trace the phone, we could triangulate its location. Depending on where the call was made, it may be on camera somewhere!"

"Yes, possibly," said Scagell. "We'll need to go through the phone records of the prince, Mr. Blanch, and Mr. Rohmer, looking for any shared callers. Once we have Pawn Smith's records, we can add that number."

"It can't just be the victims' mobile phones," said Sweven. "If there are home landline or office phones, we have to include those. Any phone line the victims might have answered."

"Or just lines they might have spoken on," said Weller. "The murder calls could have been to Mrs. Blanch's phone or the soccer player's girlfriend. You know, they get a call, someone asks to speak to the husband or the boyfriend, and they pass it over."

"And remember, the trees said that Mr. Blanch had been infected with that energy for at least a lunar cycle before he died," Padilla added. "It could have been the same for Prince Edmund and Mr. Rohmer."

"Excellent, so we have months of records to collate," said Scagell. "Let's get to work. In the meantime, we need to be prepared for the possibility that the caller will try again. Mondegreen and Chuah, I want you to look through Checquy records for previous instances of people who can affect others in this way, especially with their voice. We need an idea of the mechanism at work and what defenses have been used. When we confront this man, we want every possible advantage."

"On it," said Alix. She turned to Chuah. "We're going down to the Reading Room."

Two floors down, past a pair of sliding (bulletproof) glass doors, a nice little lobby with a (heavily armed) receptionist, and a gigantic metal door that looked like it should be doing service in a nuclear bunker, was the Rookery's in-house library. It was the most highly fortified part of the building. Of course, the entire Rookery was essentially a fortress, masquerading as the world's blandest office building. But the architects had determined that, in the case of a siege, invasion, or disaster, the library would be the last place to fall. It contained detailed records of secrets that, if released to the wider world (and believed), had the potential to rip society apart.

Accordingly, safeguards had been put in place, not only to keep the wrong people out and the documents in, but so that, if there was any danger of the records falling into the wrong hands, the librarians would have time to trigger various protective contingencies. It meant that every glass-fronted bookshelf and filing cabinet had built-in reservoirs of napalm and ignition devices for destroying the contents, which always made Alix a little nervous, even though the mechanism could supposedly only be activated by the intricate, multipronged keys carried by the senior librarian on duty.

The library was also home to the office's digital servers, hulking behind massive bulletproof glass windows. These devices could be commanded to wipe themselves clean electronically, multiple times, just before massive hydraulic presses crushed them into smithereens.

The whole place was a strategic labyrinth of concrete, glass, and steel, but primeval librarian instincts had reared up in the face of the architects and security experts, so that Alix and Chuah were first greeted by a cozy carpeted reading room with green leather armchairs and polished wooden tables topped by brass lamps, all of which had been forcibly inserted between a refrigerated vault for specialized subzero storage (librarians had to don massive fur-lined suits to go in and were required to enter in pairs in case one of them was immobilized, to ensure that no one was left to freeze to death among the bound periodicals) and a room-sized tank of hydrochloric acid.

Alix explained that the records were vast, but not all of them had been entered into the Checquy's idiosyncratic computer system, which was completely air-gapped—unconnected to any external networks—and was based on a bespoke programming language from the 1980s. This meant that what people were looking for was sometimes not available at the languid touch of a button, but rather was in a moldering paper file that had to be laboriously retrieved, sometimes from an offsite location.

"I assumed everything would have been digitized by now," remarked Chuah.

"A lot has," Alix explained. "But there are centuries of records from all over the world—not just the UK and Ireland, but also the British Empire, which for a while included America. Well, bits of America. We've been very good at acquiring histories and accounts of supernatural events that we weren't involved in at all."

"So there are a lot of facilities like this?" asked Chuah.

"Heaps," said Alix. "Archives all over the place. We've got records in Ogham that were chiseled into columns."

They signed in with one of the librarians, who took their photos and fingerprints, then passed them a little slip of paper with a onetime access code for the antique-looking computer terminals. Alix guided Chuah through the search engine for the catalog. He entered a search for VOICE/SOUND.

Unsurprisingly, especially given the broadness of the search terms, there were dozens of returns. The first entries to pop up were about people who had been employed in the Checquy.

In the 1960s, the voice of a pawn named Christina Bucktin had been known to crystallize into formations of vivid purple amethyst mere seconds after it left her vocal cords. She'd used it to create barriers, launch razor-sharp projectiles, and retile her bathroom.

There had been a Lady of the Checquy in the 1940s whose power had, rather chillingly, simply been that people would die if she told them to.

"Interesting, but not exactly what we're looking for," remarked Alix. "Let's refine it a bit more."

Chuah added CONTROL (OF HUMANS), CONTROL (OF EMOTIONS), and she suggested BERSERKERGANG. They surveyed the results. Encouragingly, there was not much, although she did sigh when she saw that Grace Merritt was first on the list. *And all we established on that mission was that we can't rely on the Grafters' mood stabilizer.*

They divided up the entries and worked their way through them. "This one is kind of promising," remarked Alix a few minutes later.

In 1565, there had been a peasant boy with a "grotesquely twisted mouth, so sore riddled with holes and flaps that he could not eat hard food, and subsisted on gruel and mash. In his fourteenth year, he found that he could make such sounds as to compel those who heard them to sleep, to weep uncontrollably, to rut madly with each other with no concern for modesty or the laws of the Church, or to run wild like ravaging wolves, gnawing and clawing and striking at each other. The youth, who had been mocked and treated roughly all his life, took great delight in humbling, harming, and humiliating those who had tormented him. Their shock was great when they awoke and saw what they had done."

"So, how did the Checquy deal with him?" asked Chuah.

"According to this, when reports reached the Checquy, they dispatched a team of pawns from London, all of whom wore well-padded scarves around their ears to protect them from his commands. But by the time they arrived, he was gone. The pawn who led the mission noted that the villagers were all frightened and silent, and had a guilty look about them. She suspected that they had murdered him or driven him off to die."

"Sad," said Chuah.

"It is," agreed Alix, "but not unusual. I'd say the best protection that the supernatural has now is that so few people really believe in it. They're always looking for a rational explanation, even when the irrational is staring them right in the face. That said, when they *do* start believing in it, it's such a break from their normal understanding of the world that they respond really, really badly."

"So, the best defense the Checquy has been able to come up with against this kind of power is well-padded scarves around their ears." He paused. "I actually can't think of a better possibility. Maybe earplugs, or noise-canceling headphones."

"How much noise do they cancel?" asked Alix, who didn't have a pair.

"Quite a bit. But not enough that I'd want to risk it if I came across whoever made Smith go nuts," he said.

"So, we're back to padded scarves?"

"Yep. So many advances in just a few hundred years," he remarked sourly.

"You just wanted free expensive headphones," said Alix.

After three hours of fascinating but not immediately useful research, they decided to check in with the team. They had put in priority requests for a dozen indexed but undigitized records around the country to be scanned to portable hard drives, which would then be couriered to the Rookery library. To Chuah's horror, the two of them were taken to separate booths and strip-searched by burly librarians to make sure they hadn't taken any materials. When they returned to the Box Room, they found a glum-looking Padilla.

"They tracked the phone that called Pawn Smith," he said. "It was a burner bought for cash seven months ago in some place called... Middle Wallop? Is that real?"

"Yes," said Alix and Chuah simultaneously.

"Sounds like a wrestling move. Anyway, the shop's video security recording was taped over a month after the phone was bought, ditto the security cameras on the high street, and triangulation records suggest that the phone call was made from the middle of a playing field in...Melton Mowbray. Unastoundingly, no security cameras there either, and so we've got nothing useful."

"Time to requisition padded scarves from the quartermaster," mumbled Alix.

"Yeah... Wait, what?"

The next morning, Smith was back in the office, to the incredulity of Chuah, who felt that being forced to turn into a stegosaurus and then destroying a government office really ought to result in at least a week off. The doctors at the Comb had given the team leader the all-clear after, in a fortified examination room, she'd turned into a stegosaurus and back again twelve times without any loss of self-control. The trees at the Blanch residence had confirmed that her brain was clear of any cube-inducing energy. She had been issued a new mobile phone whose number no one—not even she—knew, and a pager for other people to contact her.

"Good to have you back, sir," said Scagell.

"Good to be back. Although I felt bad walking through the Box Room. It's a mess."

"These things happen," Claes said blithely. "I once accidentally infected an entire village with an airborne hybridization of syphilis, leprosy, and gout." An unnerved silence ensured, as everyone stared at her, hoping for more information. None appeared to be forthcoming.

"Any insights gained about the phone call?" asked Padilla hopefully.

"I'm afraid not," said Smith.

The team leader told them that, at the Comb, she had also undergone hypnotherapy, augmented by some chemicals the Grafters had provided, but hadn't been able to provide any additional information. She could recall the sounds she had heard down the phone line and was adamant that they had come from a person, but she had no idea how to re-create them. She tried to twist her lips and gurgle out from the back of her throat to approximate them, but in the end she laughed weakly and declared herself baffled.

"So, no new clues," said Padilla, deflated.

"It's an inexplicability," said Alix.

"This whole *case* is inexplicable," said Chuah. "Every avenue we pursue comes up blank. No real leads." He grimaced. "Honestly, if this is what working for the Checquy is like, I don't know if I'm up to it. At least with the Met, you could take a few things for granted. You could assume there was an explanation to be found. But with this case, it feels like there are no actual clues, no connections between the victims. There's not even really a pattern."

"Yeah," said Alix sourly. She leaned back in her chair and stared at the various whiteboards scattered around the room, with the ghosts of unprovable theories scribbled on them. "There *was* one connection, though," she said.

"There was? What?"

"Not between their lives, between their deaths."

"Yes, they all died the same way," said Sweven as though he was talking to a moron. "That's why we're investigating all of them."

"It's not just the means of death," Alix said. "Blanch died the day of Edmund's funeral. In fact, right after the funeral."

"But we never found anything significant about that particular day," said Chuah. "And then nothing happened on the day of Blanch's funeral. Or Alfie Rohmer's."

"But it *has* to be important," said Alix. "It's the only connection between any of the murders." For the hundredth time, she began to sift through her mental inventory of information about the three men.

You kill a man. They hold his funeral. You immediately kill the next man. Why?

If the killer wanted to kill Blanch, why would they wait until the day of the funeral? Central London was certainly a lot busier. But Blanch wasn't in central London.

Could it have been a diversion—drawing everyone's attention to the funeral to commit a crime somewhere else? But Blanch wasn't being guarded. The killer didn't need a diversion.

There must be something else, she thought. *Something I'm not seeing. Because the only thing that happened as an immediate result of the funeral was that Edmund got buried, and a lot of people saw it happen.*

A lot of people.

A thought occurred to her.

No.

Please, no.

"Pawn Smith? I've had a thought." She was standing in the doorway of Smith's office and speaking quietly.

"The most frightening words a team leader can hear," the pawn said wryly. "Come in."

Alix shut the door behind her. "It's about the case, sir. I have a theory."

"Go on."

"Proof," Alix said.

"I'm sorry?" said the pawn.

"I think Edmund's death was proof. It wasn't anything to do with the line of succession, or his wealth, or a personal vendetta, or harming the monarchy. I think he was killed by someone who wanted to prove that they could do it. Proof of concept. Proof of capability."

"Whose capability?" asked Smith, her eyes narrowed.

"Well, I don't know who they are," said Alix. "But it's a person with the power to kill anyone, and in such a way that no one knows it's murder and no one can trace it back."

"But they already know they can do that," objected Smith. "They killed that poor American kid."

"Right, but the proof isn't for the killer. It's for others."

"Who?"

"Potential clients."

"Go on," said Smith. "So, then what happens, after they kill the Prince of Wales as 'proof'?"

"It's already happened beforehand. The killer has already made arrangements. They want to monetize their ability. They've identified people whose deaths mean a profit for others. They've contacted those potential profiters and offered their services in exchange for payment. All the clients need to clinch the deal is proof of the killer's abilities: the murder of a prominent person with world-class security. Someone whose sudden death will be scrutinized as closely as anyone's on earth, by experts, and eventually announced to be the result of natural causes. A man whose burial will be witnessed by millions."

Alix could see that Smith was considering this carefully.

"I think Edmund's death was never the point," Alix said. "Ian Blanch was the point. The CEO of a multimillion-pound company. His death would have made a difference in Kabriolet share prices, especially if you knew it was coming. We looked at who would benefit *directly* from Blanch's removal, either in terms of career advancement or inheriting money. But we need to look at who profited from fluctuations in the share price immediately after his death. If I'm right, that will lead us to the killer."

Alix hated this theory. It broke her heart—the thought that Edmund had been killed solely because of his position, that he was a victim of the rank that had been forced upon him by the fluke of birth. But it made a horrible sense. She watched the pawn turning the theory over in her mind.

"Very interesting," said Smith. "What about Alfie Rohmer? How does he fit into this scenario?"

"I don't know," confessed Alix. "If my theory is right, the killer was hired by someone who stood to make money off his death. Maybe through sports betting. Or, is his football team a publicly traded company?"

"Pawn Weller's group has been investigating all the victims' financial histories," said Smith.

"Yes, they've been looking for overlap between the victims. But that's the wrong place to look." Alix paused uncomfortably. "I think we've all been making the same mistake—looking at these murders through the lens of Edmund's death." She looked down, ashamed. "It's the glow of royalty, it can color everything." She looked at Smith. "What do you think?"

"I think we should give your angle a try," said the team leader. "God knows our current approach hasn't yielded much. I'll tell Weller to point her people in this new direction."

"Are you going to tell the King?" Alix asked. The suggestion that his son's murder had been incidental, a calling card, would not be welcome news.

"I don't need to call him immediately," said Smith. "But I am obligated to include it in the daily report."

"Yeah," said Alix. She bit her lip. "Do you have to say it was my idea?"

Pawn Bertina Weller arrived in Smith's office, listened to Alix's theory, and allowed as how it might have some merit.

"We'll look globally," she said, "for evidence of stock-shorting, share acquisition, data flows, market redistribution, econometrics." She seemed pleased, even as she continued to list increasingly esoteric financial terms. Alix found herself rather pitying the accountant-serfs of Weller's private little fiefdom.

"That sounds like it's going to take a lot of time and effort," she ventured.

"Absolutely," said Weller. There was the glow in her eye of an empire builder. "I'll need additional staff. Say, five more people to begin with?"

"Easy," said Smith.

"And we'll need space for them. Can we expand our offices?"

"I'm not sure," Smith said. "What's on the other side of the partition wall?"

"I checked. Nothing. There was a team working there, but now it's just shattered walls and debris from your..." She trailed off.

"My rampage. You can say it. I'll arrange for the space to be cleared and set up for you as a priority."

"Thank you. Also, Dr. Claes mentioned that her people have developed a stimulant that allows staff to remain awake for ninety-two hours straight without any loss of cognitive function and only minimal weeping."

"Right..."

"Could we requisition the dromedary that expresses that stimulant?"

Over the next week, Weller's expanded little army of finance pawns and retainers (although, sadly, not a dromedary that lactated amphetamines) arrived in dribs and drabs, drawn from offices around the country. They were immediately sequestered away in their new annex, which had its own separate entrance, although they could access the kitchenette.

The investigation team continued with their own work. They compiled all the phone numbers that had contacted the victims in the three months before the murders into a massive color-coded list and scrutinized them for overlaps. The list was continuously updated as the time frame was pushed back and more possibilities considered. Claes continued to examine the brains of the victims, while Scagell updated his profile of the killer.

At that morning's meeting, Weller had provided a recap of the work her cadre of accountants was undertaking. "We have two primary focuses," she said. "The first is within Blanch's company. We had already been looking into who gained power or money as a result of his death. It hasn't proven terribly helpful, not least because the board hasn't yet replaced him, and there doesn't appear to be a clear successor. The second avenue of investigation is much broader. We're looking to see who *outside* Kabriolet profited from his demise. That includes shareholders," she said, "but also competitors. This means a substantial amount of research." A pause ensued. "I may need more staff." She hesitated under Smith's steady gaze. "But I may not."

"Hmm," said Smith. "Keep me posted. And let us press on with our tasks."

Now the office was quiet, with everyone's heads down over their work. They all looked up when a shouted exclamation suddenly came reverberating through the door to the Financial Team's annex.

"*Yes*! Motherfuck-*aaaaahhhh*!"

They waited, but nothing more eventuated.

"That sounded promising," said Alix.

"Maybe a breakthrough on the case?" suggested Scagell.

"Or it's someone's birthday in there, and they have cake," Claes said.

"Unless they're actually having those accounting orgies that Sweven keeps insisting are going on," said Chuah.

"Gross," said Alix, wrinkling her nose.

"They're *always* in there," said Sweven. "And no one can be as boring as those people appear to be."

"If it was a breakthrough, surely someone would come rushing out with news," said Scagell.

"If it was an orgy, someone would come out all sweaty to rehydrate in the kitchenette," said Padilla.

"If it's cake, maybe someone will come out and share with us," said Claes.

They all stared at the door to the annex, mostly hoping for cake or a breakthrough but willing to accept evidence of a saucy scandal. The door opened slowly, and everyone held their breath. Weller emerged, holding no cake, and too composed to have just emerged from an orgy. She looked a little taken aback to find five people and a quokka looking at her expectantly.

"We've found a possibility," she said.

21

There are several promising leads," Weller said to the gathered team. "First, we found instances of strategic shortings of Kabriolet shares." She glanced around and saw that several of the team members were looking at her in polite, glassy incomprehension. "Um, that means that someone bet ahead of time that the company would lose value."

"How common is this strategy?" asked Alix, who knew next to nothing of the stock market.

"It's not that unusual," said Weller, shrugging. "But it depends on the size of the bet. Shorting can be very risky, because if the price goes up instead of down, you're obliged to pay the difference. It can mean very significant losses. But these transactions were ideally timed to take advantage of Blanch's death."

"Does the death of a CEO really make that much of a difference?" asked Scagell. "I mean, I can see how it might for one of those tech celebrities out of Silicon Valley, where it's all about their vision and their mildly unsettling mannerisms, but I'd never heard of Mr. Blanch until we were on the way to investigate his murder."

"Economy and business are a complicated web," said Weller. "Major bodies, like corporations and even countries, can turn out to be massively dependent on very small elements. And a lot of the market and valuation is based on human perception, which is notoriously unreliable. Just a tiny shift, or even the *rumor* of a tiny shift, can result in major movement. So something as big as this—the murder of a man who is known in his field for his vision and competence, whose leadership has seen the value of the company increase steadily over the years? That can offer opportunities, especially if you know that it's coming."

"And someone made money when the price fell?" asked Smith.

"*Several* someones," said Weller. "And a great deal of money. Shares in Mr. Blanch's company were shorted by multiple parties."

"Meaning multiple suspects?" asked Smith.

"That's what we thought at first. But as we looked deeper, we saw that these transactions had been spread out through various intermediaries and subsidiaries. Investment funds owned by seventeen different separate companies turned out to be owned by nine holding companies, which were subsidiaries of four companies, and so on." Weller hit a key on her laptop and a complicated graphic that looked like an upside-down family tree appeared on a drop-down screen behind her. "We traced the lines back to their ultimate owners and found that two distinct parties acted to take advantage of Mr. Blanch's death."

What? TWO?

"The first," Weller went on, "Party One, was responsible for the largest shorting in terms of cash value, although it was spread out through numerous convoluted transactions. Those transactions began after the prince's death, starting small, and then increased in number and amount each day until the funeral."

"Were you able to identify Party One?" asked Smith.

"Yes. Despite their efforts at diffusing their transactions, which were rather well executed, we identified them as Baffles & Co. They're a British company, an investment firm."

"Party Two's endeavors were on a much smaller scale. Two shorting transactions of equal value. A substantial amount of money for this kind of bet—we're talking a year's salary for a pawn—but nowhere near the total size of Baffles's. Also, they were much less cleverly disguised. There were only a few layers between the publicly listed short seller and the actual final party, a man named Thomas Vilanch."

"Who?" asked Alix.

"Exactly," said Weller. A photo of a man flashed up on the screen. An unremarkable-looking white guy, beige hair, brown eyes, late twenties, in a blue suit. The only vaguely interesting feature was his large (though not implausibly large) jaw and forehead, which made his head look vaguely like the number 8, if you were feeling uncharitable.

"Thomas Vilanch is in the Emerging Markets section of Baffles & Co.," said Weller. "Age twenty-seven, born in Middlesex. Studied finance at the University of Hull, worked for several different companies, always in finance. His tax records show he's doing very well, although his shorting of the stocks consumed most of his savings. Of course, it paid off handsomely. No criminal record. He's been to America a couple of times, but his first trip was several years after the first murder. No known connection to Prince Edmund, or to Blanch or Rohmer. It's unclear what his role in all this was—whether he was actively involved in Baffles's plan to eliminate Blanch, or just knew about his company's intentions and took the opportunity to make himself rich."

"So, what do we do now?" asked Sweven.

"Now we scare the shit out of him," said Smith.

"*Excellent*," said Padilla.

Thomas Vilanch?"

He looked up warily. He was twenty minutes into his lunch break, and they had been observing him ever since he left his office. He had gone to a sandwich shop, ordered a roast chicken on multigrain with lettuce, avocado, aioli, and capers, and sat on a bench in Canada Square, watching the other financial denizens of Canary Wharf on their lunch hour.

Now, looming over him with the sun at their backs were Detective Constable Chuah and Pawn Weller, grim-faced and foreboding in severe dark suits. The rest of the team was in a van parked twenty-five meters away, watching the feed from a camera concealed in Weller's spiky brooch.

"Yes?" he said, squinting up at them. He was smooth in his good suit and his carefully styled hair—the kind of smooth that comes from making a great deal more money than your parents had ever dreamed of. The kind of smooth that you get from running with a pack of people who have convinced themselves that they're conquering the world.

"We're the police," said Chuah. He showed his warrant card, and Weller displayed one that had been fabricated for her. "We're hoping you might assist with our inquiries."

"I think I—What inquiries?" he asked.

"We're investigating the murder of Ian Blanch," said Chuah. Vilanch looked as if he might throw up his sandwich. His smoothness was wiped away, so that he was now a frightened man with expensively fixed teeth. "I see that name is familiar to you?"

After a hesitation, Vilanch whispered, "Yes."

"It should be," said Weller. "You certainly profited from his death. Quintupled your investment—the one you made on your own behalf, that is. Not the one your company made."

"Nothing illegal about any of that," said Vilanch. His image on the monitor caught the glint of some sudden perspiration on his forehead.

"It's not illegal to short stock," said Weller. "Depending on the circumstances."

"I didn't know he was going to be murdered!" Vilanch blurted out—it was almost a shriek. "He said it would be natural causes! Oh, God."

In the battered-looking van thirty meters away, this was met with so many sharply drawn-in breaths that the ceiling crumpled in a little.

Vilanch was distraught, his breath was heaving, and sweat sheened on his forehead. Clearly, he'd been waiting for something like this, torn between hope that it wouldn't happen and terror that it would.

"He's ready to talk now," said Smith into the microphone that fed to Chuah and Weller's earpieces. "We won't take him to a facility... yet. Do this here."

"Why don't you tell us what happened?" said Chuah. He sat down next to Vilanch, but Weller stayed standing in front of him, partly to keep the brooch-camera trained on him, and partly to have a standing start if he bolted.

"He was a psychic," said Vilanch. "That's what he said."

"Who?"

"Kevin Spansberg."

"How do you spell that?" asked Weller. As Vilanch spelled it out, Padilla and Sweven repeated the name on their phones to people with access to various databases.

"How did you meet him?" asked Weller.

"A lecture at the LSE," said Vilanch.

"What's the LSE?" asked Padilla.

"The London School of Economics," said everyone else in the van simultaneously.

"They had one of those tech-bro CEOs over from Silicon Valley," Vilanch was saying. "His talk was about how in the future everyone would be their own bank, but most people were there just hoping to meet him and make a contact that might get them a job or a couple billion in start-up capital thrown their way."

From the dispirited way he said it, it was clear that Vilanch himself had made no contacts and gotten no billions.

"Afterward, everyone was clustered at one end of the room trying to get near the tech guy," Vilanch went on. "I'd given up, was just getting another free crap wine in a plastic glass, and this guy joined me. American, maybe midthirties? We chatted and introduced ourselves. He said he was a photographer. His wife was a financial consultant over in the scrum around the billionaire. We traded cards, just to be polite. Then he said, 'all those people sucking up is pointless anyway.' I asked him what he meant. And he said the billionaire was going to die in nineteen days."

Vilanch stared at Spansberg, confused. He'd had a few wines by that point, and his thoughts were coming rather slowly. The foyer in which the billionaire and his audience had gathered for complimentary drinks and nibbles was echoing with a lot of people talking at each other.

"What?" he said.

"Yep," said Spansberg. The American was tall and muscular, with silver flecks in his black hair.

"That's a weird thing to say," Vilanch said. "Is he sick? I haven't heard anything." In the world of international finance, an unwell visionary multibillionaire with majority ownership of his corporation would be a big deal. "How do *you* know he's going to die?"

"I'm psychic," said Spansberg. Despite himself, Vilanch gave a little incredulous giggle. "Yeah, I know," said the American. "But I get these flashes about people's deaths sometimes, and I'm never wrong. I shook that man's hand"—he nodded at the billionaire—"and he is going to die in nineteen days, from natural causes."

"Okay," said Vilanch. "Right. Interesting."

You didn't think to call the authorities?" asked Chuah.

"I thought he was crazy," Vilanch said defensively. "Not like psychotic murderer crazy, but come on. I mean, psychic? What was I supposed to think?" he asked plaintively.

The Checquy operatives remained silent.

"Anyway," Vilanch went on, "I don't know what I said, but from there I went out drinking with some mates. It got a bit full-on. Then the weekend came. I forgot about it."

"And then what happened?" asked Chuah.

"And then, a few weeks later, the billionaire died."

All eyes in the van turned to Padilla, who was blushing flaming red at the thought that an American billionaire had presumably been supernaturally murdered, and the Croatoan hadn't caught it.

"Chuah, what was the billionaire's name?" Smith asked through the coms.

Chuah asked Vilanch and the answer came back:

"Peter Ledbury."

Everyone in the van looked again to Padilla, who shrugged. Alix couldn't blame him. The name was maybe vaguely familiar. But there were so many tech billionaires, who could be bothered to remember them all, especially if you weren't interested anyway?

Padilla was typing briskly on his rugged U.S. government–issued laptop. "Okay, yeah, here we go. He died about three months before the prince." He paused. "Oh, thank *God*. He died in Spain, in Cádiz." He looked up guiltily. "Sorry, but the autopsy would have been done there." The others nodded in understanding. "Cause of death was found to be an undiagnosed heart defect." Everyone looked to Claes.

"Perfectly plausible," said Claes. "Something like that could be coiled away in your body, the result of a genetic error, and you could be fine until suddenly you're not."

"Easily confused with a cube in the brain?"

"No."

"So, a cover-up by the Spanish?" said Smith.

"What's the deal with Spain?" asked Padilla. "Supernatural-wise, I mean?"

"We can't officially place agents on the Continent," said Smith, "so the information we have is spotty. There are no Checquy-equivalent organizations there that we're aware of. And we can't reach out to the Spanish government to ask if they concealed the supernatural details of Ledbury's death. Either the Spanish missed the brain cube or they kept it secret, for which I can hardly blame them. It can't be good for their tourism if foreign billionaires keel over on the beach with abruptly fossilized brains."

Everyone turned their attention back to the interrogation of Vilanch, who was continuing to spill his guts. It seemed that Weller had asked him why he had made no report to the authorities.

"I didn't know what to think. But who would I call? What would I report?"

"You didn't think the prediction was too much of a coincidence? That it might have been murder?" Weller pressed him.

"I mean, I thought about calling the cops." Vilanch didn't seem to notice that he had just contradicted himself. "But then the authorities said it was from natural causes. And the press was all about the effect on the guy's company. Stocks plunged, investors were going nuts, and I thought how, if I had believed the guy at the reception, I could have made a bundle."

"So you contacted this Kevin Spansberg?" said Chuah.

"I spent an hour tearing the flat apart, looking for his bloody card," said Vilanch. "Couldn't remember his name. Finally found it, called him, reminded him who I was, and asked him to meet so I could explain my idea. I didn't want to do it over the phone."

"If he was married to someone in finance, surely he was aware of the possibilities," said Weller. "Why did it take you to open his eyes?"

"He said he'd struggled with his ability," said Vilanch. "That he'd been frightened of it and it took him years to come to terms with it. He didn't tell people about it, only mentioned it to me because he'd had too much wine that night."

"Had he ever tried to prevent the deaths he'd...foretold?" Chuah asked, skepticism coating the final word.

"Yeah, he said it never worked. People didn't believe him, got angry, and then died anyway, so he stopped."

"But he was open to your proposal? Which was what, exactly?" said Weller.

"Yeah, he was very interested. He was up for it right away. Especially when I explained how, if my firm got involved, there could be some serious money. I asked if he had foreseen any other deaths, and he said no, but he'd let me know. A few weeks later, he called me up and had two names. I nearly had a stroke when I saw that one of them was Prince Edmund. Then I recognized the second one and saw the profit implications."

"And your higher-ups leapt on board with this plan?" asked Weller.

"Well, I didn't just write up a proposal and send it to the whole board," said Vilanch. "It took some strategy, some words in the right ears, but there was interest. Especially when I pointed out that we could use the prince as a test case."

Alix hissed. At that moment, if she'd had the power of the girl she'd shared a dorm room with at the Estate, she would have reached into the monitor and strangled Vilanch.

"And no one thought to contact the authorities and say they had reason to believe Prince Edmund's life was in danger?" asked Chuah.

"Spansberg said it was only ever natural causes!" exclaimed Vilanch. "Never a hint of murder or accident, or anything like that. What were we going to do? Call up the Buckingham Palace switchboard and tell them the prince ought to get a physical because a psychic thought he might not be well?"

"Did Spansberg say how he'd come to shake the prince's hand?" asked Alix, and the question was relayed.

"Just said it was some reception," said Vilanch. "He went to events as part of his wife's consultation business. That was how he met Ian Blanch."

"He seems to have shaken a lot of hands," said Chuah.

"He was on the lookout, wasn't he?"

"Go on," said Chuah.

"I'd laid the groundwork with a couple of the boys on the twelfth floor," said Vilanch. "They were dubious, but when I mentioned Ledbury's death, they could see the potential. So, when the prince died, they threw some cash toward shorting Blanch's company. Nothing they couldn't afford to lose if it turned out to be a scam. We were all watching the press very closely. If word had come out that the prince had been murdered, we'd have been on to the police immediately." He looked up at them, pleading with them to believe him. When there was no response, he shrank in on himself and went on.

"But word came down, natural causes. An aneurysm. Spansberg had been right about the prince, so Blanch started to seem likely. They threw some more money into the shorting effort. And then more."

"And you laid down your own money as well," said Weller. "Separately."

"I knew it was going to work," said Vilanch. "But the guys upstairs made it even better. They spread out the transactions, hid that it was us making them. We didn't want to tip anyone off. When Blanch died, they put out word about how bad this would be for the company. Some planted comments in online industry articles, some remarks on social media about how good Blanch was, some unnamed sources putting words in the ears of financial journalists. All through dummy accounts and back channels, never linked to Baffles, but it did the trick. People were already jumpy, the stock fell, and the money came pouring in. Them upstairs were ecstatic, *and* I got a bonus."

"In addition to your own investments," said Weller.

"Yeah, but they didn't know about that," said Vilanch. "I had to be a bit sneaky—didn't want them thinking they should give me less, just 'cause I'd made a tasty pile on my own bat. And there are rules about us doing our own trades. But it was too good an opportunity not to take. Anyway, I called Spansberg, told him he was bloody amazing, paid his fee immediately, as we'd agreed. Best day ever. He was laughing, said he'd keep an eye out for any other possibilities."

"And then what?" asked Chuah.

"And then the twelfth-floor lads and I went out and got pissed," said Vilanch. "Bloody amazing day. And it looked like it was going to just be the start."

"But then word came out that Blanch was murdered," said Chuah.

"We freaked," said Vilanch. "We'd just made millions, and now it looked like we'd been involved in a crime. I was called up to the twelfth, and they were sitting there, ashen, convinced we were all going to prison."

"What about Spansberg?"

"I called him immediately, but the number was disconnected."

"No one called the authorities?"

"How would we look?" asked Vilanch, his voice pathetic. "Insane profits, based entirely on Blanch's death? No one would believe we thought Spansberg was a psychic. It looked like conspiracy to murder." He eyed his sandwich, half uneaten, in cling film on his lap. "But someone pointed out that because of all the work we'd done to conceal the transactions, odds were that no one would come knocking on our door. If we kept quiet, then it would probably be all right."

"Let's talk about Spansberg," said Chuah. "Do you have the phone number, the one that was disconnected?"

"It's in my phone," said Vilanch. He quickly found it, and it was sent to the Rookery.

Under continued questioning, Vilanch told them that he had no pictures of Spansberg, and had no idea where he lived.

"We just met that one time, at the pub," said the trader. "He never came into the office, and we did everything else on the phone or electronically."

"Were documents signed?" asked Weller. "A formal agreement?"

"Yeah, but not with Kevin Spansberg," said Vilanch. "We were all careful not to draw attention, not just from outside, but also within the firm. We didn't want questions getting asked. So, we paid him as a consultant, to his own little company, with electronic signatures."

"Not cash?" asked Chuah.

"Not the amount we were paying him," said Vilanch, looking surprised. "And besides, what if we'd gotten audited or something? We've got to be able to account for every penny, don't we?"

"Chuah, we're going to have a lot more questions for this loathsome toad," said Smith. "I want to dig deep, get every detail, have him work with a sketch artist. Let's shift him to our facility. Put the fear into him, and make it clear that his cooperation may be all that keeps him from a lifetime in prison."

There was obviously a good deal of fear in him already. The trader had looked quite glossy when they first approached him, but over the course of the questioning, he had deflated. Even his hair looked lank, as if his styling products had fled in fear, and his eyes were haunted.

"We'll squeeze him for everything he's got," Smith said, "at least in terms of information. I expect he'll be permitted to keep the money. And his freedom. He's disgusting, but for now I'm buying his story. I think he really believed this Spansberg was psychic." There were murmurs of reluctant agreement around the van. "Still, we finally have a lead on the killer."

Vilanch was escorted to a Checquy facility, which was really just a fortified back room in the Bethnal Green police station. Chuah gave him a cup of tea and Weller applied a modicum of pressure, whereupon Vilanch proceeded to thoroughly spill what was left of his guts. It was clear that he'd been living in dread ever since Blanch's death had been announced as a murder.

His phone yielded details of all the calls he'd made to Kevin Spansberg, and listed the location of the Fox & Cheese — the pub where they'd met. Sweven was tasked with requisitioning the high street security camera footage from that day, in hopes that it had captured Spansberg entering or exiting.

Claes went in and worked from Vilanch's weepy description to produce a sketch of Kevin Spansberg. It revealed a white man with dark hair tumbling over his forehead, magnificent cheekbones, rather prominent teeth, and surprisingly large and gentle eyes. He looked like the human embodiment of a very expensive horse.

As far as Smith was concerned, it was imperative that all the new information be included in that evening's briefing package for the King. Thomas Vilanch represented their biggest break yet and she was eager to show the progress they'd made in their investigation.

The problem was that the daily deadline was nearly upon them, but they had only just begun following their many new leads. Everyone was running around frantically, but the updates were mainly about information they did not yet have.

Sweven grimly advised that no Kevin Spansberg had been assigned an NHS number or a National Insurance number.

Padilla grimly advised that no Kevin Spansberg had ever been assigned a U.S. social security number.

Those grim advisories delivered, there were any number of other databases to search: law enforcement, visas and travel records, social media. It would take time to review them all.

The contract Kevin Spansberg had signed in the name of his "consulting company" was filed back at the offices of Baffles & Co. Once retrieved, it would be rigorously examined for fingerprints, DNA, and analysis of Spansberg's signature, even if it turned out to be a pseudonym. Plus, it would be wafted under the snoot of the quokka, to see if its scent profile could be tracked or matched.

Vilanch pleaded that he was unable to remember the name of Spansberg's consulting business, only that it was something unremarkable. Weller was champing at the bit to unleash her horde of forensic accountants.

Kevin Spansberg's original business card was also back at Vilanch's office. The odds of getting fingerprints off it after all this time was slim, but they'd try it.

All these avenues of investigation were added to the report.

"Where are my pages?" Smith said. "We have to have the briefing package approved and in the King's hand by six thirty! The courier will be here in ten minutes!"

The courier was actually there in two minutes, but the briefing was still being proofread before printing.

"You're early," said Smith accusingly.

"Traffic's bad tonight," said the courier. "I need to leave now if I'm going to get it to the palace by the deadline."

"How long, people?" said Smith.

"Seven minutes, if we stop editing now and are willing to hand the King a document riddled with typos, grammatical errors, and shitty formatting," said Padilla, who seemed to know the most about it.

"Hell," said Smith, her every instinct visibly rebelling against the prospect.

"I need to go now," said the courier, with the unconcern of one whose problem it was not. "I've got other stops."

Smith closed her eyes for a moment. "Unhelpful Courier, you can go. Mondegreen, you'll deliver the report once it's ready."

"What?"

"The King will be less pissed off at *you*, if it's a few minutes late."

"I'm not sure he will! Plus, my car isn't here."

"I'll drive you," said Smith.

"Oh, *God*."

Alix's fingers were clenched so tight around the oh-shit handle that she needed to use her other hand to uncurl them. The terror of being a passenger as Smith drove through rush-hour London traffic had left her drenched in perspiration. It was clear that the team leader had taken the Checquy's advanced driving classes — the ones that treated traffic as a combat situation — and was using her knowledge to cut dangerously through London's end-of-day congestion. As they pulled in at one of the palace's service entrances, the security guard in the armored booth recognized Alix but paused uncertainly when he saw the tension on her face.

"I'm fine," Alix said, tautly wiping her brow. "Really." He waved them through.

"Go!" ordered Smith as they pulled up at a side entrance, and Alix sprinted into the palace, flinging herself up the steps, dodging around staff, barreling up staircases, and ricocheting off corners. Red-faced and sweating, she came to a skidding halt outside the King's study. Bent over to gasp back her breath, she knocked on the door and checked the time. It was just turning 6:31.

"Come in." She practically fell through the doorway, but caught herself enough to curtsy. "Alexandra, good evening. You look"—the King paused, years of diplomatic adjectives offering themselves up for consideration—"well."

"Your Majesty," Alix wheezed. She held up the envelope, which she'd managed to crumple during her sprint. "Today's briefing package."

"Oh, good," he said, looking a little taken aback. "Productive day?"

"Quite a bit of new stuff, yes."

"Excellent." He took the envelope gingerly. "It feels a good deal heavier than usual. That seems promising." He looked at her questioningly.

Alix hesitated. It all *did* seem promising, at least at first glance.

"We're following all the leads," she said. The King nodded, motioned for her to sit, and began to read through the report. At points he looked up at her in surprise, and she smiled weakly, ready to comment if he asked any questions. But he didn't. Finally he put the document aside.

"As soon as you learn anything about this man, I want to know," said the King. "And I mean immediately."

"Yes, sir."

Bad news," said Weller. "We've done an investigation into Spansberg's little company."

"And is the bad news that you couldn't locate Spansberg?" asked Smith wearily. It was three days after Vilanch had told them everything he knew, and so far, they had found barely any trace of the reportedly psychic photographer. His name did not appear on any database they could access. Whatever visa had enabled the American to reside in the UK was not in the name Kevin Spansberg. Security footage covering the pub where he had met Vilanch had been erased after thirty days.

"The company's name is North Mast Holdings, based in the U.S."

"That's a weird name," remarked Alix.

"These things aren't usually chosen for their meaningfulness," said Weller. "Quite the opposite, in fact. Anyway, North Mast Holdings is owned by another company, one with an even less meaningful name. And *that* one was owned by another company. And so on." She clicked on her little remote, and an organizational chart flashed upon the screen. It looked like the upside-down tree through which she had traced Baffles & Co.'s shorting endeavors.

"In this case, our cousins across the waves were quite helpful."

Padilla shrugged. "Always happy to violate the privacy of individuals," he said.

"We've traced ownership to a single entity, a company called Constantus Limited."

"So, who is he?" asked Alix. "Who's behind Constantus Limited?"

"We don't know," said Weller. "We've hit a wall. The company is based in Liechtenstein, whose laws are very protective of people's privacy."

"We don't have any authority there?" asked Chuah.

"No," said Weller. "If the man we're calling Spansberg had gone for a former British colony as a haven, there are sometimes remnants of leverage we can apply. But nothing in Liechtenstein, and we can't operate on the Continent. That's as far as we can follow the trail."

"And the Americans?" asked Alix.

"Sorry," said Padilla. "There are limits even for us."

"Still, we've been able to gather some information. North Mast Holdings was not the only subsidiary of Constantus. In the week following Blanch's death, several other payments came into his feeder companies — those not housed in Liechtenstein. We traced them back and found that those payments came from various entities that were not Baffles & Co. The different entities who paid him included two in China, one in Indonesia, one in Singapore, three in the Middle East, one in South Africa, and two in Australia."

"So, there were several different companies betting on Blanch's death?" asked Smith.

"Not so far as we can tell. Kabriolet was listed on only two stock exchanges, and we've tracked all the transactions that profited from shorting it. They were all either Baffles or Vilanch."

"What does that mean?" asked Alix.

"It suggests that Blanch's was not the only murder triggered by the prince's funeral."

22

Ten days went by, and nothing much was accomplished. Pawn Weller and her minions spent hours sequestered away in their finance-burrow, striving for some way to breach the privacy of Constantus Limited. Not only were the banking details locked tight, but the company's incorporation in Liechtenstein meant that no information about its shareholders or directors needed to be made public.

They had discovered, however, that not all the parties who had made roundabout payments to Constantus Limited were players on the stock market. In fact, it appeared that Baffles & Co. and Vilanch had been the only ones to profit from a death by short-selling. Others seemed more straightforward. One of Kevin Spansberg's clients was a South African company known to be the front for a criminal organization that was doing very well, especially since the leader of its main rival had dropped dead while watching the royal funeral on television. Another payment had come from a young man in Singapore who had transferred an eye-watering amount, although presumably he was not missing it, since his grandfather had passed away unexpectedly, leaving him a vast inheritance.

"These people sicken me," Chuah said bitterly. Since these parties were all overseas, and none were British citizens, the Checquy had no jurisdiction to approach them. "We should tip off the local authorities somehow."

"With what?" Alix asked. "No proof of anything? That's not our job."

Then, at a morning meeting, when everyone was settling in dispiritedly around the table, Pawn Weller cleared her throat.

"We have very good news," she said. Everyone sat up alertly, including the quokka. "It turns out that information regarding our target was one of several thousand in a set of documents leaked to the International Consortium of Investigative Journalists."

"No!" exclaimed Alix. "Not the Principality Papers!"

"The very ones," said Weller with a cat-in-the-cream smile.

"What are those?" asked Smith, confused.

Weller described the leak of banking and business details from closed-mouth little tax havens that had embarrassed any number of prominent people and companies.

"And did we have anything to do with this?" asked Smith.

"No," said Weller. "It just happened that someone was disgusted with the great and ostensibly good who were not paying their fair share."

"And do these papers provide the name of the owner of Constantus Limited?" asked Alix.

"Yes, it does. Buried in the thousands of entries, between Constantine Corp. and Constar Investments, is the name of the company, and that of the single shareholder. Phillip Molko."

"Does that name mean anything to anyone?" asked Smith. The team members gathered around the conference table all shook their heads. "No one goes home tonight," said Smith flatly. "We're running down everything we can find about this man. Sweven, order us some pizza."

"Should we let the Court and the King know?"

"Tomorrow. I want more to give them than a name."

The next morning, as the sun started to cast its first golden rays on the rooftops of London, the team gathered at the conference table again, this time with the Lord and Lady of the Checquy seated regally in the middle. Despite the preposterous earliness of the hour, the heads of the Checquy were alert and pristine. Lady Farrier was dressed in a pantsuit that communicated French and *expensive,* while Sir Henry (who looked to be in his early seventies but was actually over a century old) was freshly shaven and wore a dark gray Savile Row suit that would, quite simply, never ever go out of style. They received their offered teas and tactfully did not remark on how shattered everyone looked, or on the empty takeaway boxes that had been hurriedly shoved off the table and were now teetering in an untidy pile in the corner.

The team had worked through the night, all of them fueled by the excitement of finally finding some answers. When given Molko's name, databases around the world had obligingly yielded up all sorts of information. The material was still being consolidated, and Pawn Smith had warned Wattleman and Farrier that this was a rehearsal for their presentation to the King and the Court later that day (except for Bishop Alrich who was an actual vampire, and had just gone to bed in a fortified crypt-bunker in Holland Park). The whole thing was being recorded, and an exhausted-looking Sweven was taking notes.

The Lord and Lady, both of whom had in their time been full field operatives, and who really hated surprises, assured Smith that they were fine with being present for an unpolished working session.

Pawn Smith stifled a yawn and absently ran a hand through some recently brushed hair, then clicked on the little remote. A passport photo appeared on the screen. Everyone stared up at the picture of a Caucasian man in his thirties, with thick black hair cut in a short back-and-sides. Clean-shaven, with a long face, and sporting a blank passport-photo expression, he looked very much like the portrait that Claes had created from Vilanch's description.

Quite handsome, really, Alix mused. If he'd approached her at a party, she'd have been inclined to let him strike up a conversation.

"This is Phillip Molko, owner of Constantus Limited," Smith said. "We showed this image to Vilanch, who identified him, angrily, as Kevin Spansberg."

"And what do we know about this person?" asked Wattleman. Smith nodded to Pawn Padilla.

"Phillip Roger Molko, American," said Padilla apologetically. "Thirty-one years old, born in Cincinnati, Ohio. He attended Ohio

State University at the same time as the first victim, Jordan Wu. Majored in English, minored in Chinese and Professional Writing. We're still checking for a confirmed connection between Molko and Wu. They had different majors, lived in different dormitories, but my colleagues are trawling through old social media and contacting some of their peers through the alumni association."

"And where is he now?" Farrier asked intently. "Do the Americans know?"

"He's here in London," said Smith. "On a long-term Standard Visitor visa."

"Doing what?" asked Wattleman.

"Well, that visa doesn't allow him to work here," Smith said. "And his application made no mention of studying at any institutions. So far as HM Government is concerned, Phillip Molko is here to spend the money he already possessed when he entered."

"Which, according to the IRS, is money he earned from working for seven years in the Ohio state government," Padilla put in. "It all checks out on that score. He was a manager in the Ohio Department of Insurance. His records from there are incredibly uninteresting: no sign of anything significant, no complaints from co-workers. He just worked away, until quitting a year ago."

"How much money did he have saved?" asked Alix.

"Enough to rent a basic little flat here and do a great deal of travel," Weller said. "Since the death of the prince, however, Constantus Limited has started paying for his much-improved accommodation and issued him a corporate credit card."

"What about this wife that your source — Vilanch — mentioned?" asked Farrier.

"No wife," Padilla said.

"And no live-in partner, no girlfriend or boyfriend, so far as we can tell," Smith added. "Although we've not yet entered his flat."

"We think the wife story was just a bit of cover to explain his presence at the LSE event," Weller said.

"Our theory is that he was at that reception trawling for potential clients, and identified Vilanch as the kind of person who would look to profit off someone's predictable death," Scagell said. "Although for all we know, Molko may have dropped his little psychic story to any number of people, and only Vilanch bit on the bait." He looked to Weller, who clicked her remote again.

While Kevin Spansberg had appeared nowhere in their systems, Phillip Molko was fully documented in both the UK and the United States. They had his birth certificate, his social security number, his high school grades, his college transcripts, the details of his visa application. His life on paper.

He was the second oldest of four children. His parents were William and Valerie Molko of Fort Wayne, Indiana. The family was middle class, no criminal records. Parents and siblings still lived in Indiana. When he was growing up, nothing about him had ever tripped any of the Croatoan's finely tuned alarms. No mysterious deaths linked to his presence, no hysterical accusations from weeping peers or teachers. No hint of supernatural capability.

"Why would he still be here in London?" wondered Padilla. "If I'd murdered two people in a foreign country in order to make a lot of money, I'd be out of there as soon as I could. I certainly wouldn't hang around and then murder a famous soccer player."

"Remember, as far as Molko knew, he was committing the perfect, untraceable crime," said Alix. "Even when we released the fact that Mr. Blanch was murdered, the investigation didn't come to anything. Until now, we were never close to him."

Except geographically. Molko's new London flat was, disconcertingly, just a couple of streets over from Alix's own. As of three a.m. that morning, he was under near-constant observation by Checquy operatives, none of whom knew why they were following him.

From scrutinizing Molko's credit card transaction history, Alix had learned that she and Molko went to the same Sainsbury's, and that he was a regular at a pub she liked to stop at of a Sunday afternoon. The thought that they might have stood next to each other at the bar was enough to turn her stomach. The only comfort was that when she'd first seen his pictures, they hadn't triggered any sense of familiarity.

"But look at all the places he's been," Padilla was saying. "I mean, in the five months leading up to the prince's death, he'd spent time in

Indonesia, South Africa, Kenya, India, Australia, New Zealand, Canada, China."

"Setting up murders for money," said Alix darkly. Weller's team had uncovered additional payments that Constantus Limited had received in the weeks following Blanch's death. Most appeared to have been payments from individuals with a lot to gain, such as the one that came from a woman in Macau whose extremely wealthy husband had passed away at the same moment as Mr. Blanch.

A significant payment had come from an account in Uruguay belonging to the incredibly wealthy owner of the South Harrow Mantids, the primary rival of Alfie Rohmer's football team, Oakmead Maulstick. This had been especially devastating to Chuah, who was an ardent supporter of the Mantids.

"All these journeys make it clear that Molko was planning this well before he met with Vilanch," Smith said. "They're all places from which he received payments. We don't know whether he needed to be there to infect his targets or just went there to court customers."

"But Molko was *here,* in London, when he somehow activated those other deaths around the world," said Chuah. "And we don't know how he does that."

Claes nodded, her brow furrowed as she contemplated this practical gap in their knowledge. Everyone else, however, seemed as unperturbed as Alix was. It was supernatural, so there might be no explanation at all. It could be as simple as Molko wishing for a cube to grow, or unclenching part of his mind. Or it might involve him looking at a picture of the victim and directing hate at it. It was clear that however it worked, it worked.

"In every other city, he'd have the perfect alibi," Chuah went on. "So why is he here? Especially if he's killing English businessmen and football players?"

"London's a very good city to live in if you're rich, and your money isn't necessarily one hundred percent moral," said Alix. "And he obviously felt secure here, even after we announced Blanch's death as a murder."

"Except that he wasn't totally secure," said Scagell. "He sent his colleague to do some cleaning up at the Blanch house. That woman with the hairy palms."

"Yes," said Alix thoughtfully. They still hadn't identified Molko's accomplice. They'd scrutinized his phone records and accounted for every one of his few calls. None of these had led them to a person who meshed with Alix and Scagell's description of the mysterious figure. The Croatoan had flexed some of their frightening muscles and connections and gotten them access to Molko's emails. Nothing significant, no communications with anyone from the countries where the other deaths had occurred.

There were so many ways to communicate secretly, though. Disposable phones, encrypted emails, secret signals scribbled in public places. It was frustrating.

And Molko has definitely shown he knew about burner phones, Alix thought. *Remember the attack on Smith that made her go crazy.*

And that is the man you believe killed my son," said the King. The same passport photo of Phillip Molko was projected up on the screen.

"Yes, sir," said Lady Farrier.

It was just after lunch, and they were in the fancy executive conference room at Apex House. The fancy executive conference consisted of the King, the seven members of the Court, Pawn Smith, and Alix, who suspected that she had been brought along as the royal whisperer, or at least the royal calmer.

Normally, the Checquy would have come to the King, but the amount of material to be presented made transporting it all something of a security issue.

In deference to their royal guest, though, the room had been freshly painted, and the table glistened with so much wax and polish that it looked like a portal into a very glossy mystical woodland realm.

"You're sure?" asked the King.

"Yes, sir. The Court is satisfied." There were sounds of agreement from around the table.

"All right, then." The King took a breath. "I wish to see the body."

Uncertain glances were exchanged.

"Um, sir," began Lady Farrier.

"I want to look on my son's murderer, and see that he is *dead*!" The King's eyes were clenched shut.

"I can understand that, sir," said Sir Henry Wattleman. "Only natural. But Phillip Molko is not dead."

"Really," said the King, opening his eyes. "Very well. I don't wish to speak with him, but I want to see him in his cell before he is executed."

"He's not *actually* in our custody," said Lady Farrier.

"I don't understand," said the King. "The Court is satisfied of his guilt. He is responsible for the murder of my son, the Prince of Wales, by supernatural means. The crime falls within your jurisdiction. So why is he walking about freely?"

"He is under constant observation," said the Lady. "We are aiming to identify any additional accomplices. We know there is at least one: the woman who broke into the second murder scene and fought with our operatives. We do not know if it was she, Molko, or someone else who placed the weaponized telephone call to Agent Smith."

The King pursed his lips. "How important is this woman?" he asked. *"This"*—he gestured to the screen—"is the person who killed my son."

"These people know about the Checquy, Your Majesty," said Sir Henry. "They struck out not only at your family but at our organization, and caused us harm. No one gets to do that with impunity. It's a matter of national security."

There was a silence.

"We began monitoring his communications today," said Rook Thomas. "So far, he has only contacted a couple of people here in London who seem to be friends, and on whom we've done thorough background checks. They don't appear to have profited from any of the deaths. The Croatoan have investigated his family members, and it seems they know nothing of their son's activities."

"But meanwhile this man is at liberty in this very city, having a very pleasant time," said the King. He flipped through the thick dossier that had been prepared for him. "He's certainly freely spending his money — the money he earned by killing my son! Look at the cost of this gym membership!"

"We see no indication that he is preparing any more murders," said Bishop Attirawala.

"How many more hours of freedom are you granting this man? How long will you be waiting for him to make an incriminating phone call?"

"Two more days," said Lady Farrier. "Then, sir, regardless of whether he's given us any new leads, we'll pick him up."

"Pick him up or kill him?"

"Pick him up," said Smith. "We need to question him."

"We'll have to be extremely careful," said Sir Henry. "We still have very little knowledge of how his powers work. We don't know how he infects his victims — whether he seeds everyone around him, or whether it's done by touch, speech, eye contact, line of sight, or even eating bits of the victim's hair."

"That last one is a disconcerting idea," said the King, sounding distinctly unnerved.

"It's how the Reverend Pawn Rice links with her targets so that she can inflict them with hallucinations of monotremes," said Lady Farrier.

"*Meanwhile,*" said Sir Henry heavily, "we also don't know how the seeds, once planted, are activated. Is there a length of time needed to infect someone, or for his powers to gestate inside them? All we know for certain is that he has the demonstrated ability and willingness to kill, so we must assume the worst and take every measure to ensure that he doesn't lash out at the public."

"To make matters worse, there doesn't appear to be a geographic limitation to his ability, nor an expiration date," said Lady Farrier. "We know from his travel history that at least two of his overseas victims were infected by his ability four months before they died, then killed when he was thousands of miles away. And at the time of the murder of the Prince of Wales, Molko was two hundred miles away in York. We lifted his location from his phone history, and he was in a café, paying for his cake and coffee with a credit card."

"Building an excellent alibi," remarked Rook Thomas.

"The waitress remembered him well," said Lady Farrier sourly. "The engaging American who tipped her three times the usual amount." It was not clear if her sourness was because of the firmness of the alibi or the idea of tipping in a café.

"So what does this mean? Will you drug him while he's sleeping, and spirit him away to a black site?" asked the King.

"That's an option, but we worry that if he were to wake up and feel threatened, he could start killing people. We don't know how many people he has seeded," said Farrier. "He could have seeded *you*, sir, for all we know."

"Instead, a Checquy representative will approach him, delicately, in a location where he feels safe, and make him an offer that is part carrot, part stick," said Wattleman.

"The carrot will be a lie," said the King.

"Of course," said Lady Farrier smoothly. "How we proceed will depend on his reaction, but this will all be to gain the information we require."

"And once you have this information, he will be executed?" asked the King.

"He will die in due course," said Sir Henry.

There was a pause, then:

"Indeed," said the King. He appeared less suspicious of Wattleman's statement than Alix was. "Now, what is the current status of Caroline Delahunty?"

Lady Farrier paused.

"There's been no mention of her in my box briefings," he said.

"She continues to be in our custody," the Lady said.

"At Gallows Keep?"

"I'd..." She breathed out. "I'd have to check."

The King regarded her. Alix very deliberately kept her eyes lowered. She knew that Caroline Delahunty had been moved to an isolated facility on Kirrin Island, home of the Checquy's training academy, where she was being evaluated for potential rehabilitation as a Checquy agent.

"Do," said the King. "I look forward to receiving a thorough report on Caroline Delahunty's status first thing tomorrow."

As the King stood and everyone else hurriedly scrambled to their feet, Alix spared a thought for Caroline Delahunty, who was going to be abruptly moved from the pleasant if fortified surrounds of the Estate to the distinctly spartan quarters at Gallows Keep. The Checquy wanted to be able to say honestly that the former actress was being held in their maximum-security prison, at least until the King forgot to ask.

"Who will you be sending to approach Molko?" asked the King suddenly, turning back a few steps short of the conference room doors. "Do you have some operative with a brain made of diamond, so you needn't worry about them getting killed?"

"No, sir," said Lady Farrier. "There are no such pawns. It will be a dangerous mission."

"Then I want Lady Mondegreen to be the one who confronts him."

What?

All eyes in the room turned to Alix.

"Sir...," began Lady Farrier.

"She is competent, yes?"

"Yes."

Do you think you're doing me a favor here? Is this you trying to give me a professional leg up?

"She is deadly," said the King. It was not phrased as a question.

"When appropriate," said Sir Henry.

"She has been part of this investigation since its beginning," said the King.

"Yes," said Smith.

"She is invested. She knew my son. I want her to be the one. If she must interrogate Molko, she will come garbed in the authority of the sovereign, and if she must take him by surprise, I have seen her with a shotgun. I know that she is quick and does not hesitate." He regarded the Court of the Checquy. "And frankly, I feel that I can trust her."

Oh, fuck me. The King was either completely unaware or completely indifferent as to how little this statement would endear her to her superiors in the Checquy. From the stillness among the Court, it was apparent to Alix that they were all outraged at this interference.

"Very well," said Lady Farrier with the kind of brightness that suggests that someone was going to suffer for this. Alix squirmed, certain that the someone was going to be her.

"And if it *does* come down to Lady Mondegreen confronting this man, I will want a full rundown of how the operation will proceed," said the King. "*Well* in advance."

"Of course," said Sir Henry. "It is being planned out in great detail."

"Good. Then we are finished?" said the King. Everyone agreed meekly that they were, and he proceeded toward the door. Sir Henry escorted the sovereign out, but Lady Farrier paused at the threshold.

"You," she said to Alix, "stay here."

"Yes, ma'am," said Alix.

"Should I stay as well?" asked Pawn Smith.

"No," said the Lady, and she turned to follow the King and Sir Henry. The rest of the Court moved out of the room, with Rook Thomas giving Alix a sympathetic look.

"Look, Mondegreen," said Smith hurriedly, "whatever Farrier says to you, just stay calm. You and I will talk about it later, back at the office."

"I'll be honest with you, sir," Alix said. "I'm freaking out a bit. I mean, all of a sudden *I'm* going to be the one confronting this serial killer? The man who killed my friend? I have no experience in this sort of thing. Combat? Yes. Investigation? Yes. Botany? Yes. But not this... what is it? Interrogation? Luring him into a *job*? He's a murderer. A mass murderer! How worried do you think I need to be?"

"I don't know," said Smith, which was close to being the least encouraging answer possible. "But try to be calm. Whatever happens, remember you're a pawn of the Checquy. You'll have us behind you."

"Okay, yeah, sure," said Alix.

"You'll be okay," said Smith. "I'd better go. Come see me right afterward."

Alix sat alone in the conference room. Her mind was whirling and kept presenting new aspects of the situation to worry about. For one thing, there was the horrendous danger to her career because of the

King singling her out. If the Lady thought for one moment that her loyalties were split, Alix's life as a pawn would be entirely screwed.

If I'm still alive to have a career.

She stood as the Lady returned. Farrier gestured her to sit back down.

"So!" said Farrier. "The King trusts you."

"Apparently," said Alix.

"Isn't that nice. And what, pray tell, do you think he trusts you to do?"

"I...like to think that he trusts me to do the right thing."

Farrier scrutinized her silently for several seconds. Under the table, Alix wiped her palms on her thighs.

"I believe I can imagine what the King would think is the right thing," said Farrier. "It's a natural attitude. Any parent would take it. And any monarch would take it. I loved Prince Edmund. I would like to wreak a terrible vengeance myself."

Alix knew Farrier wasn't finished, so she did not reply.

"I despise Molko for what he did. He has committed murder on our soil, using supernatural abilities. But that doesn't mean he is simply to be executed in the street. We have laws. And the fact remains that he is a rare, precious commodity." She fixed Alix with her gaze. "You are going to come face-to-face with him. I don't know what the King has said to you about this—"

"I really had no idea—" began Alix, but the Lady cut her off.

"But before anything else," Farrier continued, "you are a soldier of the Checquy. You will put your duty as a pawn ahead of any personal feelings, any other loyalties, any other possibility of action."

"Yes, my lady," said Alix. "Of course."

"Pawn Smith has been coordinating with Rook Thomas, laying out a strategy to confront Molko. You will need to be brought up to speed extremely quickly, with very little time to prepare."

"Two days from now," said Alix, remembering the briefing they had just given the King.

"It will be tomorrow," said Farrier. "And we will not be providing the King with the details of the operation ahead of time."

"Wh—why?" asked Alix.

"I do not want him exerting any more influence on this operation."

You mean on me.

"But what will we tell him afterward?"

"We will tell him that an opportunity arose, and we took it."

Alix stood outside the Box Room. Mounds of debris were still scattered across the floor, but there were also patches of carpet visible. In a few weeks, it would be as if a stegosaurus had never rampaged madly across the floor.

Hell, in a few weeks, it may be as if I never existed.

What a shit day.

She straightened her shoulders and put on her calm face before entering the office. Apart from Pawn Claes, who greeted her as usual, everyone very conspicuously did not look up at her arrival.

Great.

Evidently, Pawn Smith had advised them of the situation, and no one approved. No matter how Smith had presented it, the situation undeniably consisted of the King intervening on Alix's behalf and forcing the Court to give her a tremendous professional opportunity — one that she was in no way qualified for, and which would have otherwise been assigned to an actual expert who had earned it. The fact that the job was horrendously dangerous in no way diminished its importance, and if successful, the principals would reap significant honors and rewards.

Although judging by everyone's expressions as they avoided looking at her, they apparently had as little faith in Alix's ability to pull it off as she did. Even the foreigner Padilla and the newly inducted Chuah were apparently regarding her assignment as deeply inappropriate. It seemed that the Checquy's antipathy toward any form of nepotism or string-pulling was duplicated in the Metropolitan Police, and in America.

Pawn Claes, on the other hand, who had been playing this game for centuries and had probably been born in an actual feudal society, likely regarded it as entirely normal.

"Smith's gone up to Rook Thomas's office," Claes said. "You're to join them."

"Right, thanks," said Alix. She turned and walked back out of the office. Just before the door closed behind her, she heard conversation start up, and she winced.

I don't want to do this, and I'm resented for being made to do it.

She was ushered straight into the rook's office, to find Thomas, Pawn Smith, the leader of the barghest commandos, and several senior Checquy strategists standing around the conference table. Alix recognized them all, except a tall Black lady whom she was quite certain she had never seen before. *I would have remembered her.* The woman was strikingly beautiful, with thick glossy hair that hung down to her shoulder blades. She was dressed in an exquisitely tailored blood-red suit, and stood, unlike the others in the room, without a hint of deference in her posture.

"Pawn Mondegreen, please join us," said the rook. Alix took a place next to Pawn Smith.

"Are you all right?" asked the pawn quietly.

"Yes, sir." It was the only possible answer.

"Now, as I was saying," the rook went on, "Lady Farrier has advised that we now have twenty-four hours, at most." There were sounds of discontent, which the rook ignored. "We will be initiating contact with Molko. Pawn Mondegreen will be the point of the spear."

Everyone turned to look at Alix with varying degrees of insulting incredulity.

"We have full access to Molko's schedule," the rook continued. "We were planning to approach him two days from now, at a British Museum lecture, for which the Checquy has purchased two-thirds of the tickets." She sighed. "I suppose we'll now need to give those tickets out to staff." She gestured to Smith to take over the next part of the briefing.

"We are now looking at this lunch reservation he's made at Joyo's," Smith said. Joyo's was a new and very expensive restaurant that was housed in a former taxidermist's office in Clerkenwell and specialized in cuisine from Borneo. It was one of *the* places to be seen at the moment. "He'll be lunching alone."

"You haven't considered just coming to his apartment and

knocking on the door?" asked the Black woman, who Alix was startled to hear had a strong American accent. "He lives alone, right? Wouldn't that limit risk to civilians?"

"We must ensure that we have backup operatives immediately present, without having to kick open any doors or melt any ceilings," said a large man wearing an all-encompassing but tailored burqa-type garment. This was Pawn Rintoul, and Alix knew that underneath the pinstriped burqa, he wore a plastic suit filled with a fungicidal gel to ensure that lurid mushrooms didn't start growing all over the room.

"Also, we think it will be less confrontational if we approach him in a public place," put in the leader of the barghests, a compact, muscular lady of Malagasy ancestry named Pawn Razafindrakoto. "We don't yet know the limits of his power. In case he can simply kill anyone he wants to, it's better to keep everything as calm as possible."

"Joyo's will have been booked out for weeks," Alix volunteered.

"We're buying out as many reservations as we can," said Thomas. "Inform your teams of our new time frame, and I'll want all the contingencies before me by the close of business today." Everyone but the American moved toward the door. "Pawn Smith, Mondegreen, stay."

"So, Mondegreen, I expect you're a little jumpy," said the rook.

"No, sir," said Alix. Admitting she was sufficiently jumpy to do a trampoline routine without the trampoline would only make things worse.

"I would be," said the rook. "But you will have support. Quite aside from our people in the restaurant, there will be a truck full of troops around the corner. And we'll also—Oh!" She shook her head. "I'm sorry. You came in late, but I should have introduced you. This is Bishop Petoskey of the Croatoan."

"Nice to meet you," said the American, shaking Alix's hand.

"Because our target is an American citizen, Bishop Petoskey is here as a courtesy witness to the operation."

"Just covering everyone's butts," said Petoskey.

"And we're very grateful," said the rook. Alix noted that the two women had shed a bit of their formal postures from the meeting and looked more relaxed. It was clear they were good friends. "Mondegreen, you will approach Molko at his table."

"Are we not concerned he might recognize me?" asked Alix. "I don't want to sound arrogant, but..."

"But you're the most publicly recognizable member of the Checquy," said the rook. "Except possibly for Odette. It's not ideal. Especially since you have a known connection to his victim. There's a risk he'll react immediately and violently."

So I'm right to be very worried about that happening.

"But," the rook went on, "we're working on a script to address that issue."

"Okay...," said Alix, not entirely convinced. "Can I ask a question?" The rook nodded. "I know Sir Henry told the King that this was all just a ruse to get information from Molko, and that he wouldn't be permitted to go unpunished, but..." She trailed off.

"Go on," said the rook.

"Is recruitment part of the goal?" she asked. She knew the Checquy much preferred to tame a monster and bring it into the fold than kill it.

The other three women exchanged glances.

"There are people who view Phillip Molko as a potentially valuable asset for this country," Thomas conceded.

"Even though he's killed multiple people for profit?"

"We've had worse," said the rook.

"So have we," put in Bishop Petoskey.

"But that is not our priority," said Thomas. "Our priority is to identify the other people Molko works with. Quite aside from the fact that they have conspired to murder individuals all over the world, including the Prince of Wales, they seem to know too much about us. If they're able to phone one of our investigators and send her berserk, wrecking the office — no judgment there, Pawn Smith, it happens to the best of us — then they're a threat. So we need Molko to give them up. We also need to get an understanding of his powers, so we can bring him in without further incident. Once we have him in custody, what happens next won't be your concern."

"Okay," said Alix, not at all sure that it was. The rook regarded her, and then turned to the American bishop.

"Shantay, do you have anything you want to add?"

"Only that the Checquy have our full endorsement to proceed as you consider appropriate," said the American. "Under the terms of the Sororitas Pact, by knowingly using his abilities to commit a crime on British soil, Molko has placed himself beyond any claims or protection of the United States government. We relinquish any claims on his service and deny him any rights of appealing for consular support." She paused. "Basically, if you think he needs to die, feel free to kill him."

"Thanks, Shan," said the rook. She turned to Alix. "I won't lie to you, Pawn Mondegreen, you are going into a dangerous situation, but this is not a suicide mission."

Would you tell me if it were?

"Intelligence or other priorities aside, if Molko makes a move against you or anyone else, he will be put down," said Rook Thomas. "Now, you need to be touching the subject in order to direct your energy to a specific area, correct?"

"Yes."

"And if you're not touching the subject, when you unleash your power, it spreads out and can harm anyone around you?"

"That's right," Alix said, blushing.

"That is a problem." The rook paused. "We really do not want random civilians injured or killed."

"Understood," said Alix.

"You may only use your powers if you're sure of being able to kill Molko, and only Molko." She fixed Alix with a firm, flat look. "That is an order."

Even if I think I'm going to die?

"Our absolute priority is ensuring that he does not walk out of the restaurant unless he is in our custody."

So, that answers my question.

Alix and Pawn Smith rode in the elevator down to the Box Room.

"This is political," said Smith. "And it's bad. You haven't been given this task because you're the best person for it." Alix smiled bitterly. "Look, you're a good operative. You've been invaluable to the team, and I'd write you a letter of recommendation any day of the week. But I'd be lying if I said I wasn't worried. We have people who are trained to approach dangerous targets. It's all they do. You are an investigator with a specialty in plants."

"And in dealing with people who think the world revolves around them," said Alix dryly. She sighed. "The King said he wants me to do it, and the Checquy needs me to obey."

The team leader looked at her sadly.

"What can I do right now to help you?"

"I need a couple of hours to take care of some personal things."

"You've got them. But keep your phone on."

There was a coffee shop, Caffeine Conclave, down the street from the Rookery. It wasn't great, but it was magnitudes better than the café inside the Rookery, which was a cover business run by two retired operatives and was so bad as to be considered a strategic deterrent for any outsiders taking an interest in the building. In contrast, Caffeine Conclave served coffee that did not have a faint taste of blood, and pastries that did not appear to have a thin layer of dust on them.

Despite this, it was not frequently patronized by the denizens of the Rookery, who tended to arrive and depart from the office in cars via the underground garage, so as to avoid coming into contact with the protesters occupying the footpath.

Alix, however, had a fondness for the place, because it was within walking distance of work and a good place to sit. She was ensconced at a corner table, facing the wall—a move that offended every Checquy-instilled instinct within her but also meant she was much less likely to be recognized by any civilians—with her phone to her ear.

"Hello? Alix?" Her sister's voice came down the phone, surprised, but hearteningly happy at getting the call.

"Hi, Frances. I didn't pull you out of class, did I?"

"It's lunchtime," said Frances. "I'm just digesting the world's worst food."

"I'm sorry to call out of the blue," said Alix, "but I wanted to tell you something right away."

"Okay...," said Frances. "Is everything all right? Is Mummy...?"

"She's fine," Alix said, presuming that was the case. "But, look, I've gone over the numbers with some financial people, and I'll help you to go to university. You and Lillian and Cecily."

It was the thing to do. The only thing, really. Of all the obligations that she could practically feel closing around her, this was one she welcomed.

"Are...you certain?" asked Frances. Alix could hear her sister's hesitation, but also the excitement igniting underneath it. "Can you afford it?"

"We'll make it work," said Alix firmly. She'd stopped by the human resources office in Apex House and activated the option of her wergild, with her sisters as beneficiaries. Operatives of the Checquy were forbidden from purchasing private life insurance, but you could opt in for a good payout if you were killed in the line of duty. The beneficiaries were usually ignorant of why they were getting this money, and there was an office in Apex House whose sole responsibility was fabricating plausible excuses for people's unexpected windfalls. Out of satisfied spite, Alix had never put herself down for the scheme, since she assumed it would only go to funding her parents' delights. Now, however, it could be put to good use.

And if she managed to survive the next day, she'd be happy to contribute to her sisters' education from her salary. Should push really come to shove, she'd sell the flat and move somewhere smaller and less fashionable, or at least threaten to do so. The Checquy had invested so much in her persona—a persona that had only increased in value with her appointment as lady-in-waiting—that she suspected they'd provide some support. If nothing else, a loan on generous terms would probably be available, the Checquy being careful to ensure that their operatives did not become vulnerable through debt.

"That's amazing of you," said Frances, and her voice shook a little, which made Alix have to rub at her eyes. "I wouldn't ask you, really I wouldn't, if..."

"You absolutely can," said Alix. "And you will. You will study—wait. What *do* you want to study?"

"Farming."

"Gosh, seriously? I had no idea."

"Yep."

"That's really cool," said Alix. She was suddenly overcome by a mixture of envy and happiness. Her sister could live a free and interesting life. She could go to university and study whatever she pleased. She could travel without worrying about possibly sparking off some supernatural war. She could pursue her own interests and pick her own career.

And I can help her! I can help all of them!

"We will make it work," she said firmly. She would call Cecily and Lillian tomorrow—if she survived—take them out for lunch and tell them.

Maybe I can get to know all of them.

"Are you sure?" asked Frances. "Really sure?"

"I'm really sure," said Alix. *Farming. Fascinating. Perhaps she could take on the responsibilities for the Towers estate.*

And if I do die tomorrow, she'd make an excellent Lady Mondegreen.

After they said goodbye and hung up, Alix reentered the Rookery. She passed through the teeming actual lobby (as opposed to the near-deserted ostensible lobby, which was all that members of the public ever saw) and became aware that there were even more dark looks being thrown in her direction than usual. Intending to pay no attention, she stood facing the lift doors, waiting. But her hearing, honed by years of people talking behind her back, picked up her name being spoken only a few meters away.

The conversation was in low, bitter tones. Despite one speaker's lamprey-like mouth and the other's thick Yorkshire accent, she caught the words *sponsored, opportunity, big operation,* and typical *favoritism.* Evidently, the gossip had already gotten around. The fact that her assignment was an opportunity to get briskly murdered in one of London's hottest new eateries did not make it any less desirable, according to her colleagues.

The lift was crowded, and pointedly silent. By the time she alighted at the Box Room, Alix's cheeks were burning. She entered the investigation offices. A bulky envelope with heavy waxen security seals lay on her desk.

It was the briefing package for her meeting with Phillip Molko. Dauntingly thick, it definitely fit the parameters for the Checquy's classification of Improvised Fatal Weaponry (Office-Based).

Okay, let's get acquainted with tomorrow. She settled in at a desk and, with a little regret, because they were gorgeous, broke the intricate seals on the envelope. There was a schedule and a call sheet, requiring her to be at the Rookery for prep several hours before transport to Joyo's.

She read over the script. It focused on only a few key points, but there was a large amount of supporting material. The Checquy would be responsible for her wardrobe and makeup, so she pored over a lengthy analysis of Molko's possible psychological vulnerabilities.

She was so engrossed that it was a while before she realized that something was pressing warmly and softly against her ankle. She looked down to see the quokka, gazing up at her expectantly.

She lifted it up onto her lap, where it leaned back against her and sighed. She scratched the top of its head as she read through the proposed plan for securing Molko's cooperation.

"Excuse me, Mondegreen?" It was Chuah, looking a little awkward. "Would you like a coffee?"

"Thank you, that would be nice," said Alix, a little taken aback. She hadn't realized anyone else was in the Box Room.

"Come into the kitchenette," he invited. "We'll have a chat."

"Okay." Really, she would have preferred to keep reviewing the material.

But when she got to the kitchenette, she saw that the entire team (minus Pawn Weller's financial underlings) was squeezed in, holding beverages, and there was a very nice-looking store-bought cake in a white cardboard box.

"A little afternoon tea for you," said Pawn Smith. The others' faces wore a variety of expressions, ranging from mild shame (Chuah) to barely disguised resentment (Sweven) to devoted interest in the cake (Scagell).

"Oh, this is really nice," said Alix. "What a magnificent cake!"

It fell to Alix, as the guest of honor, to cut the cake and awkwardly dish out the slices. Then they all moved out to the conference table.

"This is so good," said Alix. There was a chorus of agreement.

"Chocolate-raspberry cheesecake with chocolate ganache, and a chocolate cookie crust," said Padilla. "I've been eyeing it at a nearby bakery for weeks."

"Is it just me, or is this really weird?" asked Chuah. "Mondegreen is confronting a mass murderer tomorrow, and we're sitting here having cake."

"Well, it's what you do in an office, isn't it?" said Smith. "And there wasn't time to organize a lunch."

"It's really good cake," put in Alix.

"She could get killed, though!" exclaimed Chuah.

"We all might get that call," said Scagell.

"And Mondegreen got the call today," said Smith. "She didn't ask for it."

Everyone contemplated their slices of cake silently.

"I can see how it would be a difficult situation for you," said Weller finally.

"A lot more emotional pressure than a normal operation," Scagell put in.

"Fucking scary, the whole thing," said Padilla.

"But you can actually get it done," said Sweven grudgingly.

"And, of course, we wish you the best of luck," said Claes, who seemed to be blissfully unaware that there had been any tension among the team and was more interested in allowing the quokka to lick the tiniest amount of cheesecake from the end of her finger. There was a chorus of agreement from around the room, even from Sweven. As far as Alix could tell, they all actually meant it.

"Thank you," she said. "I will do my best."

At 8:53 p.m., Alix put down the briefing package for the last time and stretched back in her chair. It was silent in the Box Room. The others had all left at the normal close of business, with a variety of farewells ranging from a flat "goodbye" (Sweven) to a hearty handshake (Scagell) to a lick behind each of her ears (the quokka). Smith had cautioned her not to stay too late, but she'd spent the past few hours drilling herself on every aspect of the next day's operation.

She had also reviewed the Checquy's psychological profile of Molko, which was the densest text she'd ever encountered. Alarming words and phrases had jumped out at her as she read and reread the document:

Possible sociopathic instincts.

The destabilizing effect of confronting one's supernatural abilities without institutional support.

The mentality of murder for profit.

The final analysis, once you stripped away all the ass-covering jargon, essentially said, *This is a man willing to kill people for money, so we are quite certain that he would be willing to kill you if he feels threatened.*

"Marvelous," she had said aloud.

Now it was time to go home. She logged out of her computer and switched it off. She packed up the briefing package and slid the folder under Smith's locked door. She put her coffee mug in the kitchenette dishwasher, already loaded with cake plates under the strict supervision of Pawn Weller, who apparently had very firm views about such things. She set it to running and then fetched her handbag and coat.

Finally, she looked up at the whiteboard. The faces of the victims looked out of their pictures. The formal portrait of Edmund in his uniform. Ian Blanch, his head cropped from a family portrait, taken at a moment when he looked proud of and satisfied with his life. And Alfie Rohmer, a glorious headshot of a young, shining man, handsome and excited, with so much more accomplishment and happiness ahead of him.

Finally, a surveillance photo of Phillip Molko, snapped by Sweven as the murderer walked past him on the street. Molko's gaze was fixed on some point over Alix's left shoulder, and a small satisfied smile curled the corners of his mouth.

"I'll see *you* tomorrow."

Alix let herself into her apartment and leaned against the door. Despite all her preparation, tomorrow was not going to go well. Molko would recognize her immediately, put two and two together, and kill her.

Or she would introduce herself, and then he would put two and two together and kill her.

Is that what the King wanted? To give me no choice but to kill Molko? He doesn't trust the Checquy, but maybe he trusts me to save my own skin.

Or maybe he thinks that if Molko kills me, then the Checquy will have no choice but to kill him.

That theory didn't seem as likely. She knew that the King genuinely cared about her. But he also wanted vengeance.

Either way, I think I'm going to die tomorrow.

She sat in the dark and thought about nothing.

She was jolted out of her reverie when her phone chimed with a text message.

Wotcher, are you conscious? it said. She saw that it was from **ETHEL**, which was really Louise.

Why is she up so late? Alix wondered, and called her.

"Lou?"

"Hi, Alix."

"Hi."

"Are you all right?" asked Louise.

"Yeah," said Alix. "Just getting my brain together."

"I just heard you weren't feeling well. Siti said that you'd canceled coming to the luncheon tomorrow."

"Yeah, flu," Alix said.

"I wanted to check on you, make sure it wasn't anything too serious, or... spooky?"

"Spooky?"

"I don't know, something from your work?" said the princess. "Magical flu or dragon pox or something."

Alix closed her eyes. "Look, Lou, I wasn't going to tell you this, but..."

"Yes?"

"It's goblin herpes."

There was a startled pause, followed by laughter down the line. Alix smiled.

"That's so disgusting. It's not actually a thing, is it?"

"Even if it was, I'd like to think I wouldn't have it."

"You never know," said Louise. "I've started getting briefings from your lot, and there's a lot of weirdness out there."

"There really is," agreed Alix.

"But how are you feeling?" asked Louise. "You don't sound too congested."

"It's nothing serious, but I thought best not to come and spread plague at the luncheon."

"That's too bad. I was really wanting you to be there." A little flush of warmth swept through Alix's chest. "Especially because I looked at the guest list, and Carla Makower is going to be there!"

"No!" exclaimed Alix, sitting bolt upright. "*The* Carla Makower from the year ahead of us? The Makower who ran off with the deputy headmistress?"

"The very one!"

"Oh my *God!*"

"*I know!*"

"Do we know what's she been doing since then?"

"Apparently, being involved in the Royal Society for the Prevention of Cruelty to Children."

"But we don't know anything else?"

"No," sighed Louise. "I had thought you could strike up a conversation with her tomorrow. You knew her, didn't you?"

"A little," said Alix. "Damn, I would have loved that."

"*I* can't do it," sighed Louise. "I didn't know her at all."

"Isn't Immo going tomorrow?" asked Alix. The little blond lady-in-waiting had been at school with them as well.

"No, she's also sick. There must be something going around."

"That sucks," sighed Alix. She got up and went to the kitchen.

"What are you doing?" asked Louise.

"I'm pouring myself a glass of wine."

"When you're sick? Is that a good idea?"

"It's a very good idea. Alcohol kills germs," said Alix.

"I could actually go for a glass of wine," the princess said wistfully.

"I'm sure there's a bottle of wine in the palace," said Alix. "Or, you know, several hundred."

"Yeah, in a kitchen fifteen minutes' brisk walk from my bedroom."

"Ring for one," said Alix. "There's a night service, isn't there?"

"I probably could," said Louise. "But I'd get looks tomorrow."

"We need to get you a mini-fridge — Wait!" said Alix. "Go check the boots in your wardrobe."

"Okay... I'm looking."

"Try the ones at the back."

"Why am I — Oh my God! There's a third of a bottle of tequila in this boot!"

"Yeah, that night when we were all singing and wearing tiaras, Siti decided it would be a good idea to start hiding bottles, because she thought the staff would judge us for all the empties and half-empties. I expect she forgot about it the next morning."

"I think she forgot her own name the next morning," said Louise. "Why don't I remember this?"

"You were throwing up in the bidet at the time," said Alix.

"That was *me*? Why didn't I use the toilet?"

"Henrietta was throwing up in the toilet."

"I had to clean that bidet myself the next day," said Louise. "It was so disgusting that I was too embarrassed to let the staff do it, and I was so angry at whoever was responsible. And it was me!"

"We should have gone down to the summerhouse. We could have just vomited in the topiary like in high school."

"Absolutely. Well, it's nice that I have emergency tequila, although I don't fancy drinking shots by myself."

"Keep looking," advised Alix.

"Okay, there's an empty horchata, an empty cinnamon schnapps, half a bottle of pavlova-flavored Baileys, and aha! A full bottle of Riesling!"

"You have too many boots."

"And I shall wash out this dirty coffee mug that someone left on my bathroom windowsill, and drink the wine from it," said Louise.

The conversation wound on, through gossip about old schoolmates, into memories of school, on to discussions of books and movies and music, and people they knew, and what was going on in the world.

Alix poured herself another glass of wine, and heard Louise doing the same. It was so easy, talking to a friend.

"Bloody hell!" said Louise suddenly. "It's past one in the morning!"

"What?" *Crap!* In five hours, the Checquy was coming to fetch her.

"Crikey," Louise said. "I have to be pleasant at that luncheon tomorrow."

I have to go to several intensive government briefings tomorrow morning. And then possibly get killed at lunch.

"I feel bad, keeping you up so late when you're sick," Louise continued.

"You should," agreed Alix. "But I really enjoyed it."

For a moment, she wavered.

These could be the last words I ever say to Louise. I should leave her with something significant to remember. A good, profound statement about friendship. What should I say?

Louise took the choice out of her hands by saying the perfect thing.

"All right, time for bed. Love you, Allie."

"Love you too, Lou. Sweet dreams."

23

Inevitably, she slept fitfully. Every twenty minutes, she jerked awake, convinced she'd overslept. So, when the operative sent to fetch her arrived ten minutes early, Alix was sitting on the front steps of her building. She was dressed in an elderly dark blue track suit with yellow stripes down the sleeves, her hair still wet, un-made-up, with a cup of coffee in her hand.

"Morning," said the pawn, a curvaceous middle-aged lady with a mane of dark hair. "I'm Karkazis. I'm responsible for you today." Alix greeted her and climbed into the car. "Have you eaten? I have pastries."

"I couldn't," said Alix. "Butterflies."

At the Rookery, in the conference room appointed for the preliminary briefing, she tried to ignore the fact that everyone else, all of whom appeared to be team leaders and executives, was dressed in suits, while she looked like she'd been held hostage for a few weeks.

Rook Thomas swept in, and everyone rose. "Thank you, please be seated. I'll assume you've all read the briefing packets that were provided yesterday," she said. "It's been a busy night for many people, and there are updates in the materials that are being handed out to you. Joyo's has agreed to allow two of their waitstaff to be replaced by our people for the first lunch seating, as long as they fit the 'Joyo's standard,' so we have sent ten of our best-looking operatives around there this morning to be reviewed. The selected two will be given intensive training in the Joyo's method of waitering, an education for which we are being billed," she noted sourly.

"How many pawns will be present as diners?" asked Alix. It sounded as if they would be selected based on how good-looking they were, rather than their fighting expertise. Of course, all pawns were given extensive training in combat, but she'd been hoping that there would be an entire battalion of full-time battle specialists sitting around her, rather than the hot young first-years from the mailroom.

"That's an ongoing process," said Rook Thomas. "We'll have final numbers at the next briefing."

That does not sound promising.

"Regardless," said Razafindrakoto, "we will have two additional soldiers on the street, and four more in the café opposite. Two blocks away will be an operations truck with a full support staff, and another with twelve soldiers disguised in a variety of civilian outfits, and three in police uniforms."

"I'll be in attendance in the operations truck," said the rook, "to provide any necessary authorizations should they arise, but Pawn Razafindrakoto will be in charge of the operation."

Next, Karkazis ushered Alix to the armory for a haircut and to get her makeup done, before being dressed at the quartermaster's department. Once she was outfitted, her schedule advised her that she would be transported to the operations truck for a final briefing.

And then she would be going in.

At the armory, the Checquy hairdresser was a slim bearded gentleman in camouflage fatigues who sported stunning shoulder-length blond hair. He thoughtfully regarded Alix's locks, which had dried by this point and resumed their usual untamed disco-lion look.

"Fascinating. First, I need to fit this device."

It was a small bone-conduction headphone that sat at the back of her head and would be invisible under her hair. When a technician spoke softly into a microphone from the other room, she could hear his voice vibrating gently but clearly through her skull.

To her disappointment, the hairdresser did not deploy any supernatural abilities to do his work. The trimming was done with scissors rather than appendages that turned into razor-sharp scythes. The coloring was done not by running his hands over her head or staring fixedly at her scalp but by applying an expensive-looking wash that smelled faintly of plums. There *was* the possibility that he possessed heightened strength, since he was able to wrestle her curls back into a ponytail and twist it into a sculpted mass that he could secure as an intricate bun. Some strategic application of product, and she was presenting what he called a "clean, polished outline."

The makeup was done by one of Alix's classmates from the Estate, who possessed the ability to condense algae out of thin air. Alix had seen her swirl great curtains of the stuff into existence and heard that she could actually grow it in people's lungs. Her primary occupation, however, was altering people's appearance through the use of cosmetics, be it applying camouflage, concealing someone's inhuman features, making them resemble someone else, or just making them look like a hotter, healthier version of themselves.

Then Claes came in and provided some incredibly fine, complexion-compatible powder for Alix's face and throat. The Grafter explained that it was toxic if ingested, just in case Molko tried to bite her. She gave Alix a small injection to vaccinate her against it, in case she forgetfully touched her face.

"Which you shouldn't do anyway," the makeup artist said sharply. "I don't want all my work ruined."

Hair, headphones, makeup, and poison derived from the elbow glands of the Kayan River slow loris all skillfully attended to, it was time for the outfit.

The Quartermaster of the entire Checquy, Colonel Neil Curry

himself, a hulking former soldier with a shaved head and a battle-scarred face that was missing an eye and a goodly notch of nose and lip, guided her to a little elevated platform and then set about directing a troupe of valets in dressing her.

Alix was so caught up in reviewing her updated notes that she didn't even look at the clothing being put on her. When directed, she stepped into something soft to be drawn up around her, or held out an arm to be sleeved. She barely noticed when corsetry was cinched, and didn't listen to the orders Curry barked to his underlings about refining the drape or drawing up the hem.

"All right," said the quartermaster. Alix finally looked up from her notes and beheld a brave new world.

"Gosh," she said breathlessly.

For the first time in her life, she found her own reflection a little intimidating.

Reflected in the mirror was a woman who looked so utterly self-assured that traffic, the seas, and even the crowds at Harrods would undoubtedly part for her.

The ensemble was black, of a costly-looking black that suggested not just money, but *wealth*. This black did not seek to merge with the shadows. It acknowledged the fact that it stood out in the world, glorified in it, and was wryly amused by the world's reaction.

A skirt rippled down to her shins, with folds that held their shape firmly but could flare out if it proved necessary to spin-kick someone in the face. The fire-and-acid-resistant blouse was of an odd dark gray color with a high, unbuttoned collar to frame her jaw. And the coat! It had clearly been tailored to her, presumably drawing on her measurements in the Checquy's files.

"This is a weird color," she remarked, her fingers reaching to touch the blouse. One of the valets squawked in dismay and tapped her hand away.

"It's *Eigengrau*," said Curry. "The color people see when there's no light."

"Okay," said Alix. "And why?"

"Partly to create a vague sense of unease in the target, and partly because it looks amazing."

"*Gosh,*" she said again.

"Yeah, it works," said the quartermaster. "Or it will, once Twitchell gets that hem right!"

"Almost done, sir," said one of the valets around a mouthful of pins.

A few minutes later, Pawn Karkazis announced firmly that it was time to go, and the cloud of flunkies peeled away from Alix, getting in a final pass of the lint roller or an adjustment of a fold. The quartermaster's considering gaze slowly raked Alix from head to toe, and he gave an approving nod.

"Thank you, all of you," she said, and there were appreciative mutters from around the room. Karkazis tsked from the door, and Alix stepped down from the platform.

As she walked through the hallways, eyes widened, jaws dropped, cilia trembled. People hastily stepped back out of her way. In one case, someone stepped back through a wall, leaving his own clothes in an untidy heap on the floor.

"Would you like some water?" asked Karkazis as their car departed the basement parking lot.

"Thanks, but I don't want to mess up the makeup," said Alix. "And I don't want to risk needing to go to the toilet."

They arrived at the site where the operational vehicles were parked, a small privately run parking lot that the Checquy had apparently booked for the entire day. Trailers and caravans were placed about, and looming over them all was the massive dark bulk of the operations trailer. A large security guard waved them through.

Inside the trailer, it was like mission control for a very small space operation. Various operatives were already busy about their work, their faces glowing from monitors or, in the case of one pawn, his luminous sweat.

In a tiny meeting room, Rook Thomas, Pawn Razafindrakoto, and a couple of other quite serious people were crammed around the table, which was bolted to the floor. Razafindrakoto was talking, but as Alix and her outfit entered, she fell silent.

"That's very impressive," said Rook Thomas.

"I'm just the canvas," said Alix.

"Sit. We've got..." The rook trailed off.

"Eighteen minutes," said Karkazis. "Plus one minute to get from here to the car and seven minutes' drive time."

"Thanks," said Rook Thomas. "Just a few updates. Molko is still booked in for his table at Joyo's, so the operation is proceeding."

"Bad news first," said Razafindrakoto. "We've only gotten two tables at Joyo's. I've been advised we have a 'deuce' on the balcony, and a 'four-top' on the main floor." She shook her head in disbelief. "Apparently this restaurant is so desirable and waiting periods so long that people are refusing aid to the security services. Pawn Mondegreen will have only eight of our people in the restaurant as immediate support."

"Everyone will be wired in to your microphone, Mondegreen, so they will hear every detail of your conversation," said Razafindrakoto. "That includes the ops room here, every operative in the restaurant, and those at the ready nearby."

Big audience, then.

"If you're in distress and need everyone to move in without alerting him, your go word will be 'cheesecake.'"

"Cheesecake," she repeated dubiously.

"Yes."

"Why cheesecake?"

"Because they don't offer it on the menu, but you could conceivably use it in a sentence. But we'd really prefer if you didn't use it."

"Right," said Alix.

The group discussed a few more details about the distribution of forces, none of which were at all reassuring to Alix, beyond confirming that if she died, she would be avenged in a very professional and organized manner. Razafindrakoto and the rook shook her hand and went off to take their places in the command room.

"Molko has arrived at the site," announced Karkazis, her hand at her ear. "He's been seated and is currently ordering wine. We head to the car now."

Are you ready?" Razafindrakoto's voice vibrated in Alix's head.

"Yes, ready."

"Commence."

The driver opened her door and Alix stepped out. She nodded a thank-you and began walking toward Joyo's, her back in perfect Whyteleafe-instilled posture. She could have balanced a tray with a full tea set on her head.

As Alix approached the former taxidermy shop, she saw herself in the glass of the door. Sunglasses hid her eyes, and her face was schooled to calmness. Even with all the nervousness roiling in her stomach, Alix was deceived by her reflection's poise.

She was met by the maître d'. A majestic Spanish man, he wasn't one of the Checquy operatives, both of whom were posing as waiters somewhere in the restaurant, but he knew exactly who she was. He smiled and, with a gesture, wordlessly turned for her to follow him.

The restaurant was lovely, all white paint, dark wood, and gleaming brass. Some of the old taxidermy remained on shelves and plinths, but it was all clean and bright, as if the owners had had the foxes, parrots, and ermine dusted and retinted. A peacock on a plinth positively glittered.

The place was full but did not feel crowded—everyone could see and, more crucially, be seen. The balcony that circled the room was broad enough for tables of two, and each was occupied. Alix scanned it and found a man in a striking purple blazer. He and his dining companion were some of her backup. Under his coat and in her handbag were smoke grenades that could fill the restaurant in moments, if such a scenario proved necessary.

She passed but did not acknowledge Pawn Bayada, in waiter garb. His chiseled good looks and ability to create a small, localized weather system in someone else's mouth had not been enough to get him any of Joyo's waitering responsibilities greater than pouring water.

The dining room conversation ebbed appreciatively as Alix and her outfit made their way through the restaurant. Even the stuffed boar's head on the wall seemed to be regarding her with porcine admiration.

Directly ahead of her was Phillip Molko. There was a shock at seeing, in person, the face she'd scrutinized so closely in photos. He was reading something on his phone and was one of the few in the dining room who had not noticed Alix's approach.

I've been hunting you for a while, sir.

Her eyes flickered to the table next to him, where three pawns and an unpowered agent were enjoying their first course, having arrived a meticulous fifteen minutes before Molko's reservation.

"Mr. Molko?" He looked up at her and his eyes widened. "I'm sorry to disturb you at lunch, but I've come to offer you a vast amount of money."

"I—Oh?" He was still taking in her existence, her outfit. The outlandishness of her offer hit his brain like a bucket of cold milk.

"Yes. May I join you for a little while?"

"Well...certainly," he said. His Midwestern American manners kicked in, and he stood to welcome her as the maître d' pulled out a chair for her. Molko waited until she was settled before sitting. She accepted the maître d's offer of water and a menu.

"This is lovely," she said. "I've heard good things. Have you dined here before?"

"No, I haven't," he said. "I've wanted to, but reservations take a while."

"Of course," Alix said. "Have you already ordered?"

"Not yet."

"Apparently, the laksa is outstanding."

"I've heard that. Now, forgive me," he said, rallying his wits, "but I don't believe we've met before."

"No," agreed Alix. "But I know who you are, and I bring a tremendous opportunity for you." She smiled brightly.

"Right," he said. Alix could almost see the thoughts flicker through his mind, and then he smiled, amused and curious, secure in the impossibility and undetectability of his powers.

"Would you like a drink?" he asked, gesturing to the nearest waiter, who had been on Alix's volleyball team at the Estate.

"Thank you," said Alix. "A Thai iced tea, please?"

"You say we haven't met," said Molko, "but you look familiar."

"Do I?" she asked.

Come on, enjoy the mystery. You're safe, you know you are. So indulge me in a little verbal jousting.

"Yes. Who are you?"

Goddammit.

She had hoped to engage and distract him with her offer before he twigged to her identity, but it was already here, the first moment that everything would hinge on.

"We're with you, Mondegreen," Razafindrakoto's voice thrummed through her skull.

At the next table, the diners were still, and one pawn was holding her fork so tightly that her knuckles were white. Their proximity might have been something of a comfort, but Alix knew they'd only move if things went terribly wrong, by which time she'd likely be dead.

"I'm Lady Alexandra Mondegreen." Molko's eyes widened. "You're the lady-in-waiting to the Princess of Wales."

Here it comes. It took all her self-control not to tense.

If he makes one move toward me, I am shoving this table into his gut, clocking him in the head with that carafe, and then beating him unconscious with my chair.

"That's one of my roles, yes," she said. "But I'm not here to represent the princess."

"So, who are you here to represent?"

"The Establishment," she said lightly. He looked around, confused, for a moment. "No, not the restaurant." His eyes narrowed as he processed her words, but he made no moves, and she felt no cubic sensations in her head.

"When you say 'the Establishment'..."

"I expect you can guess the various parties." She shrugged. "Individuals and groups with power. They confer, they come to understandings, they contribute to various endeavors. Nothing formal, of course. Or at least not formally written down." She laughed a little—the very idea! "It's an arrangement built on centuries of tradition, and connections. That's generally enough to prop up kingdoms and churches and trading companies and empires and so on. A nice, comfortable, profitable status quo."

"I see," he said. "And what does the Establishment want with me?"

"The Establishment"—and she smiled conspiratorially—"has become aware of what you can accomplish."

"Me?" he asked innocently. She half expected him to place a startled hand on his chest.

"Yes. And they are impressed."

"What do they think I can accomplish?"

"Money moves about, Mr. Molko."

"Please call me Phillip."

"That's very kind, but let's keep this a little more businesslike for the moment," she said. "Now, as I was saying. Money moves about, and the Establishment monitors its ebb and flow. And a tasty amount of money has flowed into your coffers recently."

"My coffers are in another country, where your Establishment has no right to look."

"There was some curiosity about this money," she said, as if he hadn't spoken. "Your clients were identified and their lives scrutinized. Conclusions were drawn about why they'd paid you so deliciously."

"I don't know what you're talking about. My business consultancy is perfectly legi—" She cut him off with an upraised hand.

"Mr. Molko, people paid you to remove obstacles. Those obstacles were other people. We can see that it was you, although we cannot see how you did it. Which is what makes you so interesting. Ah, lovely!" Her erstwhile volleyball teammate had brought her beverage, and she sipped the orange-brown milky tea while Molko turned things over in his mind.

"That is a very serious charge," he said. "Especially when you have no proof."

So, he doesn't know about the cubes.

"Why, Mr. Molko! No one's *charging* you with anything!"

"But you're suggesting that I killed people."

"Yes, but no one of consequence to us. No one who will be missed." It was bitter in her mouth to say it, but this was the bait.

Of course, it was completely unbelievable that a shadowy power elite of the UK would be unconcerned about the murder of the Prince of Wales. Edmund's death, however, was different from the others. No one had specifically paid Molko to kill Edmund, and so there was no trail connecting the two men, especially as Molko did not know that his murders left a hallmark.

"And you would be interested in..."

"Retaining your services," she said. "Exclusively. Unless you were interested in selling us the *means* of such services?"

Is there an artifact tucked away in a safe-deposit box? Or even up your sleeve?

"It's only I who can make such arrangements," he said. He smiled a crooked, self-satisfied smile that put her in mind of a fish that doesn't know it's just been hooked.

So it's you, then. Your powers. You fucking animal.

"All the more reason that we are keen to secure your services," she said. "As I said, we are willing to offer a significant amount of money."

"Then I'm very interested," he said.

She smiled. Behind him, the table of Checquy operatives recommenced eating their meal.

"Well done, Mondegreen," Razafindrakoto buzzed in her head. "An important step. But we're not clear yet, so all teams remain poised."

"Lady Mondegreen," Molko said, "would you join me for lunch?"

Why, I'd rather eat my own entrails. I'd definitely rather eat yours.

"I'd be delighted," she said. "But only if you let me buy. And now, please, call me Alexandra."

The items on the menu were eye-wateringly expensive, but the descriptions of the food were eye-wateringly delicious.

If I'm going to break bread with this maggot, it better be good bread.

Fortunately, Molko was quite the gourmand. He ordered several dishes, including starter share plates of hinava (raw mackerel cured in lime juice with chili, ginger, and onions), ambuyat (a white starchy paste) with a selection of dipping cacahs (sauces), and a bowl of sago worms (actual worms, which might or might not be served live — the menu was worryingly coy on that aspect). Then, many more dishes, including jaruk, pinasakan, and manok pansoh. Molko was completely unconcerned that it might be too much for them to eat.

"This all sounds outstanding," said Alix. "An excellent way to celebrate a new relationship."

"Could we talk a bit about how this new relationship would work?" asked Molko.

"Of course. To begin with, we wouldn't be expecting you to be working constantly," she assured him. "We would pay you a retainer for an exclusive on your services. Periodically, we would call upon you to address a problematic individual, or possibly several. From everything we can tell, you don't require much infrastructure to do your job."

He smirked.

"But we would provide such support as you require, including travel and accommodation. Of course, I won't ask for exactly how you accomplish it."

"Trade secret," he said.

Plus, you assume I wouldn't believe you.

"Entirely fair," Alix said. "But I would be interested in getting the... what would be the best word? The *parameters* of your method. So that we can set our expectations appropriately. For instance, what kind of access do you require, how close do you need to come?"

"Touching distance," said Molko easily. "I usually find that a simple handshake is sufficient to administer the process. It's a limitation, I realize, but it hasn't proven to be too troublesome. Most people will shake a hand automatically if it's offered."

Certainly the Prince of Wales would have, Alix thought grimly.

"Yes. And even if the subject was not normally very accessible, we would be able to facilitate meetings and so on," she said helpfully. "As you'd expect, we have significant resources and connections."

"That would open up the possibilities a lot," Molko said. "So, the process does require direct contact, but the, uh, the subject is not aware of anything being done to them. No unusual sensations, and they don't suffer from any ill effect until I want it to."

"And how long does that take?" asked Alix. "We've figured out that you can have quite a bit of a gap." He paused and looked a little uneasy. "We did our research, Mr. Molko. Due diligence."

"Yes, well, there can be up to about five months between the initial contact and the end result. The process can be tailored to pretty specific time frames. I have it down to the minute."

You've given away too much there, Molko. No non-supernatural method would be so specific, and those murders overseas were arranged before Edmund's death acted as proof. I'm sure those people wouldn't have died if you hadn't received payment, so you must have a way of activating it mentally, even across the globe.

"And is there a minimum time?" she asked.

He shrugged. "It could be instantaneous. But I like to leave a bit of time between my administration of the process and its activation." He smiled. "Give myself a bit of distance."

"Only sensible," she agreed. "So, in addition to our retainer, you would receive an additional fee for every problem you addressed, provided that each instance leaves no evidence and occurs within the time frame we specify," she said. "A perfectly clean, untraceable occurrence."

"Natural causes happen naturally," he said.

"Remarkable," she said. "I confess, it took our people a while to actually believe what they were discovering. There's still some debate, but I'm convinced. And you won't give me the slightest hint of how you do it? Just to assuage my own burning curiosity?"

"You wouldn't believe me."

Oh, I might.

"I'll have to settle for that," she said.

"Now, Alexandra, this *has* become something of a business lunch. You mentioned a vast amount? How vast are you thinking?"

"We know your current holdings," she said. "Your yearly retainer would be the same amount." His eyes widened. She paused to allow him to absorb the implications, and the voice of Razafindrakoto reverberated through her skull.

"Very good, Mondegreen, really well done. We now have a model for how his abilities work, which will facilitate our seizing him. We will do this once you've completed your meal and he leaves the restaurant. In the meantime, see what information you can get about his accomplices."

At that point, the first course arrived, a selection of exquisitely arranged small plates laid reverently before them.

"Lovely. Now," she added, "we're aware that we also need to compensate your colleagues." His brow wrinkled, and then his gaze shifted, caught by something behind her.

Someone dropped a glass.

And then she wasn't there anymore.

24

She was putting down a ceramic cup, and her mouth tasted foul. She licked her gums clean of the taste, her tongue a complex shape, sliding carefully over bumps and furrows.

"How is the decoction?" asked a voice behind her, and she turned to see the man with the beard and the piercing eyes. He wore a dull red coat, and his skullcap was a little askew. She felt a wash of affection and gratitude at the sight of him. Unconsciously, she stroked the fine, clean cloth of her tunic.

"Ick'sh bicker," she said. There was a twinge of familiar shame as the words wheezed and whistled out of her mouth.

"Bitter?" he said. "Yes. But do you feel clear in your mind?"

"Gyesh."

"Good. You said that your art depends not just on the sounds, but the thoughts that you link with them." She nodded. "It will be helpful if you are as defined in your thought and your enunciation as possible, so that it is fixed clearly in your memory."

"Gyesh, shir."

"Excellent," said the man. He clapped her lightly on the shoulder. "Let us go, then." He led her out onto a paved terrace. It was morning, and the air was cool. Behind them, the large house loomed. They continued to where a stone balustrade ran around the terrace's edge. Beyond it, there was a fall of five meters, and then a long, sloping lawn leading to a forest where the trees were changing color. On the grass, about thirty people stood about in little clumps, looking uncertain. A mixed crowd, of ages ranging from seven to fifty.

Off to the side, five large men stood apart. There were cloths wound around their heads over the ears. At their feet were buckets, and they held wooden staves.

"One moment," the man said. He pressed wax into his ears. "Good," he said, more loudly now that he could not hear himself. "Whenever you are ready." She nodded and fixed the pattern in her mind.

It was a tangle of thoughts that bespoke rage. It was the sensation of clenched tightness in the jaw, and the sharp jagged pain in the brow from having a rock glance off your temple. It was red and orange, fear and hate, a dog's teeth bared, and the jeering laughter of children.

She opened her lips. The people stared up at her, their faces changing as they looked at her. And then she let out a sound that was not a word but a growling, spitting, biting mishmash of noises.

As she shouted it, she pushed the thought-shape out with it. The faces of the crowd went flat for a heartbeat, before they turned and attacked each other.

It was immediate chaos. A man and a woman who had been holding hands were suddenly clawing at each other. An old man kicked out viciously at the back of a child's knees, and then two women had tackled him and were punching him, striking out occasionally at each other. A dozen little melees scattered and re-formed as the participants noticed new opponents.

Several of the victims made a move toward the five large men, who stood to the side and remained unaffected. Fended off by the men's staves, the rampagers plunged back into the conflict.

"Extraordinary," said the man. "You are valuable, lad. You have great worth." She ducked her head in pleasure. "And you can stop them?" She nodded and formed a shape in her mind. It was a conglomeration of deep indigos, the weight of a rough blanket, the yielding of straw beneath her, and the sound of a lazy sunlit brook flowing over smooth stones.

"SHLEEPF!"

Instantly, the brawling people collapsed, unconscious.

"How deeply do they sleep?" asked the man. She shrugged. He gestured to the men waiting off to the side. They stepped forward, buckets in hand, and poured water over the unconscious people, who began to rouse, coughing and spluttering. "A normal sleep, then." He carefully picked the wax from his ears.

"Shhould Aye mlake them shfugh now?" she asked eagerly.

"Not at this moment," the man said. "One lesson at a time, no?"

"Gyesh!" she agreed. He nodded and smiled. Her eyes were suddenly hot, and she felt a wetness on her cheeks.

"And now we must collect your memory," he said. She stood still as he put a small beaker to her face and caught the tears.

"—*UCK* is he?"

Alix was jolted into consciousness by the ass-end of the question pounding through her skull. She opened her eyes to find that her head was on the table, her face half in a dish of something with an intense smell of sour pork.

"Sobral, mobilize emergency services!" Razafindrakoto's voice bellowed into Alix's head. "We need ambulance, fire, and police on site now. I want a lockdown of the surrounding streets. No vehicles in or out!"

Wincing, Alix sat up and pulled the bone-conduction headphone out of her hair. She rubbed her sleeve across her face, smearing off forty pounds' worth of wild boar jaruk, which, she now recalled, the waiter had told them was prepared by being placed in a bamboo tube with rice and a specially formulated salt and left to ferment for several weeks.

Her thoughts were still arranging themselves, switching back and forth between the vivid memory of a crisp autumn morning where people had attacked each other in a wild frenzy, and the bright summer afternoon she was actually living in.

A hallucination... with the same intensity as the one on the street at Blanch's. But it was — I was a different person. She'd felt younger than in the previous vision, and the memory of the bewildering sensation of her mouth had her running her tongue cautiously around her teeth to reassure herself that she was herself. *Okay, all normal. Thank God.*

So, it must have been another hallucination that his colleague unleashed. What's happened?

With her bones no longer conducting the frantic commands of Razafindrakoto, Alix could take in the situation around her. It had changed somewhat while she was trapped in that vision. The previously elegant Joyo's was now a mad scene. An alarm was screaming from the ceiling, but two-thirds of the occupants were still slumped unconscious about the place. Diners had fallen from their chairs or collapsed into their meals. Waitstaff were laid out on the floor, and one could track the trajectory of their collapse by the trail of spilled food and drink across the polished wood and, in some cases, across tables and diners.

Some people had roused and were reacting to the situation. There was weeping and screaming and staring about in bewildered terror.

Alix's backup team at the next table were still unconscious, but the pair up on the balcony were awake and had their hands to their ears, talking frantically on hidden microphones. The man in the purple blazer caught Alix's eye and gave her a questioning look. She gave him a trembling thumbs-up and he nodded in acknowledgment.

Hanging over it all was a pall of smoke coming from the kitchen, indicating that certain foodstuffs did not do well when left unattended on burning wood over stones in a bespoke firepit.

Hell, thought Alix, looking around blearily.

Then she realized that there was no sign of Phillip Molko.

Oh, bloody hell!

It's a disaster," said Smith. No one in the Box Room disagreed.

Alix had offered to stay at the scene and help, but it was felt that her presence would only make things more difficult. Someone was bound to recognize her, the press would latch onto her, and the story would become even bigger—if such a thing were possible. So, she'd been hurriedly put in the back of a car and delivered to the Rookery to be debriefed, then to shower thoroughly with a Claes-provided bodywash to ensure that all the poison face-powder was removed, and to change back into her own rumpled track suit.

By the time she was ready to return to the Box Room, the incident at Joyo's was already front-page news on her phone. No explanation had yet been provided, and so there was lots and lots of increasingly outrageous speculation. On her way from dropping the fancy clothes back at the armory, she passed the offices of the Liars, and they looked like a Wall Street trading floor from the eighties. People were shouting and running about, others speaking into phones and typing frantically. As she'd watched, a serene-looking dromedary was being led out of the lift and into the section's kitchenette.

When she arrived back at the Box Room, there were exclamations of relief that she was all right, and then everyone turned their attention to the media. On one screen, a muted BBC was showing pictures of emergency vehicles rushing through the streets of Clerkenwell. Some people stood on the sidewalk outside Joyo's, weeping. Others were hurrying away.

On another screen, a heavily made-up woman, whom Alix recognized as one of the diners from the restaurant, was giving a distraught interview, seemingly unaware that she still had some stir-fried noodles and streaks of soy sauce in her hair.

"We've got footage from the restaurant!" announced Chuah. "The ops team just emailed it over."

"Put it up," said Smith. The news coverage was replaced with four different views of Joyo's, as presented by the cameras the Checquy had placed about that morning. Chuah fast-forwarded to the part where Alix arrived, and the entire team listened as she laid out her proposal and Molko accepted.

"That was nicely done, Mondegreen," remarked Smith, and to Alix's blushing pleasure, the rest of the team agreed. Even Sweven nodded approval. Alix leaned forward to watch as the food was placed on her table.

"There," said Chuah, pointing at the view that covered the restaurant's front door. Two people entered, a man and a woman. They were dressed appropriately for the locale, he in a cream suit with a pale blue shirt and no tie, she in a gorgeous blue dress that reached to just above her knees and was cut to perfection. Both had blond hair and the air of the wealthy and confidently good-looking. Their features were clearly visible—young, lovely, and completely unfamiliar to Alix.

The maître d' greeted them. The woman said something to him in a tone too low for the audio to pick up over the noise of the restaurant and gestured to the back of the dining room, in the direction of Alix and Molko's table. He nodded and stepped aside. The couple proceeded briskly through the restaurant. When they were only a few meters from Alix's back, the woman produced a familiar-looking glass globe from her handbag and dropped it to smash on the floor.

Immediately, everyone in the restaurant collapsed, except for the blond couple.

"The notes say that everyone in a two-mile radius of that globe was rendered unconscious," said Chuah. He peered at his laptop. "Including all Checquy operatives in the command trailer. There were at least forty civilian car accidents, a few fires, and many injuries, including two broken necks from people falling down stairs."

"Bloody hell," murmured Scagell.

The rest of the investigative team was similarly aghast, but their eyes were still fixed on the screen, where the man and woman were hauling the unconscious Molko out of his chair and carrying him — his arms draped over their shoulders — out of the restaurant. On one of the camera views, which showed the street outside Joyo's, they could be seen levering him into a car they'd left with a now-unconscious valet and driving away.

"The Checquy have reviewed camera footage and deployed trackers," advised Chuah, still reading from the notes. "They traced the vehicle's movements to an underground parking garage in Fulham where it was wiped clean. Turns out it was stolen an hour earlier." He shrugged.

"And they have no idea how or where they proceeded from there?" Padilla asked.

"It was an old structure, very dodgy, no cameras inside, and there were vehicles going in and out all the time."

"So, Molko's comrades came and got him," said Smith bitterly.

"I don't know how they knew," said Alix. She shook her head in bewilderment. "In the debriefing, they asked me if I'd seen any sign that Molko felt threatened or signaled anyone else during our conversation. I told them I hadn't detected anything. You saw on the feed: he didn't even touch his phone the entire time we were talking. I really thought we had him."

"In the recording, it all looked and sounded like it went perfectly," agreed Scagell. "And Molko looked surprised at their approach."

"Maybe they had eyes on him, noticed our people, and decided it was a trap," suggested Weller. "So they pulled their man out."

"Why did he collapse, and they didn't?" wondered Chuah. Everyone else shrugged, unconcerned — such were the vagaries of the supernatural.

"Mondegreen, do you think this is the woman you confronted at the Blanch house?" asked Smith. Chuah rewound the footage and paused on an image of the woman. Alix examined the screen closely.

"It could be," she said finally. "Except the hands are wrong. They're not that yellowy color." Still, as Alix stared at the woman, she did feel a sense of familiarity. Right height, and the posture and bearing were spot-on.

And there was something more.

"What are we going to tell the King?" Sweven was asking Smith.

"Thank God, this op was out of our hands, and that decision is above my pay grade. Last I heard, there are scores of operatives continuing the search for Molko and his accomplices," said the team leader. She looked at the clock. "It's only three, but I don't think there's anything else for us to do until they're located. It's been a shit of a day, so I'm giving you an exeat. Go home and regroup."

"Mondegreen," said a voice by her head, and she started out of her reverie. "Sorry!" said Scagell. "Didn't mean to startle you. We're going to the pub. You coming?" Alix smiled at him.

"Normally, I'd love to," she said. "But honestly, I'm knackered. Barely slept at all last night. I'm just going to go home and fall into bed."

"I don't blame you," he said, and patted her on the shoulder. She waved to the rest of the team as they departed, a little regretful at passing up the opportunity to be an accepted member at last, but there was something nagging at her.

She turned back to the image of the woman on-screen, and her eye caught on a detail she hadn't noticed before. She stared at it for a long moment, her mouth open, and then checked something on her phone. Then something else. She sat thinking for a while longer, and finally stood up.

She left the Rookery and went home. She plugged her phone into its charger by her bed, then left her flat. She walked to the nearest station to catch the Tube to Paddington Station. At Paddington, she examined some maps and the schedule, and paid cash for a ticket. While she waited for the train, she had a pasty and an apple juice.

The train ride took a little over an hour and a half, and Alix absorbed none of the scenery as the city gave way to suburbs that gave way to countryside. She just turned her thoughts over and over in her mind.

When she arrived at the station, which was one one-hundredth the size of Paddington, she consulted with a patient lady in a booth, accepted a map, and waited on the little high street until a bus arrived. It drove out of the small town past little houses and along country lanes. Eventually, she asked the driver to stop and alighted.

Alix stretched and looked around. She was in a very pretty woodland, with oaks and hazels leaning over the road and dappling it in late-afternoon shade. A long stone wall, too high to see over, ran along the road, and right in front of Alix was an entrance. There were gates, but they were open, and appeared to have been so since at least the turn of the millennium.

She walked up the long pebbled drive that curled back and forth, and came to a large house. She scrutinized it with a practiced eye. Three stories, sloping red roofs above white stone walls. At least ten bedrooms, more if there were wings off the back.

Early twentieth century, she thought. *Very nice. Very private.* The last house the bus had passed was a good three miles away. She rang the doorbell and heard a grating buzzing inside the house. She waited and then rang again, holding the button down for ten seconds at a time, until footsteps came and the door opened.

"Alix? How—What are you doing here?"

"Hi, Immo. So, where have you got Phillip Molko?"

25

Alix was looking for a reaction, and she got one. Astonished horror, swiftly masked, so that if she hadn't been scrutinizing the little lady-in-waiting's face, she could have easily missed it.

"Who?"

"I recognized your ensemble, Immo. The dress, the shoes, the bag. You wore it to the luncheon the first time we all met together. You looked really good, the best turned-out of all of us. So, it was an entirely appropriate getup for walking into Joyo's, even though you weren't actually going to be eating there." Alix smiled a little. "I understand—we've all got our favorite outfit, the one that gives us that extra bit of confidence. And I expect that you dismissed any concerns about it being recognized because you'd be safely wearing a completely different face."

Imogen's expression gave nothing away.

"But you didn't count on me, who knew the outfit and was trained not to rely on little things like people's faces." She looked up at the facade. "Whose house is this? Because I checked online, and it's not yours, and it's not your family's."

For a moment, Imogen looked as if she were going to have a reasonable answer, and then she sighed.

"You'd better come in." She stepped aside, and Alix walked into the black-and-white-tiled foyer. "How did you find me here?"

"The lady-in-waiting app," said Alix. "The one palace security made us install so we could find each other." The blonde rolled her eyes.

"The irony is sickening, because that's how we tracked you." She led Alix into a sitting room. "So, are there going to be armed troops tumbling in through the windows any minute?"

"No," said Alix.

"Why not?" asked Imogen intently.

"Because I wanted to find out what in God's name was going on. Because if you're working with Molko, then it might mean Louise is involved. And I..." *And I didn't trust the Checquy to approach things with any sort of diplomacy.*

"We're not working with Molko," said Imogen.

"Then why did you rescue him?"

"We didn't rescue him, we kidnapped him." She looked over Alix's shoulder and nodded a little. Alix was turning when:

"SHLEEPF."

"—lix, can you hear me?" The voice was very gentle and calm. A soft hand was warm on her brow. "If you can hear me, don't say anything, don't nod, you don't even need to open your eyes. Can you just wrinkle your nose for me? Please?"

I can do that, Alix thought dreamily, and wrinkled her nose.

"Good. Now, as you wake up, we shall go very gently. Because there's no hurry. No need to even move. Just slowly become aware of your body." It was a kind voice, soothing—a familiar woman's voice. "Breathe in and out through your nose, long and deep."

Alix felt as if she were on a bed that was rising up out of a delicious, warm bath into a room of golden summer afternoon light.

"That's very good, Alix. Stay still and calm, because if you move, you'll hurt yourself."

What?

Alix's eyes flew open. Imogen was leaning over her, her hands on Alix's forehead.

Instinctively, Alix tried to sit up, but couldn't. Those hands were firm on her brow, holding her head against some padded surface, and as she jerked her arms and legs, she felt firm resistance at her wrists, chest, waist, and ankles, pinning her down. She tried to twist her head away from Imogen's hands, but there was metal pressing on her cheeks, holding her head straight.

"*Don't* move, Alix," said Imogen firmly. "Really don't. Especially your mouth."

My mouth? She realized there was a taste of metal on her tongue and then froze. She abruptly snapped from comfortable unquestioning drowsiness to panicked wakefulness. Now she could feel thick iron hard against her teeth, preventing her from closing her jaw, and something sharp and irregular protruding into her mouth and pressing on her tongue.

What is this? She tentatively moved her tongue, just to get an idea of the shape of the thing, but a prong nicked her, and she could suddenly taste the copper of her blood along with the iron of the intrusion.

Suddenly, she was gasping and wheezing around whatever medical apparatus was in her mouth, perhaps to keep her from swallowing her tongue?

"Allie, calm down," said Imogen. "You're all right." Alix could only make a strangled moan. "Breathe with me. In…out…in…out… that's good."

Alix strained her eyes to look around her.

"Chlut ve fugh?" she choked out around the thing.

"This is going to be hard, but we'll get through it," said Imogen.

Okay, establish the situation, because right now nothing makes any goddamn sense at all. She did her best to assume her calm face and regarded Imogen expectantly.

"Okay, good," said Imogen. She leaned forward and kissed Alix gently on her brow. Alix thought of the poison that had been coating her skin earlier in the day, and half regretted washing it off.

"Now," said Imogen, "I have to say this first." She paused. "Don't even think about using your power, or it will end very badly for you."

Alix felt as if the world had flipped a brisk 360 degrees around her.

How do you know about that? she asked with her eyes, because there was no point in trying to say it with her mouth.

"Yes, I know what you can do. I know you can break people's bones without even touching them. I know you can kill me right now, but *you* should know that if you do that, there's no way for you to get free. And apparently no one else knows where you are."

I really thought I was being discreet and clever with that, thought Alix grimly. *I thought that I could step away from the Checquy for a few hours, and use my courtier subtlety and the connections between Imogen and me to get some answers without dragging in a whole army.*

And now I am strapped to a chair with a muzzle locked on my head.

Alix had made no sign, but Imogen continued. "So, if anything happens to me, you will starve to death here, in this house where no one will be coming for several days, pinned down securely with a spiked bit in your mouth." Alix felt a stab of horror. "But that doesn't have to happen. So, be calm, and listen."

Alix did her best to be calm, even though it felt like she could choke on the thing in her mouth at any moment. There was a gag reflex waiting for its chance, and she squashed it down. The thought of throwing up was too horrible for words. She focused on the ceiling, which was unhelpfully boring, just white plaster without even a cobweb to distract her.

"You are wearing a brank," the little blond lady-in-waiting said. "It locks around your head, and a metal tongue goes into the mouth so you can't talk. It's a disgusting idea. They've been around for centuries. They were used mainly on women, which is just"—she breathed in—"fucking appalling. If some woman was found guilty of gossiping, or being a nag, or otherwise speaking in a way men disapproved of, they were fitted with the brank, which is why one of its names was 'the scold's bridle.'

"I hate it, and I hate that we've had to do this to you. But it's necessary, to make certain that you sit still, don't lash out with your powers, and listen." Imogen now moved to the side, out of Alix's field of vision. "Okay. You are on a reclining chair, and we are going to ease it up." She heard movement on her other side, too—someone else was in the room—and then Alix's perspective was shifting. She had never been here before, she was fairly certain, but she'd been in a hundred rooms like it.

I'm being held captive in someone's drawing room.

It was a large, airy space. Sofas and chairs were placed about, upholstered in well-faded stripes of light and dark blue. Large picture windows showed a garden riotous with flowers, and a lawn curving down to a broad sparkling stream. There was still late-summer daylight, though it was fading some; shadows were lengthening. Oil paintings hung on the walls. On a low table nearby, a tea service was set out, with steam coming out of the nozzle of the delicate china teapot.

Sveven would have a field day with this. Even my abductions are upper-class. She assumed she was still in the same house she'd entered.

There were snapping sounds behind her, presumably as Imogen and her confederate secured latches to keep the seat upright, and then her friend came around the front. She was wearing a floaty light green summer dress, and looked as fresh as a very wealthy daisy.

On her other side appeared a blond man, and with a start, Alix recognized his face from the video of Joyo's. He was younger than Imogen—Alix would have put him in his late teens—but taller, with the build of a swimmer. He was wearing khakis and a short-sleeved white shirt. They looked like they were about to step out for an exquisitely catered picnic.

"Alix, this is my brother Jimmy. He's wanted to meet you for a long time."

This is the brother we never see? The one who has the special needs, and all the carers? He looks unremarkable.

Jimmy waved, and then pulled off his face.

Alix gave no reaction, but it took all her strength not to make a sound as he peeled away a thin veneer of a normal-looking face to reveal his own. She'd seen some things in her time. She'd gone to school with a boy with a large sucking starfish for a head. She'd attended morning teas with Grafters whose faces and bodies had been twisted so extremely that one hesitated to think of them as human. She liked to think that, in each case, she'd kept her composure. But she'd never seen anything as distressing as the face of the young man who stood over her.

From the nose up, Jimmy Canley-Vale gave every impression of being a normal, even handsome chap. He had the same blond hair and dancing blue eyes as Imogen. But his mouth and cheeks...

What did they do to you?

His features had been cut and twisted and... sewn and welded?... back together. Part of his top lip was missing, and she could see the scars of old stitches. They looked deliberately ragged. Through the three irregular holes that had been sliced precisely into his right cheek, she could see his teeth, white but irregularly spaced, with gaps. His breath whistled through the holes.

Under her horrified gaze, his mutilated lips drew back in a warped smile that puckered his left cheek and crumpled the pillars of flesh that were his right cheek. He opened his mouth and turned his head from side to side for her perusal. She saw that his tongue had been divided lengthwise into three tonguelets that waggled at her independently of each other.

What am I looking at? What is this madness? It all bespoke a very purposeful, very meticulous, very expert mutilation.

"I know it can take one aback," said Imogen, as Jimmy closed his mouth. "It was done to give him certain capabilities. The type of capability that you possess." Alix stared at her in disbelief, and the lady-in-waiting smiled. Thankfully, the brother did not, although his eyes crinkled in pleasure.

They're insane, Alix thought faintly. *I'm in the hands of insane people.*

"You don't believe me," said Imogen. "Such an idea doesn't mesh with your understanding of the world, but it's true. Now, I'm going to take off the brank." She reached forward and undid the latches behind Alix's head. "Open wide," she said, and Alix felt the metal tongue slide out of her mouth. She gasped and worked her aching jaw, trying not to cry with relief. "Do you want some water?"

Alix nodded, and Imogen brought her a water bottle with a straw. She sipped carefully, took her time, but finished it.

"Who are you?" she croaked. "What *is* this?"

"We're what *you* should have been if there were any sense in the world," said Imogen. "We are the Scramasax."

Scramasax? The word *did* tickle her memory. It was...a type of sword? *Old English? Saxon.*

"We are a group that addresses threats to the kingdom. Threats that common people cannot know about."

"How original," Alix rasped.

Imogen smiled. "You're thinking of your Checquy."

"You know..." Alix's mind was reeling. Bewildering enough that Imogen knew about Alix's powers, but the Checquy? She'd even pronounced it correctly!

"We know all about it. We know its history, much of it anyway, and its scale and operations. We've known for a very long time." Imogen's lip curled. "A monolithic parasite that has been feeding on the system for centuries. Acting as it sees fit, stealing children...its priority always to maintain its position." Alix opened her mouth to object, to defend, but Imogen pressed on. "Dedicated to maintaining the status quo, and its place leeching off it!"

Alix regarded her with horrified fascination—her easygoing friend, the girl she'd known practically all her life, was animated by a hate she'd never seen before.

"But while the Checquy is an apparatus of the bureaucracy, we are loyal to something we actually believe in. A power that is dedicated, before the divine, to law and justice, in mercy."

Law and justice, in mercy. I know those words. They were part of the coronation oath of a British monarch, administered by the Archbishop of Canterbury: *Will you to your power cause Law and Justice, in Mercy, to be executed in all your judgments?*

"We serve the sovereign of this land," said Imogen.

"The King," Alix whispered.

"Our families have been sworn to his. Just like yours has, Alix."

Alix could say nothing, only stare as thoughts ricocheted madly through her head. *Does the King know? But of course he does.* Suddenly everything was clicking into place.

The Checquy had thought the attack on Pawn Smith was Molko and his shadowy accomplices trying to stymie the investigation, but he'd given no sign that he felt hunted and looked confused when she'd mentioned paying his colleagues.

It's been these Scramasax all along. A group sent on a mission, given orders and fed information by a King who didn't trust the Checquy to avenge his son.

It all made a terrible amount of sense.

When did he set them on this mission? Was it from the very beginning? Or did he slowly come to the conclusion that the Checquy's desires did not align with his own?

The King had reason to doubt that the Checquy would punish Edmund's killer, once apprehended. She winced at the memory of the pickpocket who'd been apprehended during Edmund's funeral procession. His skills had seen him enlisted into the Checquy as a resource—a fact that had been included in the daily report to Buckingham Palace.

And there was Caroline Delahunty, who had come close to seducing the King and leading him around by the nose. The Checquy was still evaluating her to see if she could be folded into the organization. The Court's vacillating about the fate of Phillip Molko would only have confirmed his suspicions.

Alix thought of the meticulous reports that had been delivered daily to the King, giving him every particular of the investigation, every detail. He could then have passed it all along to this Scramasax, which she now somehow recalled meant "wounding-knife." Every scrap of information, every theory had been fed to these rivals.

"Was it you at the Blanch house?" she asked. She overlaid that dark figure in the kitchen with Imogen's slight form, and they matched.

"Yep," said Imogen. "We needed to investigate, utilize certain tools, and we couldn't wait for the Checquy to release the site. The guard at the front was easy, but you nearly gave me a heart attack when you came out of nowhere. And then you blew up the car!" There was no resentment in her voice, just fond amusement.

"But your hands?" She was staring at Imogen's smooth white fingers, which were nothing like the yellowed skin she remembered. "The hair that came out of them?"

Does she have powers?

"Artifacts from our arsenal," said Imogen. "Gloves made from the skinned arms of a man who terrorized a village near Newquay. The Scramasax caught him and, after some experiments, found a way to activate the powers in his pelt even when he was no longer occupying it."

"And when was this?" asked Alix weakly. She couldn't recall hearing about any such event.

"1768."

"1768!"

"Oh, yes. We've been around for some time," said Imogen. "Not always being used, admittedly. A weapon kept sheathed, but maintained razor-sharp until needed."

"And the call to my boss?"

"To Pawn Hannah Smith? The one that made her go berserk? Yes, that was Jimmy," she said. Her brother winked from the sofa. "We needed to delay anyone arriving at Alfie Rohmer's flat, so that we could do our investigation. We had the pawn's number—"

Of course you did, thought Alix, remembering the dossiers on the team that had been given to the King. *We handed it right to you.*

"—and she seemed like the one who would cause the biggest fuss by running amok."

"People could have died!"

"That would have been terrible," said Imogen. "But only if it had been you who died, Alix. I love you dearly, but I hate the Checquy. We all do."

"Why?"

"Because they tried to destroy us," said Imogen.

"I've never even heard of you."

"I'm not surprised, the Checquy is self-serving, and I expect they were keen to sweep the events of 1567 under the rug."

"Wait," said Alix. "1567... I *do* know this story."

It was taught at the Estate. Checquy students received all the elements of a standard history curriculum, but heavily supplemented with supernatural annotations. And 1567 was notable for several events, including the eruption of a very small, very exclusive supernatural civil war.

As best Alix could recall, a cabal of courtiers and nobles in the court of Queen Elizabeth Gloriana had been jealous of the Checquy's resurgence in power after their influence had waned during the reigns of Henry VIII and Bloody Mary. They were appalled that power and authority was put in the hands of peasants and tradesmen.

The plot had started small, with unflattering rumors being spread about court and poisoned words whispered in the Queen's ear. The heads of the Checquy were no longer received with enthusiastic courtesy. Indeed, on occasion, Elizabeth Gloriana was not available to them!

Then cuts were made to the Checquy's budget. Meanwhile, the rival faction (they came be known among the Checquy as "the Rivals") used their own wealth and influence to build a small force that reported directly to the Queen. The Queen's own spymaster, Sir Francis Walsingham, was one of the leaders, and the Rivals used his intelligence resources to conduct their own operations against the supernatural.

Finally, the antagonism had culminated in active strikes against the Checquy. After the death of two pawns, the Checquy Court had decided to demonstrate why the Rivals' ascendancy as an alternative power was absolutely not an option.

The ensuing conflict had been very localized, with only a few Rival operatives being variously incinerated, desiccated, and evaporated before their commanders' horrified eyes. The Ivory Lady of the Checquy had presented herself to the two leaders of the rival group by bursting out of the head of a servant as he was pouring them a drink.

Covered in wine and viscera, they had hastily agreed to cease all their activities, and that was believed to be the end of it.

But the Checquy histories had never mentioned the name Scramasax. *Maybe they hadn't known it.*

"It was John Dee, wasn't it?" Alix asked. "He was the other leader."

"Yes!" said Imogen. Her eyes were bright with enthusiasm. "He was a genius! People now think he was a charlatan, or deluded, but he had the brilliance and creativity to combine science and the occult."

"That was him I saw in those hallucinations!" said Alix, remembering the bearded man with the intent eyes.

"Those hallucinations were memories. Dee created an alchemical process to extract memories and store them in distillations—liquids that we can reproduce so that generations later, our members can experience the insights of our predecessors. We use them to learn from the experiences of our best operatives, and can even unleash them to affect areas around us without being overwhelmed ourselves."

So I lived the memories of a man from the sixteenth century, thought Alix, awed despite herself.

"We have hundreds of such memories in our archives," said Imogen, "but the one I used on you back in Winchester was the very first one that Dee ever extracted, from an assistant of his. We use it for such things because it doesn't give away any dangerous information, but it's also important to us." She met Alix's gaze with shining eyes. "I'm so glad you got to experience it. Please, Allie, just take a moment and recall it."

Alix did. The scene was still incredibly vivid in her memory, perhaps because of the way it had come into her mind. The candlelit room, the ceiling with the painted eyes, and the bearded man working carefully with his subject. Now, with context, she could appreciate what an astounding thing he'd accomplished.

"Think about it, Alix. Do you see what a miracle of science it was?" Despite herself, Alix nodded a fraction. "And accomplished hundreds of years ago! *That* was the kind of genius and vision that John Dee had. And even after the Checquy tried to destroy us, he and Sir Francis Walsingham ensured that we would endure through the centuries!"

"How did you know about the operation at Joyo's?"

"The operation that was very deliberately kept from the King?" asked Imogen. "Well, he's not a stupid man, and he could see that Farrier and her Court were planning something smelly. So he insisted on your being the one to meet with Molko, and I was able to track you through the lady-in-waiting tracker."

"And the faces?" asked Alix.

"Cauls," said Imogen. "Skin-masks. It's how Jimmy is able to go out without attracting attention. It's like wearing someone else's face." She made a little grimace. "It's why I didn't bother turning off that lady-in-waiting tracker. One really does feel invisible in those masks. It never even occurred to me that you might think to check the app."

"*Is* it someone else's face?" asked Alix, thinking of the skinned gloves.

"No," said Imogen. "That's disgusting. They were cast from living faces, centuries ago. We just keep them in their little casks, topped up with pond water for nutrients, and apply them when we need them."

"Yes, that's much less disgusting," said Alix.

"I shouldn't think we'll be using these ones for a few decades, now that the Checquy has recorded them, but we have quite a few. We have many tools," said Imogen. "We also use the distillations for other things. It's how Jimmy was able to learn how to use his modifications."

"Right, his modifications," said Alix. She was trying not to look at the mutilated boy on the sofa, but her eyes were caught by the spectacle of him very, very carefully drinking a cup of tea.

"There was a boy in the sixteenth century," said Imogen. "He was born with mouth deformities, very severe ones. A peasant in a small, ignorant village. He survived, but his life was not easy. Our records show that his little community did not treat him kindly. But eventually he discovered that he could use the features he'd been born with to control others. Particular sounds combined with a specific thought pattern could prompt certain responses. Mindless rage. Uncontrollable lust. Unconsciousness. He used his abilities to get revenge on the villagers who'd mocked and tormented him."

I know this story too! I remember reading about him! It was one of the historical cases she and Chuah had found in the Rookery library.

"Word got out, eventually, and of course made its way to the Checquy of the time," continued Imogen. "But word also made its way to Sir Francis Walsingham. So the Scramasax dispatched a team to retrieve the boy."

Which is why the Checquy found him gone.

"The Scramasax took him in and gave him a purpose and a sense of worth. And a new name: Henry Paston. He became one of the most important agents in the service of the Crown. His powers were studied, and John Dee discovered that they could be duplicated. In every generation, there are volunteers to receive those modifications. Dee's own memories are used to ensure that the procedure is done correctly, and then the recipients receive Paston's memories to learn how to use their powers."

The Grafters would be fascinated by this. But I've got to stop getting distracted.

"What did you do to Molko?"

"He's nearby. We'll keep him secured until we have all the answers we want. Then we'll put him down."

Am I also going to be put down? One of the hated Checquy, excised from Louise's inner circle like a tumor? But Imogen was looking at her with affection.

"I know what you're thinking, but you're one of us, Alix. You come from a family of tradition, and I know you. You believe in service, you're loyal to this nation, and you know how rotten the Checquy is." She paused. "I've seen your personnel files, Allie. The King requested them, and I read them. I know about the bullying at the Estate, and I know how they treat you now." Imogen bit her lip. "I'm so sorry. Did you know that you won't be permitted to advance further in their ranks?"

"I — What?"

"It's been decided, I saw it in the dossier. There was always doubt, because of the general resentment toward your situation, but now that you're a lady-in-waiting, they won't let you do anything else. You won't ever be made team leader, you'll never climb into management, let alone their Court. I know your work has always mattered to you, but you also have ambition—you told your superiors that. But the Checquy has decided that you won't be allowed to pursue it. You're locked into your position. Forever."

Alix could tell Imogen was telling the truth. It was the great fear that had lurked in the back of her mind, emerging sometimes in the dead of night. She'd been deluding herself—*they'd* been deluding her. Yet another restriction in a lifetime of them. All her hopes dashed. She closed her eyes, desperate not to cry, but some tears leaked out. A soft cloth handkerchief gently wiped at her eyes, and she felt a hand in hers.

"But there's another option," said Imogen. "Come work with us." Alix opened her eyes and stared at her. "Be a part of something that you can actually put your trust in. The people who matter will know the truth. The ideals we serve are ideals that I know you believe in, Allie."

"What would I do?" she asked, sniffing back her tears. "You want me to leave the Checquy?"

"They'd never let you," said Imogen. "And they can't know the Scramasax still exists."

"Which is why you broke into a major operation in the middle of London and stole their target," said Alix. "And you're not worried?"

"They'll never find out what happened," Imogen said confidently. "Remember, *you* had no idea. And we're kept up to date on everything they know."

Because they tell the King, and the King tells you.

"We've come up with a story. You'd reappear, having been abducted by Molko and his 'accomplices.' After all, you used your real name when you met him. You killed them and escaped. The Checquy would find a house burned down with three corpses inside, including Molko's."

"Whose corpses?" asked Alix. "What house?"

"Well, not this one," said Imogen.

"Whose house *is* this?"

"It's off the books. The Scramasax has used the property for centuries—it's one of many. There was a farmhouse here, and then someone decided to build a bigger house for occasional gatherings and councils, training. It's not the only one. We have resources, not just supernatural ones. We're able to make an actual difference. You'd get kudos from the Checquy, even if somewhat begrudgingly, and then you'd go back to work. Except you would know that you can endure all of their snideness and unfair limitations, because you're doing something worthwhile."

Alix had to work to keep her face still. It was such a tempting prospect, to continue doing her work for the Checquy, but not to have to feel so separate from everyone around her. So alone.

"These people are not worthy of your loyalty, Alix," Imogen continued. "And one day the Checquy will cease to exist in its current form. Then the dedicated members of the Scramasax will step forward to take up their rightful duties, no longer hidden." She said it reverently, as if she were quoting scripture.

"What would you do with the information I got you?"

"Serve the country, serve the crown. Do what the Checquy won't. They stand by and let the worst kind of evil happen. They wash their hands of anything that isn't supernatural, no matter how dangerous it is." Alix shifted in her chair, vaguely aware of the restraints, which she saw were modern, evocative of a hospital. But her mind wasn't on them. Imogen's words resonated uncomfortably with thoughts she'd had herself. "Have you never watched the news and wished you could step in and use your powers to solve those problems?"

"Rebuild the British Empire?"

Imogen shrugged. "It would be enough if they rebuilt this country."

"Imogen, there's so much potential here. Couldn't you consider an alliance with the Checquy?" Imogen's expression went flat. "It's been centuries since they fought the Scramasax. Things have changed. I don't know if you know about the Grafters, but—"

"Oh, we know all about them," Imogen said bitterly. "The only foreign invasion force that the Checquy ever stepped in to do something about, and then only to protect their comfortable feathered nest. But they did nothing about the Armada, *nothing*. When Oliver Cromwell's New Model Army marched over the land, overthrew the King, and *executed* him, the Checquy stood by. Again and again, they failed Britain and its monarchs. They let the Nazis bomb our cities! They don't care about anything that's not supernatural, they don't care about regular people without powers. They don't care about this country."

She was shaking with rage, but eventually she took a deep breath. Her hands were still clenched into fists, though. Her cheeks were flushed, her mouth was tight, and there was a look in her eyes that put real fear into Alix's heart.

"I can see that you're not willing to leave them behind. Even after everything they've done, when you know what they are, you're still loyal to them, like a beaten dog. It's too late for you, Alix." She shook her head, her mouth twisted in regret. She turned to summon her brother. "Jimmy."

The young man was already standing, his mouth open and the vents in his cheeks fluttering as he drew in breath, presumably to cast some spell. Imogen picked something up from a little table, and when she turned back, there was a glint of metal in her hand. She stepped forward.

You stupid fucks. I didn't want to do this.

Alix released the energy she'd been gathering up since Imogen reacted to her proposal.

It surged out of her, into the room, and found the siblings. She could see the moment it struck them. Jimmy's body twisted sharply — Alix's practiced eye diagnosed a broken shoulder blade — while something gave way in Imogen's left ankle so that she was sent stumbling.

But it hadn't been enough, and they recovered quickly. There were no bewildered looks — they knew exactly what had happened. Their eyes promised murder.

Again! More! The power was already climbing. It roared inside her, as Imogen took one faltering step after another. Her blade was bright in her hand, while behind her, Jimmy wheezed where he stood, one side slumped hideously. Alix could hear the air whistling through the gaps in his face. He narrowed his eyes at her, and as he breathed out, she could hear him begin to speak.

Now!

The power cascaded out of her, so intense that Alix could almost see the air in the room ripple as the wave slammed into Imogen and Jimmy. Undirected, without her guidance, it tore about inside them, and the brother's and sister's bodies jerked and shuddered.

Jimmy collapsed to the floor like a puppet whose strings had just been cut. Whatever sounds he had intended to make were lost as hoarse staccato yelps burst out of his mouth. He thrashed about, visibly jolted by each new smashing impact, until a loud crack snapped his neck and he lay still.

Imogen somehow remained on her feet, even as Alix's power ran rampant through her body. Her knife was sent flying from her hand as something snapped in her elbow and her arm jerked about. Her eyes remained fixed on Alix's, even as her body shuddered. She took a step forward, and another.

How? Alix herself was gasping, trying to recover from the unleashing of her power. *What kind of insane fanaticism would enable someone to do this?* The little blond lady-in-waiting cried out as something else snapped audibly inside her, but still she came at Alix. Her fingers were curled into claws and her teeth bared.

Alix struggled weakly. Thanks to her restraints, she could be killed easily, even by her friend's broken hands. Imogen dragged herself forward.

Fall! Fall!

"Fall!" Alix screamed. Behind Imogen, she could see the death-still form of the brother sprawled on the floor, his head twisted at a gruesomely unnatural angle.

Alix tried to summon up more energy. She could feel a trickle seeping out of her soul, but not enough to do anything more than irritate. And just that effort set her slumping back in the chair.

All she could do was watch as her friend came ever closer. Alix's power was still slamming around inside her, the muffled sound of fractures and cracks stomach-turning. Imogen's body jerked and her left side suddenly slumped as if she'd been struck with a club, but she barely paused or let out a sound. Her hand reached out, two fingers dangling unnaturally out of their sockets.

No!

Imogen lunged forward and half collapsed on Alix. The weight of her punched the air out of Alix's lungs, and she flinched when she felt the impact as another of Imogen's ribs snapped. Their faces were pressed against each other.

"Die, traitor! *Die!*" Imogen choked out into Alix's ear. Her hands crept up to Alix's neck, and Alix writhed helplessly against her restraints. Fingers closed around her throat and began to squeeze.

No! Alix's hands clenched madly, uselessly in their cuffs. She flung her head back and forth and jerked her body about, doing her best to fling her attacker off, but she was held fast, and the pressure on her throat was hideous. The corners of the room seemed to be going dark, and her lungs were burning.

Alix weakly called the power, and it came from inside her. She poured it out, into the hands that were choking her. She met Imogen's eyes and held her gaze as she directed that dreadful energy to a weakened spot in the other girl's spine. Imogen flung her head back as her body twisted, her eyes staring up at the ceiling, and then she fell sideways, off Alix, and smacked heavily onto the floor.

Is it over? Alix strained against the strap across her chest, leaning forward as much as she could to see if there was movement. She could see just a little part of Imogen's slumped body, a curve of arm and shoulder. *Is she breathing?*

"Now *you'll* die," wheezed Imogen from the floor. Alix jerked back. "A long, slow death."

There was another crack, almost earsplitting, and then the unmistakable sound of a death rattle.

26

Alix slumped in the chair. The effort of repeatedly using her power had left her physically drained. The terror of helplessly being strangled had left her mentally stunned. All she wanted to do was sleep, but that seemed like a very bad idea.

I'm only going to get weaker. No food, no water. Her muscles were already starting to ache in the confines of the restraints, and she shifted uncomfortably.

The room was eerily silent, no ticking of a clock or hum of air conditioning. No sound of anyone else in the place. Just her breath echoing off the walls and two people dead on the floor. Through the windows, the world was going on about its business, the sun was going down, completely unconcerned by her predicament.

Okay, take stock of the situation.

Alix hadn't yet examined her bonds closely—she'd been distracted by more pressing concerns. Her wrists were fastened to the armrests. The Scramasax hadn't used handcuffs but something modern that looked frighteningly clinical—a soft, squashy cloth wristband that fastened shut with a broad white leather cuff buckled around it.

She moved her arms experimentally and found that there was no give, no helpful straps that might let her move her forearms a bit. The cuffs seemed to be bolted to the armrests. She tried to wriggle her hand out, and the cuffs politely but firmly declined to release her. There was no hard edge, just a rounded, soft, immovable barrier.

We'll come back to the cuffs.

A strap crossed her chest, curved to go just above her breasts and then under her armpits. There was a plastic latch in the center, and she tried to reach down with her chin, but it held her upper body firmly against the chair, keeping her face a frustratingly tiny distance from touching it.

A set of broad vinyl straps crisscrossed her waist and went down between her legs, keeping her from moving her lower half in any helpful way. She couldn't see the cuffs at her ankles, but when she essayed a tentative stretch, she found they were just as unyielding as the ones at her wrists.

She could see the fastenings for each restraint. Buckles at the wrists (and presumably) ankles, latches for the chest and hip straps. There were no locks to be picked, nothing welded. She could easily undo each one, if only she weren't the one wearing them.

The chair was thinly padded but rigid underneath, like a dentist's chair. She pushed against the armrests and jostled her body with all her might, but the structure did not flex or shift. If it was on wheels, they were locked.

Her skin felt sticky and itchy from the sweat she'd shed during her struggle. Her bladder was also making itself known. *Perhaps I shouldn't have accepted that water.*

She thought of yelling for help. Imogen had said there was no one else in the house, but perhaps a passerby might hear? She hadn't seen any houses nearby, and had no idea how close this place was to any paths, so she decided to essay a yell, feeling ridiculous as she did so.

You'll feel even more ridiculous if it turns out you could have summoned the neighbors all along.

"HELLLLP-uh?"

Nothing, except the ringing of her voice off the walls.

"HEEEELLLLP!"

Then:

"FIRE! FIRE! HELP ME, THERE'S A FIRE!" Now she was just screaming wordlessly, a long, unbroken unmistakable sound of a human in distress.

She forced herself to stop and listen for any sound of someone coming.

Nothing.

"All right, what next?"

Think back to your training.

...

...

...I don't remember anything useful.

The Checquy's instruction for its students was wide and varied. Layered over its Harrow-level standard education was all the preparation one might need for being a supernatural warrior-bureaucrat. Alix knew what to do if she was swallowed whole by a giant beast, or found herself in the middle of a burning forest, or suddenly floating in an airless void. Patient instructors had shown her how to efficiently saw off her own limbs if she was slowly turning to stone, or how to position her body if she found herself falling from several miles above the earth. There had been some basic escapology, but it assumed you had a handy item with which to pick the lock, or at least some freedom of movement. Alix had neither of those.

She could vaguely recall an action movie in which the hero had escaped from handcuffs by dislocating a thumb. Unfortunately, because her schooling at the Estate had included an extensive study of human anatomy, she knew that thumbs didn't dislocate as easily as *Blood-Death IV: Death Reflected* suggested.

Still, she was willing to try. She experimented, but because her hands were secured to the armrests at the wrists, and the armrests projected out beyond her hands, it seemed impossible.

"I just don't see how I could manage it," she said grimly. Then she realized that she was either talking to herself or to the two dead bodies in the room, and shut up.

The room got darker as the sun sank lower and lower. It was stiflingly warm, and made worse by the smell from the two dead bodies in the room. It was too soon for any decomposition, of course, but it was clear that some muscles in the corpses had relaxed, with unfortunate results. As the light faded, she could no longer see the garden, and the room felt like it was closing in around her.

Stay focused, take stock of the situation. How long until one dies of thirst? She remembered a lecture on that. *I think it can take as little as two days, but that was probably for the desert, not a tastefully appointed drawing room in the English countryside. Victims get lethargic, suffer headaches, dizziness, cramps, confusion, brain swelling, possible seizures, going into shock... You need to get yourself free before all that kicks in.*

She was so tired, though, even after the sleep that Jimmy had forced upon her. The repeated use of her powers, after a long day, a night of troubled barely-sleep, and the terror that had coursed through her—it was all taking a toll.

She pictured herself getting sluggish, and then perhaps raving, and then slumping in the chair as the bodies of Imogen and Jimmy rotted on the floor. Eventually, she would die and start rotting too. Then, presumably, Scramasax agents would arrive, remove the bodies, and hose everything down.

Don't think about that. Think about possible ways to escape.
Instead, she fell asleep.

"Oh my God!"
She woke in utter darkness to find that her sleeping brain had produced the answer to a question she hadn't realized she was still asking.
VRI!
Victoria Regina Imperatrix!
Holy crap! I've been wearing Queen Victoria's walking boots!
No wonder they're such good quality.
Wow.
Satisfying as this revelation was, it did not prove useful to her current situation, which had not improved.

She felt less exhausted but more disgusting. It was night now, no moonlight in the garden, and the world was silent, not even the sound of a clock ticking. She had no idea how long she'd been asleep. The smell from the corpses was definitely riper, though.

Though you're not in a position to judge, if this bladder gets any fuller. And you've been wearing this track suit for hours and hours.
She tried the restraints again, but nothing had changed.
I wonder when the Checquy will realize I'm missing. Could they track me? I tried not to leave a trail, but I talked to people. I took the bus.
Maybe I should have accepted Imogen's offer.

Eventually, the pain and tension knotting inside her became too much to bear, and she had to empty her bladder. Allowing herself to do it was difficult. Then she shifted itchily and squelchily in the darkness.

This feels horrible, worse than last time, 'cause I'm just sitting in it.
I have pissed myself more since I took this job than in the previous twenty years. They talk about the glamour and the service of being a lady-in-waiting, but they never talk about the urine.
She swallowed roughly.
And now I'm really thirsty. Which is only going to get worse and worse, and I'll get worse and worse, and it'll take a long painful time.
She stared blankly for a while, contemplating what would happen to her.

*I can't move. Help isn't coming. I've got to do some*thing.
Because otherwise I'll die here.

Squatting in the back of her mind was an idea that she flinched away from. The knowledge that, if things got too bad, she could try killing herself with her own powers. If she summoned it, and it had nowhere to go, then it would run wild inside her, damage *her*. She'd never reached her limit, but during testing by the Checquy, she'd once gotten to the point where she'd vomited a little blood. The scientists had examined her, done some calculations, and projected that she might be able to hold enough energy inside herself to shred her own insides.

But you're not going to do that, she told herself firmly.

Not unless things get very, very bad indeed. She tried not to think about how likely it was to get very, very bad.

But the power's there, and it's all you've got right now. So, see what you can do.

She opened herself a little, and the power came. It poured forth, eager, and she held it tight inside herself. She had to clench down to keep it from spilling out into the world.

The power crackled resentfully, denied its escape. If it couldn't go into another living thing, then it wanted to burst out into the air and seek out prey, but Alix couldn't allow that. There was no other prey. She knew if she released it, it would only rush back into her a moment later, a maelstrom that would rip her flesh.

Instead, she tried to direct it elsewhere. She pushed it against the substance of the chair beneath her, hoping that perhaps she'd been wrong all her life, and that it would flow into metal or plastic and crack them as easily as it did bone. But it refused to go where she wanted.

How about the restraints, then? Maybe the fibers would split if she tried hard enough, if she focused clearly enough.

Instead, the energy bounced back from the padding around her wrists, and the pressure inside her increased.

She moaned a little. It was churning inside her, almost frantic to escape. She'd never held it this long before, and she knew that she was going to have to release it in a second. It wouldn't be enough to kill her, but she was afraid of how much it was going to hurt.

"Oh God, oh *God*!" her voice echoed in the dark room.

And then a moment of shock as, held tighter and tighter, denied escape, the power found an outlet, squeezing itself somewhere new, squirting into the matter of her own bones.

What?

She almost lost control then, stunned by the sudden shift in everything she thought she'd known about herself, but years of discipline rallied, and she clamped down her control.

It still hurt, but it was diffused now, coursing joyfully through her skeleton, so vivid that she could see it; she felt like a network of fire and light. She could see every one of her bones. It hurt, like static crackling inside her skin, but it was bearable. *Can I still direct it?* Experimentally, she urged it toward the palm of her right hand, and the energy streamed to it, spiraling around the spot like a nebula. It was still buzzing, ready to be unleashed.

I have an idea.

A terrible idea.

How many fingers will I need to keep?

She was trying not to get her hopes up, and was helped in that effort by acknowledging how painful this was going to be, *if* it worked.

Plus, if I lose control, then I will undoubtedly kill myself.

But I am going to die anyway.

So, this is a win-win situation.

Except that one win is definitely better than the other.

"First, the thumb." Holding her breath, she guided the coursing energy to that pesky trapeziometacarpal buried inside her left hand.

Might as well go for the nondominant one.

Now go!

The energy seethed into the saddle-shaped joint and joyfully snapped it in two.

It hurt exactly as much as she had expected.

"Fucking fuck-hell!" She clamped down on the energy and took a deep, shuddering breath. For all the bones she'd broken magically in the course of her life, none of them had ever been hers. She forced herself to look down at her hand, and then looked away. She tried dragging her hand through the cuff. The bones of her thumb grated and shifted, and she screamed in pain. But it wasn't enough.

The bones all take up too much space, even when they're not in position. I'll need to do more.

As it turned out, the sound of a bone shattering into a hundred little pebbles was quite different from it breaking.

It took more than the destruction of the thumb, and there was a lot of screaming and weeping, but all throughout, Alix had to keep a tight rein on her power, in case it escaped and ran riot through her body. Even worse, she had to watch it happening, direct it, so she could see her skin jumping about as horrible things happened inside her hand.

When she was finished and the last vestiges of energy had gone, her left hand featured a little finger, a ring finger, and three limp, purpled appendages with the consistency of rubber glove-fingers filled with aquarium gravel, which is essentially what they were. Just looking at them made her want to throw up, which she had promptly done, mostly onto herself. But some had gone on the floor and, probably, Imogen's corpse.

She set her teeth and dragged her hand inch by agonizing inch out of the cuff. Tears streamed down her cheeks, and she sobbed as the leftovers of her bones grated against each other. But in the end, the feeling as the material passed over her final two fingertips and cool air washed over her sweaty wrist was magnificent.

She allowed herself a moment of agonized satisfaction and then set to work. It was awkward, using the two fingers of her nondominant hand, but she managed eventually to unbuckle her right wrist, and then she used her good hand to unsnap the straps across her chest and waist. Her back muscles shrieked as, with her left hand laid gently on her thighs, she leaned forward, peeling herself off the chair to undo the buckles at her ankles.

Free!

She carefully stood, carefully shielding her poor mangled hand, and carefully fell over onto the carpet on her side.

This feels so good. Her hand was a little ball of agony on the end of her arm, but she could bear it for the moment. As long as it didn't touch anything, it was endurable, and when she forced herself to look at it, she could see that there was no broken skin.

So sepsis isn't an immediate danger.

Bit by bit, she hoiked herself up onto her knees and crawled one-handed, her smashed hand tucked to her stomach, across the carpet, around the dead and stinking Jimmy, and over to the coffee table. She took the teapot by the handle, and then, fulfilling a lifelong ambition, drank directly from the spout. The tea, which had been soaking for many hours now, was tongue-dissolvingly bitter, and exactly the temperature of the room. It was utterly delicious.

She knelt there for a while. Then she mustered up the strength to get to her feet and totter through a door. She fumbled for the light switch and found that it was the kitchen. There was a bowl of fruit on the table, and she snatched up an apple and tore at it with her teeth.

Not so fast. She managed to eat the second one slowly, without sounding like the Cookie Monster. The fridge was empty, except for a bottle of champagne chilling. She eyed the bottle thoughtfully, but decided to drink directly from the tap instead. Then she took another apple and, chewing, moved cautiously out into the house, turning the lights on as she went. It was furnished, with art on the walls, but it did not feel like someone's actual home. It had the strange feeling of a place that was usually rented out, occupied by a series of inhabitants.

Feeling disgusting, she found a bathroom and ducked her head under the shower. She thought about taking an actual shower, but the prospect of being naked in that house was not appealing. And besides, there was only her urine-soaked track suit to get back into afterward.

In the hallway she found a table with a landline phone on it.

She stared at it for a long time, sorely tempted. But there was still something to be addressed, so she pressed on.

The house was large and rambling. Hallways tended to have closed doors at either end. She opened every door she came to and turned on the lights. There was a library with long tables on which to lay books. There was a gymnasium with all the equipment covered in dust sheets. There was a room with several locked gun cabinets, and a large cupboard full of boxes of ammunition. She climbed the stairs, and found many bedrooms where the beds had no sheets or pillows.

Finally, she opened the door to a hallway that took her to the most distant part of the house. At the end was a door. She opened it carefully, and turned on the light.

It was a perfectly pleasant room, with a queen-size bed and comfortable chairs. There was a plush rug on the polished wooden floor, and a vase of flowers on a side table, although they did not quite cover the smell of urine. Clearly, the man shackled to the bed had not been able to hold his bladder either. He was blinking in the sudden light.

"*Finally!*" he exclaimed. "You can't *do* this to me, I'll—My God!" He took in who she was, and her general state. His eyes were caught by the mangled mess of her hand. "Lady Mondegreen, what did they *do* to you?" Apparently she was sufficiently disheveled and discommoded not to be mistaken for a captor.

"Mr. Molko," said Alix. "Hi."

"Do you know what's going on? What is this?"

"We were abducted."

"By who? Where are they? But you got free!" The relief in his voice was palpable. "Thank God. I've been here for hours and hours. Please help me before they come back!" He gestured at an empty plate and a half-empty bottle of water on the floor next to the bed.

"It was a group unhappy that you'd murdered the Prince of Wales." Her voice was astoundingly flat, given the hatred that welled up when she said it out loud.

He flinched, but then his eyes narrowed. "Is that what they told you? Because that's crazy." He jerked his head toward the shackles on his wrists. "We need to get out of here. You've got to let me out of these."

She took a step back.

"I agree it's insane," she said. "But it's also true."

"It's not! I swear! The prince died of natural causes. Everyone knows this."

"It is true," she said. "There was a cube in his brain, just like in all your other victims."

"A cube?"

"Your ability leaves a hallmark."

"But—" He was utterly bewildered.

"I know, it's shocking when you find out your powers aren't what you thought. You put in all these years of practice and experimentation, and you think you've gotten a handle on the impossibility of it all, and then you find out your ability has got a whole thing going on you never knew about. I really do understand." She held up her mangled hand. "It just happened to me."

"But... the Establishment! The offer you made me." He sounded broken as he realized it was all a ruse. She imagined all the things he had thought would be his. The power. The money. A future.

"Honestly, I think the people I work for could discount the prince's death," she told him. "Your abilities are valuable, possibly world-changing, and who knows what people might overlook for that kind of opportunity. There could very well be a place for you in the hallways of power."

He looked up, hopeful.

"And if I brought you back, alive and willing to work for them, they'd reward me. Maybe I'd get what I want too. Finally." His eyes were wide with hope. "But you deliberately killed my friend. For profit. And I'd be profiting from it too. He wouldn't get justice. And I'd have no honor."

"Alexandra!" She could see him frantically trying to come up with some plea or argument that would sway her.

"I've realized, I couldn't rest as long as you were allowed to live, to benefit from what you've done."

"I'll—I'll give you the money."

She turned and began to walk away. Her body was trembling with all the energy she'd just summoned up inside her.

"Everything I've been paid! All of it!" he shouted at her back.

She released the power and it erupted out, seeking prey and finding it. She tottered a little on her feet, but kept walking, as behind her, every bone in Molko's body exploded.

The house proved to be quite, quite flammable.

Alix sat under a tree and waited to see how long it would take for the fire brigade to respond to the call that a relatively isolated house in the countryside was aflame. She was not overly concerned that they would appear too early. Before she set the house alight, she'd done some prep work and destroyed the Canley-Vale siblings' phones and any ID. Also, after a strengthening drink of whisky, she'd returned to the room decorated with the former Phillip Molko, removed the chains that had kept him bound to his bed, and laboriously dragged him, one-handedly, down the stairs to the room with Imogen and her brother.

She'd thought about taking the van she'd found in the garage and driving away, but she was exhausted and didn't know precisely where she was. The Checquy would need to come to the house anyway. And besides, the van was a stick shift, and she didn't fancy trying to shift gears with two-fifths of a hand.

Instead, she sat on the grass, her hand a throbbing mass of pain, and watched as the flames spread through the house and a thick black column of smoke twisted up into the night sky. She was obliged to move back twice because of the heat before the fire brigade screamed up the driveway, just in time to witness the roof collapsing.

"Christ," said the first firefighter to emerge from the engine. "Well, that's already had it. All we can do is make sure it doesn't spread." He saw Alix and hurried over to her. "Miss! Are you all right? Was there anyone else in there?"

"You need to get on to your chief, and tell him it's a code Quandary," she said. She channeled Louise and Lady Farrier at their most imperious, but it wasn't necessary, since it turned out *he* was the chief, and he blanched at her words.

"Is being here going to hurt my men?"

"No, it's a standard, natural fire," she assured him. "You're fine to put it out. But don't enter the site, and do call it in, please." He was on his phone immediately, calling the number that was given to strategically selected professionals around the country, including fire chiefs, pediatricians, bishops, school counselors, psychiatrists, harbor masters, librarians, and bouncers at particularly popular nightclubs.

"They're on their way," he said. "They want to talk to you." He handed her his phone.

"Hello? ID code 45 Fatalistic Aureate 85 Zulu... No, I'm fine."

"Oh my good *GOD,* what happened to your fucking hand?" exclaimed the fire chief, who had apparently just noticed it.

"Oh, yeah, my hand is hurt," she said into the phone. "It's not life-threatening." She looked to the fire chief. "Could I maybe get some painkillers, please?" He bolted off toward the fire truck, and she returned to the call. "I think it'll need Grafter-level care. And a ride back to London."

The Checquy arrived hurriedly in the form of the nearest pawn, a middle-aged lady who didn't *quite* screech to a halt in her extremely muddy Range Rover but did brake abruptly. Pawn Mahoney, who apparently constituted a plump one-woman regional office three villages over in the hamlet of Little Rumpling, was clearly frantic to get Alix back to London.

As she pulled out of the driveway onto the main road, she asked, "First, are you all right? Do you need any immediate medical attention?" Alix held up her hand, rather shamefacedly, and Mahoney almost swerved off the road. "Jesus *Christ!*"

"It's fine," said Alix. "It'll keep until we get a Grafter to look at it."

"Are you sure?" asked Mahoney, in the tones of someone who was trying not to be sick on her steering wheel.

"Yeah," said Alix. "It isn't getting any worse, and I took an aspirin."

"Okay," said Mahoney. "So, what happened back there?"

"Oh," said Alix wearily. "Just weird shit."

"Well, that's inevitable," said Mahoney.

27

She was brought to Apex House. Waiting in the underground parking lot was Dr Claes.

"Hi," said Alix, climbing out of the Range Rover. "What are you doing here?"

"I am here to make certain you are alive and well. You do not look well." The Grafter took her gently by the elbow. Claes leaned forward and sniffed her. "Did you know that you smell like smoke and have quite a substantial amount of dried human urine on you?"

"I did know that, yes," said Alix.

The Grafter sniffed again. "Ah, it's *your* urine," she said. "At least there's that."

Alix turned back to the car, and Pawn Mahoney rolled down her window. "Pawn Mahoney, thank you again. I'm sorry, but you might want to get the inside of your car cleaned—I forgot that I've got quite a bit of piss on me."

The pawn regarded her levelly. "I wondered what that was," she said. "Anyway, it was my pleasure to pick you up."

"Let's get you inside," said Claes. "Do a quick examination." She led Alix to the lift, and they ascended to the medical facility, which occupied half the ground floor and was effectively a miniature hospital. As they entered, the staff and some patients were clearly alarmed by Alix's appearance and odor. Claes led her to an empty cubicle with an examination table and briskly drew a curtain around them.

"First," she said, "let's see that hand." She gently eased Alix's arm out from its defensive curl and regarded her fingers with a fascinated horror mixed with sympathy. "Oh, what *happened* to you?" she breathed.

"*I* did," said Alix.

"Amazing. You know bones, right? What are we looking at here?"

"I don't think there's a name for it," said Alix. Not thinking about it was one of the things that had kept her from screaming for the past few hours. "At the very least, it's several comminuted fractures, but I think it goes well beyond that."

"Not immediately life-threatening, though," said Claes. Her hands were moving all over Alix, feeling her brow, checking her pulse, palpating her earlobes.

"I don't think so."

Claes sniffed at Alix's breath and shrugged.

"Well, *they* want to talk to you immediately."

"The hand can wait," said Alix. "It's already waited."

"Fine," said Claes. "But let me give you something for the pain."

"I took an aspirin." The Grafter regarded her with pitying contempt and dug out of her purse something red and slimy that looked like half a tennis ball covered in evil. Before Alix could make nervous inquiries, she placed it firmly on the back of Alix's neck, where it suctioned on loudly and wetly.

The sudden and total cessation of pain was the most pleasurable experience of Alix's entire life. It was so good that her body went limp, she almost slid off the bench, and she actually made a little moan.

"That will get you through the meeting," said Claes.

"It's amazing," said Alix, once she'd got her breath back. "What is it? No, actually," as the Grafter opened her mouth, "I think I'm happier not knowing."

"How do you feel about a semi-sentient amalgamation of snake glands and cow brains insinuating fungal threads into your spinal column to deliver domesticated neural-inhibition bacteria?"

"Is that what it is?"

"...No?"

Alix resisted the urge to rip the thing off her neck. "Is it going to be okay in the shower?"

"The shower?"

"I can't report to the Court like this."

"You must. They want you immediately. I'm sure they've seen worse."

"I'm not sure they have! Do they really want me to go before them stinking of sweat and smoke and *piss*?"

"They didn't specifically request that, but they did specifically order that you come at once."

Alix sighed. "Okay."

As she walked through the corridors of the Apex, she had never been more aware of her own personal odor. Nor, apparently, had anyone else, since she got some appalled looks. Although the looks may also have come because her track suit looked like she'd been restrained in it for many hours, and the portions of her hair that had escaped their bindings had been denied their usual drying routine of leave-in conditioner and scrunching-by-towel, and frizzed patchily, giving, she vaguely assumed, the impression of her brain exploding out of her skull.

Once, she would have been worried about the effect this would have on her reputation in the Checquy. Now that she knew about the Court's position on her professional advancement, she didn't care at all. It actually made a nice change.

Claes ushered her into a small conference room containing Lady Farrier, Rook Thomas, and Pawn Smith.

"Mondegreen, thank God," said Pawn Smith, rising to her feet.

"Yes, we're all relieved to see that you're..." Lady Farrier trailed off, obviously looking for an adjective that didn't clash too horrendously with Alix's shattered appearance. "...present." She regarded Alix dubiously. "Can you report?"

"I can."

"Please sit, then, and proceed. Are there any immediate threats of which we should be made aware?"

"No," said Alix. "Phillip Molko and his colleagues are dead."

"You are certain?" asked Farrier.

"Completely," said Alix firmly. "It was done by my own hand. Well, by my own capabilities."

"Where are the bodies?" asked the rook.

"Burned in that house." They regarded her with the expectant air of a schnauzer when the cheese compartment of the refrigerator has been opened. More detail was obviously required. "They abducted me from my flat. They must have been waiting. I just remember arriving at home, plugging in my phone, and then nothing." Alix had had plenty of time to concoct this story while waiting for Pawn Mahoney, and then in Mahoney's car. "When I woke up, my head was foggy." Alix frowned. She described the chair and the restraints, but not the room or the house. "There were three people: Molko, and the man and woman from the Joyo's footage. I had the feeling they were the entire group. They asked me questions about the Establishment."

"Do you know why they abducted you?" asked the rook. "I've reviewed all the footage we recorded at the restaurant, and Molko gave every appearance of wanting to accept the offer."

"Something must have tipped them off," said Alix. "Maybe they spotted one of our watchers?" She shrugged.

"What can you tell us about them?"

"The other two—the man and woman—were English," said Alix. "In their twenties, good clothes, middle-class London-area accents. That's about it, really." She was not terribly concerned about the bodies being identified—the fire had burned hot, and the Canley-Valeses' dental records and DNA were not going to be in any government databases.

And the Scramasax can cover their own arses if need be.

"Do you think the woman might have been the one you confronted at the Blanch residence?" asked Rook Thomas.

"Yes, she confirmed it." *I might as well tie up that loose end.*

"What did they want from you?" the Lady asked.

"Mainly to find out what we knew about them," said Alix. "The man and woman were badly rattled by the authorities having identified Molko, and very concerned that they, too, might be identified."

"So they didn't buy the story about the Establishment?" wondered the rook.

"Apparently not," said Alix.

"But how did they know we'd approached him at all?" asked Lady Farrier.

"I don't know," said Alix, who was trying not to concoct more lies than she needed to.

"Perhaps they kept him under observation themselves," speculated Smith.

Sure, let's go with that.

"They felt comfortable talking in front of me," said Alix. "They were going to kill me."

"You're certain?"

"The woman pulled a knife," said Alix. "That's when I killed them."

After a long pause, Farrier spoke. "Was anyone else involved, do you think?"

"No," said Alix. "I didn't see any sign of anyone else."

There was a thoughtful silence, broken only by a quiet, repetitive sucking sound.

"Sorry, does anyone else hear that?" asked the rook. "Is it the pipes?"

"It's the Grafter thing on the back of my neck," said Alix, turning to display the pulsating lump. "It's keeping me from feeling pain."

"Christ," said Thomas.

"We won't keep you much longer," said Lady Farrier hurriedly. "So, to recap, you're confident that everyone involved in the plot is dead?"

"I know for a fact that Molko, the woman I confronted in the Blanch kitchen, and the one other man are dead," said Alix.

"How did you escape?" asked Rook Thomas curiously.

"I did *this* to myself," Alix said, and she held up her hand. There was a collective intake of breath. "A new application for my powers."

"How did the fire start?" asked the rook.

"The Englishman, he did something," said Alix. "Just before my powers killed him."

"Another artifact?" asked Farrier. Alix shrugged vaguely.

"Well, we've secured the site. We'll see what we can find," said Rook Thomas. "For the moment, the threat appears to have been eliminated, and we have an operative who needs immediate medical attention. Thank you very much, Pawn Mondegreen. You should go down to the hospital wing. We'll talk soon." Alix recognized her cue and departed.

The Grafters opined that it would be much easier just to have the hand off and stick another on in its place.

"It wouldn't have to be permanent," Claes said. "Just while we took care of the old one. Then we could swap them back."

"You just have spare hands hanging around ready? In jars? And how long would I have this strange hand on the end of my arm?"

"It'll be a while," admitted Claes. "A team of nine doctors, including two regular Checquy, examined the scans. Everyone was fascinated. I learned a new word! It happens so rarely now, but this is a very charming one: 'smitheroons'!"

"Smithereens," said Alix faintly.

"Well, that is even more adorable. Smithereens." Claes nodded to herself. "Anyway, we've agreed that we'd need to grow you some new finger bones." Alix winced. "I'm sorry, but some of your bones were essentially liquefied. The musculature and tendons are all in very bad shape as well. There's significant ripping and shredding." She shook her head. "Whatever you did, it was devastating. An absolute demolition. It will be a long process to repair and reweave, if we want to get the hand back to prime condition."

"But you could do all that while it was still attached to me?"

"Yes, but it will take weeks."

"I'm fine with that, I'd just... I'd really like to keep this one on me," she said firmly. "It has sentimental value."

Lady Mondegreen," announced Sir Alastair.

The King was standing by his desk, light streaming from behind him into the large, formal office. Alix dipped in a curtsy while the private secretary backed out and closed the doors behind him.

"Your Majesty," said Alix. She waited to see how he would greet her. Would it be a formal shaking of her good hand? But he smiled and crossed the room to kiss her on the cheek.

"Alexandra, my dear, it is good to see you."

"You too, sir."

"Please sit, I've had them lay on some tea for us." They settled themselves on settees. "I'll be mother." He eyed the hard black mitten-gauntlet that was held against her chest by no-nonsense straps. "How is your poor hand?"

"It's coming along," Alix said to the King. It meant several hours of surgery every day, as different Grafters took turns opening the skin of her hand and wrist and effecting a multitude of minuscule tweaks.

The apparatus she wore to keep her hand safe and stable was bulky and noticeable, and she was fine with that. It helped people remember exactly what she'd done to herself. Details were, of course, confidential, but word had gotten around about how she'd escaped from captivity, and even in the Checquy, smashing your own fingers into tiny pieces and paste was regarded as pretty hardcore.

The King's eyes lingered on it. He knew the story—it was in the report she'd dictated to Smith. They'd offered her medical leave, but she had wanted to be there for the closing of the investigation.

She contributed to the team's final report. She'd packed away her desk in the Box Room along with the rest of the team, while around them the walls of their office were taken down to make room for the next special project. She attended the farewell lunch held at a local restaurant. It had been nice. Everyone had been satisfied that they'd solved the crime, and that the guilty had *definitely* gotten what was coming to them. Smith told them all that the Court was extremely pleased with the outcome, and that she'd be writing letters of praise that would go in each of their personnel files.

And then it was goodbyes, with actual smiles and hugs. Scagell and Smith invited her to come visit them in Norwich and Limerick respectively, and Weller had booked her for a lunch in a couple of weeks, when the finance-pawn was coming back to London to attend a conference.

So I made some friends.

Sweven had stiffly said goodbye, and she'd stiffly said the same. They hadn't shaken hands.

Pawn Padilla had put in a request to the Checquy and to the Croatoan for leave—a couple of extra weeks to explore the United Kingdom. Pawns didn't usually get international vacations, but it had been granted. Alix had invited him to come spend a couple of days up at Wyndham Towers, and entranced by the idea of staying at an actual stately home, the American had accepted, even after Alix had warned him how isolated and dull it was. He had cheerfully brushed off her concerns and was currently driving a rented car through the Scottish highlands, presumably pausing periodically to be a tree in various glens and on various bens. Alix would be meeting her sisters at Euston station, as the Manticore School had just finished up the term, and they would meet Padilla at the Towers.

But first this meeting. The last time she'd seen the King was when he had demanded that she be the one to meet with Molko. He had said that he trusted her to do the right thing for his son. Now, in this large, beautiful room with art and sunlight and tea and scones, everything that had happened to her since seemed quite unreal.

"Thank you for the flowers and the grapes. They were, respectively, very lovely and very tasty."

"So glad," said the King. "I hated reading your description of what happened to you. What you did was very brave. What's the public story?"

"Riding accident," said Alix. "Horse shied, we fell. I was thrown clear but he rolled onto my hand."

"Perfectly reasonable." There was a pause. "I expect," he said, not looking at her as he stirred the tea, "that we should discuss the things *not* in your report."

"Everything I told the Court was in that report," said Alix.

He looked up.

"Really."

"Yes. But I agree that you and I really should talk about the Scramasax."

"Ah, yes. Them," he said, placing the tea in front of her. "Please don't try to juggle the cup and saucer with one hand." He smiled. "People always feel they need to be on their very best behavior. Just do what's comfortable." He sat back with his own cup. "So, the Scramasax." He looked at her expectantly.

She looked back, channeling her dog Wompus at his most inscrutable. Eventually, under that border collie gaze, the King cracked.

"Right. I was rather hoping you'd tell me everything you knew, so I could evaluate how much to tell you. But we're here, so I shall begin by saying that they are a group of soldiers equipped with supernatural capabilities. Founded by the spymaster and court sorcerer to Elizabeth Gloriana. They report directly and exclusively to the sovereign, and have done so, secretly, since the sixteenth century."

It felt ridiculous to hear such things being said in such a beautiful, civilized room. Except that it was in rooms like this—hell, it was in *this* room—that orders were given that resulted in people dying, wars being waged, kingdoms falling, and history changing.

"That much I picked up," said Alix. She took a sip of tea. "This is delicious."

"The secret is to give people more sugar than they ask for."

"Clever. So, you're saying that for centuries, the crown has had a private strike force. A private *supernatural* strike force that doesn't have to answer to Parliament or the people or laws or anything else."

"They answer to me," said the King. "It's something that gets handed down with the crown. One inherits it, along with the castles and the cars and the stamp collection."

"What do you use them for?"

"This is the first time *I've* ever activated them," said the King. "They saw some action during the wars, and they can be good for extra security. They're also handy because they don't have the same restrictions as the Checquy, especially when it comes to working overseas. They managed to get a few of the family's cousins out of Russia back during the revolution."

"My God," said Alix.

"But there hasn't been much need since the Second World War. Just because one has them doesn't mean one uses them."

"Like the stamp collection."

"Quite."

"How many operatives are there?"

"I'm not going to tell you that."

"Do I know any more of them? Is it all families?" He returned her gaze but didn't answer. "Are they all members of the aristocracy?"

"No. I understand some roles have been handed down over the generations. But they also do some discreet recruitment. They don't have the sort of enlistment capabilities that the Checquy does, especially since they operate in even greater secrecy. I'd say it's paranoia, but the Checquy *did* nearly wipe them out, you know."

"Yes, so I heard. How are they funded?"

"Such a civil servant!" He laughed. "There was an endowment put in place by Good Queen Bess, and it gets topped up occasionally." He did not volunteer whether he himself had done any topping-up. "Shall I prepare you a scone?"

"Please," said Alix absently. "The Scramasax won't be able to retrieve Imogen's body, or her brother's, although I don't expect the Checquy will be able to identify them. There was very little left."

The King winced. "That poor girl, I didn't want her to be involved in all that. I just wanted her to be with you and Louise, adding extra protection."

Alix remembered something.

"*You should probably know, I've chosen two additional ladies-in-waiting,*" Louise had said. "*If I have to have them, I'm not going to have every single one of them chosen for me.*"

And then she had named three.

So Imogen was also forced on her. Imogen, who had played with them since they were little, and been in the Girl Guides troop, and gone to school with them. Imogen whom she had seen coming out of the library where Edmund died, presumably conducting her own investigation, but on behalf of the Scramasax.

"Imogen insisted that she take part in the mission to find Edmund's murderer," the King said. "Because she had known him. And her brother was very keen to contribute." He sighed. "Well, the Scramasax will have to clean up after themselves, and come up with an explanation for Imogen's disappearance. The brother was never very prominent. I'm not sure many people will realize he's gone."

"How will they do it?" asked Alix.

"I've no idea, but they have centuries of experience in successfully hiding themselves from the agents of the Checquy." He looked at her. "Until now."

"Did Edmund know about the Scramasax?" asked Alix.

"No."

"Does...Does Louise?" she asked with dread. *Does she know I killed her friend? Our friend?*

"Not yet. It really is one of those things that comes only with the crown. It's another way to keep the number of people who know about it extremely small." He paused. "Why didn't you tell the Court?" asked the King. "The Scramasax are old enemies, and they hate the Checquy."

"I know," said Alix sadly. "I saw it in Imogen. When I mentioned the possibility of peace, she decided I couldn't be trusted. Just suggesting the idea was enough to make her decide I had to die."

"I'm very sorry you were put in that position, Alexandra," said the King.

"Thank you," Alix said.

When she didn't say anything else, he sighed and went on. "The

Scramasax do froth on about the rivalry, rather. But the Checquy can nurse a grudge as well. So why *did* you keep it secret?"

"It would lead to trouble," Alix said. "As best I can tell, the Scramasax haven't caused any problems since 1567. Except for that triggering phone call to Pawn Smith, which was practically an act of war."

The King shook his head, looking sincerely regretful.

She continued, "The Checquy would never allow a rival, especially one who had been an enemy, and who didn't operate under any laws. Action would have to be taken, a clandestine scouring of the nation, which would be hideous. The Scramasax would fight back, and who knows how that would escalate? They sound like fanatics. Just watching Imogen transform in front of me, it was chilling."

"Poor Imogen," sighed the King. "It was such a dangerous thing to do, trying to enlist you."

"So you approved that?"

"No," said the King firmly. "I authorized them to intercede and remove Molko. That was all. I had no idea you had tracked Imogen or that you were in their custody. I think they were rather hoping they'd be able to present your conversion as a *fait accompli*." He sighed again. "People tend to do that with me. They make elaborate arrangements and assume I'll be delighted. Imogen must have been certain that she would bring you onto their side. She had such affection for you, and knew that you had problems in the Checquy."

"Would you have wanted me to join the Scramasax?"

"I'm not sure. I suppose part of me would like that very much. I don't want you to feel so jolly alone. I know how dreadful it can be when you feel isolated from everyone around you. People see only the title, and don't treat you like a person."

"And I could be your woman inside the Checquy."

"There's that as well," allowed the King. "The Checquy do good work, but they do it their way." He put his cup down. "Was I wrong to doubt them? What would the Court have done with Molko?"

"I don't know," confessed Alix.

"But Molko is dead." It was almost a question.

"He is."

At this, the King closed his eyes for a few long moments. When he opened them again, there was a sheen of tears.

"I didn't know what to believe in that report," he said. "But I trust you. It's done."

"It is, sir."

"Was it the way you described, striking down everyone at once?"

"No, I was free by the time I found him. He was last, and he was alone."

He nodded.

"Why did you do it?" asked the King. "Did you not trust the Court either?"

What do I say? Do I tell you that I thought the Checquy would do everything in their power to keep Molko alive and a weapon in their service?

Because I have no doubt of it.

Or do I tell you that I killed him because you wanted it done, and you are my King, and my ancestors swore fealty and obedience to your ancestors centuries ago, and that oath is still a part of who I am, in the core of my heart?

Because, I'm sorry, but that's not why I did it.

I killed Molko because I thought it should be done. For once in my life, I acted according to my own conscience. Not because I was ordered to, or because tradition or duty or procedure required it. I did it because Edmund was my friend, and the idea of his murderer escaping judgment offended me.

"It had to be done," she finally said.

"I'm glad it was," said the King. There was another pause. "And what now?"

"Now you can tell the Scramasax that they needn't worry, once they've addressed Imogen's and her brother's disappearance. I assume that house can't be traced back to them. As long as they stay out of the way of the Checquy, I shan't tell the Court about them. They can husband their strength, be your ace in the hole, and go on as they have been."

"I think that's very wise," said the King. "And you? How will you proceed?"

"I'm not as committed to the Checquy as I was," Alix said. "Imogen told me about their policy toward my career." He nodded. "I've spent so long thinking of that organization as the core of who I was. I gave them too much power. But I'm ready just to treat it as a day job, not as my reason for being. I'm happy to continue supporting Louise, and I've actually started to develop a closer relationship with my sisters."

"I *am* glad to hear that," the King said. "I've always felt uneasy about the way you were kept separated from them. And I'm glad that you'll remain a lady-in-waiting to Louise. You've been of great service to this family, and we are grateful, Alexandra, for your loyalty, your discretion, your patience, and your kindness. In situations like ours, it can be difficult to unravel the dutiful and the professional from the personal. You've been called upon to make great sacrifices on behalf of the crown. But we do love you—Louise and Nicky and I. We love *you*. Not your role, and not your powers."

"Thank you," she said.

"I want to give you something as a token of that gratitude and love. The normal thing is a decoration of some sort, a medal or a title, but that's quite a public thing, and this is a personal gift."

"Sir, it's really not—" she began, but he raised a hand and she stopped.

"Louise mentioned that your mother's tiara was not really as suited to you as it is to her." He smiled. "I hadn't noticed, but knowing Charlotte, I wasn't surprised. So, I thought perhaps we could purchase a new one for *you*."

"I—Whatever you think would be suitable, that's very kind."

"Yes, I thought you'd say something like that. But my dear wife always said that a lady should choose her own tiara. And I worry that, out of politeness, you'd pick the simplest or least costly, and that is not at *all* what we want. Your selection will need to meet a base cost. I've consulted with the crown jeweler, and my wife's Mistress of the Robes, and they've come up with an appropriate figure." He named an amount and Alix felt her face contort in shock. "Anything less than that, and I'm afraid you'll have to try again."

"Your Majesty," she said weakly. "That's far too generous."

"It is exactly as generous as it should be."

"I'm very touched, sir, but..." She trailed off, and then an idea occurred to her. "If I may, I've learned that my sisters need help with the costs of their future education. They're covered by the Checquy for high school, but after that, they're on their own. You can imagine the consideration that my parents put into such things." This time it was his face that contorted. "Precisely. If, instead of a tiara, you could assist me with that, then it would be a genuinely life-changing gift." *And a damn sight less costly than your apparent tiara budget.*

The King pondered for a moment.

"Wonderful idea!" he said. Alix slumped in relief. "We'll do both!"

Oh, fuck.

"No, sir—"

"No, my mind's made up!" His hand slapped the armrest of the sofa. "We'll work out the details of your sisters' tuition. Leave it to me. Now, Sir Alastair has a letter for you to take to your jeweler of choice, directing that the cost of the tiara be billed to the palace."

"I'll get right on it," said Alix weakly.

"Do! I expect to see it on your head within six months." They stood, and he kissed her on the cheek. "Thank you again, dear girl, for everything. We'll have you for dinner soon." He walked her to the door, so that she needn't back out awkwardly. "I believe Louise is out for the day?"

"Yes, sir. She and Siti are attending a reception in Bath."

"That's right. And have you got the rest of the day free?"

"Yes. And then I'm on leave for two weeks from tomorrow."

"Marvelous! Go out, look in some shops. Start casting your eye over some tiaras."

"Yes, sir," Alix said. "Thank you again."

As she was escorted out of the palace to the waiting car and driver, she turned over in her mind the demented prospect of asking someone to help her pick out a tiara, because she would clearly need assistance. The problem was finding someone who wouldn't find it unutterably weird, and possibly a little alienating.

There must be someone I could ask.

Actually... She fumbled one-handedly through her handbag until she found her little case of business cards. *Yeah, let's give this a try.*

"Hello?"

"Hello, Mr. Vanacore, this is Alexandra Mondegreen."

There was a pause, then: "Lady Mysteryboots! How *are* you?"

"Very well, thank you. And yourself?"

"Doing marvelously. How am I so fortunate as to hear from you?"

"I'm looking to enlist your expertise," she said. "I was hoping to book you for a lunch, because we didn't get to talk much at the reception. And then I'd like to get your help with something."

"Sounds wonderful! Is it your fingernails? Because I have lots of ideas."

"No, I'm making a purchase, and I think you'd be the best person to advise me."

She heard a gasp.

"*Tell* me that it's..." He paused, clearly unwilling to set expectations too high.

"It's a tiara."

"*Marvelous.*"

After they'd set a date for lunch in three weeks, and he'd promised to be the soul of discretion, and to start pulling together ideas, and mentioned the startling possibility of actually commissioning a tiara, and they'd exchanged loud exclamations about how much fun this was going to be, she hung up, smiling broadly.

Almost immediately, her phone rang.

"This is Alix," she said.

"Pawn Mondegreen, this is Pawn Alderton, with the Tactical Deception Communications section. We need to call you in for immediate support in an operation."

"You're aware of my medical status?" She looked down at her slinged arm with its bulky gauntlet.

"We are, but we don't require you to assume any combat duties. There's a major manifestation in Oxford Street. We have to launch an assault on a boutique, and the area is packed with shoppers. We need a distraction."

"You want me to come to Oxford Street and break people's bones?"

"No, we, um... We want you to come to Oxford Street and wear the mystery boots." Alix closed her eyes.

"That'll certainly draw some eyes. Yes, all right. I'll swing by the flat and get them."

"Very good."

"But you'll have to write a note for the Princess of Wales, so she knows I did it for work reasons, and not just to get attention."

"...Really?" Alix didn't say anything. Sometimes, she'd found, silence worked better than persuasion. "Yeah, okay."

Alix smiled, then lowered the glass and leaned forward to tell the driver.

ACKNOWLEDGMENTS

Charles Carey remains the font of all knowledge, calmly accepting and answering queries on topics ranging from restaurant management through to mind control.

Christa Aldridge frequently answered the phone—even before she'd had coffee—and took my questions about how to investigate murder.

When one has a problem with some language, or a complaint about writing, one calls Sulari Gentill. The problem is answered brilliantly, the complaint listened to sympathetically, and then one gets an excellent half-hour conversation.

Over some very good gin and tonics, Tim and Sandra Swain discussed with me various ways to monetize the targeted murder of individuals.

Deron Edward provided expert advice on styling hair for combat situations and formal occasions.

Jon Stevens walked me through the mechanics of setting a leg bone.

Erik Davis continues to get abrupt questions about strategy, tactics, and weaponry, and continues to deliver answers that I can understand.

Stuart Wheeler provided information on a diversity of topics, no matter what exotic locale he was in, be it London, Zanzibar, or just across town.

Ross McAlpine bent his expertise to questions of a medical nature, regardless of how unreasonable my query was, although sometimes I had to wait while he finished saving someone's life.

Charles Reeves's encouragement, enthusiasm, and insights made writing this book so much more fun.

Penny Mason, Megan Holman, Charley Williams, and John Gransbury provided insights on life at different boarding schools.

For some research questions, one cannot consult the Internet, for fear of giving the algorithm the wrong idea. Accordingly, I contacted my friends Ingrid Jonach and Maria Lewis for clarification about the spread pattern when a lady pees herself (not because I thought they had specific personal experience to draw upon, but because they are both novelists, and would understand).

James Stein contributed invaluable advice on jewellery and clothing. Any fashion faux pas are entirely the fault of the author. James also kindly lent one of his fingernail designs and his wedding outfit to Caspian Vanacore. His work can be found on Instagram at nailedby_james.

Shantay Piazza (the original Shantay!) and Jim Weeks provided assistance in working out details of Molko's background.

One of the key elements in the novel-writing process is complaining loudly while playing board games. Thanks to my comrades in Gloomhaven (and now Frosthaven): Rolf Bachmann, Anthony Cutting, Ransome Mclean, and Rhys Mclean.

David Molko kindly lent me the use of his surname. When we first met, I remarked on what an ideal name it was for a villain, and even though he is not at all villainous himself, he graciously said I could use it.

Rhiannon Stewart explained to me the intricacies of DNA analysis.

Charlotte Ryan, Mike Hollingsworth, and Phillipa Bloom provided advice about neighborhoods in London.

I consulted Ingrid Southworth on English history and on the management of long curly hair.

Mika-John Southworth told me all about the challenges and requirements of purchasing a house in England.

Evan Wollen answered my questions about the delivery of military orders, and took the time to record voice-demonstrations and send them to me.

Marnie Goldberg answered my questions about cosmetics. Her channel "MsGoldgirl" can be found on YouTube.

Anthony Swift, Edmund Stewart-Mole, and David Marshall patiently explained the shorting of stocks.

Liesbeth van Alphen and Frank de Jong provided assistance with

Dutch pronunciation and phrasing, with helpful suggestions on how to make it more daunting.

Michelle Weir shared information on forensics, including the mysteries of ground markings, fingerprints, and spit.

Jon Fletcher (half of Rook Gestalt) provided information on London real estate and on the terminology of playing fields.

Cassandra Smith advised me on the tactical removal of hair.

Melanie Oldenhof's generous participation in a charity auction helped reunite a refugee family in safety. It also won her the naming rights to a character in this book, and she provided the name for Team Leader Hannah Smith.

The staff at the National Library of Australia graciously endure my ongoing presence in the Reading Room, and help with my queries about obscure and unreasonable topics.

Several people with experience in being pursued by the paparazzi told me about their experiences. Out of a desire for their privacy not to be disturbed anymore, they will remain unnamed, but I am grateful for their insights.

Amy J. Schneider was the terrific copy editor on this book, who dealt patiently with my Government-instilled instinct to capitalize practically every Word.

Special thanks to the staff at Little, Brown and Company, HarperCollins Australia, and all my other publishers, whose work and enthusiasm put this book in front of you.

Anna Valdinger, my editor at HarperCollins Australia, for her support, enthusiasm, and willingness to accept questions out of nowhere.

Asya Muchnick, my editor at Little, Brown, who tactfully and astutely made this book twenty times better.

Mollie Glick, empress of agents, makes it all possible.

And, finally, the greatest thanks go to my parents. Bill O'Malley, who helps me solve problems, and points out when they're not actually problems that need solving. And Jeanne O'Malley, who inspires me every day on the trip into the library, and who is always the first to read my books.

ABOUT THE AUTHOR

Daniel O'Malley was born and raised in Canberra, Australia. He graduated from Michigan State University and earned a master's degree in medieval history from Ohio State University. He then returned to his childhood home, where he now works full-time as a writer. He is the author of the Checquy novels, *The Rook, Stiletto,* and *Blitz,* the first of which won an Aurealis Award for Best Science Fiction Novel and became a television miniseries.